FANTASY PATCH

FANTASY PATCH

Stephen Geez

Fresh Ink Group
Roanoke

FANTASY PATCH

Fresh Ink Group
An Imprint of:
The Fresh Ink Group, LLC
PO Box 525
Roanoke, TX 76262
Email: info@FreshInkGroup.com
www.FreshInkGroup.com

Edition 1.0	2000
Edition 2.0	2006
Edition 3.0	2012
Edition 3.1	2016

Book design by Ann E. Stewart

Cover design by Stephen Geez and Anik

Cataloging-in-Publication Recommendations: General Fiction;
Media Thriller (Fiction); Advertising (Fiction); Advertising Agency (Fiction);
Public Relations (Fiction); Pharmaceutical Industry (Fiction); Psychotropic Drugs (Fiction); Television News (Fiction); News Media (Fiction); Chicago, IL (Fiction)

Library of Congress Control Number: 2011933415

ISBN-13: 978-1-936442-06-5

In memory of my brother, Gregory

Even the mournful flowers still bloom

Acknowledgements

Thanks to the following ad-mazing creativators:

Team Leader: Ann E. Stewart, Managing Director,
The Fresh Ink Group, LLC

Production Team: Anik

Research Team: David C. Moore

Content Team: Lucas Cale, Beem Weeks, Mark Allen North

Support Team: Kent D. Casey, Todd Tessin, Tom Stockbridge,
Marshall Shearer MD, Susan Stewart,
Jean Buchanan, Lendia Buchanan,
Dillard Greenwell

Member Team: All of *you* who visit www.FreshInkGroup.com,
subscribe for free updates, and share the stories.
It keeps us going when you buy our books and
spread the good word.

PROLOGUE

"*This* is the image you want?" Kristen asks, wrinkling her nose.

We gaze at the squalor that is Maywood Gardens mobile-home park: dilapidated trailers, littered weed-patch yards, broken-down cars, ratty brats . . . .

"M-Slovak's out to prove it can save the world," I tell her, "and this looks like a good place to start."

Kristen waves down the production van. She's my freelance producer on this job, a pretty but rather imposing woman with a sharp, creative eye and steel-trap mind for details. Cameraman Byron joins us while the sound man unpacks gear.

"*This* is the image you want?" Byron asks.

"Wait till we get in," Kristen says, "—nobody's home yet." Sure, the secret entrance to Shangri-la is right inside that rusty double-wide over there.

He frowns and adjusts his glasses. Byron's a rather droopy-drawered video-head whose trademark butt crack has a tendency to peek out and smile, but he's one of Chicago's best, a man who knows how to frame the perfect shot. "Isn't this supposed to be a new-product testimonial?"

"Go ahead," I urge Kristen, nudging her several times. "Give him the spiel."

She rolls her eyes, then assumes the pose of some game-show prize-pointer holding up an invisible capsule. "It's Parzilac!—the new wonder-drug from M-Slovak. Do you suffer from chronic fatigue? Obsessive compulsions? Anxiety attacks? If life's getting you down, let Parzilac pick you up!"

"Been testing the products ourselves, have we?" Byron asks, backing up a step.

"The pitch isn't ours," I explain. "We're just collecting success stories for a series of satellite programs training regional sales reps. Soon M-Slovak's foot-soldiers will embark on a mission to ensure that everybody with prescription coverage gets a chance to live in Happyland."

"Yeah, well, so who's the subject?"

Kristen paints the picture: "She's a nineteen-year-old drop-out with two terminated pregnancies, now on probation for shoplifting and bouncing checks—oh, and she's prone to bouts of severe depression."

"I wonder why," he says, looking around again.

"Hey, just six weeks on Parzilac," I admit, "and she's holding down her first job, *plus* taking GED classes."

"So you want me to shoot *around* all this?"

"No, capture it. We'll let her mom tell us the bad stuff, projecting the image of a concerned parent trapped in a crummy home in a bad neighborhood, the odds weighing against her beloved child, a ray of hope shining from those little pink capsules. Then we'll brighten the lighting and catch our girl maybe sitting at a computer or cracking the books, pausing to praise how Parzilac has changed her life."

The mom's battered old Chrysler barrels up, squeals to a stop, and coughs out an exhausted-looking tread-worn blonde, her waitress uniform wrinkled and soiled. She greets us like old friends, Kristen having won her trust when they met here a few days ago to plan the shoot. Mom's concerned her daughter isn't home yet, so she leads us inside where it's surprisingly neat and clean, inviting us to look around while she calls the girl's employer.

Byron powers up the Steadi-Cam, a counterweighted contrivance that keeps the mobile camera from jiggling, then wanders it down the hallway to test the ambient lighting and look for shots.

Mom hangs up the phone and lights a cigarette, smoke curling into the air as she looks distracted for a moment. Finally, she admits, "My daughter didn't show up for work today."

"Hey!" Byron shouts from somewhere in back. We all hurry to the bedroom.

The first image I see is the shattered mirror, then blood everywhere, our girl lying very still on the floor.

Mom cries out, dropping to her knees, shaking her daughter's arm. Kristen bolts for the phone. Byron's stunned, grabbing the shot, working from instinct, too damned many years shooting local news.

It's that shard of mirror clutched in her hand that captures me, the way it's framed by a smear of glassy crimson, a scene striped by sunlight filtering through window-blinds.

One of her hands moves! Her body shudders and squirms, but she's bleeding from slashed wrists.

Mom is hysterical now, sobbing and trying to lift her daughter's head.

I kneel beside the girl, my knees soaked in red, and I squeeze the open wounds on her wrists, trying to stem the flow. A faint hint of pulse offers her last glimmer of hope.

She's a good-looking young woman—long brunette hair, a bit too much make-up on an otherwise nice face . . .

Oh man, she slashed her neck, too, but not deep.

Mom's begging her to wake up, but the girl can't open her eyes.

My heart is pounding so hard I can't tell if hers has anything more to give.

She shudders again, her chest rising with another breath, then a pause, then another.

Hang on, I want to tell her. Don't give up.

Kristen's back now. Help's on the way. She'll be okay. Just hang on.

And Byron's still shooting, steady as a rock, every second worth thirty more frames. I've seen even the best shooters break down and cry, sometimes staggering off to vomit—but not till after they get the shot.

Her other hand is bleeding, too. It looks like after slashing her neck, she tried one wrist before switching hands and hacking at the other, ripping right through tendons and—

She shudders again.

I'm holding the best I can, but a lifetime of unrealized dreams is seeping around my fingers.

A siren in the distance.

Another breath, a gurgle, lying still . . . then a spasm.

"Oh God," the mother sobs, "she was doing so good."

Kristen gathers her in, holding firmly, both crying together now. Byron's face is screwed up tight.

The girl tries to squirm again, but there's nothing left, no breath, no more time . . .

Just blood, too much blood.

And her death grip on that shard of broken mirror loosens, exposing but a fragment of the truth, one final reflection daring us all to look.

Byron's watching over the top of his monitor now, zoomed in on the hand. It's not the image I wanted, but it sure makes this story real.

Finally the camera drifts away, a demon's eye surveying the scene, and it finds what we've all come to see.

Close-up: subject's bedroom, top of the nightstand, pill bottle tipped and spilled . . .

Like the stain of blood on my hands, an elegant spray of pink capsules.

CHAPTER 1

To capture imaginations, I start with an image.

I can't rely on clients to conjure *my* visions, so I weave telling words, set the stage, lead them in . . . then I *show* them. It might be a mock-up or storyboard or composite photo or even a video animatic—whatever it takes. If they like what they see, they imagine what that could become. Then we talk money, and if the budget's big enough, I make images real. But it all starts with a concept; they have to envision it, and they must believe.

That's why I show them.

So here we are climbing into one bodaciously fast speedboat, fully equipped with the next generation of tri-dimensional imaging—from below-surface sonar and thermal-sensor scanning to satellite mapping with course-route logic and a host of other applications. CEO Billy Sizemore and his company's top marketing muckety-muck are mid-ship, strapping down their portly carcasses. The silver-maned codger climbing in next to me aft is my account-VP, Frank Dellman. I've spent a lot of agency money on this because I can't count on these guys to *imagine* what I have in mind.

They're here to see for themselves.

The professional boat-racing champ steps aboard, greets his passengers, powers up, and activates the digital Sizemore 4000. An impressive display holographs a miniature image of our boat docked at the pier, fish schooling below the surface, stumps and brush lurking in the depths, a moss-slick log bobbing across the cove, birds gliding high in the blue . . . well, you get the picture.

"This baby," the champ says, "could top a *hundred* if we needed it—smooth, too, like a puck gliding on ice." He pats the conn lovingly, an expert obviously in awe. "This'll be a quick demo around those islands and back to the pier—just long enough to get a feel for the new Sizemore *Wave-Slicer*."

And off we go!

It's fast, and it's fun, weaving around obstacles, the projection anticipating our course. We can feel the wind in our faces, warm sunshine on our backs, all while the product impresses us with cutting-edge engineering and technology.

Sizemore and his lieutenant have already embraced the novelty of my approach, now imagining hordes of potential customers taking my ride—I mean *their* ride.

Right on cue, Frank blurts an unabashed whoop, calculated approval for one unparalleled trek. Sizemore grins ear-to-ear. So does his minion. And so do I.

So far so good.

Then all hell breaks loose! There's an explosion, a fireball on the far shore, and a man's waving his arms, calling for help.

The pilot zooms right up alongside the bank. The man jumps on the bow, shouting about people trying to get him—Go! Go! Go!

And we're out of there just as several more come running toward the shore, firing weapons—at us!

There's another explosion, now the sound of a chopper powering up. Man, this *Wave-Slicer* is really moving fast!

The 4000 is flashing superimposed images, dot-line course recommendations, obstacle warnings, readouts and sidebars, data-this, data-that.

Islands are streaking by in a blur, that chopper coming after us.

Our passenger slumps to the deck, maybe hurt, barely holding on.

"We've got to reach the main pier!" our pilot shouts. "Sheriff patrol's got a boat there!"

The chopper's gaining on us, now firing shots into the water.

"Won't make it—in time," the man gasps. "Head for that cove—leave me in the woods—they can't land there—you go for help—"

Pilot banks hard to the left. Wow!—hold on to your gotchies!

We zoom up a narrow inlet, thread more obstacles, head into the mouth of a creek, reverse hard, and glide alongside a low embankment—

"Keep yourselves strapped in!" Pilot warns us. He jumps out and pulls the wounded man ashore.

The chopper is coming in lower. What happened to my leisurely demo ride?!

Pfoom! Pfoom! More shots!

"Go!" the man shouts. "Get help!"

Pilot jumps on the bow, reaching across to paw at the 4000. A 3-D image of the channel appears. He touches a menu icon to select auto-pilot, then jams the throttle and holds on for dear life as the boat jumps back, turns by itself, and takes off.

Pfoom! Pfoom! The chopper's after us again.

Wind-whipped and pressed into our seats, we zig-zag a perfect course to the main channel, hard reality matching the image we see in that projection.

We hit open water and zoom full-throttle, easily topping a hundred.

Still the chopper's gaining on us—closer—closer!—but then we see the main pier, and our pursuers bank away, too late to stop us.

The 4000 flashes *Return?*

Pilot reaches over and swipes the *Yes* icon. We veer toward the pier, still at top speed.

Sizemore and the muckety-muck are *freaking out* by now, everybody holding on for dear life.

Pilot is shouting at us about this great state-of-the-art technology, boasting about product features while *showing* us the benefits. I'm not even a boat man, but I'm seriously impressed. The clients are eating it up. Praise be!

The *Wave-Slicer* throttles down and pulls up to the pier where a man ties us off. We unstrap and get up, wobbling on sea legs. A door appears from nowhere, so we step through . . .

And find ourselves back in the real world, surrounded by eager faces, standing in a grungy warehouse in an industrial stretch of Chicago's South Lawndale.

"Give us the go-ahead to build thirty of these simulators," I tell our breathless clients, "and we'll truck them to every boat show in North America." My virtual-ride guru is hovering nearby, shooing away his crafts-team so Frank and I can work the clients. Sizemore peers back into the nondescript box, amazed by how real it all seemed.

"Just about everybody I know is begging for a chance to come down and test out the new Sizemore adventure," Frank says, nudging his clients. "Just think of the media attention this will draw, too."

The marketing muckety-muck gushes, "Yes!—all that free publicity!—and the word-of-mouth—"

"Damn," Sizemore says, "this could be big." He grins, a far-off look in his eyes. He can almost see it now . . .

"It'll attract teens and young adults, too," Frank points out, "planting seeds of brand awareness for future Sizemore sales."

Both clients are bobbing their heads, ready to dance a jig. They can *see* the possibilities, costs be damned.

Sizemore licks his lips. "You got good ideas for other Sizemore adventures?"

I'm smiling now, too. We're a team. Vision is almost reality.

This one's a done deal.

"Oh yeah," I promise. "You can't imagine."

*   *   *

Talk about an adventure, try riding somewhere with Frank at the wheel. He's a deft but quixotic driver, always on a mission, undaunted by hulking trucks, contemptuous of stop signs, amused by amber lights. He's going to drop me at the studio on his way back to the agency.

"Score one more for the Frankster," I say. "You are the man."

"You're the one puts on the freak shows," he says, allowing a brief hint of smile. "It's been a privilege playing your carny."

I sure don't like hearing him talk in the past tense. Two work days and a final three-week vacation before his 65th birthday, Frank is winding down a long career in the media biz, his last six years at Kehoe/Lundy where I've been a VP/creative director the past four. Frank's the best, a dealmaker, an inside guy who knows the clients and their companies and their families, always making sure I have whatever I need to get the job done. His big send-off party is tomorrow night, and though I've been trying to act upbeat about it, I can't imagine doing this job without him.

He turns on the radio to check for business news, but some jockey is bleating about last night's controversial fatal accident in the "Mile-Square" community, a high-crime section of Chicago's near west side. A guy who owns a small chain of drugstores allegedly hit a pre-teen girl near the El. The media's already caught the scent of scandal, raising questions about why a wealthy white guy would be driving around this area late at night. Of course we get to hear the Reverend Falluson's latest sound bites. He's ranting about the baby-killer racist who has a history of taking from the community without giving anything back, now calling for a boycott of the man's drugstores *to send a message.*

"Free airtime," I grouse. I can't stand that self-righteous, self-styled *community leader.* Lately, he's been making noises about running for office, showing up wherever there's a camera, comforting the families of victims, preaching God's politics from the pulpit.

"And TV will eat this story up," Frank spits back. Neither of us has much respect for local news, both having played a small part in this base form of pandering earlier in our careers. It's a world that hypes for sensation, each story's importance ranked by how titillating the shots are, dragged out as long as there's *anything* to show. Worst of all, it pretends to be respectable, even while running roughshod over presumably innocent people's lives, flaunting so-called "team coverage" that ranges from silly to worse than tabloid.

"Alcohol may be involved," the radio says.

"A giant catfish wearing lipstick and a Nehru jacket *may* be involved, too," Frank interrupts, "but those aren't *facts* telling the story."

Sports scores are tumbling from the radio now.

"You looking forward to soaking up some rays?" I ask Frank. He bought a condo on Florida's Sanibel Island where some of his old connects have retired, but he sure doesn't act excited about the idea.

Looking distracted, maybe a bit frustrated, he even stops for an amber light. "I have unfinished business," he says.

That sounds like Frank, the man with a full plate always anticipating another course, but lately he seems a bit worn out. It's not that he suddenly looks older—those deep grooves lining his gaunt face aren't new, nor is that bit of paunch earned by mastering the art of client wine-n-dine, and those trademark gray wool suits of his with striped burgundy/navy ties have been looking out-of-date for years—it's that undousable fire deep inside, the one that's always burned through the competition and deftly kindled every new job . . .

It's guttering, and I think he's afraid it might simply flicker out.

"You're thirty-five years old," he says, ignoring my question.

"That's a real buzz-kill."

"There's more to life than a job, you know." Only twenty-two when his wife died in childbirth, he's thrown himself into work ever since, a lonesome man whose only family has been generations of business contacts and his cronies at the Chicago Athletic Club. "Marry her, Danté. Turn Cyn into *Mrs.* Roenik before it's too late."

"After she makes partner; that's our deal," I explain, surprised he's broaching this subject again. "Young big-firm lawyers have to prove they can run a marathon before they're put on the fast-track. We'll get hitched someday, then maybe even foist a brat or two on the world."

"Just remember," he says, "—regrets suck."

Business news is on now, so he turns it up. The lead story is about Battle Creek's big drug-maker, The M-Slovak Company, filing for FTC approval to merge with a Swiss firm and become one of the world's biggest, instantly opening many European and Asian markets for American products.

"Still the only job I regret," I tell him. We'd trained their sales reps in how to convince docs to switch their patients to Parzilac, encouraging bigger doses for longer periods, and for uses not approved by the FDA. I imagine it helps a lot of people, but M-Slovak doesn't want to shatter the illusion of complete safety by advocating better screening and closer monitoring, this despite dozens—maybe hundreds—of cases of unexplained violence. That job left us feeling like participants in a mass deception. M-Slovak won't even admit that Parzilac might be involved in one of their test subjects committing suicide the day I was scheduled to shoot her testimonial. Not related, they say.

"So do something about it," he challenges.

"I did. I refused to do any more jobs for them."

"So what? Sam's group just picked up the slack."

"Come on, Frank. Between satellite training, merchandising, and tele-marketing, M-Slovak's a big Kehoe client."

"Not anymore. As of this morning, they dropped us. It took me a long time to pull that off."

"What'choo talkin' 'bout, Willis?"

He glances over, puzzled. "I still don't know what that means."

"Lucy!" I try, my Cuban accent not particularly authentic. "Lucy, you got some 'splaining to do."

Ignoring me, he turns in at *Shoot & Die*, an old tool & die shop converted to a production center with soundstages, edit suites, animation/effects, and space to grow. Yikes, he parks and shuts off the engine. I don't want him coming in; Kristen's shooting insurance pitches with Hal Neusome, but Frank doesn't know they're also doing a surprise video to show at his party, a humorous mock newscast announcing his retirement.

"I managed to kill the account with a bit of sabotage," he finally says as we cross the lot, "—you know, unexplained problems, information slipped to our competitors, seeds of distrust planted here and there—that kind of stuff."

"Well," I say, not sure what to say. "Frank, you *are* the man."

"I put you on a job that left blood on your hands—literally. I never respected you more than when you risked your career to step aside. I felt our whole agency should walk, too, but couldn't muster the support."

"Every time I see a Parzilac ad, I still wish I could nail M-Slovak to the wall."

"Me, too," he admits, "but I was advised that could prove very dangerous, so I've been wimping out."

"Dangerous?" I ask, holding the door for him.

He pauses mid-stride and sizes me up. "Very," he says cryptically, continuing inside.

We greet the receptionist, a sharp guy who keeps track of everything. He picks up the phone as we walk by, so I know he's warning Kristen that Frank has entered the building. Bird-dog one to bird-dog two: bogey's in the field.

Instead of following me to the control room, Frank says he'll head back toward the offices and make phone calls.

"You have a cell-phone in the car," I point out.

"That's a company phone," is all he says, one secret agent to another, secret communications and all. Swallow the phone bill if you're captured.

I find Kristen sitting in the control room watching veteran Chicago newsman Hal Neusome on a wall of monitors. She's calling the shots while he shares advice with underwriters on how to sell our client's life-insurance policies. "Two pages left," she says, showing me the script. "I need you to check Frank's visuals," she adds, noticing I'm alone.

I have the still-store operator isolate a small monitor I can turn off quickly in case Frank walks in. There's a *Breaking Story* graphic, a retirement banner, then shots of Frank that will go over Hal's shoulder as he announces that a legend in the industry is toddling off to Florida for some quiet time. The pictures are all from the same photo, but altered variously so Frank's trademark suit and tie are accessorized to show a rather, well, let's call it *historical* career: caveman's pelt, zoot suit vest, Nehru collar, hippie hair with peace medallion and roach clip, skinny tie, fat tie, cowboy hat, dreadlocks . . .

"Sam's hiring in-house producers," Kristen says after a cut. "He won't be using freelancers anymore."

Sam Cox is another Kehoe/Lundy creative director Kristen's been counting on for occasional jobs. I'd like to keep her busy full-time, but I've always encouraged her to juggle other clients, too, in case something happens to me. "Are you applying?"

"Full-time working for Sam? I'd wind up in the loony bin," she admits, "but I'm worried you might start dipping more and more into the in-house pool, too."

"Then read my mind," I advise. Normally she can, too, a creative director's dream: tops at her job, loved by clients and crew, that rare performer who can capture my vision, a producer who can read my mind. "Am I thinking I'd ever let you get away?"

She just smiles and goes back to work. The rest of the visuals look good, especially the section where Hal will extol Frank's many accolades: real shots of his industry awards, then old bowling trophies, mocked-up covers of *Time and Adweek*, Frank accepting a Tony, an Emmy, an Oscar, a merit badge from the Boy Scouts, several 4-H cow ribbons, now his mugshot on *America's Most Wanted* . . . and finally the closing shot, Frank in his gray-wool suit, sprawled on the beach, half-buried in sand piled on by little kids with plastic pails.

Right now it looks too much like a funeral shot, but I'm sure it'll be a hoot at the party.

I sit back to watch Hal for a minute. He used to be a top-rated anchor until accusations started flying during his acrimonious divorce, followed by unexplained absences from his job, and finally a belligerent altercation with police during his drunk-driving arrest, the latest caught on video and broadcast by competing channels. After being fired, he dropped out of sight, then surfaced again following a stint in rehab. Now he's doing a Sunday-night talkie on the local independent station, so far a bust in the ratings. He goes way back with Frank, and that's enough for me to help the guy when I can.

"Hal wants to schmooze you," Kristen says, wrapping the last shot. "We need to light the news set, so I'll stall until Frank leaves."

Kristen talks to the grips while I join Hal on the stage, walking him over to the snack area so a local legend like him won't be humiliated having to pitch me for work in front of the crew.

"I'm not going to pitch you for work," he says with a wry smile. He just did.

"You're on the A-list, Hal," I assure him. Normally I like to banter with him, but I just approved the visuals for my mentor's send-off video, and now one of his old friends is worried about being cut loose. It's starting to hit me.

"I'll count on that," he says, clearly relieved. Hal's a good-looking guy—especially in make-up—with chiseled features, a hint of distinguishing gray through his styled coif; but he's in his low fifties now, that age where clients don't want him delivering messages for the 18-49 demographic. He eyes some donuts wistfully, then asks, "Have you seen my new show?"

"A couple of times," I admit. He's fishing for feedback, and I know he wants the truth. "I grow bored watching talking heads, you know. I'd like to see more remotes and pre-produced segments, more visuals."

"Me, too—but my director sucks."

He's right. I know the guy, and he sucks. "Then shape the format from your anchor chair, even call the rundown live on the air. Give it a behind-the-scenes feel. It'll come off more honest, less rehearsed, and make viewers curious about what might happen next."

Neusome's got that look; he can see it now. I don't have to draw him a picture. "This Sunday I've got the Reverend Falluson. We're covering that hit & run."

"You got anybody to speak for the drugstore guy?"

"No, the family's mum. If he's charged by then, there'll be a cop or prosecutor wanting to give the police version, all while pretending they don't want to talk to the media about an ongoing investigation."

I shake my head. "I hate to see Falluson get another soapbox, spinning somebody's misfortune for his own benefit."

"So do I," he admits, "but this is what I do."

The receptionist pages me up front to meet Frank, who leads me outside where nobody can hear. "We have a two-o'clock with a potential new client, something about allergy test-strips."

"Count me in, but shouldn't you hand it off? I mean, tomorrow's your last day."

"You still want a shot at doing something about Parzilac?"

"Well, yeah. But—"

"Then we'll start with allergy testing and see if that leads anywhere. Just remember, say the word and we'll walk away."

"What word, Frank? Nobody ever tells me the word."

"Until then I'll be back at the office reviewing accounts with Sam; he's taking over some of my clients."

"Let him read the files himself. You're retiring."

He looks away. "Sure, I've been trying to imagine myself lying on the beach . . ."

"Sounds like just what the doctor ordered," I offer, upbeat, trying to envision him catching those rays.

He snorts his disapproval. "Can you really see me taking it easy?"

"That would be a sight."

He shakes his head. "I just can't picture it."

CHAPTER 2

I never imagined myself preparing to pitch another drug company, but here I sit with Frank in the conference room at Briggs Pharmaceutical while some marketing VP leads us on a breathtaking romp through the exciting world of allergy testing. Soon we'll be called to the inner sanctum for a glad-handing session with CEO Rex Briggs, one of Frank's cronies from the club, a man dedicated to the proposition that no allergy shall remain undetected, especially if it's covered by insurance.

"Normally," explains VP, "it requires pricking or scratching the skin, then rubbing in various compounds and watching for reactions." He pours several two-inch appliqués from a small envelope. "This is the wave of the future, test-strips using our patented new Pene-Derm, the most precise topical agent available for delivering drugs or other chemicals without injuring the tissue."

"Who's the customer?" I ask.

"Pediatricians and allergy specialists, a segment already dominated by M-Slovak with their scratch-kits. We've learned they're trying to develop a test-strip, too, so we need to move fast. Our best shot at grabbing market share is *now* while our product is still new and unique."

"Why would doctors want to switch?"

"Higher pass-along mark-up, and it's easier to use—meaning any office flunky can apply it—plus kid patients won't find it so scary."

"Are these controlled substances?" I ask, which means requiring a prescription.

"No, but a physician has to observe and verify the reaction, and billable office visits are how he makes his money. We considered going over-the-counter, but insurance will pay a lot more than consumers." He affixes one to his upper arm, then pulls a tab that peels the backing from underneath. It looks like a multi-colored, grid-shaped tattoo. "Each of the fourteen squares," he explains, "contains a different food allergen. Other strips cover plant resins, pollens and molds, dusts and bacteria, serums and drugs, plus a mix of miscellaneous antigens."

Frank asks, "So what does a reaction look like?"

"Usually within minutes you'll see a raised bump under one or more of the squares—like a mosquito bite—but we recommend leaving them on for at least twenty-four hours to be sure."

I can tell Frank sees the obvious, too. "Take it directly to consumers with a milder dosage," he says.

"Testing their children," I point out, "isn't just an option, it's a *responsibility*. And if you package them as playful, appealing designs, kids will *demand* a chance to wear them."

"Then sell the docs a stronger, more clinical-looking version," Frank adds, "to use for verification. They'll get flooded with follow-up office visits."

VP's a bit skeptical, but he's got that look in his eyes, so it's time to *show* him.

Pulling a pad and markers from my satchel, I start drawing while Frank ratchets up the pitch: "We'll set up a Briggs Pharmaceutical toll-free helpline, plus an interactive website, both of which refer customers to the nearest specialists *who use Briggs testing products.*"

I show him a caterpillar with lovable face and long eyelashes, its body divided into fourteen segments, each matching a color on the grid-shaped sample. Next I draw a big hairy alien beast wearing crisscrossing ammo belts that hold fourteen colored grenades.

VP's on his feet now, breathing hard, gaping at my pages, so I draw more. Frank knows to keep quiet and let the visuals speak for themselves. I'm in a good mood, having found a rather fun way to hurt M-Slovak's bottom line. By the time we're called upstairs to meet Rex, I have more than a dozen sketches for "allergy tattoos," plus several print-ad concepts targeted both to concerned parents and health-wise kids who want to look cool.

Rex Briggs ushers us to low couches in his penthouse office suite. He's a big cigar-champing old-schooler who looks like he'd just as soon wrestle you as evaluate bids for a contract. We chat for the obligatory three minutes before VP spreads my drawings around the table. I can tell Rex is a poker player, but he still can't help giving up a grin.

"Yes, Mr. Briggs?" comes a woman's voice out of thin air.

"Mounting boards," he barks, "and send up Moore and Stockbridge." How—? Oh, he'd touched a button on the corner of his couch. I'll bet he could announce *Catfish wearing lipstick and Nehru jacket* and have one within minutes. "Do some more," he tells me, eyeing my blank sketch pad like a kid waiting for Mommy to frost the cake.

I start a heavy-metal skull crowned by fourteen dancing flames.

"Hot damn!" he blurts. "My grandson would *insist* on being tested every week."

A woman brings me some sticky boards for my sketches; then Moore and Stockbridge hurry in for a round of pleased-to-meetchas. Moore's an older guy, silver-maned like Frank, but with a bulbous red drinker's nose. Stockbridge is shorter and portly, with close-cropped black curls and a jolly demeanor. I could party with these two.

A spirited discussion follows, Frank keeping his fingers in the pie while I continue drawing. Finally it's decided all the departments will pull together data for a Monday meeting to coordinate an expedited roll-out. VP wants to schedule several more agencies to make pitches, a process that normally takes months or longer, but Rex has other ideas: "This one's just been awarded, so string the others for production quotes—if only to keep these two honest."

Just like that, millions of dollars in business is ours.

After the minions scurry off to cancel their families' weekend plans, Frank reminds Rex, "I'm retiring tomorrow, you know."

Rex waves him off, getting up to walk over and gaze out his glass wall. We join him for a view across spectacular grounds that include a pond with stairstep waterfall. "You sold your house yet?"

Frank hesitates. "Thought I might try migrating with the snow-birds."

Rex grunts. "Pass your days helping old ladies promote yard sales?"

Frank smiles. "Something like that."

"You'd wither and die, Frank."

"I can't stay at Kehoe/Lundy," he says quietly.

"You just picked up at least three-mill in billings contingent upon *your* participation. I think Kehoe might want to find a way to keep you on board, maybe as some kind of *consultant emeritus*, eh?"

"If I were interested."

"Oh yeah? What might make it more appealing to stick around?"

Frank shrugs. "I'd want Danté to feel better about promoting a drug company. It seems he still has blood on his hands from that Parzilac job, and it's proving a distraction."

"Is that so, Danté?"

"It's keeping me up at night," I return. Cripe, I was just having fun drawing caterpillars.

Amused and pleased by my answer, Rex says, "What I have in mind can't show on the books at Kehoe/Lundy."

"Call me freelance," Frank says.

"Hell," Rex says, "I'll call you *Daisy* if you want, long as you make sure it gets done right. I don't want legal snarls, and I sure don't want anyone getting hurt. Them boys at M-Slovak play mean." He leads us back to the couches where I can't help but watch that button, a gunslinger waitin' for him to make his move.

"Their merger with SwissChem?" Frank asks.

Rex nods, saying, "I have info that might cause 'em some headaches." He pushes that button, which I find oddly exhilarating, and asks for the "fact-sheets."

A woman appears and hands *me* about twenty pages of data.

Rex explains, "There's problems with patent conflicts and so forth, but the political hot button is their plans to move nearly all manufacturing out of the U.S., putting tens of thousands of Americans out of work, at the same time raising prices in categories where SwissChem used to be their only competitor. The part you might like is some damning evidence about Parzilac: fraudulent test-trial procedures, falsified approval applications, and a secret study on violent reactions that assesses potential liability costs. SwissChem could lose interest if that Parzilac revenue stream looks like it might dry up."

"What's our part?" Frank asks, though I suspect he already knows.

"I want a half-dozen secret videos that play like TV commercials, maybe two or three minutes apiece, designed to stir up fear and incite outrage. My people will put together a list of places we want them mailed anonymously—senators, media outlets, the FDA, FTC, major stockholders, workers' unions, patient-rights advocates, and anybody else we can think of who'll help scuttle the merger. What matters here is that Briggs Pharmaceutical has nothing to do with any of this."

Frank looks at me, which is my cue.

"Sick little girl," I say, "her mom agonizing over what to do. She can't afford medicine because dad lost his job at M-Slovak, and now the cost of treatment has skyrocketed—"

"Yes!" Rex blurts.

I go on: "A concerned voice-over briefly summarizes the facts as Dad comes in, tattered classifieds under his arm, dejection etched in his face. Mom's tucking the little girl into bed. *Mommy, I'm scared.* Mom's trying to reassure her, but Dad buries his face and wants to know how this could have happened. The narrator intones, *It's not too late.*"

Bam! Rex slaps the table. "Yes! Write 'em down, for my eyes only." Then to Frank, he says, "Figure ten- or fifteen-thousand apiece?"

"I need to bill you upfront—say, eighty-five thousand—so we can walk around with the money."

He touches the button and tells someone to cut a check for ninety-five.

"What's the other ten?" Frank asks, apparently knowing Rex well enough to assume the extra's not a bonus, at least not yet.

"I need a favor," Rex says. "You been following that hit & run at Mile-Square?"

Frank nods.

"I want you to run PR for the drugstore guy. He's an old frat brother, a good man with a good family, but that goddamn preacher's burning him up. I don't want to see him lose his stores. Here's his attorney," he adds, producing a card. "I don't need to hear what you're doing."

When a woman brings an envelope for Frank, Rex stands, which is our cue to leave. She tells Rex, "Tony Faritzka's waiting to pitch that employee-motivation program."

Rex nudges Frank. "I say find the one not doing his job, then fire his ass. That'll give 'em *all* some motivation."

*　　*　　*

Here's something you might not want to imagine: a fat old naked geezer with a bum back right now busily boffing a skinny little old woman, and it's happening in *my* back yard.

Well, inside the renovated coach house, anyway.

I live in Ravenswood, an old neighborhood just west of Chicago's Uptown. My home is long and narrow, the yard fenced, wrought iron out front, sculpted flowerbeds all around, landscaping courtesy of neighbor Hank Barnahay, the old man back there sharing an evening "libation" with Ms. Moeroff.

I swear they do it every day. A couple of gerbils, they are.

She's the one who sold me the place way below market value in exchange for lifetime tenancy. She holds the mortgage, but I'm under strict orders to tear it up after she dies.

I figure she'll outlive me.

I'm thawing prawns because Cyn just called and offered to come by for an unscheduled Thursday-night romp, and I think I might actually convince her to stay all night—that's *if* I satisfy her hankerin' for shrimp salad. For some reason, seafood has a way of putting her in the mood. I'm tempted to get myself one of those big lobster costumes and cut a hole in the crotch, then try a little muff-diving.

You know, that age-old quest for the bearded clam.

The phone rings again, Kristen calling from *Shoot & Die*. She sounds exasperated. "Sam's here!" she blurts. "He's nosing around, asking about the insurance edit!"

"It's not his place to check on my jobs." I'm not territorial—barked the hound sniffing another pooch's pee. "Tell him to get lost."

"I did, but he says he's putting together some kind of status report."

"Put him on, then be ready to boot his butt out the door."

"He's down the hall, demanding to see the billing logs."

"Page him." Damn idiot has no right barging into my edit and aggravating my crew.

I can hear an echo telling him to pick up a call from Roenik. After a minute, Kristen comes back. "He left."

"Yeah, soon as he heard my name. Next time tell him *my* orders are don't even let him in."

And she's off, armed and dangerous.

It's nearly six o'clock, so I dash around and set timers for all my DVRs. If I have to buff the image of a guy who killed a little girl, I better see what they're saying about him on the various local news shows.

It turns out to be quite brutal, exactly what I expected: shots of a makeshift teddy bear-strewn memorial, outraged neighbors gathering along the street, Falluson holding court for the cameras, our distraught mother flanked by angry kin, a graphic showing routes to the funeral home so strangers and hangers-on can swell the crowd for Monday's service. The driver's still in a coma, upgraded from critical to serious.

I reset everything for ten and eleven o'clock, then call the family's attorney.

"I am not issuing any statements," he intones. He's rather displeased to learn I'm involved. It's not exactly the highlight of *my* day, either.

"Good. Don't whack the hornets' nest when they're already stinging."

"My sole responsibility is to ensure my client's *legal* protection," he cautions.

"Look, I sleep with a lawyer," I return. Let's quit posturing.

"I can't allow this to be tried in the media."

"Good luck, pal. I know you have to pretend to rise above it, but the media will sway judge and jury whether you like it or not. At some point you'll have to paint your own pretty picture; my job is to whitewash the canvas so not so much of their ugly one bleeds through. Don't worry, I'll run any public spectacles by you first."

"Good then," he says, a reluctant member of the team now. Actually, I wish Coach would just leave me on the bench.

I stretch out and start blazing through those "fact-sheets," a lot of it boring stuff about merger ramifications. More sobering is the list of several-hundred Parzilac violence cases, including a few where the "Parzilac defense" has been used to convince juries that criminal acts were caused by the drug. M-Slovak has even reached undisclosed settlements with the families of at least three suicides. One case against the prescribing psychiatrist stirred up so much controversy that M-Slovak finally agreed to assume liability for all clinicians. It's cheaper to pay a few claims quietly than to jeopardize sales of more than sixty-million doses per month; and that might discourage potential plaintiffs from challenging a mega-corporation's legal department in what surely would turn into a costly, protracted battle.

So how do I slam Parzilac when it's a legally approved drug? Do I try to influence supposedly impartial civil-trial judges? How do I sway indemnified psychs? It seems I'd have to reduce demand, maybe by scaring the public—the *users*—but so far nothing else has.

Ms. Moeroff stops by, a mischievous twinkle in her eyes, looking like a gray-haired anorexic with that coat-hanger skeleton, droopy little breasts, and those constellations of liver spots that dapple her milky-white hands and arms. She's positively glowing in her favorite hot-pink leotard.

Pouring her a glass of wine, I begin to blanch the prawns, explaining, "I'm hoping you'll carp and kvetch about how I make shrimp salad, then demand to take over."

"If it's for that she-devil, you're on your own," she teases. She's buried five husbands, claiming it took that many to find true love. She calls Cyn my first big pending mistake. "So, you got any pretty pictures to show me?"

I gesture toward my satchel, explaining the allergy-tat concept as she admires my work. She's my biggest fan, one who thinks I should quit wearing suits and give up the demands of commerce to focus instead on painting and drawing simply for the sake of art. She doesn't quite understand that my job does allow me to be an artist, that print ads and film and video let me paint on widely distributed multi-million-dollar canvases—all paid for by rich clients.

Patronage for profit isn't so different from that time-honored practice of patronage for the sake of prestige.

"Little girls might like a pretty ballerina," she suggests.

I don't have the heart to tell her that's passé, that I'm after mass-market appeal, so I ice the shrimp and pause long enough to draw her a soulful-eyed little ballerina wearing a frilly-laced, fourteen-colored tutu. She's delighted.

I start assembling the salad, but she can't stand to watch anymore, flouncing over to snatch the spoon and take charge. I put my arms around her for a big hug. It's been a long time since I lost my mom, but I never forget how it feels . . .

Ms. Moeroff always finds ways to show me.

Salad ready, she retrieves the ballerina sketch for her collection, offering a warning on her way out: "A Thursday-nighter must mean your lawyer-gal wants to file away at your briefs. Just remember: don't let her ruin the mood by talking about her job."

It's after nine by the time Cyn finally roars up in her new Volt. I meet her outside, warm springtime air blanketing our embrace, a scent of blossoming lilacs mingling with the sweet fragrance of her flaxen hair. I give her a gentle kiss . . . .

"Woo-hoo!" shout some boys biking by, so we move it inside before someone summons the police.

"You get the food ready," she suggests, lingering for another kiss, "while I lose the power-suit."

I carry trays up to the bedroom in time to catch her emerging from the bath in a pullover nightshirt. Forget the suit; one quick water-hose spray—cold, preferably—and this would qualify as high fashion in my neck of the woods. She's swept her hair around and below the ear on one side, adding some highlights that hint of glittering gold, a mischievous tease of frondeur in contrast to her normally professional demeanor.

We race through our snacks, then find ourselves setting sail, riding the waterbed waves—which surely must be leaking, wet as we are. At one point we pause to catch our breaths, so I fetch my mask and snorkel, then dive in for some more . . .

And the bearded clam is quite lovely, indeed.

Eventually, she manages to blow the wind right out of my sails, so I slip over and open the screened window, letting the cool night breeze and sounds of distant traffic waft through the room. Back to my Cyn, I pull her close, her cheek on my shoulder, my hand massaging the cut of her jib . . .

And she glances toward the clock.

"It's almost eleven," she says.

"I'll write you a late-slip," I whisper.

"I need to watch the news."

"No rush; I'm recording all the local affiliates."

She pulls away and gives me a curious look. "Seriously? Why?"

"I'm keeping up with the Mile-Square hit & run so I can do PR for the driver."

She's aghast, shaking her head now, our ship having run aground. "I signed the mother," she practically wails. "Mr. Salterfin's going to let me act as lead attorney. I'm suing the drugstore guy."

There you have it. Ms. Moeroff warned me about talking biz, and now Cyn is getting dressed while I try to convince her to stay. Vowing to refuse the assignment doesn't work because she's always pushed me to be another career fast-tracker, and she knows I wouldn't step so far outside my usual bailiwick on a job like this unless it mattered to somebody important. She's already been exasperated lately because I refuse to apply for Frank's soon-to-be-vacant job. Hey, I like making images, not deals.

Alas, she hugs me stiffly and disappears into the night.

A rather long, sleepless night, I might add.

So the next morning I get up too early, take a rather lonesome shower—no need for the mask and snorkel, that's for sure—and head out back to find Ms. Moeroff relaxing in her chaise-longue. She makes quite a picture in that flowery frock and sunglasses, a straw hat tied down with her favorite chartreuse scarf, the morning newspaper spread across her lap. "Today you will discover opportunities amid adversity," she reads from the horoscopes. "Recognize them, and chart a new course."

"And today my course is to bail water for a client Cyn is preparing to sink."

"Ah," she says, "no wonder your ships parted in the night."

"Business and personal are separate matters," I complain without conviction.

Ms. Moeroff gazes at me over the top of her glasses, that look you give a six-year-old planning to parachute from atop the garage with a pillow-case. "Are they to her?" she challenges.

"I'd like to think so."

"I'm sure you would, dear," she says, shooing me off. "Put your suit on and go to work, Danté. It's nothing personal, you know."

It's starting to be, I know that much.

As I drive toward the Kehoe offices in Elmhurst, I call Cyn's cell-phone. She's very curt: "I can't discuss my strategies with you; that's attorney-client privilege."

"Sure," I answer, "but practicing law and manipulating the media don't *have* to overlap." I feel like a six-year-old atop the garage clutching a pillow-case.

"What's your goal?" she asks.

"To counter Falluson's self-righteous crusade before it drives the drug-stores out of business."

"You're protecting the value of my target's assets," she says, mulling the concept for a moment.

"Which is to *your* benefit. You don't want him losing his stores before you try to take 'em."

"Good point. So then, just make sure you succeed." I don't get a chance to answer before she has to pick up another call.

This pillow-case better break my fall.

As I'm pulling into the lot at Kehoe/Lundy, a security guy waves me down from the booth, saying Ms. Kirloot needs to see me right away. I park and head to her office in human resources, figuring she wants me to sign some benefits forms, but I find security-guy Tommy standing awkwardly beside boxes packed with my personal office accoutrements.

Kirloot looks appropriately sad. It's the reorganization, you see. I'll get two months' salary, plus six months' insurance, good news delivered with the bad.

This is not how I pictured someday leaving the agency.

Imagine that: it looks like I'm unemployed.

CHAPTER 3

What I'm picturing is a nice guy in his mid-thirties, blond hair, average build, devilish good looks, a twinkle in his eye—okay, it's me, but what I don't want to imagine is how I'd look standing in a long line at the unemployment office, dark circles under my eyes, my face the picture of dispirited resignation . . .

Let's try it this way: have me standing confidently beside my lawyer, Super-Cyn SiCauge, barracuda in a power-suit, champion of the downtrodden, righter of corporate wrongs, and she's suing the socks off those Kehoe/Lundy bastards for wrongful discharge. The jury is awarding me *all* the corporate assets, the company now mine, mine! Mine!

Okay, let's bring it down a notch. Picture me updating my résumé, dazzling all the competing agencies, landing the power position, then swooping back to steal away Kehoe's most lucrative clients!

Sigh.

Okay, forget the pictures. Right now as I carry my office accoutrements to the parking lot, what I really see is the hard reality of a young single mother sitting in a beat-up blue compact, face buried in her hands, and she's crying.

The Kehoe/Lundy security guard doesn't notice. "You guys always do better when it's time to move on," he reassures me while helping load the last box into the back of my jet-black Cadillac CTS-V. Stepping back, he fidgets uncomfortably. "You'll do all right."

"You, too, Tommy." I lean close, glancing about furtively, then whisper, "And I'll give you a big raise when I come back and take over this place."

He grins. "I just bet you would, sir." He tips his hat and wanders back inside.

I head toward Melissa's car. She sees me and quickly wipes her face, looking embarrassed as she tries again to start the engine.

Whir-whir-whir . . . whir . . . whoooo . . . clunk.

"Are you okay?" I ask. Her window's down an inch, tilted at an odd angle, probably forever.

Whir . . . whoooo . . . clunk.

"Stupid car!" She's near tears again, refusing to look up at me.

Whir . . . whoooo . . . clunk.

"Let it rest," I advise gently.

Clunk. Clunk.

I walk around and let myself in, squeezing into the small space without saying a word. Melissa Norrow has worked as our account administrator for close to a year. She's a pretty lady, early twenties, with curly chestnut hair teasing her shoulders. Her credentials were minimal, but she impressed Frank and me with her determination, so we gave her a chance.

And we've never regretted it.

I've seen her stand up to the bullying demands of myriad Kehoe drones, so I can't imagine car problems rattling her this much. She's suffered more than her share of personal adversity, too, barely surviving a harsh childhood, her mother long dead in the bottom of a liquor bottle, the abusive stepfather kicking her out after she got pregnant at seventeen. GED classes, night school, waitressing, cleaning offices, swapping child care with others of like predicament . . . She's worked hard to achieve her success, and to be the best possible mother to an adorable little boy who must be about four by now.

"I just got fired," she says, staring at her lap. Okay, now I'm really ticked.

"Me, too," I admit. She finally looks at me, surprised. I want to appear casual and confident; hey, these things happen. "Did they give you a reason?"

"*Reorganization*," she spits out. It's a swear-word. "They gave me two weeks, which is when my insurance was gonna bump up to full coverage."

"You'll be working again in no time."

"I have no cushion," she breathes. "I'm a month late on my rent, three weeks behind on the woman who watches Taj, and I need to take him to see an expensive doctor because his asthma is getting worse. I can't afford to keep waiting for better coverage." She's crying again. "And my *stupid-stupid* car keeps quitting on me."

"Hey, do you still have that zip with my old files?"

She nods and pats her leather-bound schedule planner, the one that probably cost more than her whole wardrobe.

"Okay, here's my offer: ride with me to the studio where you can update both my résumé and yours, and I'll have my neighbor Hank come tow your car somewhere so he can figure out what's wrong. He's a mechanical whiz who owes me some favors."

Yeah, for not turning the hose on him when he comes around every evening to share a "libation" with Ms. Moeroff.

"Something else," I point out. "Remember, you're not just cut loose to drift alone; you've got friends who'll help you search for a better port." There it is, a smile through the tears, Theta Moeroff's horoscope to the rescue.

She grabs her kid-seat, which we strap into my Caddie, and we hit the road. My phone rings; Kristen's in a panic. "I had to let Christobal take the insurance videos! He brought a signed release because *Sam* is finishing the job. Then Frank called, sounding really weird, looking for you, and now Murray's here freaking out because he just got *fired*. He's ranting about how Kehoe/Lundy is the anti-Christ. Danté, what's going on?"

"Melissa and I got tossed overboard, too."

"Oh no," she gasps, and I know it's because she's concerned about us, not about all those jobs I won't be able to give her anymore.

"I can't believe Murray got torpedoed. All those years freelancing, and not six months after we finally talk him onto staff . . . They're dismantling Frank's team before he's even out the door."

"Hey," she says, "Frank just buzzed. Hang up so he can call you."

Two clicks and he's on. "Just can't hold a job, can you?" he kids. He's a real card.

"They got Melissa, too," I point out.

He's more serious now. "Yeah, she was perceived as too loyal to you and the others who are being let go."

"Well, that's a two-way street."

"I hear you. So, have you started job-hunting yet?"

"It's only been ten minutes, Frank."

"Yeah, you always were a little slow."

"If you know where I can find something here in Chicago for the same kind of money, a position that'll let me draw pictures and have this kind of fun, sign me up."

"Don't be in a rush. Remember, the secret Briggs projects are billed through me; we can spread that money around. I'll be at Kehoe all day with Sam, so if you don't hear from me, make sure you bring our cohorts to the party tonight. There'll be plenty of glad-handing enemies surrounding me; I want my friends there, too."

Melissa and I pull into *Shoot & Die*. She reminds me to grab my old-fashioned paper-bound schedule planner, but it's not in its likely spot behind the seat, and it's not like she'll be writing in my appointments anymore. Long as I've been trying to lose that thing, maybe I finally have! She rolls her eyes, and we head inside. The receptionist is sorry to hear what happened.

"It's just a rumor," I tell him with a wink. "Unless and until somebody informs you officially, I'm still here working on whatever I want—with full access to the video library, if you catch my drift."

He does.

Kristen waylays us in the hallway. "I *know* you've got a plan," she announces hopefully.

"A couple of short-term projects to crank out, anyway," I return.

We find Murray lurking in the conference room. "Wanna freelance?" I ask.

He grins. Short and stocky with unevenly cropped black hair, he has a round face and chronic skin problems, an odd bird who's a bit bashful except when it comes to his projects. He pulls out those thick horn-rimmed glasses and perches them on his nose, his signal it's time to work.

We all grab seats so I can conduct my first meeting as captain of the good ship *S.S. Unemployed*. "Okay, none of us can afford to retire yet, so do you want to make a little money while we all look for new jobs?"

"Count me on board," Murray says. "You need a word-slinger for some client to keel-haul, I'm your man." He is, too.

Kristen and Melissa are nodding agreement, so I continue. "Then job number one is PR for the Mile-Square hit & run driver. Murray, you collect content and stay on top of the media so we'll know what we're fighting. Kristen, you grab anything visually useful and stay in the loop with our buddy Neusome; he's putting Falluson on the air Sunday. I wanted to work behind the scenes, but it's looking like we may have to come out shooting."

Kristen salutes. She's not much for agency politics, but she does know how to schmooze in a pinch.

"Job two is producing stealth videos designed to interfere with M-Slovak's pending merger, the kind you might enjoy writing, Murray."

He literally licks his lips. "Do I get to slam Parzilac?" He wrote scripts for the roll-out, a job over which he later expressed regret.

"If you promise to show no mercy." I slide him the "fact-sheets." He starts flipping through them, wagging his brows. It's payback time.

"Ooo Ooo!" Kristen says, raising her hand like a third-grader who finally knows the answer. "I could produce those, if you want."

"Hmmm," I say, feigning skepticism. "Maybe I better have a look at your résumé—which, by the way, is job three. Melissa's the document factory, so if you want to dust off your respective packs of lies, she's available to update them for you. Melissa, I could also use some help with the admin on these jobs, billing and what-not. What do you say?"

"Given your track record with paperwork, I'd have to say yes—yes, you *can* use some help." Good, she's getting the wind back in her sails.

"Hey, Wardley acted like all I had to do was draw a few pictures. Okay, job four: I'm going to lose my access to the Kehoe client footage, so somebody should fire up several DVRs and start laying off chunks."

Kristen says, "Good thing I know my way around the video library here better than anyone. So what are we grabbing?"

"Everything we did for M-Slovak, plus samples of the best work we've done for other clients, stuff any of us might want for demo reels."

"Byron's back there today," Kristen says. "I'll draft him for the heavy lifting."

"That oughta make him smile." An inside joke.

Kristen adds, "All this dubbing will take some time, so when I pick the best ones, you should sign them out using yesterday's date—you know, back when you were a somebody. I'll load them in my car, and keep them until I'm done—or until Sam catches on and demands their return."

"Sneaky—I like that."

The receptionist buzzes me; attorney Ritenour's on the line, so everybody scatters and gets to work.

"There's been vandalism," says Ritenour. He has a way of cutting to the chase. "Several stores were targeted, and threatening calls have scared a half-dozen employees into quitting. The family agrees we should find ways to blunt the impact of all this negative publicity."

"I need to talk with them, learn some background, see what they have for visuals."

"If you can meet me in Hillside—" He gives me the address.

Heading for my car, I'm intercepted by Hal Neusome driving in. "Sorry to hear about Kehoe," he says, rolling down his window. Damn, word gets around.

"All for the best, Hal. I couldn't work for Sam, so this is my way out with a nice severance package. Why quit when they'll pay you to go away."

"I've played that game." He has, too—recently.

"I want to help with your segment on the hit & run." He's clearly pleased, so now it's time for full disclosure. "I'll be spinning against the backlash."

"Works for me. The show needs balance."

"I'll put together a personal look at the driver and his stores. I'm hoping you'll do more than just powder Falluson's butt—like maybe dig up some background on his history of boycotts and other righteous crusades. Look for anything where he's turned out to be off-base or outright wrong."

"Shouldn't be hard."

I drive out to the house in Hillside, a very nice place on a secluded cul-de-sac, elegant but homey. The adult son isn't here yet, but Ritenour and the wife are ready for me. I'd say she's about sixty, a handsome woman with an air of high society, except right now she's a mess, cried out and worried sick. Imagine tumbling from the social register and discovering your only friends are a shyster billing by the hour and an unemployed fantasizer who just likes to draw.

Ritenour leads us to couches, but paces while we sit. He's a big guy, well over six feet, with an oversized head and obstinate red hair that points every which way. He projects the image of authority, very serious, but I can't tell yet if he's got that knack for engendering sympathy. "She has a trove of photos," he says, "covering the history of the stores, plus various community-improvement projects, employee picnics, and so on." He's all business. Cripe, show some sensitivity. This woman's been through hell, and it's far from over.

"I'm just here to help while your husband recovers," I tell her. "Right now I'm more concerned for you than the stores, so let me know when I ask too much." My voice is soft. I'm close to her, not crowding, symbolically reaching out. Sure, it's a bit calculated, but I mean what I said. Besides, I've just found a face to put on this tragedy, and she's sitting before me, exhausted and scared. That's a basic strategy of public relations, matching a concept to a sympathetic face. This is the real deal.

We move to the dining room where boxes are spread across the table. She answers questions while Ritenour and I sort through photos and mementos. We spend about an hour at it, by which time I can see our hostess is flagging, so we call it a day.

I'm working my way to the door when the son finally arrives. He's a fortyish yuppie-looking sort, definitely a younger version of the man whose face has been staring out from one station's over-the-shoulder newscast graphics, but he's agitated, definitely shaken up. Ritenour tells him he can talk in front of me.

"A forensic surgeon just examined Dad," the son explains, shaking his head. "Those injuries to his chest and shoulder? He says they couldn't have been caused by the accident."

The wife is confused, Ritenour baffled. I'm the one who finally asks . . .

"So what's his theory?"

The son spreads his hands, incomprehensible truth the kind of picture we never imagined . . .

"He says they're *stab* wounds."

*   *   *

Driving Melissa to her apartment in Wicker Park, I'm really not in the mood to think about where I might look for a job, but she can't afford to waste time, so she's busy compiling her own list of places to apply. She's understandably worried, and maybe not as confident in her abilities as she ought to be, but we both know it's hard to imagine either of us will find something as fun and challenging as it was to be a part of Frank's team.

We park at a building down the street from hers, waiting for someone to bring down her son, Taj. This neighborhood in the heart of Chicago has faded considerably, many of its tenements and apartments now run down, office space vacant, graffiti-walled storefronts peering through padlocked steel gates, drug exchanges and prostitution in plain view.

A woman appears with the boy, a little moppet with longish chestnut curls and big brown eyes, purple shorts and a faded purple *Monster Bin* t-shirt showing all the critters from the popular cartoon—each character and the storage bin sold separately, batteries not included. He climbs into his mother's lap for the short drive, burying his face when I greet him. I'd never imagined my destiny would be to turn into that man who scares children and pets.

"Goo-lah, foo-lah, woo-lah!" I tell him, earning a peek and a smile. Yes, I've seen the cartoon a few times, and I'm guessing his favorite of all the monsters who "live" in the bin is his quasi-namesake: "Q-Tawzh" —the big-eyed little monster covered with curly purple hair, herald of the great "Goo-lah" proclamation.

"You're sure it's okay for me to bring him to the studio this weekend?" Melissa asks.

"Long as he brings his Monster Bin," I answer.

"I'll make sure he keeps busy and out of our way."

"No, I mean so I have somebody to play Monster Bin with whenever I need a break." I give him a sneaky look, earning another grin when I add, "Goo-lah, foo-lah, woo-lah!"

I pull up to her building, a smallish five-story walk-up, and offer to escort her inside, but she's quick to insist that's not necessary. "You shouldn't leave a car like this on the street," she adds by way of explanation, but I suspect she doesn't want me to see her place.

"I'll pick you up at eight."

"We'll be here in front," she says.

"I could call up."

"My phone service lapsed," she admits, glancing away. How do you tell someone not to be embarrassed without making them more so?

I watch until they're inside, then head for The Blue Pony, picturing a few dozen people from Kehoe standing around long enough to be seen before they slip out to get on with their weekends. Maybe a few of Frank's old cronies will show up later, lingering late to drink too much from the cash bar, smoking cigars and carping about how the business ain't what it used to be.

I park and walk inside where I'm directed upstairs . . . and the place is packed! Kristen and Murray are ensconced by an hors d'oeuvres table, surrounded by production vendors. I head their way, but find myself needing a Sizemore 4000 to navigate the gantlet of colleagues, cohorts, compatriots, and compadres.

"Free munchies!" Kristen touts, wagging her brows, "—right on time for all us unemployed types!"

"I'm counting at least one-sixty here so far," Murray says, taking off his glasses, "—a lot of brass, too. I feel naked not having at least a VP on my name tag."

I touch bases with Byron, who's up front re-checking the wiring for what I'm sure is the umpteenth time. Dressed nicer than usual, he can bend over without smiling for the crowd, a refreshing new image.

Frank's across the room, surrounded by bigshots, everybody shaking hands and grabbing arms and patting backs, leaning close to whisper in hushed tones followed by uproarious laughter. He's moving slowly from group to group, a glacier carving valleys and filling lakes, still powerful enough to move a mountain or two.

Then Frank's touch-sensor, ultra-sonic, thermal-image, infrared, sonar doo-hickey Dellman 4000 kicks in and he's aware of my presence, purposefully catching my eye. He nods and gestures to wait, meaning he's working my way, don't move too far and throw him off course.

Hal Neusome has spotted me, too, and is heading toward me. As a celebrity, he's getting lots of attention, the charismatic performer playing to his audience.

"Is it coming together?" Neusome breathes, smiling and waving whenever his name is called out.

"There's a surprise twist, for which I made arrangements to net you the exclusive."

"Excellent! So what are the terms?" He glances about like he's making sure his competitors aren't pointing microphones at us.

"You give face time to the lead detective, Heath Culler, who'll appear under the pretense of exhorting people to come forward with information to help his investigation. Reality is, he's after lieutenant bars and wants to show he can handle the media."

"Why *my* show?"

"Hal, baby!" I say, acting like the stereotypical snake-oil salesman, "I'm the one cut the deal, and you're my *main* man. Besides," I add more seriously, "you're a bit outside the mainstream contacts his boss uses, and you offer a Sunday night slot before the PR machine kicks in Monday morning. Hey, I had to think fast."

Several people stop by to chat—Isn't Frank something? What a guy! Gosh, I remember . . .

"So what's the scoop?" Hal blurts after they've moved on.

"Multiple stab wounds, and a case of prescription drugs is missing from the Madison Street store. It's an ambush robbery that turned into kidnapping, or maybe a carjacking. He either ran over that little girl while struggling with his attacker, or he was left to die, bleeding badly, and he hit her while trying desperately to drive himself to the hospital before passing out."

"This is big," Hal says, and he's got that look, already painting his own picture.

"Falluson's got his symbol backwards; it's *my* guy who's a victim, the victim of that neighborhood."

"You're sure no leaks before Sunday night?" I swear Hal is about to hyperventilate, no doubt imagining this going national . . . *According to reports on Chicago's "Neusome on the News"* . . . *Video courtesy of "Neusome on the News"* . . .

"You need to promote this," I tell him, "without revealing the surprise. Start Sunday morning with a blitz touting, *Startling new developments you won't want to miss.* Detective Culler will make himself unavailable for comment all day, and I'll arrange to shield the family and the Madison Street store."

"Falluson will be suspicious."

"Act like the drugstore vandalism is what's new, and we'll be obvious about collecting shots to support it. He'll welcome the chance to portray it

as outraged citizens; then he'll advocate taking the high road with his organized boycott. Just before airtime you'll learn from Culler that those vandals
suddenly appear to be predators taking advantage of a victim while he's
down, a good man who supported the very community that's now failing to
help him protect his stores. You get the picture."

Frank is close now, keeping an eye on us while we talk. Rex Briggs has
just shown up, another surprise.

"The affiliates will scramble to cover this on the eleven o'clocks," Hal
says.

"To help your show get the credit, I'll put together media kits with footage, background, easily verified fact-sheets, and so on. Your competition will
jump on those to avoid being the only station in town stuck with nothing
but a live remote and no cut-aways."

Neusome is flashing me that endearing smile, the one that makes people
believe everything he says. "What do you need?"

"Reasonable costs, and I want press credentials for myself, Kristen, and
Byron's crew. We need access, especially in case something else breaks at the
last minute."

"First thing tomorrow," he promises.

"Good. Now, don't be seen hanging out with me all night."

He turns and nods to Frank, then wanders off to glad-hand his adoring
fans.

Frank seizes the chance to come over with a man I've never met, introducing him as Flynn Durbett. "And this is Danté Roenik, the ace I've been
telling you about." Maybe he's trying to scare up some job prospects for me,
not that I'm sure I want to jump right back into the conniving world of
agency politics, artistic integrity valued somewhere below a nickel's worth of
sell, sell! Sell!

"You're a man of integrity," Durbett says, surprising me with both the
offbeat greeting and his country accent, very southern but not quite a bayou
drawl. His voice is deep, sonorous, ideal for narration and voice-overs,
maybe even for singing.

"I've heard you and Kristen made a video," Frank accuses, feigning in-
dignity. "We'll have to listen to a speech by Dib Wardley," he adds more
seriously, referring to the president of Kehoe/Lundy. "Then you're supposed to get up, spin a nice lie or two about me, and introduce the vid."

"I'm not the speechin' type, Frank."

"Wing it," he says with a wink before breaking off to intercept a group of well-wishers. I suspect leaving Flynn Durbett and me alone was his plan.

"Frank speaks highly of you," Durbett says, somehow seeming to look right through me. He projects an interesting image: bald on top with a fringe of gray just above his ears, longer hair pulled into a pony tail in the back. He's medium height with what appears to be a medium build under that precisely tailored European-cut suit, but he moves with the smooth assurance of power, the kind of guy who might break you in half without missing a dance step. I'm the center of his attention, but something tells me he's also watching the crowd, eyes in the back of his head, listening to everybody at once.

"It's been an honor to work for the master," I answer in keeping with the spirit of send-off banter. Gosh, that Frank's a helluva guy—except I'm not exaggerating.

"I've been a client of his four years now," he says, watching for my reaction.

"Apart from Kehoe?" Obviously, but he caught me by surprise.

"That Wardley feller didn't want the agency to take my business, so Frank's been handling it on the side." Kehoe/Lundy not want business? What's this guy sell—botulism? "He showed me how to launch a catalog system with websites and in-bound telemarketing."

"Have I heard of you?"

"Maybe. Most of my subsidiaries fall under *The Weisman Company*."

"What do you sell?"

"Services play a small part for the high-end clients, but the biggest chunk—seventy-million in sales last year and growing steadily—is sporting goods, hunting and camping and adventure supplies."

"Why did Wardley not want the account?"

"He don't like that I started out with gun shops throughout the south, then added other defense supplies—you know, alternative weaponry and clandestine communications. Private-detective and corporate-espionage technology, specialized information gathering, customized encryption software, laboratory supplies, and other low-profile goodies make up a nice piece of business both here and overseas. Discretion is part of our niche, even on the everyday stuff, and Wardley would rather focus on *prestige* clients." Another swear-word.

"Where you located?"

"Main headquarters is south of Waverly, Tennessee. I keep an office here for working with Frank; plus the catalogs and other print work is mostly done up here."

I'm picturing a clutch of ole militia boys in camouflage fatigues: they're hunkering down in a bunker, eagerly tearing open a plain brown wrapper to gaze at the new Weisman catalog—like schoolboys with a dog-eared *Hustler* magazine. I can understand Wardley's reluctance.

"I'd like to see what you and the old buzzard have been doing."

"I'm glad to hear you say that," he says all genteel-like with a slight bow, "but that's as much business as I'm willin' to talk in a place like this." He grins.

I can't help but smile, too. You have to admire somebody who's successfully tapped the paranoia market. It's gotta be a big one, especially among the *true* patriots.

Wardley's up front calling for attention. Everybody falls quiet, the liquid crowd propelling Frank forward. He steps up beside the podium.

Everything seems to blur for a minute, nice words from Wardley, Frank accepting a gold clock, extended applause, me talking about Frank's commitment to his work and the people on his team . . . and finally the video rolls.

The crowd is loving it, laughing and shaking their heads, Frank glaring at me in mock outrage. For a hokey script, it's coming off funnier than I expected. Come on—Frank selling cross-trainers to kangaroos?

But then I step back from myself, and suddenly the world is surreal, the people laughing in another dimension, and there's one image I dread ever seeing again. It's that last shot, Frank on the beach being buried by youngsters.

The funeral shot.

I don't want this show ever to come to an end because it means that Frank as I know him is coming to an end.

Will this be me someday?

What am I even doing in this business?

When Ms. Moeroff asks me to draw, it's the intrinsic beauty of an image I created that she appreciates, its form and style, the color and texture, the *art*. And yet I can't even draw her anything so simple as a little ballerina without recasting it in my mind. Is it sellable? Can it be an allergy tattoo? Do a million faceless little girls demographically charted and focus-grouped want to *buy* it? Ms. Moeroff doesn't care . . .

Why do I?

The video is ending, but I can't look.

More laughter, applause.

Frank is thanking me and Kristen and everybody who helped put all this together, imagining how much fun we must have had planning ways to skewer the old geezer.

But it wasn't fun, and I'm ready to chuck all this in. I don't want an audience anymore, and I don't want my dreams packaged for commercial appeal.

I want to be an artist.

I want to draw butterflies and let them flit away unseen as they seek their own place amid uncharted realms.

And Frank is saying that despite leaving Kehoe/Lundy, he refuses to roll over and play dead. "So I've taken over *Shoot & Die* with plans to expand," he says from that other dimension, "and I'm launching my new agency from there, too."

The room is abuzz, some clapping, a few cheering him on, many too stunned for words.

He's looking toward Durbett, who glances at me and nods.

Frank surveys the room, then announces, "And I won't be satisfied until I've recruited the best creative director I've ever had on my team, bar none."

Now quite a few are turning to gape at *me*.

Someone shouts, "What are you gonna call the new agency, Frank?"

He winks at me and grins. "If Danté agrees, I hope to call it *The Dellman/Roenik Group*."

CHAPTER 4

"What does *your* choice of socks say about *you*?!"

I hate local newscasts, all those hard-hitting fashion investigations, doggedly ferreted *facts* telling the story.

"This is Letta Chunoe, *live*, here at the new *Fat Piggies* in Elmhurst, the ultimate gift store for all things pig!"

Million-dollar remote trucks, news choppers, in-your-face reporters, all the information you need to know!

"A behind-the-scenes look at the making of tonight's *very special* episode of *Rock-slide!* Are those big rocks real?"

Gee, do you think *Rock-slide* airs on a competing channel?

"Next up, Psychic Sally! She's here, live in our studio, taking *your* calls!"

Ohmigod! I should've stayed home this morning and called!

It's way late now and I'm beat, but here I am scanning my recordings of today's news while the remnants of Frank's party smolder over at The Blue Pony. He and some of his cohorts are planning to stop by here sometime in the wee hours. Oh joy.

One channel's showing the makeshift memorial in Mile-Square, but at least it's yesterday's video, meaning they must not consider this story worthy of another live remote—yet. Now they're cutting to the drugstore on Madison while telling us there's no change in the driver's condition. Rats. That fixes this image in the minds of people who might want to lash out in revenge.

Here's something new: a shot of the wrecked car, then a graphic depicting its path. It seems it careered north under the El, veered right, hit the girl, then swerved and continued east before colliding with a marker and concrete bench at the corner of one of those dilapidated neighborhood parks.

Now we see several school pictures of the victim, a young African-American girl with a shy, pretty smile and tiny pink bows woven into her braids. They're putting a face on the tragedy, and it's working; I'm both sad to see her robbed of the chance to discover her place in the world and furious with the criminals who caused such a senseless death. It's almost powerful enough to make me forget that a young child never should have been allowed to roam the streets after 2:00 a.m. on a school night.

Now they're soliciting comments from outraged relatives and friends, cutting away to shots of a crowd gathering at the funeral home, Reverend Falluson in the background running interference for the mother. At least there's no mention of the boycott. I don't know if he's holding back because Hal will give him a lot more face time than one of these eight-second sound bites, or if the affiliates just want to see what kind of legs this story grows before they decide to buy it running shoes.

Oh no, in the final shot I catch a glimpse of Cyn hovering near the mother.

My phone rings, Cyn calling from the office. These partner-wannabe's work way too many hours.

"Heard I made the news," she says.

"And you looked very lawyerly," I confirm. Now, how do I say this? "Listen, Cyn, you need to back off from the public-spectacle aspect of this. I have reason to believe the driver will soon become a sympathetic figure, too."

"That would be quite a PR accomplishment for you."

"No, it's what the facts are going to reveal, and I don't think you want to end up looking like a meanie. But hey, you can still make some money; go after the car insurance, maybe some business liability coverage."

She says nothing for a moment. "I'll take that under advisement. So how was the party?"

"Frank announced he's opening a new agency."

She sighs. "It must be hard for the old guy to let go. I feel sorry for him."

"He's planning to offer me a partnership."

"You told him you're not available, right?"

"Well, actually, I am—available, I mean. I got laid off this morning. Dib Wardley and Sam Cox are cleaning house."

She's quiet again. "Tell me you didn't accept Frank's offer."

"We haven't had a chance to discuss it yet."

"There's nothing to discuss, Danté." She sounds exasperated now. "You have to consider your career progression."

"Well, I've also been thinking about quitting the business to become an artist."

"You *are* an artist—a successful one. Very few creative people ever achieve the kind of clout you have, which means you have to keep stepping carefully from stone to stone. If you take a break—or worse, fall in the wa-ter—you'll have to start over again. Right now you need to land somewhere prestigious fast or you'll stop being perceived as a player."

"But if Frank pulls this off, I'll be a *major* player." Here I am defending a choice I haven't even made. I think there's a lesson for parents of teens in here somewhere.

"Come on, Danté; Frank's an old man." Now I feel like that six-year-old atop the roof with a pillow-case. "He's got heart problems, and I've heard you say new production technology goes right over his head. You know he's a relic, and you can't afford to risk letting him gamble your reputation."

"But sometimes we have to take chances, Cyn." Heck, Ms. Moeroff says I don't take enough.

She sighs again. "We've already had *that* discussion." Yes, I know the script, except she gets most of the lines. Problem is, this time she's right.

My doorbell rings. "Oh, people here; have to go. How's the weekend look?"

"I'll be home early tomorrow, but I'm working Sunday, and I have a thing Sunday night." Rats, another *thing*, one of those law-firm functions that make sure no associate has time to cultivate a potentially demanding personal life. I wanted to invite her to watch Neusome's show with me from the control room.

Flynn Durbett's at the door, carrying some sort of small case. He holds up a hand and gestures for quiet before I can say anything. I follow him to the dining room where he reveals a cache of high-tech equipment. Powering it up, he watches various needles and scopes, then eases to the back door and lets in a black man who's dressed all in black and carrying another case. They signal each other, then move to the dining room, study the instruments again, and unpack various hand-held devices.

Now I'm hearing that theme from *Mission: Impossible* in my head as I follow this pair of sneaky snoops through my house, watching them point wands here and there, my appliances and phone lines and computer interfaces earning particular attention.

Durbett's satisfied the house is clean, so he finally introduces us. "Jankety," the man's called, nothing more.

Jankety nods and smiles.

"Frank'll be along soon," Durbett says, joining me for seats in the living room. "Mind if we talk about my business until then?" He doesn't seem to notice that Jankety is quietly slipping out the back door.

"You do a lot of corporate espionage?" I ask.

"It's a big market, especially foreign." I can only imagine.

"So what are your marketing goals?"

"To sell more merchandise, but a lot of people don't trust internet access, and catalogs are expensive unless they're targeted just right. It's identifying the right people that's a trick."

"Let's expand the definition of *right* by repositioning your goods for wider appeal. For example, how much of your inventory could be used for increasing child safety?"

He thinks for a moment. "Now that you mention it, a lot. Tracking and communication devices protect against kidnapping, safety gear keeps 'em safer during sports and recreation, and there's home detectors for smoke and carbon monoxide and asbestos and black mold and water chemicals—" He's growing excited in his unexcitable way.

"So we make the consummate thirty-minute video on keeping children safe in a dangerous world. We'll showcase your products wrapped in helpful tips and expert advice, finishing up with the various ways to learn more about Weisman products—and how to place an order. One version can run as an infomercial, another as a free video available at or streamed through your website, toll-free number, and outlets that carry your products."

He's eating it up. "I bet you could come up with other topics, too."

"Hunter safety and first-aid, eco-friendly camping and adventure, smart travel for domestic or international tourists, next-generation do-it-yourself home security, self-defense—especially for women . . ." His head's bobbing now. He's got that look, and I've not even drawn him a picture yet.

"But we can't do one on corporate espionage," he says.

"We could on ways to protect yourself from it."

He grins like a kid with a brand-new toy. The paranoia market; you gotta love it.

I hear a car pulling up, then notice Jankety's back in the dining room wearing headphones and manipulating equipment, taking notes on a pad. When did he slip back in?

Durbett peeks out, then lets Frank inside. "Danté knows exactly what I need," he says. "I hope he decides to ride with you on this." He excuses himself to don headphones and sit with his cohort.

"So how long have you been planning this?" I ask Frank.

"Since this afternoon." Now I'm surprised, puzzled, befuddled, fiddle-dee-deed.

"But you've known for years this day would come."

"And I knew my clients would hate to see me go, but now they're upset because Sam and Dib are bad-mouthing me in a pathetic attempt to shore up the accounts. These are *my* clients, Danté—many of them good friends, something those bastards don't understand. I was gonna go quietly, turning over all my years of work, but now they're trying to take my respect and dignity. That's when I had Durbett do a little surveillance and found out that you, Murray, and Melissa were to be fired, and that Rupert is next to go. And get this—" He's showing his anger now. "They laughed about Melissa being cut off before Kehoe had to pick up the top tier of her insurance coverage."

I give him a moment to calm down. "But Frank, starting a new agency?"

"Here's the deal," he says, waving off my carefully cultivated expression of thoughtful concern. "Hendon's tired of Chicago winters, so he's moving to Sanibel Island full-time." He's referring to the owner of *Shoot & Die Studios*. "He likes these terms, so if you agree, we're in business."

"Do I need my lawyer here?"

"She'd be more fun to look at than those two," he says, gesturing toward the pair of secret agents toppling third-world dictatorships from my dining-room table.

"I'm very reluctant," I warn him, "but I'll hear you out."

"Imagine a privately held corporation owning two operations: *Shoot & Die* and The Dellman/Roenik Group. Hendon, you, and I each own twenty-six percent of the stock; the rest is held for employee options. Hendon's fully vested now since he built and equipped the facility; you and I vest incrementally over the next twelve months."

"Any two of us will have voting majority," I point out. Duh.

"That encourages consensus. Hendon trusts us to run it, so he butts in as the tie-breaker only when you and I can't agree."

"The overhead to operate *Shoot & Die* costs a fortune, Frank—especially the full-time crew of, what? Fifteen or so?"

"But having that leeway to control production costs will make our creative more competitive, and with you on board, our creative should generate enough work to keep the studio running long enough for us to build a bigger client base." Yikes, I've never been fond of constant pressure to generate numbers, so Cyn's long view of career building is showing new luster.

"Are y'all ready?" Durbett calls to us, saving me from having to answer Frank right away. I don't know what to say, except maybe, *Sorry to dash your dreams, but . . . .*

They doff their headphones as we join them, Jankety attaching two small speakers while Durbett explains, "We miked ten locations at The Blue Pony and saved the conversations to disk. Just now we auto-scanned using phonetic identifiers *Frank, Dellman, Danté,* and *Roenik.* After Frank's speech, most is saying they don't think you'll pull it off, but a few plan to watch close and maybe throw some work your way if it looks like you're in for the long haul."

"Unfortunately," Frank says, "long hauls depend on getting the early business fast. Anyway, all I want to hear is what Sam Cox and Dib Wardley had to say."

"They talked about you five times. Three boils down to calling you a son of a bitch. You'll be interested in the other two." He nods to Jankety, who punches instructions into a tiny keyboard.

Now we're listening to muted party noise. "I bet he's been planning this for months," Dib growls from the speakers.

"I told you we should've bounced Danté sooner," Sam responds, "then parked Frank at a desk so he couldn't goose our clients on his way out."

"We'll have to bury their asses now, no matter what it costs."

"How?" Sam asks. You always have to draw this guy a picture—then he'll think he's the one who drew it.

"Pull all our jobs out of *Shoot & Die.* We'll hook a deal with Bower over at *Colorfix,* then cut-rate it for anybody we can snatch from Frank. When *Shoot & Die* goes under, his little agency will fold right along with it."

"We need to know what all he's planning," Sam says.

"I'll call Ellmata in the morning, see what he can set up."

Somebody approaches them to chat, so while Jankety changes disks to locate the fifth conversation, Durbett explains, "Henry Ellmata runs a small investigations agency here in Chicago. He buys spy gadgets and other toys from my company, so even though he's a hack, he's got good technology."

Frank says, "Flynn, if Danté throws in with me, I'll find a way to make this work. You know I'll put your business front and center, and I'll be more than fair on the deals."

Durbett waves him off. "How long I been ridin' with you, Frank?"

Frank's satisfied, so both turn and look at me.

Think hard, Danté. Can I see this happening? Can I make vision reality? Would Cyn stand behind me, my Dulcinea cheering me on as I tilt at windmills? Can I find a way to tell Frank *no* and somehow manage to avoid any hard feelings?

Jankety hits play, and Sam's voice fills the room. "Screw that bitch Kristen, and that faggot writer, too."

Dib says, "I'll make sure *nobody* at Kehoe ever uses either of 'em for anything."

"But Danté's gonna be a problem; the clients love him."

Dib answers, "Tell them we expected to run the same team after Frank retired, but once we got into the files, certain questions arose that for legal reasons we can't discuss. Hint that we couldn't keep somebody around who can't be trusted with our clients' confidential information."

Sam chuckles. "That's perfect. If Danté really is stupid enough to throw in with Frank, I'll make sure *nobody* in this town wants to work with him."

Jankety stops the disk.

Frank sits back and looks at me. "I'm putting Melissa on staff," he says matter-of-factly. "If you want Kristen and Murray full-time, they're yours."

All three are looking my way, and Jankety finally breaks the tension with a wide grin.

Frank leans forward and says, "So what's the deal?"

He already knows the answer: "Twenty-six percent."

$$*\qquad*\qquad*$$

Buzzzzz . . .

I feel like a tired old bumblebee after a long night of, well, buzzing, but I drag my stinger out of bed and hit the sunshiny road on this beautiful springtime Saturday morning. Melissa, Taj, and his Monster Bin are ready and waiting, so we strap the youngster in and head for *Shoot & Die* while I buzz her up with the latest developments. She's ecstatic, of course, because she believes in us.

Oh, to be young and naïve again.

It does feel good, in a way, but it's also scary as hell. I'm used to lots of responsibility—spending huge sums of somebody else's money, having other people depend on me—but I always had the option of buzzing off if too many Parzilac-type jobs left me feeling cold. The hive could always regroup, the bees finding a way to get along without me. King Bee Frank will always be a master at gathering pollen, but now a lot of my good friends could starve unless I constantly come up with new and exciting recipes for transforming it into honey.

The hive is buzzing by the time we arrive.

Neusome's waiting with the credentials, and the hornet's here, too—Flynn Durbett, along with his sweat-bee sidekick Jankety, both zipping around with those devices, debugging the place, I assume. Hal shakes my hand before Murray commandeers him and lures him into his lair.

It turns out Frank's already set aside a kiddie room to be supervised by the technical director's sister, a junior majoring in child-psych who took a year off school to save some money. Taj pauses in the doorway and watches in wonder as two slightly older boys and a cute, golden-haired girl about his age help her set up a play area stocked with new toys. Byron's hooking up a monitor, testing the channels . . . Yes! It's time to watch Monster Bin!

Taj is still shy, but Byron motions him over and shows him how to use the remote control. Kid'll be running the satellite uplink by the time he's ready for kindergarten.

Faritzka Partners are keeping two of our edit suites running, a big job doing training videos for an equipment-leasing company. Ka-ching. Frank catches us in the hallway and whispers, "They gave us all their production biz for the next year when I guaranteed our rates and promised you'd make them a free, fully animated video for pitching new business."

"At least you didn't have to give up a kidney," I point out.

"Not mine, no—but you don't need both of yours, do you?"

He leads us back to our new work area, a mess with boxes piled everywhere, supplies being carried in by two deliverymen. I'm starting to picture this, and it looks like Shangri-la!

Well, better than a rusty double-wide, anyway.

"I've already negotiated contracts with Kristen and Murray," Frank says, "—subject to your approval."

"I approve."

"Good." Then to Melissa, he says, "I'd like to offer you ten percent better than Kehoe, plus all the same benefits—except that full medical insurance will kick in just as soon as you can get us added to the plan already covering the Shoot & Die employees."

She's overwhelmed a moment, then finally says, "Okay, but I'm not sure how you expect me to work in a madhouse like this—" She waves around at all the mess, adding, "So if you'll excuse me, I've got a job to do."

By the time Frank and I clear places to sit in his new office, she's managed to round up every able body to form a moving posse, our queen bee directing the arrangement of desks and cabinets and supplies into an organized hive.

Frank sits back and smiles. "Billy Sizemore's already pledged to pull all his business from Kehoe and bring it here. That's Briggs allergy tattoos,

Sizemore simulators and merchandising, Weisman Company promo videos—plus the catalog work I already had from Flynn—and Ollum DeForest over at Parmenter Publishing called and said she's looking for a new agency who can handle some merchandising. You need to find your planner; I'm planning to fill it up." Sounds like Melissa ratted me out.

Murray wanders by and pokes his head in, his laptop under one arm, sheafs of paperwork under the other. "Hal's making phone calls while I find us somewhere to work," he says, rolling his eyes. "It's not safe out here with Melissa and her marauders tearing up the place." Melissa's calling him, something about having a desk for him. "Before I go," he says, handing me a disk, "here's drafts of the first three M-Slovak scripts. I'm cranking on Neusome's show right now. Is somebody going to get some footage for that, like maybe with the family, preferably bedside at the hospital?"

"I'll set it up for this afternoon. Tell Kristen to get a crew together."

And he's off.

"I hired Rupert, too," Frank says, "before they could fire him later today." Rupert Allup was one of Frank's assistant account executives. "It's the same salary, but here he gets to jump straight to account supervisor. He's out picking up some software he wants to use in designing us a new client- and job-tracking system."

Buzz buzz.

Frank takes a call, so I pull a chair off to the side and notice Taj peeking in. Clutching his Q-Tawzh "action figure," he's studying Frank. I motion that it's okay, so he moves closer, curious about the folderol piled atop the desk, until all we can see of him is a mop-top and two big brown eyes peering up at the old man. Frank waves him around, and soon the boy's sitting in his lap, fiddling with Frank's "toys," office supplies apparently more interesting than anything in our kid-room.

Durbett and Jankety poke their heads in, a signal from Frank giving them the okay to join us. "Building is clear," Durbett says when Frank hangs up.

"You mean no bugs?" I ask.

"No wire or equipment taps, either, but we still need to check your satellite uplink."

"We use encryption," I point out.

"The kind a ten-year-old with a laptop can get around," Durbett says. "With your permission, Jankety and me would like to bump you up from basic to state-of-the-art. We wanna do the building, too—full security, infiltration prevention and surveillance detection. We'll set up your home and cell-phones, remote computers, microwave transmitters—whatever y'all use in the field. You gotta watch for pirates, competitors, and even hackers just looking for a conquest."

"The proverbial bad guys," I say.

Durbett isn't amused. "I've seen M-Slovak be very dangerous with some of their enemies overseas."

Melissa pokes her head in, spots Taj, and leads him away by the hand. He gets a monster growl from me on the way out.

Frank's phone rings again, so we scatter, our mercenaries off to do battle with the phantom spy-monsters. I head back to check on the remote vans where Byron's loading gear and assigning jobs, one crew for me, another for Kristen. Everybody's as wired as the equipment. This is real video work, slogging around town with a million bucks in circuit boards and chips, a coterie of techno-heads who can take this stuff apart and put it back together again, and sometimes do—just for fun.

Hal Neusome arrives, ready to appear in some of the shots, field investigator extraordinaire. He could do without the cliché flak-jacket, but hey, it's his show. I run some ideas by him for remotes, then make a few calls to set it up.

Durbett appears just as we're about to load up. "Jankety'll be doing the install, so I was thinking I might tag along with you awhile—you know, see for myself."

"Sure, okay." Maybe we'll have time to toss around some ideas while Byron and the techies string cables and fret over things like time-base correction. "Is there anything in particular you're interested in?"

"Not really. It's just that before you work up too powerful a trust with someone, it's always a good idea to do a little ridin' together first, find out how the other one works, like a couple guys who think they might be a good fit for huntin' partners. It tells you what to expect, helps get you ready in case there comes a time you can't afford no hesitation."

Hesitation?

"All right, then," I tell him, "let's hunt for good video and see what we can flush out."

Truth is, I already know what I'm after, and just how I want it to look.

It's time to paint the big picture.

Frank appears at the last second, barely containing a grin. He exchanges knowing glances with Durbett, who just shrugs when I look his way, then pulls me aside and whispers, "If you really want to do something serious about Parzilac, it looks like we might just get a shot."

Or get shot, I'm starting to think. Durbett does look like he's packing heat, and I'm wondering if hesitation might not sometimes be a good thing.

"A shot at what, Frank?" I whisper back.

"It's two words that could change the world."

"What words, Frank? Nobody ever tells me the words."

"Put them together, and it's called the Fantasy Patch."

CHAPTER 5

Here we are, hitting the streets of Chicago, and in my head I keep hearing a sort of TV theme song I just made up:

> *Picture this! Better check those lies!*
> *We'll zoom on you, and varnish true!*
> *We got colors to paint your world,*
> *So watch out! We're The Image Crew!*
> *Ooo yeah! The Image Crew!*

Now I'm picturing the show's opening credits: Danté Roenik, Image-maker; Handsome Hal, News Hound; Smilin' Byron, Lens-master; and special guest Flynn Durbett as . . . The Watchman!

> *Ooo yeah! The Image Crew!*

Riding up front with Byron, Hal's going through his satchelful of sundries, which is mostly make-up, retrieving a foreskin for the microphone—one of those sleeves that fits over the top to ID a show or network. It's sporting the "NN" logo for Neusome on the News.

Opposite me in the other crash seat, Durbett's shifting things around various hidden pockets, surreptitiously letting me glance that he is armed, a weapon holstered up under his field jacket. He opens a case and hands me a miniature phone with an unusual red button at the top. "I gave another one to Kristen. That button will insta-dial hers with a secure signal."

"Encrypted?" I ask.

"Redundantly, and satellite trackable, but with GPS ghosted through scrambled land lines to Waverly so we're the only ones know how to look for it," he confirms. "If somebody takes it from her, we'll go get it back, and maybe keep the hand that's holdin' it, too." I wonder what he does with the bloody hands.

Growing bored as we ride, I pull out the phone and punch the red button. When Kristen answers from the second-crew van tailing us, I whisper, "Pssst! Code purple! The catfish in Nehru jacket has applied the lipstick. I repeat: the catfish is wearing lipstick. Be careful out there." *Click.*

Hal's confused. Durbett just looks me over. Hey, he wanted to see what kind of guy he's riding with.

We unload at the hospital where I'll be getting shots of the injured guy, then of his wife being interviewed by Hal. Kristen and her crew will shoot exteriors, then help cover the funeral home before heading off to collect footage supporting the drugstore history. Of course there's much ado about getting into the hospital with TV gear, this despite having made arrangements in advance—a typical remote shoot.

We find the wife sitting by her husband, talking to attorney Ritenour and his associate Cricket LaRayne, a tiny black lady with a big-toothed grin. She's a bundle of concern, practically hugging everyone, fluffing the comatose man's pillow, frustrated she can't do more to make the world's pain and suffering simply go away.

Ritenour explains, "I only handle criminal charges, so I'm including Cricket because her specialty is civil litigation." I wonder if he's expecting her to play offense or defense. The way he keeps glancing toward Byron and the camera, I think he wants to be interviewed.

"He's stable," the wife says, turning our attention back to the important stuff. "That's all they can tell me." He's surrounded by flowers and cards, tethered to IV's and tubes, vigilant machines, beeping blippers and blipping beepers. I hope he can sense she's here for him, that we all are.

The son arrives, surprised he has to talk his way past Durbett, our sentry guarding the entrance. Hal remains quiet while Byron steals a shot of mother and son hugging each other, both reaching down to hold the injured man's hand. I glance away, studying the hospital equipment, these marvels of modern medical technology. I'm both impressed by and suspicious of life-preserving devices nudging nature and doing what nature does. Our TV-production gear is also state-of-the-art, and I'm very good with it, but people like Byron quickly learn how to stretch every technical capability of anything they use, forever suffering the limitations of even the latest and the best. Still, technical problems arise, but with ours no life hangs in the balance. Could I trust my very survival to machines I don't understand? To me, this looks like so much college-dorm stereo; all that's missing are a pair of tower speakers and a graphic equalizer.

We decide to interview only the mother, saving the son for a live appearance on the show. Hal does an excellent job, Byron catching all the right shots, the best angles, a soft look, that mix of hope amid despair that I'm trying to portray. At one point, the mother cries, then steels herself with new resolve to defend the man she loves, a man who can't speak for himself, and I have all I can do to keep from misting up myself.

Theta Moeroff wants me to be an artist, but isn't it art to start with reality and sculpt your own abstractionist slant? Or to do what we're doing here: bringing reality to the surface, showing audiences what they might look past without ever truly seeing? Giving people a chance to gaze openly at the unvarnished truth when they might otherwise look away?

The wife provides two excellent must-use lines. The first: "We've been after him to retire since our son took over, but he still spends most of his time at that first store on Madison, the one he opened just out of pharmacy school, still loyal to the people who supported us, still caring for their health and their children's and now their grandchildren's." Her best line, a good closer, is punctuated by a pause where she glances toward her husband, the machines beeping like ticking clocks: "It's a tragedy for two families," she says, a tear tracing forlornly down her cheek, "but I know he would trade his life in an instant if it would bring that sweet little girl back home to her momma."

Nobody says anything for several beats. I make a mental note to recommend to Hal that he allow for a similar pause in the show, a moment for the line to sink in. I think he already senses it.

Ritenour looks disappointed when we start packing the gear, but Cricket seems pleased with what we accomplished. The son follows Byron out to talk to Kristen about which drugstores and where else to shoot.

Durbett pulls me aside and quietly points out, "There's no security on his room. Anybody could walk right in." He seems to be taking it personally.

"He'll become a sympathetic figure after tomorrow night's show. Besides, with as much trouble as we had getting in, I doubt axe-grinders barging in off the street will be a problem."

"Maybe not an axe-grinder," he says, "but a professional . . ." He follows me out, still not satisfied, but not pressing the issue.

My crew follows Kristen's to the funeral home so Hal and I can talk to the Reverend Falluson before we go meet Detective Culler. "I want Kristen," I tell Hal, "to collect sound bites and shots depicting the community's outpouring of support, Falluson presiding, but I don't think we should let him speak today. As much as I'd like him to spout off before we play back his own words proving him wrong, I can't afford any trashing of our guy on the air. Too many people have short, prejudiced attention spans. The negative is all they'll hear and remember."

"And it wouldn't be impartial reporting," Hal adds. Oh yeah—that, too.

I call Kristen on Durbett's spy-phone to explain what we're after. She's up to speed now, and—I might add—no saboteurs were able to eavesdrop. I think Durbett takes this stuff way too seriously, so I guess I'll owe him an apology if I let my guard down and the enemy obliterates all my space invaders or captures the inner chambers of my castle.

We find the packed funeral home just six blocks from the accident scene. A large poster is directing contributors toward a stack of envelopes beside a drop-box, a fund to help pay expenses. It's a good cause, so I'll encourage the reverend to mention it on the show. I might even write a check myself.

"It is a sad tragedy," Reverend Falluson cants. He's shorter than I pictured him, an immaculately dressed black man, a bit portly, with pudgy jowls. "It has hurt this family and this community deeply, this innocent little girl robbed of her future, all of her hopes and dreams snuffed out in an instant of senseless violence."

Yeah, whatever. "That's what we want to show," I tell him, Hal standing beside me, both projecting grave concern.

"How we gonna shoot this then?" His facade melts as he kicks into his own PR mode.

"Mostly cover shots showing the depth of this tragedy and how many people have been affected," I say. "We'll catch you comforting the mourners, the community leader who puts the needs of his people first."

"Yes," he says. "That's what I'm seeing, too." This guy's mine already. He trusts me to paint his picture.

"We need you to help Kristen keep the commentary focused not on who's at fault, but on the loss of this wonderful, innocent child. You'll have a chance in the studio to discuss why this happened."

"Yes," he agrees. "Such a tragedy." The facade is back, every word a dramatic pronouncement. "There will be time for blame later. First we must stand up for the victims, to give aid and comfort in their time of need."

Amen.

Kristen's already set up in a small anteroom off the main chapel. The mother is small, not much bigger than Cricket. Her eyes are swollen from crying, and she looks nervous about all the TV and attention. Kristen shoos us away. I'm glad she's here to handle this part; she'll guide her with compassion and help her feel better about showing others how much her daughter was loved. Kristen will get the job done, and the message will be something she believes in.

The only job she ever refused from me was editing the Parzilac testimonies. We'll never know if Parzilac was the reason that girl killed herself, or maybe just a contributor, or if the drug should have stopped her but failed, but those are big ifs. Kristen just couldn't paint that picture anymore. I pushed on and finished the job myself, relieved when I could finally walk away. I still envy her that.

We finish up with a shot of Hal talking to the mother, proof he was here investigating.

Ooo, yeah! The Image Crew!

It's time to move on. We're late, already behind schedule, too many shots in too many locations and not enough time . . .

Your typical remote shoot.

*   *   *

The Wood Street Station, 13th District. Cop Shop. You have the right to remain silent.

It's an unassuming tan brick building smack in the middle of Westown, about five minutes from Mile-Square. We leave the van parked out back, guarded by one of our techs, and head inside.

Byron's horsing around, pretending to frame shots by dipping and shifting his head. No, we'll not be using frenetic shaky-cam pan-pan jiggle-and-lock, none of that nervous-perp point-of-view spying the action. If I wanted to be hokey, I'd depict the distraught wife perspective, tears trickling down the camera lens, hands wringing at the bottom of the screen.

"Detective Culler had to step out for a minute," we're told at the desk. "Wait over there." Maybe I'd rather wait outside, or down the street, perched on a bar stool.

Durbett disappears down a hallway as if he owns the place—maybe he does—while Hal chats up two old ladies who recognize him. He's not interested in why they're here; everyday crime is blasé, and the victims rarely provide sensational visuals. *Newsome on the News* is a man-bites-dog operation, so *please*, when the man starts chomping, *try to get it on camera!*

Impatient, I head out to the van to call Frank. I want to see if we're still in business.

"He's in the men's room checking for vampires," Melissa reports. Now there's an image.

"Okay, this I've gotta hear."

She chuckles. "One of the kids told Taj it's where vampires hide. Now he's afraid to go in there by himself, and he's getting too old for me to take him in the women's, so Frank is showing him it's safe."

"Think how bad you'll feel if Frank winds up getting all his blood sucked out."

"I think it's the vampires who need to worry; he'll wind up pitching them a PR campaign to improve their image."

"I'd rather work with vampires than M-Slovak."

"At least you'd know what you're dealing with. So how's the shoot going?"

"Way too slow."

"You always say that about remotes."

"They always go way too slow."

My bleeping beep-beeper phone beeps, a signal from Byron that Culler's available, so I head inside where Durbett introduces us to our detective, apparently somebody he already knows. Heath Culler's a black guy, likely forty or so, with an unusual bend in his upper back that pushes his chest out, maybe scoliosis or some kind of injury in his past. He wears a grim expression like it's his badge.

His walk an uncomfortable-looking shuffle, he leads us back out toward the parking lot. "I'll show you the car," he says, "and the scene of the accident, but I don't want you recording me yet." He speaks fairly well, with just a hint of the streets in his delivery.

"We prefer catching you tomorrow anyway," I explain, "so it'll look like Hal got the last-minute scoop, not that you've been cooperating all along."

"That's my way of thinking," he agrees, nodding several times.

"Off the record for now," Hal says, "what's your theory?"

Culler thinks, then nods again like he's agreeing with himself. "It was a robbery. He still had his wallet, but the trunk was found open, which is where he'd have been carrying prescription drugs. The pharmacist said when other stores was low on something, our man would take 'em home and drop 'em off the next morning. We had him check the inventory and, sure enough, a case of Parzilac is gone."

"Parzilac?" That was me. Seems like I've heard that name somewhere before.

Hal surmises, "The robber must've thought it was something stronger, like painkillers." Keep a wary eye on any news reporter who does a lot of surmising.

Culler disagrees with him. "The narcotics task-force thinks Parzilac is what he was after."

I have to ask. "He wanted to perk up depressed junkies?"

"No, to use for making Pozies."

"I've heard of Pozies," Hal quickly points out. Yeah, he's got his finger on the pulse. "What exactly are they?"

"It's the latest designer drug," Culler says, pulling out a spiral pad and flipping through the pages to find what he's after. "You inject a small amount of LSD mixed with something they call atropine into a Parzilac capsule, and that makes a powerful strong high. There's a brain chemical for perception and creativity called sara-something—" He's having trouble deciphering his notes.

"Serotonin," I supply, Culler nodding agreement. "It's a neurotransmitter, a chemical that fires brain cells." I did pay attention to the M-Slovak satellite training programs. "And Parzilac's a re-uptake inhibitor, meaning it slows down how long it takes serotonin to be absorbed. That's why people feel a boost and seem to think more clearly, even if it's just managing to relax better."

Culler takes over. "And LSD is a chemical shaped like that sara-stuff. It acts the same way, so it makes Parzilac way stronger while causing hallucinations."

Rats! Too bad I need to keep this on-topic. I wouldn't mind firing a few shots across the bow of M-Slovak's flagship, the *U.S.S. Parzilac*. I can see it now: *Four out of five addicts agree—blowing your mind starts with a little pink capsule!*

Culler invites Durbett to ride in the unmarked cruiser, so we pile into the production van and follow them to a combination impound lot and junkyard. Our subject is an aging Cadillac sedan, its front end smashed in, the passenger compartment covered with a blue tarp.

Byron sets up the Steadi-Cam while Culler and Durbett strip off the shield. Far from ideal, our shots will be cluttered by a distracting background of barb-wire fence, piles of parts, shells with no hearts, musty husks and rusting hulks. Durbett is examining the trunk latch and door handles, whispering quietly with Culler. He climbs into the back seat for a minute, looks around, then checks the front, but says nothing.

I'm trying to picture what happened. "Why settle for one case of drugs?" I ask. "Why not rob the whole store?"

Culler answers, "Well, one case is a lot; that's twenty-four bottles of a thousand each. Besides, there's a trigger alarm inside, plus a building alarm that was set before he came out."

"It seems like once he was stabbed, he'd have tried to set off the alarm to summon help rather than get in the car and drive away."

"Evidence shows he was stabbed *inside* the car, the angles suggesting it was somebody reaching around from the back seat, and it happened away from the store."

"So it's an opportunity robbery," Hal says, trying to follow our discussion and watch Byron grab shots at the same time. "Somebody saw him put a case of Parzilacs in the trunk; then he beasted his way into the car and held a knife on him, making him drive someplace where he couldn't call for help."

Culler shakes his head. "A sub-shop employee working two doors down was loading the Dumpster when our man come out. They waved good-night to each other before he drove away. Everything seemed normal."

"Somebody hid in the back floorboard," Hal guesses, "before the sub worker emptied the trash—somebody who knew the victim would be transporting drugs."

Culler says, "But he kept the car locked whenever it was parked out back."

Hal amends his scenario: "So the robber broke in."

That doesn't sound right. "Even if a break-in caused no noticeable damage," I point out, "surely our guy would see somebody hiding in the back, especially since the interior lights would come on when he unlocked the doors. Most people make a habit of checking back there when parked in dangerous places at night."

Durbett nods agreement, adding, "He even had to walk past the rear seat twice to put a box in the trunk."

"He *let* somebody into the car, is my way of thinking," Culler says. Durbett's watching Hal and me to see if it's our way of thinking, too.

I have to point out the obvious: "I can't picture him making somebody he knows ride in the back seat." I can tell Durbett agrees.

Culler shrugs, glancing over at the car. Byron's trying to get a better shot of the smashed front end. "Well, it's the only way that makes sense. At first I thought maybe a stranger caught him by surprise and jumped in when our man was stopped at the end of the alley, waiting to pull out, but the dealership says this car automatically locks its doors when it's put in drive."

Durbett shakes his head. "Back door, passenger side," he pronounces, "—it don't lock." Byron pauses to load another disk, so Durbett walks to the car and triggers the power locks several times. The little thingies on three doors are moving back and forth, but the right rear's remains still.

Culler is surprised it got by him, but clearly pleased by Durbett's contribution. He's not worrying about being upstaged; he wants to solve a crime.

"To exploit that," I point out, "the robber would have to know in advance it was broken . . ."

Durbett finishes, "Which'd be easy when he's the one who disabled it."

Culler's skeptical. "There's no sign of deliberate tampering."

"Ah, but there is," Durbett says politely with a twinkle in his eye. He looks around—to make sure we're not being watched?—then retrieves his case from the van and walks down several rows, his entourage tagging along as best as Culler can keep up. He finds another wrecked Cadillac with similar handles, its rear doors intact. "This is a Lock-Slaver," he explains, showing us a small hand-held device from the case. "It probes inside keyholed devices, learns the tumbler configuration, detects security triggers, then follows commands to open, close, jam, or destroy."

He puts it over one of the rear door-locks, then folds out some miniature bar-clamps and hooks it under the handle, the slightest hissing sound barely audible as he tightens it into a solid hold. Durbett pushes a tiny suction plunger against the paint and decompresses. When a red dot lights on its panel, he punches a sequence into three tiny buttons. The whole device vibrates silently for about five seconds . . . until a green dot lights.

Click. The door unlocks, and the light turns red again.

Durbett repeats the process with a different sequence, green light, *click*, red light. We're locked again.

Culler's impressed. I want shots of this, but Durbett gives me a look and shakes his head. Nope.

Durbett removes the device, then demonstrates that all the doors lock except that one. This is way cool. Motioning us to look closer, he indicates two spider-silk-thick scratches on the bottom edge where the clamps grabbed. He pulls a pinch of talc from one of his secret pockets and blows it on the handle, revealing a circular smudge where the suction had held.

Culler gets a head start, beating a path to the drugstore guy's car. A similar smudge is obvious in the white dust where lab-techs checked for fingerprints. Two hairline scratches appear underneath the handle.

Durbett tells Culler, "This little demo never happened. You want to ask the forensic boys to explain the scratches and smudge, or do you want an anonymous tip?"

Culler bobs his head. "Anonymous tip."

"You don't have a problem," Durbett asks, "with Hal here receiving the same tip?"

Culler grins. "I got no control over my sources *or* reporters."

Hal is nodding, Durbett looking satisfied, Byron and our tech packing the gear, and I'm thinking what a great concept this is, the *anonymous source*. If you want to spread a message, make sure something verifiable corroborates your story, then leak it to a reporter who'll do the dirty work while tenaciously shielding your identity, protecting you from the responsibility of making accusations.

Just before we leave, Durbett examines a barely noticeable gouge in the corner of the Caddie's rear bumper guard. Culler produces an evidence bag into which Durbett scrapes some particles, holding them up for a better look. Durbett produces a miniature scope, examines the grains, then pronounces, "Red-orange brick." He hands the bag to Culler, then measures the height of the bumper against his leg.

We load up and head out to the Mile-Square area. The makeshift memorial is already gone, so we settle for shots of the damaged marker and the area where she was hit. Oodles of kids are playing in the streets, adults hovering on corners, small groups gathering to sit on stoops in the warm afternoon sunshine. The tiny park is piled with used tires and other refuse.

Byron is grabbing B-roll footage—background shots—of Hal examining the scene and talking to neighbors, telling the story, showing sympathy, gathering facts, filling cracks, seeking truth and tweaking sooth. I notice Durbett is gone. Nobody saw him leave, and both vehicles are still here, so he must be on foot.

He finally appears just as we're ready to leave, and I'm hearing *Twilight Zone* music in my head, Rod Serling intoning, "To all outward appearances, Flynn Durbett is a simple man . . . but is he?"

"It's about three blocks from here," Durbett says, pointing behind himself.

And we're off.

He leads us to an alley behind some shuttered businesses, its motif one of Dumpsters and trash, ratty crap and two or three crappy rats. There's space to drive through, just enough room to park out of sight, and an exit at the other end heading toward the intersection where the girl was hit. At just the right height where the car would have to turn, there's a slight scuff in the red-orange brick. Byron breaks out the Steadi-Cam, grabbing a few shots including point-of-view out toward the street.

Culler takes several photos and collects a sample from the scuffed building. "The lab boys will have to confirm this," he says.

"It'll confirm," Durbett says.

Culler loses his grim expression just long enough to allow a hint of smile, nodding several times.

Everybody satisfied, we part with our detective and head toward *Shoot & Die* where we'll have dinner and plan the evening's session. On the way back I'm still thinking about this concept of the anonymous source. I already have what I need to make it work for me: a paying client, production capability, a crew, the right information . . .

And a news reporter in my pocket.

Forget shooting across the bow; maybe it's time to load the torpedo bays.

I'm thinking Hal might want to break out with a major investigation of M-Slovak . . .

And Parzilac.

CHAPTER 6

It's like scuba diving.

Mile-Square after dark reminds me of night diving. A coral reef during daylight teems with life, but when the sun sets my favorites come out: the wily hunters such as octopuses and eels, and the intrepid scavengers like lobsters and crabs. That's when the day-fish all hide, when even the corals themselves come alive. The landscape looks familiar, those very same structures and caves and maybe a decrepit relic or two, but it's a neighborhood transformed, electric with furtive activity, a palpable risk in daring to intrude on all you can see, even greater apprehension for what else might lurk just beyond the unflinching glare of revealing light.

So it is with Mile-Square, but now we're here, after dark . . . and me without my wetsuit.

As we drive around to survey the scene, I'm quite pleased that Durbett decided again to ride along, our very own monster moray threatening one helluva nasty bite. The families we saw this afternoon are in hiding, replaced by the predators and scavengers: roving gangs, drug dealers, pimps and prostitutes, thugs and thieves, pistol shooters, dope shooters, purse snatchers and snatch pursuers.

It doesn't take Byron long to collect our neighborhood shots. He's motivated to move fast, what you might call *shoot & run*. Finally we head for the drugstore on Madison where the son was planning to meet us, except that he rushed to the hospital where our guy has stirred a few times. I'd rather get shots of the victim waking, but his family prefers some privacy for now, which is fine—as long as Hal's top of the list for that exclusive interview.

We pull in and park behind the place next door so we can shoot the back lot without our van showing. Kristen shows up in the second van, coming straight from a three-hour editing session, which means she got ten hours' worth of excellent work done. She once told me she wished she could edit her own life as neatly as she cuts clips. Wouldn't it be grand simply to keep the best parts and run each day like a montage or highlights reel?

The pharmacist has been expecting us. He's an old dude named Walt, grizzled and gray, his ears sporting big bushy tufts of hair that remind me of coral polyps waving in the current, trapping plankton for a nightly feast. The bored-looking cashier is a young lady most likely from the neighborhood. A lad of twelve or so is trying to look casual about buying a box of condoms, and an older woman seems determined to squint at the fine print disclaiming every cold remedy on the shelves.

Kristen and I help Byron set up while Durbett examines the security system. He's paying particular attention to the front windows, looking out at the street as if to check routes of attack. Let's see, we could mount anti-aircraft artillery over there . . .

Byron collects some B-roll first, then begins prepping for Hal to interview Walt. Kristen will be running sound, so while Byron works on the lighting she joins me to relax behind the counter.

"I've been watching Taj," she says, smiling, maybe a bit wistfully. "I keep wanting to gather him up and give him a big hug. Melissa is so lucky to have him, but I can't imagine the pressure, the worrying about her situation, the lack of a safety net if—for whatever reason—she can't always take care of him."

"She's smart," I point out, "and resourceful—and she's got people."

"Yeah, she's got people," she agrees, nodding her head as she looks off into an uncertain future. "Sometimes I think I could be a great mom . . . but I'd definitely need a dad around for my child, somebody I could count on to help, and to be there if something should ever happen to me . . . ." I don't know much about Kristen's family, except that she stays in touch with her mother in Florida. I've never heard her mention her own father.

Byron's ready, so she joins them for the shoot, Hal starting with fluff about what a great member of the community our guy is, eventually working up to the case of missing Parzilac. He's got the old feller leafing through inventories, shipping logs, and invoices to confirm the disappearance—our reporter sifting those pesky details to bring our viewers the straight skinny, documented and corroborated.

Durbett comes from somewhere behind the counter and slips outside, then returns with a small case. He motions for me to follow, leading me to a small office behind the shelves. "Try to give me a few seconds' warnin'," he says, "if you see anybody comin' back here." He removes that Slaver device from his case, pointing toward a door with two security locks.

I raise my eyebrows, secret code for: *What are you doing?*

"The boss's private office," he says. The device suctions into position, red light, green light, *click*. One to go.

I give him a scowl, international body language for: *Should you be doing that?*

Red, green, *click.*

It's a tiny room with a desk and chair, plus two gooseneck lights mounted overhead, but no phone or other amenities. A small safe hunkers down in one corner while three seven-foot metal cabinets stand tight-lipped like Easter Island statues along the side, all reinforced and padlocked. Durbett puts his shoulder to one, then whispers, "Bolted to the wall."

The Slaver does its job, and the first cabinet reveals at least a dozen cases of Parzilac, each box printed with *M-Slovak Company* and the drug's generic name, *Pi-ethym-lorenazol.*

I peer out and see the pharmacist back to work filling a prescription, Byron setting up the Steadi-Cam, Hal using a small desk-topper to photocopy the shipping logs and invoices. Gesturing that he's taking the copies to the van, he follows Byron out.

"It's nearly time to close up," Walt says. "You wanted to film me locking the security gate?"

"Twice," I tell him. "Byron will show it from inside, through the window; then you need to open it again and wait for him to cross the street so he can shoot it a second time from outside, the neighborhood perspective, its lifeline to caring pharmacists and healing drugs shutting down for the night."

He sends the cashier home, then heads outside to rehearse his big part. Durbett and I slip back inside the priest's hole where he carefully opens one of the boxes, then several more, all containing bottles of Parzilac.

The second cabinet is empty, but the last one holds six large brown boxes with no markings, all unsealed. Inside the first, the second, all six . . . tens of thousands of loose, very familiar, little pink capsules.

Durbett and I look at each other, asking the question at the same time: "You think he's making Pozies?" His sounded cooler, though, southern accent and all.

I pick it up from there. "Start with cases of real ones, doctor 'em up, fill the plain boxes, then deliver them to some middle-man . . . more than a simple robbery, maybe he got double-crossed by his customer that fateful night."

"I don't see any sign of the drugs he'd have been adding, though," Durbett points out—like we're going to find a big jug marked *LSD 64 oz.*, its label advertising: *Play the ACID CHALLENGE and win a fabulous TRIP!*

"Maybe he used them up."

Durbett doesn't look convinced. Then, examining one of the loose capsules, he says, "This is still sealed, and I don't see evidence of a puncture. How 'bout, while I take some pictures, you check the ones out there and see if they look the same?"

I find Kristen crouching behind the counter, waving me down out of the shot. "Byron's about ready for the outside-in angle. Nobody wants to watch *your* mug all over the news."

I can see Hal out there following Byron and his Steadi-Cam up the cross-street, our fuzzy-eared pharmacist poised in front. I locate that familiar Parzilac bottle on the shelf, check the contents, and note that these are also sealed, no obvious difference.

Durbett comes out to see what I learned. He examines the capsules while I peer around the corner to watch Byron.

Walt starts to close the gate, but Byron signals him to wait because a car's cruising through the shot. Silhouettes of the driver and one passenger appear to be watching Walt. Durbett's peering around me now, and I can sense him tensing.

The car turns onto the street toward Hal and Byron, but they've disappeared into the shadows, probably not wanting to attract the nuisance of curious gawkers. Big honkin' cameras have a tendency to do that, you know.

Suddenly the car backs into an alley, turns around, and heads this way again.

The driver punches it, tires squealing.

Durbett lifts Kristen and literally tosses her aside, then yanks me back the other way.

The pharmacist panics and tries to run—

Thump! Crash!

It hits the old man and carries him through the shattered window, racks and displays smashed and scattered, a shelving unit landing on Kristen, the car coming to rest between us.

Durbett yanks my leg and pulls me down just as two men jump from the car, one hurling some kind of tube toward the offices, the other setting fire to a bottle.

Durbett's under a rack, now scrambling out and up—

Whoosh! Molotov fire erupts behind as, both men climbing out through the gaping hole in the front—

Pfoom! Pfoom! Pfoom! Durbett's firing, one man clutching his leg and stumbling as another car zooms up to grab them. I see Hal running our way,

Byron farther back.

"It's a pipe bomb!" Durbett yells. "Take cover!"

I crawl under something, shouting, "Kristen! Kristen! Are you—?"

Booom!

A deafening compression blows down the fire for an instant, but it blazes up stronger, smoke choking the air. Durbett's shouting something, but my ears are roaring. I pull myself up and see Hal trying to climb in through the wreckage. The pharmacist is right beside me, pinned against the front of the car, covered with oozing red dots—bomb shrapnel? There's no sign of life, and no reason to hope.

I crawl toward where Kristen went down. Durbett's already there gesturing to Hal to pull the other end of a massive aisle display.

"Danté?" I hear Kristen call through the roar. I'm helping Durbett push and lift, Hal straining against his end.

"Get her!" Durbett yells in my ear.

I've got her hand, but can't get any leverage. I drop to the floor and squeeze underneath. I can hear better now, Kristen calling weakly. "Danté . . ."

I get a better grip and pull carefully, but she's hung up.

"Hurry!" Durbett shouts. The fire is spreading faster, the heat horrendous, Hal choking on the smoke, his end beginning to wobble.

Kristen's struggling, and I'm pulling as hard as I can, but her leg seems caught, her jeans snagged. "Try the other way!" I shout, pushing now as hard as I can. She manages to twist around backwards—

Rip!

And she's free, squirming out behind Hal.

Whoosh! The car's in flames now. Durbett motions Hal and Kristen toward the storefront, both disappearing into the smoke as flames spread between us. I turn and see Durbett trying to pull the pharmacist free, but he shakes his head and gives up, motioning for me to follow him to the back exit. The heat is unbearable now, my very clothes hot to the touch, and I can't breathe, my eyes stinging with smoke and sweat.

I trip, go down, feel Durbett yanking me up, and we're at the door, but it's locked, so he kicks it until the dead-bolt breaks, then body-slams it open. I stumble out behind him, flames licking our backs, smoke billowing into the sky.

"The car's gonna blow!" Durbett warns, pulling me away from the building—

Boom!

"You okay?" he shouts.

"Yeah—"

And he's gone, running down the alley and around the building. I'm trying to keep up, desperately hoping Kristen and Hal got out in time, and that Byron wasn't too close.

Durbett gets there first, finding them all across the street, Byron recording the conflagration. I motion for Hal to get into the shot, so he runs across to peer into the store, braving the flames as if to look for others he might heroically save.

Kristen struggles to her feet, smudged and smoky, her pants torn, still gasping for air. "I'm fine," she insists. "Get the shots."

Satisfied, Durbett barks, "I need van keys." Kristen tosses him one set, Byron the other; then he and I race around back and pull the vehicles away just in time, parking them down the street, not so close they might interfere with fire trucks.

Sirens are wailing in the distance. I grab the "NN" microphone and run with the cable, handing it to Hal. "Keep it generic," I tell him, still trying to catch my breath, my heart pounding. "We'll give clips to all the affiliates, *Newsome on the News* here at the scene when vigilantes retaliated for the Mile-Square accident."

He runs into the shot again, backlit by flames, red and blue flashing lights strobing the scene as help arrives, firefighters swarming like ants, great streams of water now playing over and into the building. Hal briefs the captain about the situation inside.

"Almost out of memory!" Byron calls, so I run to the van, grab another disk, and make the switch.

"Send news crew my way for dubs," I tell him. He grins with big teeth. After all those years shooting local news, right now, this night, he's the man capturing it all, copies available to those who bow and scrape.

The authorities shoo us back and start setting up barricades. Other news crews begin arriving and setting up. I give the cut signal, so Hal wraps and we all head for the van where Byron sets up to lay off dubs. If we had our own daily news shows, I wouldn't give this away, but we don't, and tonight is our best chance for maximum exposure.

"Let's hold back some of the footage," I say.

"No gunshots," Durbett insists, keeping his role out of the story.

"Right. We'll give them a short set of clips, highlights of the crash and explosion, then of Hal rushing into the burning building, escaping with Kristen, and finally directing the fire captain. There's no way local news can tell that story without promoting *Neusome on the News*."

Hal heads over to talk to the other stations' crews, bringing them up to date, offering his eyewitness account while Byron and I edit shots. It's not long before salivating production assistants are lining up at the van, grabbing dubs and running back to their own microwave trucks to feed footage back to cadres of waiting editors and news directors.

It takes about half an hour to get the dubs out, nearly ten o'clock now. Hal's collected a stack of business cards and accepted two invitations to be interviewed "live on the scene" during the eleven o'clocks.

I go looking for Kristen, pushing my way through large crowds gathered around the perimeter. The building's more smoke than flames now, the street a disco of flashing lights.

But our coral reef is toast.

I turn at the sound of a low whistle. Flynn Durbett is at the intersection behind me, nodding toward the side street. As I round the corner, he says quietly, "She's over there." He's been keeping an eye on her, but letting her be.

Across the street, several doors down, Kristen is propped with her back against a wall, her eyes closed. I walk up quietly, noticing how tears have drawn lines through the smudges on her cheeks. She's trembling.

"Kristen," I whisper. I reach for her hand.

"Oh, Danté," she whispers back, squeezing my hand hard.

"Are you okay."

"Yeah. I just needed to get away from the mayhem for a minute." She hesitates. "The pharmacist—Walt—he's dead, isn't he?"

"Yes," I confirm quietly.

She takes a deep breath. "I could hear you—when I was under the shelf. You were trying to find me. I thought— I didn't know—"

"It's okay." I gather her in, both of us holding each other tightly. She trembles again for a moment, then seems to calm, to steel herself. The hug is over, but we're still holding hands. It's better now.

Durbett is still watching us. I nod confirmation that she's all right, so he comes over to stand with us, nobody speaking for a moment. Finally, I break the silence. "I'll be up half the night editing," I mock complain, "and at it again first thing in the morning."

"*Both* of us, Roenik," Kristen warns with a hint of mock petulance.

"We're gonna share that Emmy." Yeah, she's okay.

I look at Durbett and shake my head. "Too bad, though. We were this close to breaking the biggest story of all, that our guy was manufacturing street drugs."

"But you might have alienated Briggs," Kristen cautions.

I shake my head. "Not once he found out his frat brother was an illicit dealer." I sigh and shrug. "We can't tell that story anyway, not without proof, and that just went up in flames."

Durbett snorts, the slightest smile giving him away. "You ever sing that song when you was a kid, that *Ring Around The Rosie?*"

"Ashes ashes," Kristen adds, "all fall down."

Flynn nods. "Let's all sing it now because—" He pulls something from his vest pocket and opens his hand.

My eyes are wide. "Are those—?

An elegant spray of little pink capsules!

"I grabbed me a pocketful of Pozies."

*   *   *

Picture a pen full of swine, dirty and smelly, snorting and wallowing, pleased as pigs in . . . well, you get the idea.

We look a sorry sight gathered here in the conference/viewing room at *Shoot & Die* as we scan the eleven o'clock newscasts from all the affiliates. Hal Neusome is the star, the big pig, boss hog, shown again and again as he braves flames to save lives. More than Hal bringing you the news, tonight Hal and his show *are* the news.

Hal's station is forwarding calls here, including two from national networks who want to interview him via satellite during their Sunday-morning talkies. Everybody wants to belly up to the trough.

"Call your manager," I suggest, "and have him buy radio ads all over town. Tell him to have traffic at your own station clear as many slots as possible, too. In the morning we'll shoot promos touting that you'll be airing exclusive footage and giving the inside story. Run those between programs, blanket the station's website, and put a tagged shot of the car crash on YouTube. Tomorrow night's *Neusome on the News* ought to grab its biggest audience ever.

Now it's half past eleven, so I insist Byron and Kristen go home, clean up, and *sleep.* They agree, thinking I won't notice when they double back and head for the edit suites, probably to log shots so they'll know what to lay down in the morning for Hal's segments.

Trailed by an older blond woman, Jankety arrives with three large cases. Durbett appears out of nowhere to greet them, telling me, "Forty minutes," then leading them back toward my office. I thought we'd be doing this tomorrow, not *right now*. Silly me.

Cyn arrives next, horrified to see me so disheveled, grimy, sweaty, and smelling like smoke. She hugs me anyway, her expensive blouse be damned. "I had to see for myself that you're all right," she whispers. "I never know when you're serious."

"We're okay," I promise her, "except for the pharmacist."

"You had me so worried."

I walk her down the hallway, talking quietly. "I have some info that'll impact your lawsuit big-time. It looks like the drugstore guy might have been manufacturing and delivering illegal street drugs."

"You have *proof* of this?" she blurts, looking not at all happy about it. I thought she'd be thrilled.

"Not yet, but we're setting up to do spectro-chromatography on some samples we found before the fire. We should have data within an hour."

"Do the police know about this?"

"No, not yet. We want to be sure."

"But you're supposed to be doing PR for him. Maybe you should've just let those samples burn up."

"I don't understand. I thought you wanted to squeeze nickels from this guy."

"It's his insurers who have the deep pockets. I need them to cover a major part—if not all of—the judgment, but if hitting that girl occurred during the commission of a felony, then they're likely off the hook."

Detective Culler and his grim expression appear, so I introduce him and Cyn to each other. He's gracious, but down to business. "I'm gonna need some video, is my way of thinking," he says. "I know there's First Amendment issues about that, so I'm hopin' our spirit of mutual cooperation—"

"No problem," I tell him. "We have an edited version of all the important parts. We can lay that off for you right now."

He nods and allows a knowing smile, that look you get when everybody's backs have been scratched. Kristen joins us—so much for her getting some rest—and offers to run it through an edit suite so he can watch from a comfortable chair. She may look like she's been through a blast furnace, but she always shows that inexhaustible capacity for grace and consideration.

After they're gone, I ask Cyn, "You want to watch the analysis with us?"

"No way. As an officer of the court, I shouldn't have any direct knowledge of that, especially if it's something that winds up going away."

It turns out what she prefers is to watch the video with Culler, at least to see what's been on the air, or will be tomorrow night, but I suspect she's scoping a potential witness, too. I leave her at the suite to work her considerable charms on our inveterate detective, then head for the front desk to call the hospital.

The son has already heard. "Are you and the crew all right?" he asks, a weary sadness in his voice.

"Yeah . . ." Man, this is hard. "We got out okay—barely," I admit, "but your pharmacist . . ."

"Walt was a good man. He went all the way back with Dad. You know he just lost his wife to cancer a few months ago? Took time off to care for her, right to the end." Ignorant people lash out at mislabeled symbols, and an innocent man pays with his life. I have to wonder, what if we'd given the story to Hal's competition sooner . . .

"How's your father?"

He sighs. "About the same. The docs are hopeful, but, well . . ."

"You should stay with him tomorrow instead of spending all day at Hal's station."

"Well, yes, I'd rather do that, but the show's important."

"How about we establish a remote feed? We can talk to you there, live from the studio."

"That would be great." He means it, too.

Durbett's signaling me, so I wrap the conversation quickly.

"Two things," Durbett says. "One, we need to set up a secure computer back where the fiber-optic line comes in to your uplink. Is it okay to work with Byron, to let him know what we're doing?"

"Trust him," I say.

"Good. The other is, I understand Culler's here getting a video."

"I made sure it's the edited version that won't reveal gunfire."

"Good thinkin' ahead. Still, though, you need to suggest he alert hospitals to watch for any man with a left-leg wound."

"Won't he want to know what kind of injury?"

"Tell him penetration, like maybe the bomb shrapnel mighta caused. He'll know not to press it."

"I guess he'll find out it's bullets anyway, once he locates the guy."

"I'm figurin' he won't find him 'cause it's something a private doc could handle. I was just trying to slow him down, not take him out."

"In other words, don't tell the cop something he may never need to know." See? I'm catching on.

"You're catching on," he says. "Likewise, don't tell him I got Pozies yet."

"Why is that a secret?"

"I wanna do our own analysis first. Once Culler knows, he's responsible for immediately preserving the chain of evidence. He'll have to confiscate 'em, tag and bag 'em, then write up *how* he got 'em—which is me. I don't like to be involved unless I know what I'm involved in."

"It's just as well. On the off chance it turns out they're not Pozies, I don't want the lingering impact of accusations—even if they're unfounded."

"Yeah, accusations have a way of developing a life of their own, and livin' a lot longer than the truth—if the truth ever be told."

I check back with Culler and find him seriously impressed by the clips. For a guy who spends so much of his time trying to *picture* crimes, I've managed to *show* him one. Better yet, Kristen's using digital video effects to zoom in on key places, creating stills of the license plates on both the crash car and the escape vehicle, plus surprisingly good shots of the men's faces as they stagger from the smoke. She's even laser-printing them so he can put them on the wire.

Cyn's looking a bit green around the gills, so she follows me out. "He won't talk," she says, "and it's kinda hard to watch that video knowing it was you." I guess reality is a lot uglier than those myriad statutes that try to govern it—though not *that* much uglier.

Still, when she's painting this picture for a jury someday, she'll be glad she had a chance to see it for herself.

"I'm going home," she says. "Please, think hard about whether or not you want to involve that detective in, you know, something nobody knows about yet."

"I will," I promise, and I'm surprised to find I mean it. Durbett seems to be rubbing off on me, the way he decides what's prudent before taking action, weighing the effect on him and those he's looking out for, deciding the best of all possible courses.

She kisses me on the way out, pausing to say, "Make sure you record the show for me." Yeah, like I'd never think to grab a copy after all this work. "I wish I didn't have that thing tomorrow night." And she's gone.

I wish she didn't have that thing, too. I'd rather we have a thing together, maybe explore each other's, well, you know, things.

Culler comes out, one DVD and a folder full of digi-prints in hand. He thanks me several times, then heads off for the Wood Street Station, 13th District, cop shop.

I walk back to my office, rap on the door, and let Durbett know it's me. I must have gotten the password right, because I'm admitted before the door is ceremoniously sealed.

Durbett introduces us. "Barb, Danté." 'Nuff said.

Various lab equipment is strewn around my desk and work table, Jankety running another cable, Barb checking something on a computer screen. "It's makeshift," Durbett admits, "but quicker than waiting on a portable." Heck, I wish I'd known. I could have brought one of my pocket spectro-chroma-thingies.

"Well, it's ready," Jankety pronounces, stepping back.

"Thanks," Durbett says. "Now I need you to relieve Ed's post at the burned-up store, and arrange to have it watched around the clock. There's a safe in the ruins. If anybody takes it or empties it, I wanna know who and where, plus find out what-all's in it."

With a smile and a nod, Durbett's dark-skinned sidekick vanishes.

Barb is pouring the contents from several pink capsules into their own glass vials, then adding some kind of solution.

"Distilled water," Durbett tells me. He's narrating this documentary for those of us whose eyes glazed over during Chem-Lab 210.

She attaches one vial to a suction device that pulls the liquid into a tiny coil attached to a shimmering plate. Then a graph of wavy lines with lots of numbers and symbols appears on the computer screen. She repeats the process eight times, all eight graphs appearing identical to my untrained eyes.

"They're the same," she pronounces, raising her brows at Durbett. Turns out she can talk. "That speaks to the integrity of the readings." Durbett nods and looks pleased. Integrity sounds like a good thing, so I'll ride along. She copies the data to a mem-wafer, then pops it out and says she'll be right back.

"Transmitting to a mainframe?" I ask Durbett after she's gone.

"A secure one," Durbett says, already packing up the equipment. He's nearly finished when somebody raps on the door. He lets Barb back in before I can demand the password.

She pops in the wafer, then begins streaming data, gazing at the screen. Something tells me she can keep up with it all, though I can't imagine how.

"Whatta you got?" Durbett asks when she finally sits back.

"Well, it's twenty percent buffer."

"The inert part?" I ask.

"Yes, something to give it volume, fill up the capsule, make it easier to measure."

"What's the active?" Durbett asks patiently.

"It's just one compound," she says, shrugging her shoulders like she's disappointed we didn't present her with a bigger challenge.

"What?" I blurt.

"Pi-ethym-lorenazol."

Durbett looks at me, and we both know the truth even before she can say it.

"Using its trade name, I'd say you've got pure samples of Parzilac."

CHAPTER 7

It's a wonderful life . . .

Sleeping late on a warm, sunny, Sunday morning. Birds singing, the fragrance of flowers and fresh-cut lawn . . .

Nnnnn— Nnnnn— Nnnnn—

Back to the real world, it's my alarm clock, way too early, not enough sleep . . . I take a deep breath and climb out of bed, then ration minutes to race through my face-the-world routine so I can monitor for Hal's interviews on the network Sunday-morning newsies. We're the big story, now with Hal live via satellite from the affiliate's Chicago studios. The woman in New York is breathless as she interviews him, caught up in the drama and raw excitement. She's exhausted herself, working hard to bring you this story. Her whole team has, leaving no stone unturned, these seekers of truth, purveyors of sooth, a cadre of professional fact takers and tacit fakers.

Hal does a great job painting the picture, dropping hints this is but the tip of an iceberg. He can't expose his sources or reveal *all* the facts yet, but tonight on *Nuesome on the News* . . .

After Hal's wrapped, our spent anchor promises she and her comrades will probe tirelessly to keep us up to date. It's news about the news, but not until Hal deigns to open his bag of cat.

I check in with Ms. Moeroff before I leave, finding her reading her paper in the early-morning sunshine.

She looks me over. "You need more rest."

I sit across from her. I'm in a hurry, but I try never to blow by her without pausing for a moment, if only out of respect. "Yes, ma'am," I agree with a sheepish grin. Respect needn't always be delivered somberly.

"What have you been creating? Do you have anything to show me?"

"You'd have to turn on that old TV of yours. The footage of Chicago's big news story is my work—my *team's* work."

I can see the briefest glimpse of disappointment. She nods, then seems distracted for a second. "I don't follow the news," she says quietly. "It almost never applies to me."

That's a good point. Coverage of important developments in the legislature, court rulings that affect citizens' liberties, anything dealing with taxes or government services or the infrastructure . . . these are things that affect many. But they're rarely interesting and almost never come with exciting footage. So what constitutes *news*—something that panders? Something that entertains? Something that offers drama and suspense? *Catching the crash, explosions, fire, and rescue with a camera?*

"After Hal Neusome's show, I'll have the evening off—without Cyn because she's got a thingie-doo at her firm—and I'm going to want to debrief myself." Actually, I'd rather Cyn debrief me. "Since I'll be involved during the broadcast, probably as first-assistant director, when I get home I'm gonna watch a dub of the show and imagine the reaction of an everyday viewer."

She nods. "Late in my career I saw a film of one of my performances. There is much to be learned by studying your artistry from the cognoscenti perspective."

"Will you watch my Neusome video with me?"

"I look forward to it."

I stand up to leave. "What's the advice?" I ask, referring to the horoscope.

"The harder you try to find solutions, the more likely underlying problems will change."

That earns her a kiss on the cheek and I'm off to—cue the French horns . . . *The Dellman/Roenik Group!*

Of course the place is already buzzing. Find my missing planner and write in "Mayhem—all day."

I start with Byron, explaining what kind of shots I want at the drugstore fire scene this morning before he sets up at the hospital for tonight's live remote.

"What about interviewing the cop?" he asks.

"I assume he'll go live in the studio—" I start, then realize that's a very big assumption. Stupid me—that's not how it's done. Police never come to the newsmonger's turf. It makes 'em look like they're seeking glory, like they're taking valuable time away from investigation to chase media attention. They're supposed to look harried, busy, in a hurry, willing to pause only a moment to answer our questions. That or they hold impromptu press conferences with important people flanking them on each side. But you can't do that without inviting *all* the media. "No, I better call and see what he's willing to do."

The intercom buzzes. "Frank's pulling in," our reception dude alerts me.

With Mel and the monster, our whole agency family is here at an ungodly hour on this beautiful Sunday morning. This is what they call being in business for yourself?

I check on Murray's progress writing Hal's voice-overs for tonight's roll-ins. He pushes up his glasses and assumes an authoritarian voice. "What drives a successful businessman to honor his commitment to a fading neighborhood? Is it simply to make money? For the prestige? Waiting for a conglomerate to buy him out? Because it's easy—?" He changes to his own softer voice, gesturing toward the shot log. "There's quick cuts that contradict each question as it's asked." Back to his Hal voice, quieter, empathic, understanding: "Or is it the people? Standing up for a community—in good times *and* bad?"

I can see it in my mind, the shots of people who depend on this drugstore, who come out for the free screenings and blood drives, the older folks who can't get around so well anymore.

"Impressive," Frank says from the doorway. Melissa's beside him, Taj peeking from around her leg, his Q-Tawzh doll clutched under his arm.

"Morning, colleagues," I greet. Then with a wink to Taj, I proclaim, "Goo-lah!" and collect a shy giggle for my reward. Melissa smiles.

Frank just doesn't get it.

Hal comes in, looks at some footage for the segment being edited, and skims through the scripts, clearly impressed. "This sounds just like me," he repeats several times.

Murray's good at picking up people's styles. That's why he's invaluable doing corporate stuff. Those presenters usually aren't performers; oftentimes they're nervous and hyper-aware that an entire career is judged by a moment in the spotlight. Crafting scripts that sound like they speak, that are easy for them to read, that's our ace for successful biz communications and our key to client loyalty.

"This is how I picture the open," I tell Hal. Here in the suite surrounded by videos, if he can't see what I imagine, I can *show* him. "You open with a posterized, strobed montage of shots, tense rhythmic music building in intensity, your voice announcing, *Street drugs, armed robbery, a vicious stabbing, pause, Struggling for help, tragic accident, a community torn apart, pause, Misplaced blame, blind retribution, the wrong scapegoat, pause, Senseless violence, brutal murder, a daring rescue, pause, pounding music, A double tragedy, casualties of Chicago's illicit drug trade,* pause, shot dissolving to pretty posie flowers in the sunshine, then morphing to little pink capsules, *A story of Pozies, and death in Mile-Square*, music stops dead for a second, then resumes, fading down and under."

"Yow," is Hal's reaction.

Murray's been scribbling it down. He'll have it refined and improved by the time we're ready to record the voice-over.

"I started to say *heroic* rescue, but you can't blow your own horn *too* much. An act like braving flames to save Kristen should be treated as if it goes with the territory, that it's not so important what role *you* played. Just keeping Chicago informed is, for you, of paramount importance."

He nods enthusiastically. Murray's enjoying this in his perverse wordsmith kind of way. Kristen's still calling shots for the editor, telling the assistant which disk to load next.

It's almost nine, so I call Detective Culler.

"No injured legs at area hospitals and no ID on the bombers yet," Culler explains. "Both cars, the crasher *and* the getaway, were reported stolen two days ago. That's odd, and it suggests pre-meditated planning, is my way of thinking."

"What does that accomplish?"

"A hot car is most looked for right after it's reported. After a day or two, we figure it's been chop-shopped if it hasn't turned up somewhere. If you want to drive a hot car while committing a crime, one that's been missing long enough to be forgotten is the best—unless the plates or VIN have been changed."

"Any other developments?"

"The lab guys couldn't get prints from the blown-up car. That's all I know so far."

"Hal and I want to be careful to preserve your image of an impartial detective who's pausing only long enough to answer our questions in the hope somebody saw something and will come forward. You got a good place to shoot that?"

"How about at the burned-up drugstore?"

"Hmmm . . . No, there'll be other news crews out there today." Think, Danté, think. Out by the wrecked car? The hospital? "How about if you come to the studio this afternoon to compare your digitized blow-ups with the original shots? Since Hal Neusome is the one who stepped forward with this critical evidence, here is where you'd obtain another chain-of-custody lay-off anyway. We can put you and Hal in front of the monitors while a tech enhances and lasers the shots. That'll be our cue to show them to our audience and ask people to call your office if they can identify these men."

"Excellent! That's exactly my way of thinking. And while I'm doing this, Hal will ask me questions about the stabbing and robbery and so forth?"

"Now you're thinking like a producer," I kid him.

"Thinking like a detective who needs the story to get out," he corrects. Yeah, right. Sure.

We set a time and let him get back to work. Hal's grinning.

"We'll work up the questions," Murray offers. Him and Hal, pals, colleagues, cohorts, compadres. Murray seems to enjoy himself most when deadlines loom and the do-list grows faster than items can be crossed off.

"I think you should lead off with quick highlights," I explain to both, though I'm looking at Hal. He is, after all, in charge here. "—A review of what people already know with exciting—but very quick—clips, then go to the Culler interview and learn what's new. Paint the picture like you've been investigating and already had put much of this together, waiting for Culler to confirm because you're being a responsible journalist who wants corroboration before taking the story on the air. Hold the big explosion footage till nearly the end, but tease it before commercials so they'll keep watching. Let's put together a piece on Pozies, what they are, what they look like, why they're bad bad *bad*, and what role they played in this tragedy. Follow that with re-enacting what-all happened; then get the personal story of the girl, her friends and family, the funeral, support from Reverend Falluson, and let Falluson talk live about that and solicit donations for the fund. Then we tell the history of the drugstore chain, its role in the community, the man and his family behind it, weaving in the quotes and footage of the kids' soccer team they sponsor."

"There's enough to keep this moving fast," Hal grins.

"A lot of visuals," I agree. "Let's wrap that section with the first good quote from the wife, how her husband is a victim, too, then deride the vandalism and show the big crash and dual explosions and rescue, the unadulterated version that's Neusome exclusive; then quickly hit them with the digitized cut-outs, then the fire and you telling the captain what he's up against. Let Falluson talk about such a loss to the neighborhood, how tragic it is to continue the senseless violence when we should be starting the process of healing."

"He'll jump all over that," Hal concurs.

"We'll walk him through this before airtime and seek his input. He's a sharp media player. He may find other angles and places to horn in, so let him. We'll balance him with cutting to the hospital if we need to."

"The son will be seeing it all on a monitor, right?"

"Just like the nationals, Hal."

"And what's the ending?"

"The son said they'll rebuild the drugstore. Let's get him to pledge that, to stand by the community while Falluson pledges the community's support, working together, warm and fuzzy, hands across Chicago. Then we'll fade into a live shot of our comatose victim in the hospital and bring in the wife's final quote about how her husband would trade his life to bring back that little girl. We'll fade it into a montage of the man and the girl and those insidious pink capsules over a still of the explosion. You thank Falluson and the son and promise you'll stay on top of this story, then close with a wide shot showing crew scurrying around like everybody's getting right to work on the next show."

Reception dude buzzes me that a Mr. Barnahay is calling about Melissa's car. "It's worse than I thought," my gardener/auto mechanic reports. "Hairline cracks in the head—I couldn't tell until I got it apart. I can fix everything else—and it'll run for a while—but it'll strand her someday."

"What do you recommend?"

"Rebuilt engine—now. Look, I want to hold this to the three-fifty I promised, so if I got a few more days, I can run down a good deal on one and have it delivered."

I buzz Melissa. She's overwhelmed by it all, but says as long as she can find rides to work and bring Taj along, she can get by for a week or more.

Another buzz, Mr. Durbett on the line. "I was out there poking around, helpin' the fire investigator, when the son showed up to see about getting into the safe."

"The investigator is letting you—?"

"Anyway, he wasn't dressed to climb through that mess, so *I* offered to for him." I'm picturing Durbett in a nuclear bio-containment suit with helmet and gas-mask, Geiger-countering his way through the rubble. "So he gave me the combination," he continued. "I warned him too many would see him leavin' with valuables in his car; then I offered to have one of my guys put it all in a protective box and follow him to the bank or wherever."

"He liked that?"

"Yeah. He's jumpy, though. Say *boo* and he's up a tree. The safe contained a dozen lock-bags. We carried 'em to a bank where he put 'em in a safe-deposit box."

"No idea what was in the bags?"

I could almost hear Durbett grinning over the line. "Just between you and me, our lock-box had X-ray capability and we accidentally got shots of each bag."

"You're accident-prone," I accuse.

"Can't be careful *all* the time. Anyway, one was papers, the rest was paper cash-money. Can't be sure, but prob'ly somewheres between fifty and hundred-thou."

"Is that suspicious?"

"Don't hafta be. Still, though, with most of the store's big transactions bein' insurance and all—not much cash changin' hands—I gotta wonder how many weeks' or months' receipts that kinda loot is."

"And why they'd keep it there?"

He pauses. "Maybe 'cause that's where he worked most, kept it close to him. They's a lotta people like that—don't necessarily mean nothin'."

"What's next?"

"I'm gonna keep pokin' for a while, at least see what the investigator turns up. He's bein' real friendly, sharin' things with me." I'm not surprised. "I'd like to get over to the hospital when you do that remote, see how it's done and all."

"That'll be late-afternoon. In the meantime, watch for Byron. He'll be out there pretty soon where you are, getting next-day shots. If you don't want to show up on camera—"

"I'll watch for 'im."

Time to see what Frank wants, I pause at the kiddie room on the way, just long enough to make faces at Taj and the little golden-haired girl, today's only young'ns in residence; then I stop to see Melissa. She's printing out presentation summaries, quotes for advertising production and placement costs, Briggs Pharmaceutical, Allergy Tattoo. Knowing Rupert and the deal-meister, the *whole* package probably runs toward ten-mill.

I find the two of them in Frank's office crunching numbers from my list of program topics for Flynn Durbett's *The Weisman Company*.

"If you get Murray running on his scripts," Frank asks, "and have Kristen shoot the blind videos on M-Slovak after I get Rex's approval, can you get the rest of the tattoo package together in time to present Wednesday?"

"Of which month?" I know when he means.

"This week," Rupert clarifies. He takes me too literally.

"Sure, what the hey."

"Good," Frank allows. "Rex is *extremely* impressed with what you did on the drugstore PR and what you've done so far on the allergy tattoo. He said he'll flip us another fifty-K to work with if we can come up with more anti-M-Slovak and anti-merger ideas."

"I'll have to ponder that."

Frank sits back, a slight smirk on his face. Rupert keeps glancing between him and me, trying to conceal a grin, not doing a good job of it.

"Rex called me about something else, too," Frank explains. "He said he knows this tattoo account will mean having to bring in a team, especially media buyers, and that we'll be growing fast, but he definitely wants us to take a crack at his big one, the Fantasy Patch—even if it's just creative and PR planning. But the sky's the limit," Frank emphasizes. "He said they're looking at breaking the billion-dollar sales mark within two years, and doubling or tripling that within five, especially after the international roll-out."

I swear Rupert's drooling. "Agency billings of fifty- to a hundred-million a year!" he blurts.

"Start thinking concept," Frank says. "At the same time he wants us to make the whole world scared of Parzilac, he wants 'Fantasy Patch' to become synonymous with a safe way to empower people to solve their problems and take control of their destinies."

"What is this patch?"

"It's a tiny thing you stick on your skin. It uses that new Pene-Derm stuff they developed. The drug is a synthesized version of some fungus from South America that gives people voluntary control of autonomic responses—things like anxiety, fear, depression, attention problems, obsessive-compulsions, hyperventilation, attack-rage, debilitating grief, you name it. Instead of a drug that does things *to* your mind, this one gives you more *control* over your own mind. Instead of having to take doses that last for long periods and are uncontrollable, this patch starts fifteen minutes after you put it on, keeps a steady effect going, and can be removed at any time. The effects fade after about thirty minutes."

"It's a wonder drug for psychological problems," Rupert sums up.

"Over-eating, compulsive gambling, drug and alcohol addiction, behavior problems in kids, treating criminals—the applications are unlimited," Frank breathes.

Wow. Imagine how you would like to be, then put on the Fantasy Patch and your ideal self becomes reality.

Heading back toward the edit suite, I make a face at Taj and our Chyron operator's little girl, earning giggles again as my reward. Kristen rolls the fully edited accident re-enactment segment for me, complete with Hal's voice-over. This woman works *fast*. It looks great, riveting, compelling, fraught with tension and drama; I was on the edge of my seat.

"Well, that tears it," Hal pronounces, stomping into the suite. "My director just quit. He's in a huff that I'm putting together all this without bringing him along to slow us down and contribute nothing."

"Oh, well," I console. "They can just run a couple of episodes of *The Nanny* instead."

"Like hell. Who can I hire? Who's available and sharp enough to get up to speed and pull this off?"

Don't say it, Danté. Don't even think it.

Cripe, Kristen speaks up. "I recommend you contract with the Dellman/Roenik Group. Request Roenik—he's already up to speed." She gives me a sneaky grin and, I swear, sticks her tongue out at me.

"Done," Hal agrees.

Wait a minute . . . Looks like I'm going to direct news. I don't like the looks of this.

What would Ms. Moeroff think?

*   *   *

Like a college term paper.

This reminds me of pulling those all-nighters, six hours' worth of work to squeeze into the last three hours before deadline, trying both to fine-tune as I work and to get it all down for editing with whatever time I have left. I always managed to beat those deadlines, sometimes well in advance, sometimes just barely in time. I was doing a double major and an internship, plus working a part-time job, so it wasn't unusual to find myself with six hours' work but only three hours to go.

Like preparing for my first directorial stint at *Newsome on the News* here in the cracker box they call a studio at Hal's station.

Byron calls in when he gets to the hospital. Surprise!—they're hassling him about bringing in the equipment. The son intercedes until we reach a compromise. We'll set up in a waiting-room lounge down the hall from the private ICU.

"I'll use a long cable on the camera," Byron assures me on the QT, "so I can sneak down and shoot into the guy's room." Nudge-nudge, wink-wink.

"Grab a cover shot at the beginning, then stick with the son in the lounge unless his father starts to wake, hopefully sitting up and announcing the butler did it."

"Actually, they do think he really might wake up. His eyelids have been fluttering and he's moved several times."

"We might get that exclusive interview yet."

"He's got one of those trachea things, though, plus lung damage from the stabbing. The doc told me it'll be at least a few days before he can talk."

"Hmmm . . . Well, at least you could shoot the joyous family reunion. I guess we don't need words, or Hal can wing some quiet voice-over, but visual impact will carry it. I sure hope it happens whether we catch it or not," I add. To think, last night I was ready to hang this guy as a street-drug manufacturer. Too often, perception runs way ahead of reality.

And too often reality never catches up.

Falluson arrives with a small entourage of handlers, a tall black man who could be a bodyguard, a waspy white woman who seems to be in charge of acting suspicious, and a youngish, chubby black fellow who does most of their talking. I really want to spring the big developments on this guy after he's spouted off on the air, to let him make a fool of himself, but I can't risk the potential for residual backlash against the guy I'm being paid to gussy up.

"There are big developments," I explain. "The detective confirmed it was a *robbery*, that the drugstore guy was driven to an alley near Mile-Square, robbed of prescription drugs used for making street drugs, then stabbed and left for dead. It looks like he tried to drive himself to get help but passed out at the wheel from blood loss, then accidentally ran over the little girl."

"Another police cover-up!" Waspy announces.

Falluson is surprised and clearly suspicious, Chubby thinking it through, Big Dude clenching his fists in silent outrage.

"It *could* be a ploy," Chubby points out, "to put down the boycott. They're scared after last night's violence."

"It's because he's *white*," the waspy white woman spits out. It's a swear-word.

Chubby advises, "Don't take *his* word for it—"

Falluson holds up his hand to cut off their comments. Turning to me, he asks, "The lead detective will confirm all this on the air?"

"Yes."

"And you have reason to believe what he says?"

"I watched a lot of the investigation myself, saw him collecting the evidence."

"You waited until the last minute to tell me," Falluson says quietly, but it's accusation, right in my face.

I don't want this guy to walk out. The show really needs him for balance, and to prove he's back-tracked on his earlier pronouncements. "I'm not even supposed to release this information until air-time—"

"You knew yesterday, didn't you? When we did the shoot at the funeral home."

I nod. "I couldn't be sure yet, but that's how it was looking."

"That's why you didn't want me to talk about blame."

"I didn't want to take a chance you would look foolish if you turned out to be wrong. I tried to let you know, but without violating the confidentiality of my sources."

"Yes, you did say new information would be released before air-time, that it was important right then to focus on the girl and her family."

Chubby tells his boss, "He was looking out for you."

I nod slightly, silent acknowledgement we're all in this together. Waspy still looks suspicious, but all the steam's blown out of the engine of her prejudice. The really big guy relaxes.

Falluson looks toward Chubby, his aide nodding in return, then turns back to me, takes a deep breath, and makes the call. "The drugstore owner, the little girl, the pharmacist—all victims. This is a triple tragedy."

Whew!

"Exactly." We're on the same page. "I think it's important that you seize this opportunity, step up to your role as a community leader, and help us find some way to understand this, to make sense of this awful tragedy." See, I can use that word, too. "These people need your help to start the healing process, to ease the burden on that little girl's family, to rally support for another family who must decide if they'll rebuild and continue to serve the sick and elderly who have no place else to go."

Falluson makes his pledge. "The healing *must* begin—and it will, with us, here, tonight."

Amen.

Chubby's into it, already firing off suggestions. We go through the run-down, quick descriptions of my roll-ins, samples of what Hal will say, the important role this good reverend will play. Yes, tonight we will begin to heal.

"If you brought the information for making donations, I have a nice background ready."

Chubby's got it in his satchel. I suspect he also has where and when to meet for the big boycott-protest in there, too.

Now that Falluson has changed gears so smoothly, I'm more impressed by him than I expected, not feeling the contempt I always held for his public persona. He's a smart man, good at what he does. I don't always like his goals, but I can't fault his relentless pursuit of them.

Putting all this together, like working with Hal Neusome, has been more interesting than I expected. Hal let me take charge because he trusted me enough to let me run—though if I were going the wrong way, I'm sure he'd rein me in or cut me loose—and he's been very professional in fulfilling *his* role. After all, he *is* the front man, the one whose image and reputation and remnants of career will live or die on how he performs both in front of the lens and behind it. I sure wouldn't want that role.

I like to make images, not *be* one.

Hal finally arrives with the last of the edited elements. He talks to the reverend-plus-entourage while I eavesdrop on their conversation and review the videos.

Neusome definitely has finesse. Falluson has finesse. The son has proven to be pretty sharp.

My director's elements are grade-A. I have confidence in our equipment and in Byron's ability to handle problems on the fly. Kristen will deftly juggle the myriad elements at the hospital. My control-room crew is the best, used to working with me, a team that knows how to hum.

It's show time!

I'm sorry, *news* time . . .

Just another term paper.

*   *   *

I'm pleased and proud with how the show is going. It's fast-paced except for those emotional pauses, filled with information and images, a mix of investigational intrigue and human interest, entertaining even to me—and I've already seen all this in pieces.

I'm not sure if it's Hal's penchant for digging out the real story or that he just wants to enjoy tweaking Falluson's nose, but at one point he challenges the good reverend about his earlier calls for a boycott.

"I'm embarrassed to say I was taken in by the local news establishment."

Yow! I'm calling that one a counter-tweak. "There was a rush to judgment, a quickness to declare guilt through irresponsible journalism, that unfortunate pattern of believing and blindly reporting the first thing police say," he declares with the remorse of a little boy with contraband cookie crumbs on his chin. "It's not just the suppression of our African-American brothers and sisters—" He's preaching now. "It is *all* the disenfranchised and the poor, the people outside of the mainstream, excluded from the status quo, who are so often victimized by this—"

"Victimized by what?" Hal asks.

"The police, when they target a scapegoat. Then they focus on obtaining a conviction, rightfully or wrongfully, and stop investigating for the truly guilty party."

Hal nods and starts to say something, but he's cut off.

"But not you, Mr. Neusome," Falluson praises. "That's why I waited before starting the boycott. That's why I come to you to learn more about what *really* happened. *You* were the one working to uncover the *real* story, the one who looked beyond easy explanations in a *tireless* search for truth and justice."

"Much of that credit goes to the dogged efforts of Detective Culler."

"He is a good man, the detective. His work has been an asset to our community."

Ka-ching! It's payday for Culler—public relations our good detective can take to the bank. This will be one telecast where everybody wins.

Another interesting development is when the subject of Pozies is explored. Falluson's chubby handler had made two phone calls, then briefed his guy so well that the good reverend is able to speak quite authoritatively about the subject.

"Just last week, two little boys, not much older than ten or eleven, they were pressured to try these Pozies. They didn't know better; they didn't understand the danger; they didn't know of the potentially deadly consequences. We need more funding, for education and prevention—"

"What happened to the boys?" Hal is very concerned, ready to step in and help.

"It was a *long* and terrifying night, them boys seeing all kinds of horrible visions, crying out and begging it to stop." Falluson's shaking his head grimly. "There's already too many examples of people taking these Parzilacs and committing acts of violence. Mixing in other drugs, that just makes them even more dangerous."

I could kiss the good reverend.

Our cutaways to the hospital are equally successful. My favorite line is when the son thanks Falluson—*thanks* him! "I know you spoke of a possible boycott back when emotions were running high, back when it looked like my father had done something wrong, but what we've suffered ever since—the vandalism, the bombed-out store—it could have been much worse if you'd not provided a calming presence. That poor little girl's funeral could have erupted into even more senseless violence, but you kept people focused, reminded them there would be time for blame later, that what mattered at the moment was to celebrate the life and mourn the loss of that beautiful child." He's choking up, and I'm convinced he's not just dramatizing, that it's how he really feels.

"On behalf of our community," Falluson announces, "I pledge our support for your family. We hope you'll stand by us and remain an important part of a neighborhood who needs you. We hope you'll rebuild, and help us all work together to heal."

"We will, Reverend. Even if my father is unable to go on, my family pledges our support. We *will* rebuild. We'll never abandon the people we've served for generations."

This is wonderful. Of course, it's seven minutes sooner than it was supposed to happen, and it takes the wind out of my big ending, but I can still make this work.

Now we're in commercial and Kristen's talking in my headset. "Danté! Something's happening! He's been having violent convulsions." I can see on my monitor that the son has run down the hall, Byron's camera following, a phalanx of doctors and nurses and equipment rushing into his room.

I open the channel to Hal's earpiece. "Something's gone wrong at the hospital! *Byron*, stay on the shot, but don't pander to the family's grief if it goes bad. *Kristen*, you're the reporter on the scene. *Chyron*, gimme a super of her name! *Hal*, you be ready to recap events in the lulls—"

"Five seconds," the technical director announces. "Four, three, two . . ."

"There's been an emergency at the hospital," Hal announces. "Kristen Aurbach is on the scene. Kristen?"

The camera angle is from the hallway, first on Kristen, then into the room. It looks like one of those emergency-room shows with gowns and masks and rubber gloves, instruments and tubes and machines.

"He started convulsing about eight minutes ago, Hal, and now he's in cardiac arrest," Kristen says sadly but professionally. "The crash team is involved in a heroic effort to revive him."

"Have they succeeded?"

"Not yet, Hal. The medical staff appears to be baffled by what's happened. Somebody just shouted, *Total failure.* Now I'm hearing others saying it's not working; it's just not working."

The activity continues at a feverish pace, Byron inching closer, the camera carefully avoiding the scared wife and son. Our view is distracted by the machines, the blipping and bleeping, the respirator wheezing, now that thing that pumps something or other, a second crash cart rushing in.

Hal is recapping events. I'm cutting to shots of him and Falluson, both grave and concerned. Now Falluson is saying a prayer, the perfect image, everybody pulling together.

And the doctors struggle. And we can hear the wife crying. And the machines are squealing.

Now the paddles. "Clear!" *Woomp!* "Clear!" *Woomp!*

Frustration, resignation, crushing disappointment.

And they call it.

Kristen quietly says, "Time of death, five fifty-seven, p.m."

And the camera's distracted by the heart monitor, a steady hum, a flatline.

Back to Hal, repeating grimly that our man has just died despite the most heroic efforts of hospital staff. He is survived by his wife, his son, and many good friends.

"Such a tragedy," Falluson bemoans.

"Give him the one-minute," I tell the floor director through his headset. "Signal that we have a clip first."

"A man who gave his life to a neighborhood," Hal says. "This is what his wife told me . . ."

We roll the video, the quote about how he would trade his life for the little girl's.

"Forty seconds."

Hal needs to wing it. What will he—?

"Thanks to the Reverend Falluson for being here, Kristen Aurbach reporting from the hospital—"

Turn to camera two, montage of stills over his shoulder.

"Street drugs, armed robbery, a vicious stabbing—" He's repeating the opening text. Excellent! "—A double tragedy, now *three* senseless deaths—"

He's added a line.

"—Casualties of Chicago's illicit drug trade, a story of Pozies, and death in Mile-Square."

Push in tighter.

"This is Hal Neusome, with *Neusome on the News*."

Wide shot, credits rolling, Hal with his hand on Falluson's shoulder, the reverend shaking his head sadly.

Fade to black.

"And we're clear."

CHAPTER 8

"Oh, that poor man." Ms. Moeroff holds her hand to her mouth.

I stop the video, hit reset, and mute the volume. "A million people died today," I say quietly. "But this show made you experience, made you *feel* that particular one."

She nods understanding, then turns and regards me curiously. "Danté, how is this *art*?"

"How do *you* define art?"

"Esthetic expression?"

"Creative interpretation?" I counter.

She nods agreement. "Both—and more."

"For some, art is capturing what we see, like a photographer. But the photographer also interprets, choosing angle and framing, adjusting for lighting, showing us *his* perspective on something anybody can *look* at, but which nobody else sees his unique way. Then he clicks the shutter to capture that and—most importantly—he displays or distributes the photo and *shares* that vision with others."

She gets up and does a spirited pirouette, then sweeps her arms toward me, tilting her head gracefully. "That's the difference between dancing for my own pleasure and performing for others."

I'm smiling now, tilting my head to agree. "For others, art is seizing an experience, something they see or hear or taste or feel, then exerting their will on it, changing it, making it their own." Now she's doing a Fred Astaire with a stand-up lamp. "That might mean taming it," I continue, "or it might mean setting it free. Maybe it's dressing it up; maybe it's stripping it bare. Unless the artist destroys what he creates, the ultimate goal is to share the result with others—his *audience*."

She twirls and dips low, holding, lower, lower; she's about to fall, so I grab for her— And she's up and smiling before I can touch her. "Everybody responds differently," she points out. "Whatever reaction an artist gets varies from person to person, or from time to time in the same person."

"Yes! The artist can strive to evoke a similar response from everyone, or he might intentionally craft ambiguity so every interpretation is unique. Likewise, beauty needn't be its inherent goal; sometimes it's exposing the ugly, the profane, evoking revulsion in order to move an audience."

She's holding both of my hands now, her eyes glistening. These moments are golden, when Theta Moeroff can dance the dance of the minds, exploring ideas and concepts nobody else in her life considers or cares about. It's not a Hank Barnahay discussion. It's not for the ladies of the garden tour. It's between this gentle old woman with the soul of an artist and her ersatz son, two people who care about and look out for each other. Leading me into the kitchen, she pours me a soda and herself some Zinfandel, then asks just like a mom, "Danté, why suddenly do you want to be an artist of news?"

"I don't," I admit. "It's a temporary enabler, the financial security for our new agency that will allow me time and resources to play later, but I must admit I'm enjoying the philosophical challenge of it."

We take seats at the table. "And what is this challenge to you?"

"To become master of the metaphor."

"You'll have to explain that, too."

"It's not easy. Communication, whether for art or otherwise, has been moving away from what's literal, moving toward the symbolic. Attention spans today grow shorter while a tidal-wave deluge of information competes for them."

"What you're describing is advertising."

"The underlying art of which is to equate goods or services with concepts. A door-latch equals safety. An allergy tattoo means loving your child—or to the youngster it's being cool among your friends. Other products equate to healthy or sexy or secure or smart or informed or comfortable or classy or—you name it. If you have an established product and want to remake its image, what's the first thing you do?"

"Call it new and improved!" She knows the drill.

"Ah, but not so much anymore. That becomes trite. Now it needs a modern buzz-phrase designed to evoke *today's* images. You call it low-fat, or tag it low-calorie, all-natural, biodegradable, Made in the U.S.A., fresh-cut though it's canned, and this is my favorite—" In my narrator's voice again, "*Now!*—with added tetra-moola-goobie-whatever-zol! Like we're all bio-chemists."

"But now *all-natural* is unpopular," she spars, "if you're talking about fur."

My narrator recites: "No polyesters were harmed in the making of this coat!"

She's up swirling around again, this time modeling her invisible mink coat and giggling. "So you, Danté Roenik, want to create your very own symbol, or a metaphor, or something that evokes meaning simply from a word or a visual image?"

"Somebody's willing to pay handsomely for me to transform one and create another." I jump up and spread my arms in a magnanimous gesture of self-mocking. "Call me Danté! *The Imagemaker!*"

She laughs. "And what will these images be?"

"One is of danger, unpredictability, loss of control. Violence, suicide, murder . . . Little pink capsules . . . *Parzilac.*"

"If such artistry results in saving lives, then that would be a noble endeavor. What's the other one?"

"Then I'll craft the ultimate symbol for taking control of one's destiny, for exerting mind over body, the means for remaking the self however one desires."

"What could possibly do that?"

"Fantasy Patch!"

*   *   *

Woooo! Woooo! Sounds like a toy-train whistle.

"You're listening to WU-WU radio! W-U-W-U 490 A.M., Chicago's all-talk, ride or walk, info-mation info-station!"

"I'm Pook!"

"And I'm Kook!"

"Bringing you the WU-WU Pook & Kook show!"

"So Kook, didja see Hal Neusome's show last night?"

"Ka-*Boom!* Just goes to show—if you're gonna be fire-bombed, bring your *camera!*"

"He sure took the wind out of Reverend Falluson's big boycott!"

Imitating Falluson: "*Now* we don't know *who* to blame—that's the *real* tragedy!"

"In case your wu-wu's not up on the latest, Hal Neusome—your favorite former drunk driver—climbed up out of the gutter long enough to put together some *real* news, exposing the scandal behind the Mile-Square accident—"

"And got in the middle of that retaliation crash-boom-boom fire-bombing of the drugstore down there on Madison Street—"

"Seems the owner was robbed of some Parzilacs used for making street

Pozies—"

Kook's singing: "Ring around the rosie, pocketful of posies—"

"Don't make an ash of yourself and fall down, Kook."

"I yam what I yam—nyuk nyuk nyuk."

"The reverend was calling for a boycott to get even, but it turns out the owner was a victim, too. He was in a coma till last night; then he cashed in his chips, right there live—"

"No pun intended!"

"Right on Hal's show."

"Now he's pushin' up posies—"

I shut off the car radio and pull in at Chicago's new agency, The Dellman/Roenik Group.

"Hal Neusome is waiting in your office," the reception dude greets me. "Frank wants to see you in *his* office first. Oh, and good morning, Mr. Roenik."

As I pass the kid-room, I hear a "Goo-lah!" for my second greeting of the day. I shout one back without breaking my stride. I find Rupert in with Frank, both shoving around stacks of papers. It wouldn't be Frank's desk without piles but, seeing as how we have few jobs and fewer clients— "This is scrap paper—admit it. You've piled up scrap paper just so you'll look busy."

Rupert closes the door.

"Hal's waiting for you," Frank says with a mocking smile. "I think you've got, shall we say, a new *friend*."

"Cripe. I'm ready to work on caterpillars and flaming skulls. I need a break from this guy."

"Well, that job is done. We made enough off Briggs's dime to stay in business for eleven more days. Give Hal a pat on the back and tell him we'll be in touch."

Rupert thinks this is funny.

"Can't do that. Hal's our ace up a sleeve, our entrée to the news media. Deep-pockets Briggs is willing to pay for PR and I've got my collar on the news hound."

Rupert asks, "Are you planning a *Neusome on the News* about Pozies and Parzilac violence?"

"We're seeing Rex at two today," Frank says, waving his finger toward me like I should be writing that in my lost planner. "Why don't you sniff your news hound before we try to sell him the idea."

"Hal's a strong outlet," I point out, "as long as he can ride this wave of recognition from the Mile-Square show. If we let him flounder the next few Sundays, his audience will drop off before we do a Pozie show."

"We can't afford to carry the guy," Frank cautions.

"But with people on salary and underutilized equipment and facility, we might as well do favors for Hal and Faritzka and whomever's butts you two kissers sniff out."

Frank sets his mouth, then nods. "Follow my lead with Rex. He might want to contribute toward making sure Hal stays popular and is beholden to us."

I find Hal waiting patiently for me, jumping up to shake my hand. "More than three-hundred calls, the hot topic on radio, and the big story on morning newscasts!"

"Congratulations, Hal. You really pulled this one together."

I take the seat at my desk, so he sits across from me. "Don't blow smoke up my skirt, Danté. I've finally managed to get rid of the smell from that fire."

"Okay, *we* pulled it together."

"And we're not through yet."

"Oh? You've got a budget?"

Hal lets that hang for a moment, a sneaky look on his face. "Let me tell you the other news first."

"Keep it quick. I'm billing you for my time, you know." When did Frank take control of my mouth? Call the exorcist.

"My station's independent, so nothing's stopping me from climbing in the sack with a network for a one-night stand."

"Network talk makes me all hot and sweaty."

"You joke, but—truth be told—*I am*. Hot and sweaty, I mean. NBS is pulling me in as special correspondent to do a segment on the Mile-Square triple tragedy for Thursday night's *NBS Newsline*."

"You're kickin' butt there, Hal. Just remember, I knew you back when you were just a broken-down has-been."

"And drunk driver, according to Pook & Kook. Anyway, *Newsline* wants to use the rest of the footage, so I told them I can't clear the rights until I settle your bill."

"How much is that?" I'm wondering, *What bill?* Briggs paid for everything and then some—has Frank been guilt-tripping Hal with numbers?

"You think Frank would go for, say, eighteen-thousand?"

Frank sticks his head in. "Hal!" He smelled the money.

"Hal's trying to buy our friendship," I report, gesturing it's okay to join us.

"Eighteen-thou won't get him a roll in the hay," Frank says, pulling up a chair, "but we might play spin the bottle."

"Frank, you're a serpent who'd shed a dozen times a day if he thought there was good money in snake skins."

"Is there?" Frank looks eerily serious.

Melissa slips in and leaves a tray of juice and snacks, smiling at Frank's retort.

"I've got production budget, too. *Newsline* will cover reasonable costs for this segment, plus my station will pay to add roll-ins and beef up my show each week. Apparently, they like me reminding viewers there's a channel down at that end of the dial."

"You should shoot at the guy's funeral," I suggest, "and interview Culler to update the investigation."

"I'd like to book your crew for those," Hal agrees.

Rupert pokes his head in. His money-smeller's not as good as Frank's yet, but these additional remote jobs must have been just pungent enough. Frank gestures him to sit and soak it up.

"I'll write the piece myself," Hal says, "and supervise the edit if you have an open suite for two days." *Ka-ching!* "Plus, I need a small *Newsline* stand-up set and backdrop so I can shoot my narratives and go live from *your* stage Thursday night to banter with the anchors in New York."

Buzz. Frank hits the intercom, reception dude reporting, "Misters Durbett and Jankety are here. They want to meet with Byron, but thought they should okay that with you first."

Flynn Durbett saved our lives. Hell, he can date my girlfriend.

We hand Hal off to Kristen to put together a production plan, then get waylayed by Tony Faritzka stopping in to check on his edit. Frank leads him down to animation to talk up our offer, so I head back to find Durbett and his sidekick.

They're in the equipment room where Byron's explaining, "I didn't have a disk in the camera because those minis only run twenty or thirty minutes, but I did have a one-eighty recording in a portable, just in case something interesting happened while we weren't on the air. I was just about to erase it."

"I'd like to watch it first," Durbett explains. "There was a nurse there lookin' too jittery for my liking. Nervous folks make me nervous. I stuck around for a while afterwards, but I never seen her again. I wanna see if we got a shot of her."

Byron answers my look. "I'll set him up."

"We'd like to use an office, too," Durbett requests. "I need to run some mass spectrograph gas chromatographs. I collected some souvenirs after the commotion died down." He opens a case to reveal syringes, an IV bag and tube, several instruments, some kind of print-out covered with wavy lines, and other miscellany.

"How did you get all that out?"

"I was quick-like," he says, allowing the slightest grin. Call him Flynn Copperfield.

Buzz. "Sam Cox and Dib Wardley are here from Kehoe/Lundy with two others and a truck. They want to pull out their tape and disk library. Also, two people from Hale-Bopp Graphics are here to see you, Danté."

"I'll be right there." I sure could use a planner today.

"One more thing," Durbett says. "My product guy'll be landing within the hour. When can we hook him to whoever's gonna write my scripts?"

"You lookin' for me?" Murray asks, wandering in at just the right time. He hands me a sheath. "Here's the latest Briggs scripts, including the new one on Pozies being the first domino in the downfall of civilization." Murray never laughs, but he's acting like he would if he could. He's enjoyed writing these.

"You ready to jump on Flynn's infomercial series?"

"I thought you'd never ask," he says, batting his eyes demurely and pushing up his glasses. "I've got a few concept outlines going already."

"Set here with us while we watch this video," Durbett offers, "and let's talk."

Frank leaves Faritzka with our animator, and Kristen leaves Hal to edit so we can discuss how to deal with Sam and Dib.

"I can oversee giving the library to those loathsome vermin," she offers. I picture her spitting. Cox and Wardley are swear-words.

"Did you finish laying off all the samples we want to keep?"

"Pretty much. I've still got most of the M-Slovak source disks in my car, but all they'll want are the edit and broadcast masters." She heads out, adding, "Give me a few minutes to run through the shelves and make sure it's all in order."

Melissa brings in bound copies of the scripts and says, "Mr. Briggs's secretary just called and said he wants a set faxed over."

"Darla and Hans from Hale-Bopp are waiting," I say. "I need five minutes to get them started."

Frank tells Mel, "Fax those scripts; then when Danté's ready, go bring Sam and Dib back. Make sure you point out your little boy in our day-care center as they pass by. Show them how much happier you are working here."

"I'll try to fake it," she says. We're rubbing off on her.

"Then go help Kristen with the library. I want them out of here as fast as possible."

I rush over to my office and spread out the tattoo and ad artwork, telling Darla and Hans to start thinking about what they'll charge to compose, render, and format them for PDFs. I leave the door open so the Keholers will see big goings-on when they come through.

Mel fetches our former cohorts plus those two goofs from their graphics department. Frank makes a show of shaking Dib's and Sam's hands, so I do, too. I'll probably get warts.

"You two can follow Melissa to get started," Frank tells the graph-holes. He gestures for us to sit, blatantly not offering refreshments from the tray Mel brought in earlier.

"You're not serious about making a go of this, are you?" Sam starts. What a dick.

Frank ignores that, opting to cover business before we tell Mr. Cox where to go. "Our client is willing to reimburse you for the simulator program if you'd like to recoup the eleven-grand," he offers.

"*Your* client?" Dib returns. "Kehoe/Lundy is still agency-of-record for Sizemore *Wave-Slicers.*"

"You don't have that in writing," Frank spars.

"It's a verbal understanding."

"I'll arrange to have it become a verbal misunderstanding."

"Even if you manage to take Sizemore, we'll need that demo for other simulator clients."

Frank glances toward me. "We have exclusive rights to the hardware," I counter.

Frank adds, "So that disk is worth nothing to you. We can spend eleven-grand making another or do you the favor and reimburse your costs. We're trying to make a friendly gesture here."

Dib looks like he's ready to bite, but Sam always gets ahead of himself.

"This little agency of yours will go under in no time; then the hardware will be up for grabs again. We'll keep the disk."

Dib looks at him like maybe they should have talked that over, but he has to back his top employee. "Frank, you can't be *serious* about trying to compete with us."

"I have no sense of humor. You know that." Actually he does, but these two have probably never seen it.

Now Rupert's hovering in the doorway. Frank gestures for him to join us. "You all know each other," is his introduction.

"You really stole the cream of our crop," Sam sneers, glancing at Rupert and out toward Melissa's desk.

Now I'm annoyed. Rupert's embarrassed. Frank's getting pissed. It's not often I see the old man get red in the face.

Dib changes the subject quickly. "I could see you running the production house—hell, maybe we could even help. But if you persist at trying to be an agency, too . . ." He shrugs like there's no telling what might happen.

"We're already down that road," Frank says, gritting his teeth. He's not going to let the barb drop, either. "As for who's joined our team, I'm holding four aces and all you've got is the joker." His glance toward Sam is unmistakable.

"Yeah?" Sam blurts. He's getting louder now. "You just—"

Dib waves him quiet. "You're still an employee of Kehoe/Lundy, Frank. This is *very* improper."

"I'm on vacation, my termination's been processed, and Miss Kirloot *took my building key*," Frank grinds out. I think he's about to pop this guy.

"You know we'll have to take legal action over this blatant conflict of interest," Dib threatens. Sam is smirking. I think *I'm* about ready to pop *him*.

"Then you better cover your ass or I'll kick it so hard it'll hurt next time Sam kisses it," Frank practically shouts, "*then* sue your board of directors, *then* bury you under bad publicity—" Frank's on his feet now, jabbing the air. "—And scare your employees into jumping ship!"

Dib's up now, so we all stand up. *And in this corner, weighing in at . . .*

"We know about the Weisman work you've been doing for that podunk hillbilly militia nutcase," Sam accuses.

"He's just down the hall right now. You care to repeat that to him?"

"It looks like we may have irregularities," Dib cuts in, "in your handling of Kehoe accounts. Outright fraud, maybe some embezzlement. If we file criminal charges, there's not a client anywhere who'll trust you."

Here's where Frank is his most eloquent. "*Screw you!*" He should write scripts.

Dib's fairly creative, too. "Yeah, well screw *you!*" What a plagiarist.

Frank's beet-red, coming around the desk now. "You son of a bitch! I'll—"

I step toward him, but he stops dead in his tracks, looking toward the doorway. We all turn to see . . .

A scared little boy with tears in his big hazel eyes, clutching his Q-Tawzh doll, sucking his thumb.

Frank is shaking, breathing hard.

Melissa rushes up from behind her son, whispering, "Taj, there you are. Come on." She takes him by the hand and leads him away.

But he's looking over his shoulder at Frank as they round the corner.

We all look at each other; then Dib tilts his head toward Sam, and they quickly leave without ceremony. "We'll be in touch," he growls.

Frank leans back against his desk, breathing hard, sweat on his brow.

"Frank, are you—"

Melissa's back without her son. With business-like proficiency, she takes a bottle of capsules from Frank's top drawer and grabs an apple juice from the tray. "Here," she says quietly. Frank hesitates, so she practically shoves it in his mouth, then opens the juice and insists he drink. His hand is shaking.

I've never seen this before. I knew he had heart problems, but he's been very low-key about it. I've never seen him take medication.

"Now sit down," she says like she's talking to her son, firm but loving. She leads him gently around to sit in his chair. "Take another drink."

He complies dutifully. I feel awkward standing there, so I sit down and try to look calm. Rupert follows my lead.

Frank takes a deep breath, then looks at us, embarrassed. "Thanks, Mel," he whispers.

"Drink the rest of the juice," she admonishes good-naturedly. "Don't make me come back in here." She glances at me. "Sorry Taj got in your way. He's quite the little escape artist. I'll be in the back with Kristen," she adds before turning to leave.

"You okay, Frank?" Rupert asks.

The old man waves him off, mad at himself, I think, for getting carried away.

"Don't let those dicks get to you, Frank," I advise.

"I've got forty-five years in the business," he says quietly, "and *nobody* questions my integrity."

"It takes real scumbags—" I start, but I notice Durbett and Jankety are moving around Melissa's area, each holding some kind of scope. They look like Trekkers with tricorders. Now they're coming into Frank's office, moving toward the chairs where Dib and Sam were sitting, looking closer, Durbett now down on the floor. He points up under the seat of one, then touches his ear and gestures me to follow him out, motioning for Frank and Rupert to keep quiet.

"There's been a simple listener planted under the chair," Durbett whispers in the hallway. "I suggest we move it somewhere neutral and don't let on you know about it. You might want to use it to your advantage later. Are those two gone?"

"They headed back toward the video library." We walk to Frank's door where I disguise my voice. "Excuse me, Mr. Dellman? We're ready to work on the carpet now. Okay if we move this furniture out for a day or two?" I'm nodding vigorously, prompting him.

"Yeah, go ahead."

"We'll be out of your way in a minute."

Durbett makes a show of banging and moving furniture, then gingerly picks up the spy chair and carries it out of the room. I lead him back to a storage closet and pronounce in my disguised voice, "We'll leave these in the spare conference room for now."

Durbett grins, making more noise like furniture is being moved. He shows me where a tiny silver box, just big enough for a dozen matches and screened at one end, has been slid up along the cushion seam and stuck against the seat support. He rolls his eyes like he's unimpressed. We lock the chair away and head back to Frank's office.

"What was that about?" he demands, looking much better now.

"Them fellers planted a short-range audio transmitter," Durbett explains matter-of-factly, like *What did you expect?*

"That's illegal!" Frank declares.

"So's taking your dog out for a beer in some parts of Tennessee."

It's my turn to chime in. "That's discrimination against Canine-Americans!"

Rupert adds, "I read it's illegal in Atlanta to tie a giraffe to a telephone pole."

Frank's glaring at him in disbelief, so he clams up.

"Who sat in that chair?" Durbett asks.

"Dib Wardley."

Durbett shrugs. "Well, you can't *prove* he was the one to leave it," he points out. "So ain't no reason to let him know you're on to him."

Frank thinks a second, then starts to smile, his expression matched by Durbett's. Jankety grins like a Halloween pumpkin.

Durbett asks, "These guys got hands-free phones in their cars?"

Frank nods.

"Show me which cars. Jankety, you go pretend to help 'em with the videos and blip me if either one heads toward the lot."

Frank's confused. "What—why—?"

"You just show me, then get back to your office." It's almost an order.

Frank shrugs and follows our secret agent.

I finally have time to fly my tail in to work with the Hale-Bopp people for a while. Then I give our notes to Rupert so he and Melissa can put together a summary for the meeting with Briggs.

Next, I check on Murray and meet Durbett's product guy, a lumberjack-looking fellow who could probably wrestle a bear—but who speaks like an English professor. He and our writer pause just long enough for the formalities, caught up in flinging ideas at each other.

Durbett comes looking for me. "If you got a minute, Jankety needs a list of words."

Huh?

With the door closed to intruders, Durbett's assistant explains, "Remember how we searched for buzz-words when we recorded Frank's party? Well, we need words those Kehoe guys might use which'll cue us to when we'd be interested in what they're saying."

"Did you—?"

Durbett holds up his hand. "Now, we didn't open the floor up for questions. We just need some words, names of clients, names of your employees, anything else to search for in case we accidentally have a chance to, you know, overhear 'em."

This guy's *very* accident-prone.

I write out what he wants, a longer list than I expected, but he doesn't act like that's a problem. "I suggest you run this by Frank and see if he wants to add any."

"We got his list," Jankety says matter-of-factly, typing my words into a micro-computer. "Overlap's okay."

Durbett's vest beeps, a signal that his cell-phone—scrambled no doubt—has an incoming call. "Yeah," is all he says before writing down some codes and what looks like a phone or fax number. "We just got the chemist," he tells Jankety. Then to me, "We can't use the university people for something this confidential."

He plugs his phone into a port on the computer, then watches Jankety transmit some data. "We'll know soon enough," he says cryptically.

Frank buzzes me into his office and puts a call on speaker, introducing me to the voice of Ollum DeForest from Parmenter Publishing. She sounds African-American—though I can't be sure—with a deliberate, precise diction.

"Frank described your fabulous ideas," she says from the box, "from which I would like to develop proposals for my supervisor. Might you be available to meet with me sometime after Thursday?"

I still wonder what happened to my planner. "Any time Friday would be good."

"May I come there and see your facility? I am fascinated by the television-production process. Maybe someone could give me a tour?" We agree on ten o'clock and close with the usual pleasantries.

Then Frank taps his copy of the Briggs scripts and says, "He called and gave the go-ahead with only two changes. One, he wants a line tweaked in the one about a depressed guy who takes Parzilac then goes back to his seedy apartment and gets violent. The other is, he killed the one on Pozies. Says he'll explain later."

Good—Briggs has the vision.

Kristen and Byron are through dumping videos down the Kehole, so we sit down for a production-planning meeting.

"Looks like with a few set pieces and five actors," I explain, "we can shoot all the Briggs bits on the stage here, except for the one set in a run-down apartment building. Are you clear to produce these ASAP?"

"Should be able to shoot them day after tomorrow," she assures me. "Can I use Melissa as an assistant line producer? She's been curious, and I know she'd be good at it."

Line producers do the booking and scheduling, pulling together crews and, in this case, actors. "If she wants," I agree. Like she wouldn't . . .

"Didn't you say she lives in a dump?" Byron asks. "Maybe we could shoot the apartment one there. It's mostly stairwell shots."

The piece he's describing puts the camera in the point of view of somebody taking a Parzilac with trembling hands, standing in front of an old sink. There's a woman nagging him from behind. He turns and walks to the door, the shot blurring and strobing, increasingly unsteady and leaving trails. A gentle voice-over uses words from Parzilac ads about coping with depression.

The camera works its way down a dirty stairwell, holes in the walls, an incoherent drunk on the floor. The voice-over is urging him to take charge and do something about his depression. The camera stops, sees his fist tapping the wall, now punching harder, then harder yet. The camera whirls around and charges up the stairs, flings the door open, storms past a scared, tearful child and into the face of a terrified woman as if to attack.

The picture goes dark while statistics on Parzilac violence scroll past, the voice-over pointing out that M-Slovak hopes to move their manufacturing to Asia and avoid strict U.S. standards of quality control, at a loss of U.S. jobs. It ends on the image of a tipped-over pill bottle with little pink capsules spilled out.

Kristen brings in Melissa and explains to her what we need.

"I'm not proud of where I have to live," she admits, "but it would be perfect for what you describe."

"We would pay you a location fee," I quickly point out.

"I could play the drunk," Byron offers.

"We need you to shoot," I counter.

"Then I've got friends who are naturals for the role," he says, grinning, "especially with a case of authentic props and some time to focus on their motivation."

"All this woman does is turn and look terrified?" Melissa asks. "Would *I* look right?"

Hmmm . . . Amateur talent. The fewer people in the biz who are involved, the better we can keep this job a secret.

Byron reads my face and runs to fetch a camera. We do an impromptu screen test and Mel's perfect, better than I expected. She makes me want to come to her rescue.

Taj appears at the door, curious, looking for his mom. She picks him up and hugs him. "Here's the little kid you need," she offers.

"Can he look distraught on cue?" Kristen asks.

"Show 'em what you'd do," she tells him, "if I said I was fixing you Brussels sprouts for dinner."

No question, our little method actor *can* look distraught—*very* distraught.

"If you do a good job," she whispers, "maybe I'll make fish sticks instead."

And he's the picture of joy!

"I'm going to remember this trick," Kristen says, chuckling.

"Since you need a ride home," I suggest, "let's drive you in the remote van today and shoot this after work."

That decided, I check on all the various projects around the building, then go in and update Frank on our plans. That's when Durbett pokes his head in, Jankety right behind him. Frank invites them to sit. Durbett shuts the door.

"We didn't find the woman on the video," he reports, clearly disappointed. "I didn't expect to, but it was a hope."

"It was probably nothing anyway," Frank says.

"Are you two up on your poisons?" Durbett asks. Frank and I look at each other. "The four most toxic substances known to man," he continues, "not necessarily in order, are ricin, plutonium, botulism, and venom from the Black Mamba snake." Jankety shudders and makes a face. I picture Durbett putting Black Mambas under Dib's and Sam's car seats. I'm starting to wonder just how dangerous this guy really is.

"What was that first one?" I ask. Will this be on the final exam?

"Beans from the castor plant—the ones used for castor oil. They're boiled with several other compounds to make ricin. It's toxic to the liver, nervous system, kidneys, you name it. You start convulsing; then your body shuts down. It's nearly undetectable in an autopsy, especially since a toxicologist wouldn't be looking for it."

"Let's invite Dib and Sam over for coffee—and let *you* make it," I suggest. That's a plan: *Poison* your rivals to gain that competitive edge.

Ignoring me, Durbett continues, "I recognized the reaction."

"Where?"

"We just confirmed that your drugstore guy's nearly empty IV bag has a trace amount of ricin."

"But how long does that—?"

"He was poisoned *while* you were on the air with Hal."

CHAPTER 9

Picture a herd of zebras.

Gathered in a tight-knit group, each is dressed to blend in, barely discernible from the others. They're powerful animals, and smart, too. They may look confident, but they're uneasy, wary, watching. These are the survivors . . . or they wouldn't still be here.

Now picture a stalking lion choosing its prey, looking for the weak. The herd grows restless, but stands firm. They're in this together, except there's no loyalty. It's every zebra for himself.

Maybe this time the lion will pounce, the herd bursting into fevered frenzy. If one is felled, he'll be mauled by predators, devoured by scavengers. And the other zebras will look on, the immediate danger passed.

But they never relax . . . or they wouldn't still be here.

The Briggs Pharmaceutical herd is gathered in the executive conference room adjacent to Rex's office. Here, proper zebra stripage takes the form of $1,200 gray wool suits—two-piece, double-breasted if you dare—silk ties in blue or red. Under this camouflage, all but two are white men. There's one woman and a single black, but you don't notice them. They blend in.

So does Frank, my favorite zebra, the one with bushy eyebrows and silver mane. He's made me dress the part, too, but I'm a horse of slightly different color. My shade of gray shies toward green and my silk tie boasts the hand-painted image of a red octopus, the knot forming its head, eight streamers as tentacles.

As Rex Briggs stalks through the room, *I'm* the one who stands out. But I'm allowed this silken badge proclaiming creativity because my success depends on grabbing people's attention, on reaching out to millions of cash-laden consumer-fish. Give me room to swim, and the world will feel my sting.

And Frank will submit the invoice, commission included.

There are fifteen executives in this herd, yes-men and no-men, thinkers and doers, from snooty suits to lickers of boots. I recognize Doug Moore and Ted Stockbridge, the silver-haired gladiator and his portly cohort. I still want to party with these two someday. I hope they turn out to be important so Frank will arrange some recreational schmooze.

Rex takes a seat and announces us. "Our agency-of-record to launch the allergy tattoo. Frank handles the account; Danté's the creative director." He goes around the table, naming each zebra and his role. Frank's learning who they are—or already knows—while I make a little chart for myself in the shape of a conference table. Turns out Moore runs market research and customer relations while Stockbridge has full control over distribution.

"It was their suggestion," Rex continues, "that we take this over-the-counter and package it as a cartoon tattoo, something the kids will *ask* to wear, and something parents will purchase out of curiosity as much as concern. Show us what you mean, Danté."

There's a plastic board with markers on one wall, so my octopus and I swim over to do a demo. I ask Stockbridge if he has kids, and wind up using his son, the computerhead, as an example. "Does he have any allergies?"

"Blaine gets winded sometimes, which *I* think is from not enough exercise, but my wife's starting to worry it might be asthma or something."

I'm drawing a computer screen surrounded by CD's, each in different colors. "What's recommended retail for a set of these Aller-Tats?"

"We're looking at just under fourteen dollars," somebody answers.

"Would you pay fourteen bucks to find out once and for all, to know if your kids have allergies, and to have the answer *today?*"

"Yeah!"

"Definitely!"

There's a sudden ripple of enthusiasm spreading through the herd. I'm showing them, each imagining in his own way, and they're taking *this* one home.

"Would Blaine wear one of these on his arm?"

Stockbridge is grinning now. Frank's grinning. The whole table's grinning. Grinning zebras, they are.

And the lion cracks a smile.

"I want you to sit in on the approval meetings, Les," Briggs tells one of his henchmen. He nods importantly, making a note in his planner. He's a tall fellow, lanky, with a sun-pink hairless pate. Put a beige turtleneck dickey on him for that uncircumcised look.

Corporate counsel asks, "Are there any new liability issues? Side effects, damages from misuse? What if a kid swallows one and his lawyers argue that cute cartoons made them an *attractive nuisance*, that we disguised dangerous products to look like toys?"

Briggs waves him off, but an older man speaks up. Compared to the others, he's a bit rumpled, a thick shock of graying hair that looks like he's been sleeping on it—wet. According to my little chart, he's in charge of the product-development program, a pharmaceutical biochemist or some-such. "Anaphylactic shock," he says. It's a swear-word.

Anna F'Lactic . . . I'm picturing a gal with big hooters.

"There were no recorded incidents during the clinical phase," another guy argues, looking exasperated.

"Your sample was too small," Messy-hair counters. "You will when this goes mass-market."

"But the estimated numbers are within acceptable boundaries," another chimes in. "All we have to do is include an emergency procedure in the directions and put a warning on the package."

"That's a legal determination," the lawyer huffs, defending his own turf. "Explain this risk factor." Surely a company lawyer knows this stuff. He's just assuming nothing, making them explain in front of Rex.

"Anaphylaxis is the skin-testing process," the researcher explains. He runs a hand through his messy hair. "What we call *delayed* allergies and most of the *immediate* allergies will cause a small blemish like a mosquito bite—which is an anaphylactic reaction."

"So what's the *shock*—what are we worrying about?" The lawyer's not interested in the long version. Tell him why customers might file lawsuits.

"It's a violent, sudden collapse—gasping from bronchi spasm, a drop in blood pressure from small-vessel dilation, skin turning blue, maybe some itching—a rare antibody/antigen reaction causing cells all through the body to dump histamine."

"Is it dangerous?" I ask. This isn't my discussion, but if I'm supposed to sell this thing to kids and trusting parents, I want to know.

The researcher nods, directing his answer to me rather than the lawyer. "Sometimes there's spontaneous recovery, but without intervention it could be fatal."

Fatal?

Well, that pops the balloons at *my* party.

But Rex is nonplussed by the info, maybe even annoyed at the researcher. "I thought this was settled. What's the anticipated rate of incidence?"

"Probably about one in seven- or eight-thousand."

"Ratio of spontaneous recovery?"

"Maybe nine out of ten."

"So only one every seventy- or eighty-thou *could be* dangerous."

Messy-hair nods almost reluctantly.

"And intervention will take care of those, right?" Rex asks, his glare fixed on the researcher.

"A fast dose of epinephrine should counteract it." Messy-hair shrugs, conceding, "That and antihistamines would even get rid of the itching."

I have to ask the obvious. "Can't you put a dose of epinephrine in each box—just in case?"

"It has to be injected," the insurrectional researcher explains. "It's that little kit people with severe bee-sting allergies carry when they're out where they might get stung."

"It's expensive," another adds, "and requires instruction to use properly."

"A lot of people wouldn't understand the directions," the lawyer points out, "even if it were a pill. They might think that's part of the allergy test."

"Not cost-effective," Briggs says, dismissing the idea.

"Part of the package warning," Messy-hair cautions, "should say *not* to use the tattoo on somebody who has ever had a severe reaction to *anything*. Anaphylactic-shock victims almost always had a previous negative experience."

"Is there any other way to reduce the risk?" Rex asks.

"Physician supervision," the researcher asserts.

Dead silence. Rex stares at him, jaw clenched. The pinstripes stir uneasily. Messy-hair blinks, looking away, his shoulders drooping.

Turning his attention to the lawyer, Rex sums up, "So if we try over-the-counter, we'll need to keep it *very* tight on the legal—especially with our ads. Let's loophole our claims and tag 'em with disclaimers."

The attorney looks appropriately skeptical. Cyn once told me the art of corporate lawyering is never to commit; voice objections, point out options, worry over details, do a lot of costly research, but avoid actually blessing something if there's any chance it'll come back and bite you in the butt.

Rex gets up and strolls slowly around the table, studying his herd. He pauses at the window and looks across his grounds, the landscape of ruffled green and glassy pools, the lone hawk circling under sparse wads of lazy late-afternoon cloud . . . His back to us, he quietly pronounces, "Let's do it, and put it on the fast-track."

"*How* fast?" somebody asks.

"Fast as we can put it out. Nobody else has Pene-Derm, but when word spreads that we're launching, there'll be copycats. An inferior competitor who manages to hit the shelves first could kill our niche before we lock it up. Let's dominate the market fast, then fight off imitators as they come along." He comes back to his seat.

What follows is an hour-long run-through covering every aspect of launching this product, from packaging and manufacturing and distribution to marketing and merchandising and advertising. The name Aller-Tat sticks, though Doug Moore is planning to run it by a focus group. Frank's media-placement presentation, punctuated by my visuals, is enthusiastically embraced. The kind of numbers they're talking, it looks like nearly six-million dollars' worth of biz for Dellman/Roenik over the next nine months. Briggs's idea of fast-track is to start tattooing kids' bodies in seven to ten weeks.

Wow.

There's a flurry of conversation, business cards passed around, Frank setting up various appointments for us. Heck, I don't need my missing schedule planner, I've got a Frank.

Rex shoos out everybody except us and pink-domed lanky Les, the corporate PR guy.

"With no Pozie spot," Rex starts, "how long before the rest of the M-Slovak anti-merger videos are ready?" We're taking seats around the low table, our CEO on his couch with the hidden magic controls.

"End of the week," I predict.

"Stay away from Pozies from now on," PR says.

"It's secondary to your goal of interfering with the merger," Frank prompts.

"We don't want the backlash," Rex admits. "Parzilac is dangerous and causes violence when taken *as directed*. Mixed with street drugs, any product could be dangerous. Since we're getting ready to launch the Fantasy Patch, we don't want people afraid of *all* psychotropics and associating their use with *illegal* drugs. It's Parzilac we need to vilify, not Pozies."

"Have we already done any harm?" Frank asks.

Rex shakes his head. "No, you did what you had to. I was *very* impressed with that, and I count on you guys to impress me with this tattoo—handling the creative for it, at least."

"We want it all," Frank says bluntly.

"I want to give it to you, Frank," he says, "but how can you put together such a big team with the right people that fast?"

"Take it to where there's already one in place," Frank counters. "We can subcontract all the print production and media placement. It happens in the agency biz more than you might think."

"Maybe even take it to Kehoe?" Rex wonders.

Frank shrugs. "It's a good team. I hired a lot of them myself."

Rex nods, then looks around conspiratorially, leaning forward slightly. "Confidentially, Kehoe's gonna be scrambling for some biz soon anyway."

"Oh?"

"I played eighteen holes with Woot Wooter the other day. He says he's gonna call for agency review."

Yow. Wooter Home Products is Kehoe/Lundy's biggest international account. Agency review is when the clients are so unhappy they ask their agency and several others to pitch new creative and try to win the business. Sometimes the original people manage to keep the account, but only after some kind of shake-up or major concessions on commission rates or personnel changes. Usually, though, it means new players on the block.

"Knowing him," Frank says, "he's already got a few of the big ones in mind."

"Oh yeah," Rex is quick to agree. "It's not something you could go after, but Kehoe might kiss your ass to sub my tattoo business if only to prevent having to lay off their top two floors after losing Wooter."

Frank smiles. Rex smiles. My octopus and I smile, though it's hard to be so cavalier about people's careers being sucked out from under them.

"When?" Frank asks.

"Few weeks. Woot said he could shift the timing a few days, maybe a week, if I asked him to—you know, to help you grab what you need to launch my allergy kits fast."

"We could knock Sam Cox off his box because we don't need Kehoe creative on the tattoo account," I point out.

"But Dib Wardley . . ." Frank continues, leaving his thoughts unspoken.

"Funny you should name those two," Rex grins again. "They've been trying to get in to see me. I sent them to my best vendor-spinner down in marketing. They'll get nowhere but frustrated."

"Look," Frank says, sitting forward to shift gears. "I don't know if we'll use Kehoe, somebody else, or more than one, but Aller-Tat will be humming this week, no problem handling your entire launch well within deadlines." He's fixing Rex with a dead-serious expression. More than earnest, more than a boast, more than a promise . . .

It's a fact.

"We prove that to you," Frank continues, "and you give us the Fantasy Patch account, top to bottom, not just bones for the dog, not just creative. The whole shebang. We launch Dellman/Roenik on your tattoo—and on Sizemore and Weisman and Parmenter and Faritzka and Sally's friggin' lemonade stand if we have to—but we take our new venture big league on your patch."

Rex sits back and strokes his head several times, looking nowhere in particular. "I think you just might pull off the logistics, Frank, but has your boy got the nuts?"

Okay, a testicle metaphor.

"I mean," he continues, not looking directly at me, "Fantasy Patch is my baby, and I got only one shot at making her pretty. How you gonna do that?"

Picture Danté thoroughly exasperated but trying not to show it. Does he want a creative pitch—*now?* Okay, picture Danté *showing* his exasperation—a little, anyway—then affecting the aura of a confident smart-aleck. "I have the utmost confidence in my testicles," I assure him, "but I've not prepared anything—"

"So think out loud."

I swear Frank's holding his breath. I can't remember what Ms. Moeroff's horoscope said about me today.

"You've been thinking about it—haven't you?" Rex asks.

"Keeping me up nights," I return. "Tell me, what exactly is this patch?"

"It's a fungus that grows around the butt holes of Brazilian caterpillars," Rex says.

We all look at each other. I'm waiting for the other shoe to drop, but it just hangs in the air. He's not kidding.

"Butt fungus." That's my summary of his complex physio-pharmacological explanation. "Okay, well . . . That presents some interesting images. Several potential celebrity spokespersons come to mind."

Rex chuckles. I think Frank's still stunned.

"*Brazilian* butt fungus," I clarify. "So how's it work?"

"We found out it stimulates neurotransmitters that connect the brain-stem to the cerebral cortex," Rex explains. "That's the simple way to put it. Brain-stem is where that fight-or-flight stuff is, the source of stress, hunger, instinct, fear— You can learn to control your physical and psychological responses better than that flaky biofeedback crap ever hoped. Just imagine how you want things to be—wish away your stress, your anxieties, your self-doubt. It's *real* easy with kids. Junior can't pay attention, slap a patch on him and teach him to practice better listening—"

"A *fungus* does all that?" Frank interrupts. He's having a hard time getting his arms around the concept.

"The basic stuff, yes," Rex boasts. "Complicated goals, like overcoming obsessive compulsions or sexual perversions or whatever, those still need psychological help, but the patch makes 'em dramatically easier to accomplish."

"So it doesn't replace the psychs?" I ask.

"Hell, it's the best thing ever happened to their business. Somebody's gotta write the 'script; then the patch gives them a way to get real results—not this mumbo-crap where if your problem is wanting to shoot all your neighbors the shrink says let's talk about your mother twice a week for the next ten years."

"Brazilian butt fungus—"

"Actually," Rex points out, "the Real McCoy causes hallucinations. We've synthesized it, stripped off the alkaloids that make you see and hear things, added a strand that regulates the rate of serotonin transfer, and *voila!*, you've got Briggs-patented *Lokistarrinane*. The rate of absorption has to be kept low, though, so we spent the big bucks developing Pene-Derm. Aller-Tat was just another way to take advantage of that research."

"And it's perfectly safe," Frank puts out for confirmation.

"Perfectly," Rex assures. "Clinical trials have been running for three years with incredible results. Now it looks like FDA approval could come way sooner than we planned—as in later this week."

"If you want PR and image on top of advertising, we should start documenting this," I point out. "Collecting footage on the trials, success stories, behind-the-scenes, the research, shots of caterpillar butts—stuff we can use in documentaries, provide to news services, support training and info media, you name it."

"Show me how to sell the image and generate consumer demand for it," Rex challenges, "and I'll give you a blank check to collect anything you think might be useful now or later."

He does that trick with the magic couch again and I'm brought a stack of tagboard and colored markers. "What's it look like?" I ask.

Magic couch and we have samples. It's a little round patch about the size of a quarter. Peel off the back and stick it on your skin. "I don't suppose you can show me some of those caterpillars with fungus on their butts," I kid.

"It would take fifteen minutes," Rex says seriously.

"Never mind."

Frank asks, "How long to get a catfish wearing lipstick and a Nehru jacket?"

Rex arches his eyebrows, then as dead-serious as I've ever seen a CEO, decides, "*Twenty* minutes."

But I'm staring at blank boards, white on white, three-dimensional nothing. Like trying to laugh on cue . . . Think out loud, watch for reactions . . . "Control," I think aloud. "Steering wheel, in the driver's seat, hand on the tiller, a road map for where you want to be—"

Rex is watching. Frank is watching.

I'm looking at the patch. "Where do you stick it?"

Rex shrugs. "Most'll put it on their shoulder. But you can hide it anywhere there's complete skin contact with good vasodilatation."

"Can we put little bevels around the edges?" I ask. I draw a round shape with little round indents and spikes, like looking at the underside of one of those metal caps from old-timey glass soda bottles.

Rex shrugs. "Sure," he says tentatively.

"It's easy to lose your way when your world is fog," I explain. I'm drawing wisps on the board. "Words don't say it right, but I can see it happening. Burn away the fog, let the light shine through, find your way to become anything your heart desires—" I'm drawing feverishly on one board, then another, then another.

Rex is intrigued, hanging off the front of the couch, vein pulsing in his forehead, actually licking his lips in anticipation.

"Junior is thirteen now. He wants to do better in school. He wants to have confidence making friends. He wants to win the heart of pretty Cathy Sue— I see him frustrated in class, awkward around the boys, shy with Cathy Sue, but then he imagines how it could be, the fog is lifting—" I'm showing the face of an earnest boy, then my symbol of sun shining through the clouds, and it's on the boy's shoulder, and he's clutching an A-paper under his arm, and the other boys are vying for his attention, and Cathy Sue is over by the lockers smiling shyly, and he smiles back, and he knows— "He *knows* it's going to be all right. Now they're holding hands, and she's wearing the patch, too."

Rex lets out his breath. Frank looks pleased. I'm scribbling fast.

"Martha wants that promotion at work," I start another. "If only she could speak in front of groups, run those staff meetings, have the confidence to advocate her own ideas. Her career—her life—is a series of images with fuzzy edges, living through the fog, a cloud hanging over her dreams. But there's a break, and shining through—" I hold up the same board. "Shining through," I whisper, "the Briggs Fantasy Patch. And it's on her arm, and now it's covered by a crisp business suit, and she's running the meeting, and it's all her idea—"

"Yes!" Briggs blurts, slamming his palm on the table. "Yes!"

"It's a shifting 3-D animation applied to all the versions, a unified look carried into print, a music track that marries the image with the sound and carries into radio so when you hear it, you can see it, and it looks like—" I show them my bottle-cap shining-sun shape again, hastily scribbling *Briggs* under it.

"I can see it," Frank says reverently.

"I can, too," Briggs agrees, his voice practically cracking with emotion. "It needs refining—"

"It needs Danté," Frank says.

Rex nods. "I'm looking at more than thirty-mill just for the launch," he says quietly.

"For that," Frank promises, "we'll make sure every soul in North America sees your patch—sees that *shape*, and knows it's the shine of dreams, your fantasies come true . . ."

"Yes!" Rex breathes. "Yes." I think he needs a cigarette. Leave a twenty on the dresser on your way out.

There's a faint buzz, a "Hmmm?" from Rex, that ubiquitous voice reminding him of some meeting.

"Tony Faritzka," Rex explains.

"Throwing him a bone?" Frank nudges.

"A big one, actually. We're upgrading our communications software, so his people will be training us company-wide on how to use it." He's up now, the lion prepared to resume his prowl, to stalk his territory.

"Gonna talk about buying one of his motivation seminars, too?" Frank kids.

"That's like begging these sons of bitches to do their jobs." He's dead ser-ious. "People get too damn relaxed about their work, don't do enough to stand out, to make the company stand out. I got two slackers I'm gonna take down hard at the end of this week, make a real bloodbath of it. That always rattles everybody, makes the rest of the herd more alert."

Herd?

We're shaking hands to leave, our meeting a success. The zebra image isn't working for me anymore, though. I'm locked on the new shape for Fantasy Patch.

But I don't have to wear one to make my dreams come true. Just get a million others to slap one on. That's my part.

And Dellman/Roenik and *Shoot & Die* will soar.

And Cyn will become Partner SiCauge.

Through the fog I see my fabulous future, fantasy come true, my wife and family, my friends and colleagues, time enough for love, time enough for art.

And it's shaped like a circle, little bevels around the edge.

*   *   *

The gorilla stays with the van.

Melissa's apartment building should be ideal for this shoot: old and run-down, decrepit and dirty, plundered and trashed, raided, grated, jaded and faded . . .

We scout the location before unpacking the equipment. Byron will shoot. His friend is dressed as the bum; two hefty guys are on tech. Melissa is excited but nervous, Taj clutching his Q-Tawzh doll, wide-eyed and curious. Hal Neusome is following me around, business to discuss. We leave the biggest guy down on the street to guard our vehicle and gear. The gorilla stays with the van.

From the outside, it's sooty tan-brown brick; five stories, rusty-black fire escapes on either side; slide-up windows, many open, some barred; one big entranceway; several people idling on the broken concrete out front; a lot of kids running around.

It's still daylight here on the urban reef.

We attract a small pack of urchins as we go in, friends of Taj. Yes, he's gonna star in a video. Wow! Kid'll probably want more money now—and a bigger trailer.

"Let's do the stairwell shots first," I decide. "Use the light while we have it, get it done before the crowds pick up toward evening. Then we can take our time in Melissa's apartment and light as needed."

We move the equipment up to Mel's place as our base of operations. It's a small apartment, two tiny bedrooms, mismatched garage-sale furnishings, that haute style known as modern-American college dorm. It's a rathole, but it's the neatest, most immaculate rathole I could imagine. She's living the lemon-ade life in this, her lemon world.

Gawd, I hope Dellman/Roenik succeeds. Melissa deserves her shot at success, too. I don't want to cut her adrift again. Kristen and Murray would land running. Byron, too. Rupert would work his way up somewhere. But Melissa's got no safety net, no margin, no slack. She's on the edge, grasping with one hand while the other holds her little boy.

Byron and I try walking through the descending-stairwell shot several times. It'll be one continuous take, hesitate on this step, look around, seven more deliberate steps, distracted, down farther, barely noticing the drunk, moving again, stopped, here's where the fist will pound the wall. Byron's buddy strews around some trash, pulls on a ratty overcoat, then assumes his position as the passed-out drunk against the wall. Byron starts rehearsing with the Steadi-Cam. Melissa's running interference, explaining to curious neighbors what we're doing, Taj reveling in the excitement and attention. Get him a Sharpie; he's ready to sign autographs.

Hal takes the opportunity to talk biz with me. "Detective Culler's been trying to arrange a Pozie bust," he says, "a chance to tag along for footage, but the info their narcs are getting is that Pozies are scarce. That's all right, though—I got enough for Thursday's national segment."

"Pozies aren't the story, anyway," I tell him. I'm working for Briggs now, trying to influence the media. "It's about a tragic accident and the community's rush to judgment. It's about the robbery of a drugstore, the black market for all pharmaceuticals, the dedicated businessman trying to survive in a fading neighborhood—"

"Yeah yeah, I read the brochure," he interrupts impatiently. "That one's in the can. I got something else to chew, but this is *very* confidential."

I nod. Byron's coming down the stairs, the Cam close to his face, a glaze in his eyes. He's becoming our Parzilac zombie.

Hal lowers his voice and glances around. "NBS is buying my station," he says, "and six others, to be announced sometime next week. They need a local presence—fast." He's grinning.

"A news operation!" I'm grinning, too. "It's a prestige thing."

"And a money thing," he adds. "They're licking their nuts over losing the affiliate after next Friday, so they need to grow some hair fast." That's two testicle metaphors in one day.

Byron's glaring at me. Far from directing, I'm distracting, ruining the mood. Good cameramen, in character and chasing their motivations, can be just as persnickety as actors.

Several residents watching from lower levels are waving at Hal Neusome, local celebrity.

"I'll be down there." He excuses himself to let us work, anointing adoring fans with his glow. Bask away, bask away, all.

Byron nods that he's ready, so we walk through it once with me right behind him. I like it, so I tell him to roll. He shoots it six times; then we stop to change disks.

"I remember you," says somebody. He's talking to Byron from the landing below. Melissa's beside him, quietly encouraging him not to interrupt us.

Byron looks, then nods. "Um, yeah. You doin' all right?"

The man shrugs. He looks familiar somehow, but I can't place him. He's a big white guy, overweight; picture him as a prison guard or professional wrestler. He appears to think it over. "I dunno," he decides.

"This is my neighbor Gordie," Melissa explains awkwardly, sorry for the intrusion.

"I'm famous," he says, "used to be on TV." He runs his hand across his head, wavy reddish-brown hair brushed straight back, beads of sweat on his forehead. His hand is shaking.

"Let's do the ending," I suggest, leading the crew back to Melissa's apartment. We block the shot and do a dry run. Taj knows where to stand. Mel knows when to turn. She's doing an excellent job looking scared, then terrified, cringing as the camera rushes past the child and into her face. She's very good.

"Karo tears?" Byron asks. He's wondering if clear syrup down Taj's cheeks is needed.

"Taj, honey," she whispers, kneeling to his eye-level, "can you cry about Brussels sprouts every time Byron rushes in with that camera?" He nods sadly, then tunes up to prove his skill. We paint a streak down each cheek so it'll show better. I glance out the window, check our sunlight, and notice Hal's down by the van surrounded by a dozen or more admirers. I have the tech add another soft light in the corner so Taj's tears show up better.

And we roll.

The camera bursts into the apartment, glares around, then spots the scared child—who turns toward his mommy and starts to cry. Then our POV lumbers at a terrified Mel—

Cut.

We do three more to make sure we've got it. Another would be too much for our actors. We watch the shots on a bigger monitor where all can see.

Perfect. Cheers and applause.

Melissa grabs up her son and hugs him and kisses him. "I'm so proud of you! Now we can afford to buy you more Monsters for your Bin!"

Our little star beams through Karo tears while Mel fishes out a tissue and dabs her tongue to clean his face, a ritual of the ages, mother and child. I'm tempted to grab the shot.

"You were great," I tell her. Everybody agrees. She's proud of what she did, but even more so of her son.

We do five quick takes of the opening shot, starting in the bathroom, the sink, the turn. "Try one where you keep going, right into the second shot out and down the stairs," I tell Byron.

We shoot one, two, then one more, and this baby's ready for edit. I'll be able to spend the evening with Cyn for a change. A yummy treat. Better than another Monster toy.

Byron's two landings below, end of shot. I look down, give him the okay, then notice our pal Gordie stepping from the hallway at the level between us.

He's panting, crouched slightly, almost simian. He's pointing a handgun at Byron!

"Gordie—" our cameraman says.

"Hey!" I shout.

Gordie whirls, looks up and—

Boom!

Flying plaster. I duck and look through the rail.

Mel shouts, "What—?!"

"Gordie, *don't!*" Byron implores.

I can barely see. The gunman's staring down *my* shooter, Byron framing him. A dot of red light says we're still rolling.

Gordie reaches into the hallway and grabs something. It's a five-gallon gas can, the old metal style, round, red, *Caution: Flammable.* He waves the can, sloshes some liquid on the floor, the other hand still clutching the gun. "You're one of 'em," he accuses Byron. He looks up toward me, louder, "You are, too!" Screaming now, "You *all* are!"

What do I say? I call out, "Gordie—!"

Boom!

A woman screams, people in the stairwell below us. Gordie looks over the rail and aims.

Boom!

Another scream. "My baby! He shot my baby!"

A child's crying, panicked people running.

"He got a gun!"

Gordie's voice, growling, broken, "You—*did*—this!"

I look over the rail, trying to see. The odor of gas is strong. Byron's backing down the stairs.

"Wait!" Gordie orders him. "Why'd you do this?" he demands. "Wait, I said!"

Byron stops. "Do what, Gordie? I didn't do any—"

"*Why'd you do this to me?!*"

He sets the gas can down and—

Boom!

I have no idea what kind of gun it is or how many shots it holds.

Byron's moving again, still pointing the camera at Gordie. How many men have recorded their own murders?

"Stop!" Gordie orders.

Byron freezes. "Gordie, I don't know—"

"Yes you do!"

"Tell me," Byron soothes. "*Tell* me."

Gordie's crying now, weeping, sobbing, a plaintive plea. "Why'd you do this?"

"If I did something, Gordie, I didn't mean to."

Gordie picks up the gas can, then sets it back down. He's forgotten about me. I ease down several steps. The man's blubbering. Could I sneak down behind him?

He holds the gun to the side of his head. His crying stops, replaced by sniffles, a strangled noise. The shaking stops, too, and he's calm now, resolute, aimed . . .

And time stops.

"Gordie," Byron whispers. "Don't. Not now, Gord. Not like this."

"You should'na," he says calmly.

"Gordie!" Melissa shouts from her doorway. "Put that down. It's okay."

"It was *him!*" he shouts, whirling to look up.

Boom!

Plaster rains on me. I drop flat on the stairs.

"Danté," Melissa whispers. "Get in here."

"No, Gordie!" It's Byron. "Not *that!* You'll kill *everybody*."

I sneak a peak. He's holding a lighter over the gas can. The gun wavers, starts to quiver, moves slowly away from his head, dangles at his side. He shakes his head.

"Gordie—"

He kicks over the can and jumps into the hallway. A flood starts down the stairs. The lighter—

Whoosh!

Byron's running down now, out of sight.

I scramble up, dive into the doorway, knocking Melissa—

Ba-whoosh!

A fireball races up to where I'd been, thick black smoke dancing a strangled dervish.

We reach for the door, slam it, and scramble up. She grabs Taj and pulls him to the window, but bars are blocking our way.

Thick black smoke is curling around the doorjamb. These bars are framed, held by bolts and wood screws. "Screwdriver!" I've got the window open. She's rummaging through a kitchen drawer, then rushes me a large flathead.

Prying, twisting, splintering wood, I'm getting it loose, but can't push it free. She brings a baseball bat. I wedge it between bars, pulling and twisting, looser, still won't come out. Smoke is thick across the ceiling, pulled toward the window, dipping to break out, to dance and flee into the sky. I can see Byron running into the vacant lot, camera pointed up at us. Hal's running toward the fire escape where people are spilling to the ground and scattering away.

I run into Mel's room, into Taj's. He's got a solid-wood nightstand. I drag it to the window, hoist it up, and side-fling it at the bars. They groan and give, but not enough. Heft and throw. Heft and throw.

Melissa's coughing now, putting a wet towel across the doorjamb. It's getting hot. I can hear the fire. The smoke smells chemical.

Fling—and the bars pop out!

A voice down below: "Danté! Look out—!"

Boom! A bullet flips my hair. In that glimpse, I see Gordie on the fire escape, one switchback below. Hal Neusome is one level under him.

"Oh Gordie," Melissa cries. It's hard to hear her now, the roar in the stairwell, the roar in the walls, the roar in the vents. She runs to Taj's room. Straight back with clothes, she starts bundling him. A winter jumpsuit, gloves, mask, a scarf, layers. She disappears and returns with blankets. "No time, Danté," she shouts. "Down through the fire!"

She throws a blanket at me, sweeps Taj into her arms and wraps herself in another. This fragile girl who wept at the loss of her job is now the fierce mother prepared to die saving her child.

The door is buckling, flames licking through the crack along the top, dragon's tongues tasting their next meal.

Gordie's inching his way up.

"It's too late, Mel! We can't!"

She's staring at the door, and she knows I'm right.

"Gordie!" Hal calls, distracting him for a second. "Let them out!"

"He's one of 'em!" Gordie screams.

Boom-Ping! He fires down wildly.

"Canned food!" I shout at Melissa.

She rushes to the cabinet, lowers her son, scrabbles for soups, beans, Brussels sprouts.

Taj is crying now, fear and confusion washing Karo down to his chin.

Gordie is four steps below, now only three.

"Hal!" I shout. "Call him again!"

I grab several cans from her.

"Gordie!" Hal yells.

Gordie turns. I throw hard and hit him in the side of the head.

He bellows, blood spurting, "You're one of—"

Smack! Direct hit, knocking his gun to the pavement. He looks at his empty hand, confused.

No weapon, it's him and me.

"Melissa! Let's go! Stay behind me!" I'll throw him over the rail if I have to.

I'm climbing out, Taj's breath on my neck—

Ba-woosh!

The door blows in, flames erupting into the room, a cloud of soot and smoke, blistering heat. I drag Taj through the window, pulling Mel right behind. I'm looking right at Gordie now.

I take a step. He balls his fists, assumes the prizefighter stance.

Whack! Got him! Direct hit, chunky tuna in water, economy size. Gordie yelps, turns and runs down, then jumps inside through an open window.

"Let's go!" Flames race across the ceiling, groping their way outside, tasting their freedom.

I grab up Taj, pushing Melissa in front. Hal takes her hand and leads her down.

Then Gordie's screams of anguish pierce the air. Once, twice, the third but a strangle, finally a plaintive wail consumed by the basso howls of exploding inferno.

Byron shoots us racing to the van, then turns again to frame the building.

Sirens in the distance, a police car roaring down the street, a hundred or more people are running around, hysterical. I don't see anybody in the windows, so it looks like everyone got out.

"Need blank disks!" Byron shouts.

The techs are piling gear into the van, helping Melissa and Taj in.

"Get the van out of here," I order, grabbing several blanks from an open box, "before we're blocked in. Over to the next street."

Hal and I get back to Byron just as the first fire truck is racing up. We switch disks, then work our way around the front. Again, Hal's performing, telling the fire captain and police where it started, that the gunman is still in there, pointing with authority.

More trucks, more police. It's dusk now, the flashing lights and bright flames front-lighting dark sky, smoke billowing out open windows, tendrils whirling low in the humid air.

The microwave van from one station arrives, parking behind the barricades, a reporter out and doing a stand-up. Another van is pulling in.

"Damn I wish I had a transmitter to go live!" Hal bemoans. We're shooting spectacular footage as the roof collapses into the structure, a wall breaking apart, a broken fire escape crashing to the pavement.

It's time to go for more disks . . . or wrap it up. "Hal, let's get back to the studio where we can transmit. You've got the premium footage. Anything we shoot now, everybody else is getting. I think maybe a phone call to NBS in New York first . . ." His face lights up. "Of course," I add, "we hold back some—you know, for *Newsome on the News*." He's grinning and nodding, nodding and grinning. "Byron! Let's wrap and run!"

Heading back to the van, Hal says, "I didn't tell you the best part about NBS wanting me to grow a news operation. We need a production facility already up and running. I mentioned *Shoot & Die* and they're *very* interested in cutting a deal."

"Good man, Hal. Steer 'em toward Frank, our deal man."

The van had moved another street farther to avoid being locked in. The conflagration is really drawing crowds now.

"Did you get the shots, Byron?" I ask.

"I got it *all*—from when he stepped into the hallway till the last people came down the fire escape!"

"Footage a newsman can only dream of!" Hal practically shouts.

We're at the van, pausing to high-five each other. The door slides open, and there's Melissa huddled in the corner, dirty and bedraggled. Stripped of his jumpsuit and extra layers, Taj is cuddled on her lap, sucking his thumb. She's rocking him, cooing gently, assuring him everything's okay. She looks up at me.

And this tragedy has a face.

All Melissa owns now is a broken-down car and the clothes on her back, yet Hal and I dared have the audacity to celebrate because it was *our* camera first on the scene. Gunshots, flames, smoke and flashing lights—these are the images we chase, now to commence our mercenary blurring of fiction and fact. But to capture the visage of terror, the camera must focus on somebody real, the face of a person, someone who matters.

It's different when it happens to someone you know, the people you care about.

It's what they mean by cutting close to home.

We *will* make the best of our lucky opportunity, parlaying it to the pinnacle of media success, but of all the frames we grabbed, the shot I'll remember most is this one, the one that never got recorded. It's my friend who came this close to losing what she cherishes most, or to leaving him, motherless and alone, to grow up without her in this harsh world where it takes only one Gordie to destroy all we hold dear. It's the image of this mother with the strength and resolve to promise her child that everything is all right, when she knows in her heart it's not.

Sure, we got the shots, but Melissa and her son lost their home.

And this big-eyed little boy lost his Q-Tawzh doll.

CHAPTER 10

Be it ever so humble, *Shoot & Die* is like a second home. We burst in, techs grabbing and hauling the gear. Frank, Kristen, and the gang surround us, touching, inspecting, assuring themselves we're all in once piece. Taj lets go of his mother for the first time, reaching out to Frank. The old man takes him into his arms for a bear hug, now a three-way with mommy, too.

"I'll call NBS!" Hal's rushing to a phone.

"Let's log shots," Byron tells Kristen. Turning to me, he asks, "Highlights? What're we holding back?"

"In the stairwell: show him firing the gun, holding the gas can, accusing you of being one of them—but not all of it, not tipping the can or setting the fire. Same outside: one or two gunshots, not me beaning him with the can or knocking away his gun, then the best of all the rest."

Our receptionist, staying late since my call, is hovering. "Give 'em some space!" he's ordering. "They're exhausted, might be hurt—" The Faritzka people have come from edit-three, news traveling fast.

Everybody pauses to breathe and take stock. *Is* anybody hurt? Should we go to a hospital? Smoke inhalation? What about Taj's asthma?

"We're okay," Melissa assures me, a quaver in her voice.

"Did you lose anything irreplaceable?"

She's caressing Taj's head, her son riding side-saddle on Frank's hip and holding horsey's silk-tie rein. "I have only one thing that matters."

"You have no place to live," Frank says quietly, reality dawning.

"What about footage that lets on why we were shooting there?" Byron rushes back to ask.

"No— No!"

"NBS is *frothing!*" Hal announces, trotting in. "Besides the footage feed, they want to cut to me live for the story. They're going to interrupt programming and go to the remote truck their current affiliate has on the scene."

"We can do that. Don't explain the reason you were out there. In fact, you weren't even there for *my* shoot. You were investigating, 'nuff said for now. Hmmm . . . You need a background. We don't want you to look like you ran away from the crisis . . . Let's go live from the edit suite. You're here putting together the story."

Frank has Melissa off to the side talking quietly, still holding the little one.

"Is this exclusive?" I ask.

"NBS—yes. There's no conflict with my station because they don't yet have competing news. Besides, they're about to become—you know." Too many people around to say it.

"It's Reverend Falluson!" our reception dude announces, putting a call on hold. Hal and I look at each other. I take the headset, Hal picking up the side phone.

"Are you and your people all right?" he demands to know. Sounds like he's on a cell-phone.

"Yes—"

"Oh, this is such an *awful* tragedy. I understand there's at least five dead, probably more—"

People who couldn't get out . . .

"—And the tortured soul who started the fire never came out—"

Gordie. Gordie who used to be famous. Gordie who used to be on TV. He'll be famous *now*. He'll be on TV like never before . . .

"I understand you caught the whole thing on camera," Falluson says, past sympathy, now to the point.

"Yes—"

"They've closed off the area. I can't get in to help, to comfort the victims—"

"Well," I say, "I'm sure they're—"

"You'll be going on the air soon, won't you?"

Hal and I look at each other. "Yes," he says tentatively.

Falluson is very earnest. "I know that neighborhood. I have ministered in that very building. I know those people, know the victims—"

Hal says, "Well, at some point we may want to—"

"The human angle," Falluson says bluntly. "Color. Perspective. Background. *Filler* when you need it—"

I smile at Hal, finishing the good reverend's pitch for him. "You can paint the faces of real people in this tragedy."

"Such an *awful* tragedy," the reverend agrees.

"How quick can you get here?" Hal asks.

"We're pulling into the lot now."

Handing the headset back, I tell the receptionist, "Send the reverend's entourage to edit-two." To Hal, "Let's get set up."

Turning to head back, I notice Melissa cradled under Frank's other arm, tears streaking her cheeks, no Karo tonight. She looks toward me and smiles, nodding relief.

"How 'bout it, monster?" Frank's asking the little one who's now hugging him fiercely. "Okay if you and your mom come stay at my house for a while?"

Let's make news.

Byron's racking the videos, Kristen initializing the suite. "Byron, set up for remote-cam right inside edit-one. Hal's going live to New York, separate feed for footage."

"Ha!" Byron loves it. Circuit freak, he is.

Kristen's scanning the first disk, our shots in the bathroom, down the stairs, Gordie. Pause and mark time-code. She looks at the monitor, then looks closer, surprised. "Gordie?" she asks. "Gordie Pollikey?"

"You recognize him?"

"Recognize? I *shot* him. Me and Byron."

"When?"

"We wound up only using one quote, but he was one of those Parzilac success stories."

*   *   *

"You sure you don't need me?" Frank asks. "I could come back."

"*No, Frank.* Right now they're more important than business. Take 'em home and stay there with 'em."

He takes a deep breath, still reluctant. "They've been through a lot," he says quietly.

"And it's not over. If media comes snooping around, don't allow any more access than Melissa wants—which I assume is none. If police want to question her—well, that's up to Mel, too, but keep a rein on it."

He furrows his brow and nods. Clasping my shoulder, he pronounces, "Call me. Keep me apprised." I'll bet his last will and testament says put a cell-phone in the casket.

Murray's here now, notepad poised. Rupert's running coffee. Hal puts New York on the speaker box.

"We can start feeding highlights," I tell the news director, "in about fifteen minutes. Shots of how it started, the hallway confrontation, gunfire, and so on. By the time you pull that down, we can feed highlights of the fire-escape portion—"

"Hal Neusome shows up in those?" the box asks.

"Yes."

"Excellent!"

"Then we'll feed a third set of clips of the fire rescues up until your local truck arrived."

"Great. We've already broken with a live report from the scene. We'll grab your bits and keep beefing the bulletins to promo tonight's *Newsline* at nine. What can we do live before then?"

Hal answers, "Two talking heads, me and the local reverend—a Chicago celebrity—who knows the building and its people."

"Wow, that was a fast get. Let's sit you two together so he can react while you relay the facts, add some emotion. We'll anchor it from control here with our national-news set in the background, Bailey Caharent asking you the questions. We'll drop in the clips from our end. The reverend won't get much early, but we'll try him, and if he's good he'll get a bigger piece on the show. We're going to lead with this and run as long as it has legs—the full hour if you got enough good clips and it's still interesting out at the scene."

Kristen nods to me, waving a disk. "We're about ready to feed the first submaster," I announce. The sound of popping champagne corks wouldn't surprise me.

Byron's already lighting the edit suite. We're a bit crowded, no place to work, cables here, cables there, elbows and butts. Our editor arrives, freeing Kristen from the console. She joins me at the side wall where she can call the shots but still talk quietly with me.

"Gordie Pollikey," she says. "He was living with his mother in a trailer out there in Maywood Gardens, one of the last testimonials we shot. You were in L.A. that day."

It's ringing a bell now. "I *thought* he looked familiar."

"He was the quote about how he doesn't worry so much now, isn't so scared of people trying to take advantage of him—a confidence quote."

"Why didn't he get more time in the program?"

"He was never bad off before the drug. Lived with his widowed mom; they got along great; he did okay in school, had a part-time job. He was kinda shy and nervous around people, was all, said Parzilac helped but that he didn't like being on the drug, wanted to get off someday."

"Not a good product testimonial. He told me he was a TV star—"

She chuckles. "He's talking about our shoot. He was *super*-excited about the camera and being in the show. I don't think he ever did understand it was just an industrial."

"That address, the name of his mom, it should be on file."

"I'd have to dig, but I can probably come up with it tonight."

"Do it. I want Hal to be the first one out there in the morning interviewing her."

Buzz.

"Yes?"

"Mr. Roenik, Detective Culler and Mr. Durbett are here to see you. I seg-regated them to the conference room."

Cripe.

"What do you need done?" Durbett asks as I come through the door. He's just taken control of the meeting. "Everybody safe? Need clean-up?"

"We're all right—"

"This guy after one of us?" Durbett demands, "—or just random?"

"We shot him doing a drug testimonial last year. He recognized Byron, but he was whacked—acting paranoid."

Culler shrugs. "Drugs is up to the coroner to look for."

Durbett asks, "Do you think he mighta been *told* to talk to Byron? Maybe somebody else knew Byron or the rest of you was there?"

"No no. He was surprised. He got off on being on camera last year, so maybe the camera made him think he had an audience—"

"Paranoid," Durbett says.

"Watch the video. He's accusing all of us of hurting him, or trying to, or something."

"*Could* be just whacked," Culler agrees, looking to Durbett.

"Need to see the video," Durbett decides.

"Maybe ten, fifteen minutes." It's the best I can do.

Durbett nods. I think it's Culler's way of thinking.

"Coroner said inconclusive on the ricin," Durbett says, changing topics. "He thinks so, but isn't convinced enough to write it down. Make sure you don't get rid of that hospital footage. I may want to study it some more," he adds.

"No IDs on them store bombers," Culler says, shifting it again. "Not many tips even after all the times TV showed them guys' faces."

"Looks like they stayed in Chicago a day, then headed southwest," Durbett adds. He knows *something*.

"No sign," Culler continues, "I mean *no* sign of Pozies *anywhere*. Our narcs say word on the street is that everybody quit making them, and they don't think they'll ever come back after so many had bad trips. To risky, too many problems."

New slogan: *Parzilac! Too dangerous even for junkies!*

"Somebody wanted the drugstore owner dead," Durbett says.

"Or wanted to get rid of something they thought mighta been in the car, maybe even in the store," Culler adds.

"Hal made copies," I offer, "of some of their records while we were there—"

"Or maybe they wanted *you* dead, too," Durbett sums up. "Parzilac's a billion dollars a year in somebody's pocket, and you're messin' with a lotta people's livin'."

"I'm putting Hal and Kristen on Gordie Pollikey's mom with a camera in the morning," I say. "I need a victim list tonight or as they're identified—*and* to know who police notified as next of kin."

Culler agrees.

"Might be safer if I go along with Kristen," Durbett says. "Could be some bad areas. Chance maybe to hear about somethin'."

"I don't think you have to worry about Gordie being after us," I assure him. "He's dead now. It's all over."

Durbett pauses to look at me. "Ain't nothin' over till you know *why* it happened."

*   *   *

I've been floating around the studio and filling whatever role rounds out the team, determined to be home before the onslaught of eleven-o'clock newscasts. It looks like I might pull it off.

We do six live cut-ins throughout the evening, then sail through the full hour of *Newsline*. They spend about a third of the show live at the scene, and the rest telling and re-telling the story over stills and moving shots. The anchor cuts back and forth with Hal a lot, the image playing like Neusome's the journalist as much as the participant. Every time they talk about the area or its people, Falluson gets asked for three or four comments. They're using a lot of Murray's questions and topics, especially his bulleted version of the chain of events. By the end, it's a lot of slick graphics and short video clips digitized, computerized, analyzed—man, having so much New York production capacity and that many people to work with must be fun.

By the time it's all over, Durbett is gone. Culler's called three times so far with info on seven victims, including their next-of-kins' names and numbers. They're thinking at least three more to come, maybe as many as five more. Kristen and Hal will drag Byron out at daylight. I'm worried about intruding on grieving relatives, but they're going to get hit sometime tomorrow anyway, so having Kristen on the job at least means she'll do it right, and even tell them how to protect themselves when the frothing pack descends.

I never dreamed there were so many victims. The body count means this story will be really big, likely to last three days or more. I'm going to have to watch out for news vultures wanting to offer a personal look at the man who beaned Gordie, the man behind the chunky tuna.

I call again and finally catch Cyn at home, offering to head her way. No, keep it easy, she offers: let her come to my place with a snack and drinks, ready to help me unwind. Afterward, I may want to wind back up again—several times—because she certainly knows how to uncoil the old spring.

We need to wrap up with New York's news director, a *very* pleased man. *His* wife'll be happy tonight. "Flawless," he says over the box. It's just Hal and me in the other suite. "Is this the place we talked about earlier today?"

"*Shoot & Die*, yeah," Hal concurs. "And Danté Roenik's the one we discussed." Were my ears burning?

"We'll be talking," he says, presumably to me. "Look, Hal, I know you held back on the footage. You've got a helluva show coming up Sunday. I want to be involved."

"But I work for—"

"The brass'll cut a deal to pick it up nationally. You got eighteen minutes for the Mile-Square story tomorrow. That show and Thursday night's both have throwaways." He's talking about segments that can be postponed to another date without losing their impact, usually investigative or human-interest bits. "If something else breaks, I can expand tomorrow or give you time Thursday."

"We're collecting victim footage tomorrow," Hal says. "The inside track."

We close with every TV-news director's plea, on the box, from big New York: "Let me know if it looks good."

*   *   *

I'm almost out the door. I'm this close, actually heading down the hallway.

"Danté," Kristen says quietly. "I found the file. Jody Pollikey is her name, address in Maywood Gardens. I called and got her answering machine."

"I *have* to run with the tattoos in the morning, spend hours with Murray on Flynn Durbett's and Billy Sizemore's stuff—"

"Culler's list just grew by two more names. I think we need a second crew for me; then let Byron direct the first so we can split up the victim shoots. Danté," she says softer, "we can't zoom through and callously slam those . . ." Not Kristen.

"Do it your way—whatever you need."

"I already put together a freelance crew," she admits. "Are Melissa and Taj okay?"

"Yeah, I'm gonna call Frank again on my way home."

"One more thing." She motions me back to the equipment room and lifts a box of disks and tapes onto the console. "This is one I had in my car," she explains. "I wonder . . . Sam Cox signed off on the video library, delivered and accepted, received in full. They didn't want the other odds and ends—source tapes, lay-off reels, cam-disks and so on. I guess those are trash, or for degauss and recycle."

"Yeah . . ." An odd topic to bring up now.

"So who owns these, then?"

"Um, we do, I guess. Sure, *we* do."

"And who owns the content of what's on them?"

My eyebrows are arched. "I guess nobody. As intellectual property, it's discarded refuse—unless there's trade information from a client, something copyrighted or trademarked, secret formulas or something."

She nods, thinking. Then she takes the top disk and loads it into the machine, scanning past shots of a middle-aged woman talking off-cam. Then the shots switch to a young guy, a *big* fellow with wavy reddish-brown hair.

It's Gordie.

Play. "—You know, paranoid, afraid of people," he's saying. "But not since Parzilac."

I snatch up the case, label: *M-Slovak/Testimonials*. "We kept these?"

She spreads her hands. "It was on the shelf." She shows me three more, plus one of B-roll, shots around the M-Slovak world headquarters.

"I'll take 'em home. Don't mention 'em," I caution.

"Mention what?"

"Huh?"

So I finally hit the road, calling Frank. He answers just as it connects, talking quietly. "She's asleep in the guest room." He's almost whispering.

"I got a message from Hank. Her car's repaired."

"Oh good," he says. "Good. That's all she owns right now."

"That and we found her schedule planner in the van."

"We're heading out early to buy some clothes for her and the little one."

"How's Taj?"

"Scared and skittish. He kept asking when their house is going to be fixed. It's disorienting, I guess. I'm thinking of giving him the small room upstairs until they move on, but he didn't want to sleep by himself tonight."

"He's in with mom, huh?"

"No, he's curled up in my lap."

There's a tenderness in Frank's voice I don't think I've ever heard. I picture him cradling Taj gently in his arms, holding the phone with his shoulder, talking quietly, worried less—probably for the first time in his life—about business than about feeding and clothing this shy spark of potential who trusts his lap as the safe place to be on this, the scariest night of his young life.

I've never thought much about the depth of Frank's grief, how it made him withdraw, made him *re*draw the lines separating the facets of his world, to make work his passion, his cohorts the ersatz family. And I wonder which parts of him—those lines drawn firmly around and cut off from the rest—which parts found no place to be, left to whither unnourished like unwatered seeds or sprouts with no light. Can they be saved?

At what point does it become too late?

"Take all day, Frank. Get the little one a *Monster Bin* something from me, too. Rupert and I will cover if *you'll* leave your cell-phone on in case somebody tries to sell me my own shoes and I need to ask you how much I should offer."

Frank chuckles. "I'd go twelve, fifteen bucks—tops."

I'm almost to my neighborhood now, still picturing Frank cradling Taj. Stop at a red light, relax, long day. . .

Frank would be in that big recliner of his in the front room, probably tilted back, Taj's head on his shoulder. They're bathed in the soft glow of that antique lamp. I can see the shot through the window now, framed by French glass, a budding tree branch swaying gently above . . .

But I'm distracted.

It's that footage of Gordie. Imagine the impact of watching him tout

Parzilac, then seeing him freak out and kill a lot of people before committing suicide.

Fuzzy-edged shot over still background, left side of the screen, Gordie bragging, "—Paranoid, afraid of people, but not since Parzilac."

Second shot dissolved over, right side of screen showing Gordie before and after, flaming building dissolves under, Gordie now screaming, *"Why'd you do this to me?"*

And the background brightens just slightly, a freeze-frame Byron grabbed at Maywood when that girl killed herself:

Pill bottle, tipped and spilled.

Pink capsules.

CHAPTER 11

The sultan of the palace.

That's me arriving home, greeted by the most exquisite maiden in all the kingdoms. The finest wine is sparkling, nectar of the king's vineyards. Chilled shrimpmeats are inviting me to gorge, the biggest, most tender of today's catch, bounty of the sovereign harbor where ships ply under vigilant clifftop battlements. The aroma of delicate custard tarts tempts me, puffed and buttery golden, fresh-hot from the castle's kitchens.

Ah, but the royal seamstress has shirked her duties. My goddess wears little more than a wisp, a few shimmering threads, and maybe not even that, the briefest hint, portent for innumerable pleasures of the flesh that await my every desire. It is my fair Cyn, Lady SiCauge, who will carry me in rapture to enchanted realms. She greets me with a caress, a gentle kiss, her scent of honey and lilac, of springtime in a cool hillock glen.

And the royal scepter rises.

Sound the trumpets!

"It's almost time for the news," I say as romantically as I can muster.

"Enough time to eat while we watch," she admits. "Then *I* get to be creative director, and you'll be my demanding client."

The royal scepter pulsates in desperate need of air. "Let me go check on the old lady. Don't start without me—"

"I'm way ahead of you—" she's saying as I trundle awkwardly out the door, I the tripod with one leg tilted up.

I find Ms. Moeroff and Hank Barnahay sitting in lawnchairs just outside her door. No lights, he with bottled beer, she with glass of zinfandel, they're drinking the cool night air, moonlight flickering across them to the rhythm of swaying branches. The apple tree is in full bloom now, its fragrance narcotic.

"She's hot tonight," Theta whispers. "I think she wants you to couple with her."

"I must agree with the lady's assessment," Hank pronounces, holding his beer out to seal the verdict, then taking a hearty draught. He's in a white undershirt, the bottom curled up where so much belly's determined to come out and join the party. "Poke her good," is his advice. "Lawyers is used to givin' it; it's good they play catcher once in a while."

"If I want to know what you're doing lately," Theta says, tilting her head to look up at me, one hand absently straightening wrinkles down the front of her iridescent robe, "I have to turn on the news. Are you okay?"

I reach down and take her hands, kissing them both. Then I see a glint out the corner of my eye. "Hank! What did you do?!"

He's grinning. I've spotted Melissa's car parked just around the side. They get up and follow me over. Hank gets in and starts it, the engine an affection-ate purr. It's been completely bumped out, the cracked glass replaced, fully repainted—a lighter shade, I think, near as I can tell in the refracted lights from the houses behind. The interior has been detailed. There's even one of those pine-tree air fresheners hanging from the mirror. Must've been out of Elvis.

"Had some parts left over," he says. "Couldn't figure 'em, so I threw 'em out." An old joke.

"How much—?"

He's holding up his hand. "You forget the price we agreed on?"

"No—"

"Not a penny more, not a penny less. I used up some favors is all. Maybe collected on a bet or two." He gives Theta a mischievous grin.

I shake his hand, not sure what to say.

"You better get back in the house," my carriage-house gal admonishes. "We don't want her suing you for breach of britches."

I kiss her good night, shake Hank's hand again, and head back to the house, the two of them disappearing into hers. Couple of gerbils, they are.

Just in time, the news is coming on. We flip back and forth between channels. Our story's ten to twelve solid minutes leading every affiliate. The anchor on one keeps telling us her team coverage was first to bring us the news. Yeah, well, I was *there*, sweetpot. She was probably getting her nails done. More hairspray, please.

Cyn turns off the TV, taking my hands and gently leading me up to the royal bedchamber. "Too bad that Gordie guy wasn't rich," she muses. "Twelve victims so far, maybe more . . ."

She pulls my shirt off, tugs my pants down, then pushes me back onto the bed and works them the rest of the way off. She crawls in beside me, props herself on one elbow, and looks me over, her royal highness deciding if this scullery boy looks satisfactory for her evening's pleasure.

But I'm distracted. It's what she said coming up the stairs. *Too bad that*

Gordie wasn't rich. "You mean so you could sue him? Sue Gordie, I mean?"

"Huh? Um, yeah." She's caressing my chest, breathing hard.

"But what if it wasn't his fault he went berserk?"

"So? If he was rich, I'd get a piece of it anyway, just to make me go away, if nothing else. *Somebody's* gotta pay."

I'm thinking.

She adds, "And if whoever's fault it was had deep pockets, I'd go after them, too." She's looking at me, puzzled, suspicious. "Why? Whose fault *was* it?"

"He was a Parzilac case, classic Parzilac-violence syndrome—murder *and* suicide."

She sits up, intrigued. "Who makes—?"

"Are M-Slovak's pockets deep enough?"

"Wow. Juries haven't been very favorable to Parzilac claims." She's thinking out loud. "But twelve victims, sensational news . . . M-Slovak will make worthwhile settlements to avoid the fight, to avoid the publicity."

"What if you had something powerful that *would* make a jury sympathetic?"

She's practically on top of me now. "Like what?"

"That Gordie was a success story, video-produced and shown to M-Slovak employees and shrinks all across America. And what if you had access to even better footage of tonight's tragedy than what you've been seeing? And what if you had that earlier footage showing him bragging how Parzilac cured his paranoia? And what if you had all kinds of inside info, names of researchers, charts and graphs and data, background on their Parzilac testing?" She's getting hot. "And what if you had footage of another M-Slovak success story, a young woman writhing in a pool of her own blood, a violent suicide with pink capsules spilled out onto her nightstand?"

"And what if I *didn't* have this stuff—" she starts, her face right up to mine, "—during the early stages when discovery compels me to show all my cards? What if I just had the confidence that this stuff would turn up later when I needed it?" She's cradling my gotchies.

"The Gordie stuff will need to hit the news sooner than your discovery, but that should give you plenty of time to sign up all your plaintiffs and lock up the suit, before all the other shysters suspect there might be money to be had."

"Yes!" Now she's rubbing my thingie. Then she pauses, thinking. "It will look like collusion if it's my boyfriend who hands it over, though."

"What if it's the news media that comes up with it—say Hal Neusome? Aren't *his* news sources protected—confidentiality and all that?"

She rocks back. "Oh God. I need to get these people signed up before one of the sleezoids does it hoping to sniff out insurance or a reckless ambulance driver or something."

"What if you had an inside track, a list of victims' names, with *next of kin and their addresses and phone numbers?* And what if you had a secret-agent soldier-of-fortune type to go around with you in the morning and run interference—protection if needed—while you try to sign the whole class-action bunch in one fell swoop?"

"Yes! It's gotta be *my* deal, though. I *must* be a partner. If Wanamaker, Salterfin & Brock are firm-of-record and I don't have the clout, I'll lose control of it."

"Could taking a gig like this to the streets get you a partnership at another firm?"

She looks thoughtful. "It's not something you see done, but why not? This could be the lawsuit of the century."

"You should hit the streets early. Sounds like you need to cut a deal with your boss, um . . . Salterfin, and need to wrap that up *tonight.*"

"Yes—yes! Man, it's late, though."

"Aren't we talking maybe hundreds of millions?"

"He'll be up," she decides. "Let's put him on your speaker box. I'll lay it out, flat deal, full partner, full control. If we break down, the clients go with me. To keep it clean, I'll let you hint around what Neusome might be coming up with someday. That way he'll know it's not just some kind of bluff on my part." He sounds like a real trusting type.

We hug our way into my studio/office and punch up his home number on my speaker phone.

A woman answers, sleepy, annoyed. "Who is this?"

"Cyn SiCauge. I work with Mr. Salterfin. I have something urgent to discuss with him."

"I'm sorry," the woman snaps. "It'll have to wait until tomorrow. He's asleep."

Cyn hesitates.

I make a fist and give her a fierce look.

She glares at the speaker, a snarl on her lips. The queen is in a rather demanding mood.

"I said it's *urgent.* Wake him up."

*   *   *

7:00. Ahead of schedule, I call and check with Kristen during the drive.

"Already here," she says quietly. "Mrs. Pollikey's agreed to talk *only* to us because she knows me, so Flynn Durbett has six goons keeping all other media away."

"How's she taking it?"

"She's overwhelmed. Gordie was her only family. Listen, we're about to start shooting."

"Was he still on—?"

"Yes, he was taking Parzilac."

Maywood Gardens is just as I remembered it, except right now to it's too early for ratty brats and too crowded for the bratty rats. There are several TV trucks, a number of video-crew vans, at least a dozen reporters and photographers, all held at bay by monster SUVs and Durbett's rather large, intimidating men. Hand-lettered placards are displayed:

NO MEDIA
Private Property
Will protect with FORCE

Doubt ye not.

We park several trailer-streets away and walk up, Cyn with her leather satchel, me still without my schedule planner. "Flynn Durbett's expecting us," I tell the goon-of-goons quietly, giving our names. He speaks into his chest, nods, then motions us in.

We're introduced to a pair of detectives who are taking notes from kitchen chairs in the homey-looking living room. Hal Neusome is standing to the side, wisely letting Kristen's relationship with the woman finesse this delicate situation. I recognize Kristen's shooter, then notice a familiar woman comforting the one who's in tears, dabbing her eyes with tissue.

She's the mother of that girl who committed suicide. They're good friends, it turns out, now with a shared tragedy, a common bond with roots to the soul.

"Danté Roenik is the man who'll be using the media to show everybody how dangerous Parzilac is," Kristen explains, "and Cyn SiCauge, his fiancée, is a lawyer who's planning to sue the drug company so this will never happen again."

She looks up at me, tears in her eyes, a chunky unattractive woman who looks just like her son. I'm seeing polyester stretch pants, a linen blouse, hair pulled back and tied with a scarf, eyes red and swollen.

I squeeze her hand gently, kneeling in front of her. "If you want us to tell everybody about Gordie without all those other reporters, and if you want Miss SiCauge to help you find justice in court, we'll have you sign some papers, do this interview now, then leave some men outside to protect you in your time of grief."

The skinny dark-roots blonde who lost her daughter is nodding her support, reaching out to clasp Jody Pollikey's hands. "These are good people," she whispers.

Pollikey sighs, her eyes darting to a large framed photo atop the television. It's young Gordie, maybe junior high, a chubby kid with a shy smile, a cowlick at the side of his longish wavy red hair. "Mr. Roenik," she says, looking up at me again. It's hard to imagine how she must hurt. "They're saying bad things about Gordie on TV. He never hurt no one his entire life. I think Kristen was right sayin' it musta been that Parzilac. The only time he ever so much as raised his voice at somebody was when he got off his schedule and messed up his dosage. If I let you put me on that TV camera, will you try to get people to listen, to know it weren't my Gordie's fault what happened?" She reaches out with one hand and takes mine, squeezing firmly, resolute.

"Your son will take a lot of blame in the media," I tell her. "I promise, even if I'm the only one, I promise I'll make sure the truth about what happened to your son comes out."

Her friend moves over by the detectives, so Kristen sets up. She shifts the couch slightly, turns off one lamp and lights another, then moves the photo of young Gordie over onto the end table so it's in the shot, but at an angle where Jody can look over at it like she's been doing since I arrived. It's an effective image, the mother struggling to make sense of what's become of her son, her eyes trying to reconcile the deranged madman we've all watched on TV with the shy boy she raised and loved.

Durbett's at the door motioning to Cyn, so I follow. "Byron's halfway through with his first interview," he tells her. "We need to get you over there soon if you're going to sign 'em up."

"Before you go," I interrupt, "Pollikey's friend is the mother of that Parzilac girl who committed suicide. Shouldn't you sign her, too?"

We lead the mom to a back bedroom, a boy's bedroom with model battleships and sports paraphernalia and posters of comic-book characters—Gordie's room. Note: tell Kristen to get Jody back here to reminisce about what her son was like growing up.

"I talked to my cousin's nephew who was in law school," Cyn's potential client explains, "you know, after what happened to my little girl." She's speaking in the passive voice: her daughter didn't kill herself; the suicide happened *to* her. I'll mention that to Murray as a style point when he writes this story. "He said it wasn't worth trying, that we couldn't prove Parzilac done it, and that the company was so big and rich, nobody could afford to fight 'em."

"After what happened with Gordie, some new information might come out soon," Cyn explains cryptically, "that could make a difference. We're willing to spend whatever it takes, however long it takes, to make them pay you for what happened to your daughter." It's a declarative statement regarding an event described in the passive voice.

"I don't need money," she says. "It won't bring my daughter back. But everybody thinks something was wrong with her, that she was crazy. She don't deserve to be remembered that way, not for working so hard and trying to get her life together." She's crying now. "Not after all that—and when she was doing so good."

She sighs. Cyn hugs her. I hug her.

I've never had more respect for what Cyn does, for her much-maligned profession, than I do right now. The law and the system it feeds are very powerful forces. Everybody deserves justice, even grief-stricken mothers whose children can only leave truth as their legacies.

8:07. Receptionist offers a hale and hearty hello, reporting, "Phone's ringing off the hook, mostly looking for footage, interviews, et cetera. I'm referring them to Mr. Neusome's office."

Rupert appears with a stack of files and that look in his eye. I'll not be rid of *him* any time soon. He's the pup and I'm the leg.

"The Hale-Bopp people at nine, the Weisman people at nine-thirty," he reports. I've been *scheduled.* "Lots to cover." He waves the files at me.

Heading down the hall, I ask, "Can some of that be discussed where Wardley and Cox would overhear us without it hurting us?"

"The financial tracking system," he decides. "I guess some of the Weisman stuff, too—Flynn Durbett's not vulnerable to being lured away."

We start in the storage closet so the bugged chair can transmit us. Durbett wanted me to keep Ellmata Investigations listening in case we decide to send the Kehoe people chasing wild geese. Rupert says I'm already behind in filling out expense sheets. "We're kicking butt," he adds, "already past break-even for several more months." Take that, Sam and Dib.

Receptionist is at the door. "One of your contacts at Briggs is on the phone."

It's Moore; the sample tattoos are ready; he wants the artwork for the other thirty-four designs; we'll be there at eleven; sure lunch sounds good, too; you think Stockbridge might want to come along?

We leave the closet for the conference room; that's enough radio theatre for now. "Tennessee Film Commission called," Rupert reports, another file open. I notice the inside covers of each folder have Kristen's trademark *do-plan* form for writing in what and when, then checking off why and, sometimes, how much. "They expedited the permits for you guys to shoot two Sizemore simulations on Tims Ford Lake. Kristen wants to be out there by end of next week, maybe shoot into the weekend."

"What else?"

"Ollum DeForest called because Parmenter Publishing has a big piece of the true-crime genre and she says if anybody's talking to you or Hal about the Gordie Pollikey story, make sure she gets a chance to pitch before you make any deals."

A book deal? One that blows the lid off the pharmaceutical industry would be a lot bigger than a simple true-crimer. *Parzilac: The American Tragedy.* *Parzilac: Cure Worse Than Cause.* Hurt Parzilac. Frazzle M-Slovak's merger. Elevate Hal. Big advance check, royalties, residuals, movie deal starring Lance Longrod as Danté, maybe a sitcom . . . "She calls again, tell her I was rather mysterious about the idea but agreed not to make any commitments until I see her Friday. What else?"

"The timetable Frank was talking about to launch the Briggs tattoos—" He flips through another file. "It's, well, just about impossible. Les Casapell, Briggs's PR guy, is doing double-duty with their marketing guy to rush this intro; he's saying he wants full-pagers in all the magazines listed in that plan Frank and I put together, or as many as we can get. At the last minute like this, I doubt that'll be many. We're going to need some savvy media buyers to start cutting deals fast; then you'll have to have the ads ready yesterday."

Buzz. "Two people from Hale-Bopp are here to see you. Send them to your office?"

"Your other thirty-four tattoo designs are ready," Hale-Bopp founder Hans reports as I'm walking in.

"And we have sketches of your six ads," his buxom, not to mention artistic, wife Darla adds, "which is all we have so far accomplished."

The ads look great, but they'll need at least another day or two to finish them right, including laying in the type.

"Be sure to leave room at the bottom," I say, "for a one- or two-line disclaimer about anaphylactic shock."

"First of Friday morning," Hans offers as deadline. "We will try for sooner."

"They're not placed yet," I explain, "but we know it'll be a rush. Do what you can."

"Even if these are only for impressing the children," Darla says mischievously, "I will want to find out if this ballerina can tell me about my own allergies. I would proudly display her on my arm. She is very pretty."

I'm picturing Hans in the spiked punk or maybe the flaming skull. These things could be as big a hit with adults as the kids. Whooda-thunkit?

Murray's holding court in the conference room with two freelance writers, plus Durbett's product guy from Weisman, Carl something, and boxes of various items stacked around the walls, several odd-looking devices on the table. And my new running shoes?

"Not yours," Carl explains, "but you can have 'em if you want. I goofed and brought an adult size."

"This stuff is for the kid-safety video," Murray explains. "Dad says maybe they should check out the new Weisman catalog; Mom thinks there's such a thing as worrying too much. Turns out, Dad goes ahead and loads up on the goodies; then we see the kids going through a wild and crazy day where all kinds of dangerous situations are happening, all of which they're unaware. The Weisman stuff prevents uncountable tragedies, even to the point of being humorous—you know, the oblivious guy walking down the street narrowly missed by falling pianos, stepping over open manholes, that kind of stuff. Finally, at the end, when the last push for *order now* is going, Mom agrees maybe they *should* check out some of that Weisman stuff. Dad's all *Nah . . . I was just being overprotective.* Mom, now lovey-huggy with the brats, points out if you love your kids enough, you *can't* do too much to protect 'em."

"We was trying to hook *the parents* to watch," Carl chimes in, "but I think kids'll watch it, too."

Now it's time to play with the goodies. I can't believe all the stuff: secret communicators, kits for making photo/fingerprint ID files, personal defense items, data hiders for little kids, safety gear for all recreation from sports to biking to blading, educational packages for teaching/discussing drugs and sex and dangerous behaviors. What's with the shoes?

"First, there's the RFID chip," Carl explains, "—Radio Frequency Iden-
tification. You stick it under the kid's skin or on the inside of his back molar." He demonstrates, inviting me to put one on. It looks like a tiny ink-dot
on a slip of wax paper, but he swears it's really a coded circuit chip with
micro-antenna. I have to use a tissue to wipe off the tooth; then I press the
dot into place. I inspect the wax paper; the dot is gone. A probing finger
suggests maybe I can feel something there, but I can't be sure. It sure
wouldn't bother me, and I'd forget about it in no time. "What's it do?"

"It gives the ID to a scanner/transmitter in a key-ring or hidden in the
kid's shoes."

"It's built right into the shoes?"

"Naw, we put it in. Name brands and styles are too important to
young'ns for us to try to make 'em wear generic." He squeezes the sole, in-
serts a tiny tool, and pulls out a two-inch rod with several interlocking pieces,
explaining, "Here's the battery, back-up battery, short-range ID checker that
sends out a scan looking for that chip, and long-range transmitter—up to
three miles—so somebody with a tracker can follow it. It's for kids who get
lost, kidnapped, maybe snatched by the divorced parent, teens sneaking
where they shouldn't be—any situation where they'd think getting rid of their
cell-phone or other GPS devices would make them untrackable. You also
got situations with no cell signals, like separated during a hiking trip, whatever."

"How's it tracked?"

"Subscription service tapping our proprietary satellite system puts it on
your home computer, or the ones with more money can buy their own portable unit like this." It looks like a laptop with a small dish-style antenna. "Put
on them shoes," he coaxes me.

Now I'm dressed in Frank-gray with black-and-green running shoes.
He's typing in some data, asking the spelling of my name, home address,
social-security number, emergency notification with phone number and address. He shows me it's filed with the code number for the chip stuck to my
tooth, then switches the screen to what looks like a map of Chicago. He
types in my name, and a dot appears on the west side, probably close to
where we are. Then the screen goes through a series of shifts, zooming closer
and closer, until we're looking at a map of about two blocks each direction
right around the studio. There's my glowing dot right where our building
would be. Leaving our phones on the table, we walk out to the parking lot
and back so I can see the dot moving. I'm impressed. He even gives me a

redundant transmitter key-ring for a souvenir.

Byron's hovering around now, so I leave my conspirators to their work. "You want to see the morning news?" he asks. He's recorded the affiliates.

We spend nearly thirty minutes watching segments while Rupert asks questions and adds info to the files. The story is huge, garnering major coverage, but nobody else got Jody Pollikey on-cam, and so far only one victim's relatives are talking. Thirteen have been confirmed dead, not including Gordie. Most were inside two apartments on the top floor, rear. Unable to get to a fire escape, they were overcome by smoke.

Thirteen dead.

Killed by Parzilac without ever taking a dose.

We must leave now, or Rupert and I will be late for our meeting at Briggs. It's 11:30, and I still don't know where my schedule planner went, but I'm distracted. I'm struck by the hard reality that I was one of the lucky ones.

I got out.

I got to tell my story, to speak for Gordie, to run around and keep my schedule and make my plans. I feel sad. I feel tired. I wonder who these thirteen people were, these victims, these casualties, these *acceptable risks* . . .

These very real people, now with no place to go, no plans, their hopes and dreams extinguished—ahead of schedule.

CHAPTER 12

The trappings of bossdom.

Les Casapell, Briggs PR-meister: he's the man to reckon with, caller of the shots, grand pooh-bah, big kahuna, brigadier-general, doesn't need Rex involved at this level; Les will be handling things; bring all your problems and plans to Les.

"We expect FDA approval Friday," he reports. "That alone will attract some media attention, especially now with psychotropic drugs a hot topic." He bobs his head several times. I just can't shake that image of him in a turtleneck looking like something you might see in a locker room. Hand him two basketballs and try not to laugh.

"Tuesday's probably too quick," I caution, "but maybe Hal Neusome could exposé this new Fantasy Patch wonderdrug for *Newsline* next Thursday." We're at the table in Rex's conference room, Rupert poised to take notes.

Les likes the idea, but acts like he's considering all the ramifications before he agrees. "After we have the secret anti-merger commercials shipped out Monday, there'll be a surge of media interest."

I'm the one putting this together and somebody else gets to break the story? I don't think so. "Neusome's *On The News* show Sunday night is going to be about Parzilac and the latest violence. Part of that will be about a big Chicago law firm filing suit against M-Slovak on behalf of the Wicker Park victims. Another part could be about the appearance of these videos, drawing attention to the merger, making it look like M-Slovak's trying to flee to Europe so they can peddle their poison to our shores while minimizing federal scrutiny."

Les sits up—erect, as it were. "We could use couriers to deliver some of the videos Sunday. Then it wouldn't look suspicious that Hal had advance info."

"He'd just be first to break the news."

Les nods, rubbing his head vigorously. Don't rub too much; it could go off. "We want the story to imply the videos are coming from disgruntled anti-merger shareholders—of which there's a very vocal bunch, by the way—and not from a competitor like us. Briggs has to stay a mile away from this."

Rupert asks, "You guys still want your own warehouse to be responsible for video distribution?" He has his file open. Les nods, so Rupert indicates a cover page, adding, "We need a sign-off from Rex or somebody with authority to approve that. Then I'll arrange duplication and delivery."

"*I'll* sign it," Les insists, affixing our parchment with his royal seal.

"We should leave out the one shot at Wicker Park," I say. "The news footage would connect it to us and, since we're launching Fantasy Patch, cast suspicion on your company."

Les goes limp. He strokes his head again—*Look out!* "You're right. Drop it."

Rupert's noting this on the cover page, sliding it across for another signature.

"You keep things tight, don't you?" Les asks him, signing off.

"Frank always says when the shit hits the fan, whoever has the most signatures is the one who comes out clean."

*   *   *

Lunch is at The Blue Pony, Stockbridge and Moore joining us, Rupert glad to meet them.

"We have a case of these for you out in the car," Moore says, pulling out some appliques and setting them on the table. He looks proud, pleased with what he's offering. "These were a rush job to have samples for our focus groups and for you to work with, but I think they turned out very well."

Aller-Tats! Two versions: the alien with weapon-belt and a hummingbird sipping a bloom. They look great, brilliant colors, cool designs. I handle them gingerly, remembering they're serious pharmaceutical products. "When's the focus-grouping start?"

"This morning," Moore reports, barely suppressing a grin. "We've got major testing going in Atlanta, Boston, and Phoenix. I checked just before we left, and the response is through the roof!" There's that grin.

"We have the other thirty-four designs outside," Rupert says. I made him leave his files in the car. "Danté's already signed off on them." I did, too—he made me sign all thirty-four cover sheets. He *does* keep things tight. "Do you have production set up?"

Stockbridge takes a hearty drink from his beer. He'll need another one before the soups even arrive. "Manufacturing said if they can get those designs by Thursday, I should plan region-one in three weeks, two more regions the week after, and the two western regions the week after that. I'm putting together a whole team to set up that kind of distribution so fast."

"Wow," is Rupert's reaction. "I'm used to six months being a short window for a launch. Les Casapell said he wants national magazine ads and TV spots to coincide, so we're going to have to bust a nut."

"I can't dawdle and wait for you," Stockbridge says, finishing his beer and scratching his portly gut, "even if they're on the shelves before the ads. Rex is worried about competitors. He wants the trademark *Aller-Tat* to become the name you trust."

"We'll have the ads out fast as possible," Rupert assures them, glancing toward me. Yes, I know we don't even have an agency or media service working on the buy yet. Frank'll get on that soon. "Magazine ads take the longest lead time. Newspapers and TV, especially local placement, can be done last minute. We'll need to make a lot of adjustments to our media plan to accommodate the rush."

Stockbridge waves him off, pausing mid-slurp from his clam chowder. "That's between you and Casapell. Our jobs are to make sure people like the package, then get 'em out there stacked at eye-level on as many shelves as we can."

"How do you do that?" Rupert asks. I'm curious, too. Our waitress is hovering around, waiting for Moore to finish so she can whisk away our bowls.

Stockbridge shrugs. "We have five regional offices that oversee sixty districts, our sales and distribution territories. The district reps are basically order-takers. They feed the computer system weekly, and my department makes sure the right quantities are shipped to the right areas."

"Does M-Slovak work the same way?" I ask.

"Similar," he says. Yuck—the guy's eating fat and all. Down boy! That's a bone! "They have a smaller presence in the over-the-counter niche, so they don't have nearly the field sales force. They've got a bigger piece of the prescription pie, especially since they have Parzilac and Ducilam, so they do a lot more of their order-taking from regions, by telephone, fax, or 'net. As for distribution, they go through contract distributors more than we do. Briggs has a spin-off division that even wholesales for other companies in some of the major cities."

"Making a profit off competitors," Moore interjects. He's having a wa-

tercress sandwich with avocado, if you can believe that. I picture him growing a silver cottontail.

Stockbridge grins. "Cuts both ways. Ligg-Doball distributes a lot of *our*
stuff in Tennessee, Georgia, Alabama, Mississippi, and Louisiana. It's a
patchwork system that grew up over the past century."

"Why would the dead drugstore guy have cases of loose Parzilacs in his
store? Shouldn't they have been in Parzilac bottles?"

Stockbridge stops eating for the first time. "Did he?"

"Boxes full. They looked just like the other Parzilac boxes, pi-ethym-
lorenazol, but each had thousands of loose capsules."

"You saw these?"

I nod.

He shakes his head. "I can't imagine."

"You ever seen M-Slovak ship 'em that way?"

He shrugs. "I don't see their products at the wholesale level." He looks
distracted. I gather it sounds shady to him, but he's cautious, not wanting to
make pronouncements when he doesn't know what he's talking about.

I push it. "I was thinking the drugstore guy was selling 'em to somebody
to make Pozies, but why get rid of the bottles and not the boxes?"

"The bottles are coded," Stockbridge points out. "Batch and stock numbers, dated, traceable. Boxes aren't—only the pallet they're on for shipping
purposes."

Moore states the obvious. "He was getting rid of the bottles so they
couldn't be traced back to him. He could move the boxes around and look
legit unless somebody opened one, but if dealers or some illegal lab got
raided and the bottles were there, he'd be caught in the middle."

One last bite of my mahi mahi and I'm ready for another St. Pauli Girl.
"I wish I could figure out why or who wanted him dead."

"Whoever robbed him," Moore conjectures.

"Sounds like a double-cross to me," Stockbridge muses. Sure, he'll have
the chocolate fudge cake, the rest of us passing. "Or maybe rival dealers."

"But Pozies have become *druggas non grata*."

"If I were running underground drugs, I'd get rid of my Pozies after all
this attention, wouldn't you? I'll bet narcs are crawling up every dealer's butt
in Chicago."

"I have my own theory," Moore says cautiously. He looks around.
"M-Slovak. If Parzilac was *your* billion-dollar drug, wouldn't you be worried
that Pozies could hurt or destroy its image—especially after a few hundred

kids freak out, think they can fly, and take a header off some bridge or building? M-Slovak has enough problems with violent reactions to the *un*altered form of the drug."

"You think M-Slovak did their own investigating—tracking down sources where their drugs were slipping through to the black market?"

"It's a *billion*-dollar baby."

This is making a lot of sense. "Then goons were sent to shut him down and, when they learned there were probably more in the store, to destroy the evidence and keep the Parzilac name out of the media."

Moore nods sententiously, glancing around again. "Except you messed up their plans, big-time."

"They sure didn't worry if *your* scrawny butt was in that store when they bombed it," Stockbridge points out. I like his characterization of me. This discussion has taken us to a personal level.

"Frankly," Moore says, "I'm glad to see you're knocking Parzilac down several notches, exposing it for what it is—"

"Regardless of our company launching its next big competitor, that Fantasy Patch," Stocky cuts in.

"—But I hope you're being careful."

Suddenly, I don't want to go anywhere without Flynn Durbett. Worrywart Durbett, the guy who'll outlive us all because the demons he saw in every shadow turned out to be real, and he was ready for 'em.

There's an awkward silence. Rupert puts his credit card on the tray.

Everybody's looking at me, Rupert observant, Moore deep in thought, Stockbridge very earnest. The portly distributor wants to say something, but seems unsure what. I think he's worried about me.

It's an odd feeling, that shedding of the roles long enough just to be people, to share our thoughts out of school and show our concerns.

I look at the Aller-Tats again. They look great. Now that I have a whole boxful, Melissa might want to test Taj and see if she can isolate a cause for the little one's asthma.

"What's your son's name?" I ask Stocky. "Blaine?"

He smiles, then whips out his wallet and shows me a picture. Talk about an eleven-year-old mini-version of dad. He's posing at his computer with that same earnest expression as our Briggs distributor. He looks like a good kid.

"You gonna try these tattoos on him?"

He shakes his head no, putting his wallet away. "Uh, we went ahead and made an appointment next week for him—with an allergist. Do the whole nine yards."

"It wouldn't hurt to try these anyway, maybe tell the allergist what to look for."

Stocky looks embarrassed, glancing toward Moore. "Well . . ." He's hedging, finally deciding we're still out of school. Glancing around, he says quietly, "You heard what they said about that risk of shock."

"Yeah, but that's one in seven-thousand odds."

Stocky hesitates, looking at me, searching my face for understanding. "But we're talking about *my* son."

*   *   *

"Grrrrrrr!"

A monster growl from Taj—my day is complete!

The big-eyed monster is stylin' in his new outfit; plus he's been transformed from moppet to little man with a punkish new haircut. He's strutting for the golden-haired girl in our playroom.

"Danté!" Frank found me. Back to work.

"You guys finished fast."

"Mel's still shopping, gonna get her hair done. I had her drop me off and take my car. Listen, we've got a phone conference with Woot Wooter in five minutes and a meeting with Karl Ferman in an hour."

"Who?"

"He's on the board of Willard Communications—in charge of assimilating Kehoe/Lundy. Yes, they're folding in as a Willard subsidiary. That's why all the reorganization. Anyway, Ferman was somebody's guest when I stopped by the club yesterday, but I didn't meet him. I took a chance and called, dangling some insider info in front of him."

We're in his office now, Frank calling Woot's secretary to tell him we're standing by. "Listen, just follow my lead."

"You Frank Dellman?" Bigger than life, Wooter sounds like the flamboyant used-car huckster with Texas drawl who used to sell appliances on late-night TV back in the seventies.

"I'm here with Danté Roenik, also formerly from Kehoe/Lundy."

"I remember you," Wooter bellows. "You done that big-ass campaign for us that time, that what-you-call *Bless Our Wooter Home* thingamajig. If Kehoe would come up with more ideas like that, I might not be looking to throw 'em out with yesterday's biscuits."

"I had a ball doing some of those Wooter promotions, but that was before Dib Wardley started moving me around. Luckily, Frank Dellman snagged me to do product launches and corporate communications."

"Just between us, I think that sad-sack Wardley don't like havin' people around who's smarter than he is. Shows him up too much."

"You do understand," Frank points out, "that he bounced Danté as soon as I retired." Frank's playing me as the underdog, common enemy and all. It's an odd tactic to start a creative pitch by boasting your top guy has just been canned.

"That's one of the reasons we're callin' the review—Kehoe's creative's done gone stale. If that's the best Kehoe can do for their biggest client, then out with the biscuits they go." I can't shake the image of him in that big ten-gallon hat chomping a cigar and worryin' over the little lady getting a washing machine big enough to handle the needs of a growing, patriotic family.

"When you announce your review," Frank says very seriously, "I want Dellman/Roenik to be on your short list of agencies invited to pitch."

"Well now, Frank, you boys done good work—*real* good work—but you ain't got the organization."

"No, but we can put it together."

"That takes too much time, no matter *how* good you are."

"What we want is the *creative*. We'll sub all the production and placement. Kehoe's got an excellent organization, or we can take it somewhere else."

"What about Cox? And what makes you think Wardley would go for it?"

"Wardley used to have senile old Herb Lundy wrapped around his finger. There was almost no board oversight there—one of the reasons they were allowed to flounder and not keep *you* happy. But now he's got to answer to Willard's board. Faced with having to deal with me or losing a third of the business Willard thought was coming with their new acquisition, I think they'd be willing to sit down and talk. Cox could be limited to working their other clients, and Wardley would have to lie down and lick his own nuts."

The line is quiet. Finally, Wooter speaks again, mellower this time. "I don't think you can do it, Frank—but dammit if I don't like a good shoot-out, so I'm willin' to let you try. What does my announcin' the agency review next week do to you?"

"I want to leak it to the Willard people sooner, then ask your indulgence to time the announcement on whichever day works best for me."

"Done! You boys pull this off, I'll fly you down to my new llama ranch in Texas and we'll see if we can manage to ride one of them things. And if this *don't* work out, well hell, you can still come on down, but you buy your own plane tickets." Now there's an image I'll not shake for a while. Frank in chaps and ten-gallon hat, riding the wild llama.

Frank's satisfied; we'll get our shot. "Compared to the rest of this, the llama ride sounds easy."

*   *   *

Picture a little robot, elfin, smart and alert, a variety of jaunty hats appropriate for whatever he's doing. Chef, mechanic, nanny, maid, accountant, maintenance worker. He's "Wootman!"—that little guy who symbolizes how Wooter Home Products runs your house for you.

"Perfect," Frank pronounces. I have a small batch of rough sketches already, not bad for fifteen minutes. "Help me grab some stacks." He's rummaging through cabinets, gathering artwork, 'stats, story boards. "Make a pile of everything you have on the Aller-Tats."

We load into his car and hit the road.

"You set out your stacks of work," Frank says, "the tattoo stuff on top of two piles, the Wooter sketches you just made on top of a third. We're going to talk about Kehoe maybe getting our tattoo biz, but if I steer it toward Wooter, act like whatever story I spin is gospel."

We meet at Ferman's hotel suite not far from the agency, per Frank's request, so Kehoe people can't speculate about what's going on. He's a smallish sort, a white guy with short-cropped graying hair and immaculate beard. He looks studious in his wire-rim spectacles, very relaxed, friendly, the kind who touches your arm while shaking hands. We sit on couches in the office area of his suite.

"You and Dante both have tremendous reputations, and have done some remarkable work," Ferman says good-naturedly—he's done some fast pre-meeting homework on who we are. "And I'm sure you were a loss to Kehoe. I'm glad to hear you've both landed running, and that you have already started to assemble an impressive client list for your new enterprise." He's glancing at my three piles, but being very subtle about it.

"We have several big accounts already, creative and oversight, but we don't have the people to handle production and placement. You just bought out one of the best organizations in Chicago."

"I'm glad you think so."

"I know, because I put most of it together."

Ferman nods.

"I'm planning to come in and dismantle Kehoe/Lundy," Frank says matter-of-factly. "Thought you might want to know."

"I see Briggs and Wooter on your piles," Ferman says off-handedly. We could be chatting about the weather.

"Briggs is in the bag," Frank says. "I need twenty of your best people to launch their new allergy-testing tattoos nationwide, on the shelves in three to five weeks."

"That's ambitious in the extreme," Ferman says.

"Similar timetable," Frank tosses out, "for a thirty-million-dollar launch about to be announced next week. I'll need everybody on your top two floors for that."

Ferman nods. "You would. If you've got the scratch to throw around, I can't stop you from hiring some away, either. We'll adjust. It's the nature of our business."

"Or we could cut a deal," Frank says.

Yeah, I'm thinking, let's cut a deal. All this huffery-puffery makes me nervous. We're so far extended in our commitments and obligations, with such a huge payroll to cover already . . .

"You're looking to sub this tattoo business you spoke of?" Ferman asks.

"I've got millions in media-buys alone that need to be done *now*."

"I appreciate you bringing this to Kehoe first."

"I didn't," Frank corrects. "I brought it to Willard Communications, assuming we'd work it to be handled by Kehoe."

"That you did. Why are you going around Dib Wardley? Hard feelings over him gutting your group after you left?"

Frank shrugs. "As you say, it's the nature of our business. I don't mind that he's a worthless, conniving son of a bitch—and you must not, either." Frank leaves that hanging for a second.

"Buyouts have to be very stable," Ferman points out, "or the whole thing collapses. Dib has the relationships with his big clients. We put too many Willard people in there and it's a green light for clients to scramble. Besides, then it would take that much longer before I get to go back home."

"I'll tell you what I think of Dib's relationships, but first, let me make my offer. Then we'll see how long today's agenda is."

Ferman smiles and looks over at me. "I'll bet you just like to draw, don't you?" He's got me pegged.

"Something he's quite good at," Frank says quietly, a mischievous smile matching Ferman's, "which is why I enjoy the privilege of cutting his deals."

"So what are we talking here, Frank? Even split?"

"No, I was going to offer you two-to-three—with a proviso."

Ferman's *very* interested, and not hiding it very well.

Frank says, "Sam Cox can't get near it; Dib Wardley and anybody representing him or Willard stays away from my client."

"So we get the business, at a fair cut where we'd have wound up after negotiating all night anyway—" Frank nods. "And you get the pleasure of knocking Cox down two pegs and Wardley down one." He's looking thought-ful, nodding his head. This one's a done deal.

"And you get to save," Frank says, "at least part of what you're going to lose when Wooter dumps Kehoe next week."

The room stops spinning, reality freezes, and I can hear that aggravating ditty during Final Jeopardy playing *Mmm Ahh, Mmm Ahh, Mmm Ahh Mmmmm* in my head.

Ferman takes his glasses off, inspects them, puts them back on, and takes a deep breath. Finally, his words slow and deliberate, he starts to ask, "So then you have reason to suspect—?"

"I wouldn't waste your time with suspicion. Agency review gets announced next week. Kehoe will get the courtesy opportunity to spend a lot of money trying to convince Woot they'll do what they already should've been doing. Then it's Dellman/Roenik or one of two agencies in New York." I notice he called Wooter by his first name, the image of comfortable familiarity. "I can't say we've got it locked up, but Woot says it's okay I leak this to you if it'll help me set up to lease your top two floors and put about two-hundred of your layoffs on my payroll." Frank shrugs again. "That's if working with you is the way I want to do it."

"Dib knows nothing of this?"

Frank shakes his head. "And if you tell him, we're through talking about the bigger Briggs product launch or any of Wooter's work. I still want to give you the tattoo, though. We need a good team fast and I trust the one at Kehoe I put together. Besides, we wouldn't be able to absorb *everybody*, so maybe we can save the jobs of a few friends."

Ferman's thinking hard. "I can't afford to do the same percentages like this tattoo if you take Wooter, then offer to bring his work back to us," he says.

Frank leans toward him, nudge nudge. "And I'm not going to try to negotiate something I don't have yet."

Touché. "Okay, Aller-Tat's a done deal. What do you need out the gate?"

"Print and broadcast buys. Set me up to meet with Meg and her placement supers sometime tomorrow. The rest we'll grow together. I don't care if Meg's required to report to Dib every thirty minutes, long as she's *my* contact."

"Done. Now, you're offering the bigger Briggs job—"

"For the same split," Frank interrupts.

Ferman winces, but continues, "—For the same split, contingent on?"

"You make sure the tattoo work succeeds, Dib stays off my clients, Cox stays completely away from the job, and you don't tip Dib that Wooter's throwing him up for review."

"I can take all but the last one." He shakes his head. "You tell me Kehoe is going to have to compete with you to keep its biggest client, but you're trying to dictate that we can't pull out the stops and *compete*. And all this is on the if-come, no promises, maybe after we roll over and let you walk away with it—just *maybe* you'll bring it back and split the money. I'd rather just help your little agency succeed with a big tattoo job, then try to make things work for the bigger one yet, but still try to blow you out of Wooter's water."

"Then your little tip-off," Frank says nonchalantly, "was a gimme. It's the last one you get from me. Will you be there for our tattoo-launch meeting tomorrow?" Meeting's over.

Or maybe not. "Okay," Ferman allows, "I'll talk to New York, but nobody at Kehoe hears about Wooter until after I kick it around with several key board members."

Frank nods. They both look at me, so I nod. What the hell.

It's time to leave. The tenor of the whole situation has changed. Ferman's gone from looking cool and calm and in control, to having accepted us as one of the boys. I half expect him to invite us to stop by next time we're in New York so we can ride his llama or something.

He walks us and my pile of artwork to the door, lingering for a moment. "I guess you just couldn't stand the idea of retiring, huh Frank?"

"Actually," the old man says, "I was ready to go." Ferman's surprised. "But after working with so many hacks like Sam Cox all through my career, the last few years were the most fun. It's rare to have the chance to build a team around the kind of talent Danté has." Golly, Frank, you're embarrassing me.

Ferman's shaking my hand. "I just like to draw," I tell him.

He turns to Frank. "Is he really all that good?"

Frank just smiles.

*   *   *

And they're off!

It's a horse race! It's a drag race! It's a foot race!

It's a camera race, a lawyer race, a signature-snagging race . . . and we're winning! Byron beat out all his competition, six for six. Kristen's beat out hers so far, six out of seven, only one more family to approach. Cyn has signed all twelve families she's met, a slam dunk, batting 1.000, one giant leap for lawyerkind on our trek toward marriage and family and a perfect life and contentment in our old age.

Kristen recites the address so I can meet her there, our conversation confidential and fully protected over Flynn Durbett's super-duper spy phones with the red buttons.

Frank careers us into the lot at *Shoot & Die*, screeches into his spot, and pronounces, "Good meeting," for the umpteenth time. He's been praising how I handled myself, but for all I contributed, I might as well have been sitting there, you know, handling myself.

I leave right away for the north side to meet Kristen, Cyn, Flynn Durbett, and entourage. I find the house, a modest brick bungalow, just as the others pull up.

"Those two do the first approach," Cyn explains, "so the people aren't overwhelmed by a crowd of strangers." She looks up into my eyes with a sneaky smile, barely containing her enthusiasm. "I can't believe how well this is going. This one'll make thirteen families, plus Gordie's mom and the mother of that suicide girl."

Hal Neusome pulls up, then walks over to us grumbling about getting caught behind some tanker. "Sunday's show will be phenomenal," he gushes. "This footage is *de rigueur.*"

"I've got some beef to add to your run-down," I tell him. "Five-hundred anti-merger commercials against M-Slovak will start showing up at the offices and homes of influential politicians, FTC people, and shareholders during the day Sunday. It dovetails with Parzilac being M-Slovak's biggest, albeit controversial, product."

Hal's eyebrows are up.

"Also, I'd like to see Cyn on your show, announcing the big Parzilac lawsuit she's filing— When?" I ask her.

"I could file an initial summons and complaint by Friday," she answers, obviously liking the idea of appearing live.

"Then I'd get scooped before Sunday," Hal disagrees, shaking his head.

"How about Monday morning for the filing, with the lead lawyer on your show Sunday night announcing her intent?"

Hal nods vigorously, both of us looking at Cyn.

She smiles. "Perfect. So, what do I wear? I hear you're supposed to avoid white and busy patterns."

A big Lincoln pulls up. Of all people, it's Doug Ritenour, the tall red-headed lawyer who repped our drugstore guy when it looked like criminal charges would be filed.

"Danté, what are *you* doing here?" He's friendly, but tentative, suspicious maybe.

"We're interviewing victims' families for Hal Neusome's show. Doug, this is Cyn SiCauge."

"Oh!—plaintiff's attorney," he says, shaking her hand stiffly. That's right, Cyn is suing the drugstore guy on behalf of the little girl to collect maximum insurance. Ritenour's associate, Cricket LaRayne, is defending the widow's civil interests. Cricket's role will probably dwindle to little more than watchdog when the insurance company brings in its own law firm to stall, intimidate, and haggle.

"I better get inside and meet my clients before you media types inundate them," Ritenour says good-naturedly. He nods goodbye to Cyn. "Counselor."

Kristen comes out, tells the crew to start setting up, then comes over and reports, "Well, they'll consent to the interview, but they've got a lawyer in there running interference. A little black woman, very friendly—"

"Cricket LaRayne," I supply, explaining the connection.

"Looks like a bust for you," Kristen tells Cyn, shaking her head in disappointment.

Cyn shrugs. "We were doing better than the odds. I might as well come in and hover with you, get to know the family, get to know this LaRayne woman. I'll wind up having to cut a deal with her eventually, anyway. Let's be extra careful *nobody* mentions a Parzilac connection around these people."

It's crowded in the small house. Our subject is an older black woman, tiny, stooped, gray hair in a bun, a peach shawl around her shoulders. She's furious.

"Ain't right," she pronounces. "Ain't nobody done explained to me what made that man up and kill my boy," she spits. Kristen's setting up, trying to get the camera rolling as quickly as she can.

Cricket LaRayne is sitting beside her, patting her hand. "He didn't care who he was hurting when he went crazy, Aunt Tildie," she offers quietly.

Aunt?

"*Somebody* coulda done somethin', Cricket." Then to the rest of us, angrier yet, she says, "*Some*body coulda stopped it. I want me some justice, an eye for an eye, a tooth for a tooth. That's why I called my brother's girl here. She's a lawyer. She'll know what to do."

This is great for Hal: outrage, looking for understanding, spitting venom and ready to blame. We'll capture this now, then keep her at the top of our list for *after* the drug connection becomes known. Then she'll have a choice thing or two to say about Parzilac. Hopefully, by that time Cyn will have squeezed LaRayne and Ritenour out of the picture.

Kristen is rolling now, getting this on camera, tight on the woman's face to keep Cricket out of the shot. Kristen starts asking questions, getting all the right answers.

I wander into the kitchen where Cyn has cornered Ritenour. "I don't know," she's saying. "Maybe a little something from the landlord, maybe some insurance. Gordie Pollikey wasn't worth anything. I just came along and signed them because it helped loosen their tongues for Danté's interviews. Made them feel like somebody was helping."

Ritenour is nodding. "Now you're saying Salterfin, Wanamaker & Brock might be willing to pay me a referral fee, or even a percentage, if we'll sign off and let you handle the whole class-action?"

"I'd have to run it by the partners, but I'll try."

Ritenour takes a pen from his pocket, fingers it for a second, looks me over, looks Cyn over, then puts his pen back in his pocket. "I don't think so. The way I see it, Salterfin wouldn't have you racing around signing people if there wasn't something in it. Riding the publicity train? I don't think so, not something this low-end." Cricket LaRayne is coming in, curious. Ritenour finishes, "No, I think you've got a defendant, a *big* defendant, something high-profile, something up your sleeve. I think we'll keep our seat on this buggy and see which way you're driving."

Cricket shakes her head, glancing into the front room where her aunt is railing for her TV audience. "Tildie wants a pound of flesh. She won't be satisfied until she knows the truth. She won't trust anybody else's version, and I won't tell her something I don't believe."

Hal's behind our lawyers, against the wall, not pleased with how this is going. Cricket heads back in to show support for her aunt. Ritenour follows her.

Hal whispers, "Rats. They're gonna want a piece of the publicity machine, news appearances, the whole shot."

Cyn's upset. "That'll steal my thunder. I've got *all* the other victims."

"Then they'll take *their* half of the story to my competitors," Hal bemoans. "We were doing great, sign or don't sign, play or don't play. This last one wants to play with somebody else, and so far Aunt Tildie is the most flamboyant, the most outspoken, the most *photogenic*. We've got her *now*, but soon we're gonna lose control of this story."

Our horse race has two finish lines, and we can't cross them both.

We stand in the dining room and watch. Aunt Tildie is steamed and still doesn't know whom to blame. But she wants something done.

She looks pleadingly into the camera, pausing to wipe a tear, asking America to help. It's too late for her son, but we're all in danger. We should all be scared.

"Please!" she wails. "How many *mo'* gots to die?"

CHAPTER 13

Imagine.

Fantasy Patch.

What's the essence? Imagine, and change. Imagine, transform. Imagine, metamorphose.

Imagine, become.

"Hi, Danté!" Ms. Moeroff's coming up the stairs. "What are you working on?"

"I'm trying to come up with a Fantasy Patch slogan, a focal point for the launch campaign."

"So what's the concept?"

"I'm trying to keep it simple. *Fantasy Patch: Imagine, Become.* It's missing something, though. Imagining is what you do—the action step—something anybody with a problem has already done, thinking what it would be like *not* to have the problem. That's followed by a result: *Become.* But it's not strong enough, not specific enough. The reward must be bigger, the payoff on a grander scale. Become is more of a process. Problem is, there are so many uses for the patch, so many results, I doubt I'll find the essence in any one word or phrase."

"How about *succeed?*" she asks. She gets up and stretches, then does a graceful, flowing arc to touch the floor. She could turn a butt-scratch into ballet. "Set a goal; use the patch; *succeed.*"

"Well, okay, for *some* goals, but that's weak for, say, somebody suffering anxiety attacks. *Succeed* sounds active, maybe even a *cause* for anxiety. For those people, it's more like: *Imagine, Become, Relax.*" There's a light bulb over my head now. "Yow. That's it. Three or four words, the last one different for each application. *Imagine, Become, Take Charge. Imagine, Become, Create. Imagine, Become, Perform . . . Motivate . . . Learn . . . Heal . . .*"

"Danté, you advertiser types will promise people *anything.*"

"Like motivational speakers who convince them they can accomplish whatever they put their minds to."

"But that's never backed up with a guarantee," she scoffs.

"Because it's up to each person to put his own plan into motion."

"So just apply one of those patches for a little help. You could even push the things people *most* want, like love—" She grins mischievously, tousling my hair. "—Or sex."

"*Imagine, Become, Climax!*"

"But no guarantees," she teases.

"That's advertising," I pronounce.

"*If* you can deliver."

Imagine, Become, Sell!

*   *   *

It's the most beautiful car in the world!

Our lady has tears in her eyes, her hands together at her mouth, her chestnut-haired little boy's big eyes wide with excitement.

"But Hank—" Melissa says quietly.

"You're welcome," he tells her, his arm around her shoulders for a quick squeeze.

"It's wonderful. But how much—?"

"Price I quoted. I'll settle with Danté later. *We'll get in!* See how it feels." He hands her the keys.

The engine purrs. Mel dabs her eyes and smiles at me through the windshield. Taj explores the interior like he's found lost treasure, fascinated now by the dangly air freshener. She climbs out and gives Hank a big hug, kissing him on the forehead. Just watch him grin. She whispers something to Taj, who shyly shakes the big guy's hand.

Hank shakes formally, then sweeps him up to give him a big noggin noogie, a squeal and a giggle his reward. Frank and Melissa are smiling. Ms. Moeroff's eyes glisten; she's nodding approval, proud of her co-gerbil, a brief glimpse at her deep affection for this crude man who appreciates a lady and enjoys a good "libation."

Taj come-hithers his mom with crooked finger, then whispers something, pointing at the carriage house.

"No, Danté lives in this one," she explains, pointing at my house.

"Would you like to see?" I invite him. Mel retrieves a small sack from Frank's car. We leave Hank and Theta—his arm around her—waving at us from her porch, and tromp inside.

"Tours cost one monster growl," I inform the little devil, but he's distracted, tugging uncomfortably at the waistband of his shorts.

"Let me get some lotion on him first," Mel says, gesturing with the sack. "He's been without it since the fire." I show her to the bathroom. "His rash is getting worse," she explains, "but all this does is relieve the burning. Can I ask you something personal?" She hesitates awkwardly. "Does this look like what guys get, that what-they-call jock itch?"

"Jock itch is just a fungus infection, same as athlete's foot," I explain. She's got him standing on the counter now, his shorts down. He's holding his underpants up, embarrassed. "It's okay, Taj," she whispers, "just a little bit." She pulls the waist band of his briefs down a few inches, enough to reveal a nasty red welt, puffy and almost raw in several places. It's a jagged line two or three inches high that runs all the way around.

"Oh! That's no fun, is it?" I ask him sympathetically. He shakes his head, then relaxes a little, not so worried Mom's going to reveal too much. "It *could* be, but a fungus is more likely down, you know, where skin is against skin, where it's maybe damp after a bath—like athlete's foot gets between toes. I have some cream if you want to try it." Ah, the wonders of modern pharmaceuticals, the American medicine cabinet, each home stocked better than an entire sanitarium in days of yore.

I warn him it might sting a little, but only for a few seconds; then it'll feel better. She dabs some on her finger, then starts to rub it in. First a whimper, then big tears squeezed stoically; then he starts to cry. I grab a washcloth and wet it for her. "Get it off! It shouldn't hurt *that* bad. Hold on, Taj." I feel like dirt. This isn't the cry of a small boy who hates Brussels sprouts; it's real, and so sad, that plaintive anguish of countless children living in a harsh world where not even a loving embrace can erase the hurt, where kisses don't always make it better. She quickly coats him with the lotion. He tugs his shorts up, still crying, then melts into his mother's arms as she coos softly, rocking him gently, her own eyes moist.

And there in the doorway stands Frank, panic in his eyes, breathing really hard.

"He's okay," I offer, coming out. Melissa sees him and nods.

"You okay now, little guy?" he whispers. He goes in and dabs the boy's face with his handkerchief. Taj eases himself into Frank's arms, too, all three now close together.

I move to the other room, but I can see through the open door. Frank's still breathing too hard. Melissa fishes inside his jacket pocket for capsules, then feeds him one, swallowed wordlessly.

It's a scene from a movie, a TV show, a commercial, or maybe just like the real world. They're top-lit, a glow from the mauve-curtain backdrop, framed by the doorway. The tiny boy is still on the counter, his mom reassuring him, the ersatz grandpa protecting them both.

The image of what's important in three lives, captured in this singular moment.

*   *   *

Grumble, grumble.

I'm on my way to *Shoot & Die*.

So much for watching Hal's live uplink to *Newsline* from the comfort of my castle, for leaving production under the capable purview of Kristen and Byron, news-types handled by Murray, clients finessed by Rupert. Frank had planned to head back there and schmooze the NBS people, but he asked me to go in his place so he could take Melissa and her son to the 24-hour walk-in clinic to deal once and for all with a little rash.

My heart's not in this, but I arrive and do the corporate thing. There are too many people here. Besides the production crew—shootin' tapers and image shapers—there is Hal's support staff—fact takers and tacit fakers—plus three self-important middle-grade executives from NBS sniffing around to get the lay of the land—stuffy puffers and, frankly, puffy buggars.

But it's show time, so I'm saved from all the glad-handing, taking my seat in the control room, the authoritarian presence who wouldn't dream of interfering with Kristen's direction unless she keeled over and had to be carried out mid-show. Besides, she's at least as good at this as I am, which is to give me too much credit because, in fact, she's often quite a bit better. I never fail to be surprised or impressed by her capabilities.

It starts out great, follows the standard format, pleases the NBS brass—ho hum.

Then *the footage* starts, and I'm transported back to the run-down building in Wicker Park, Gordie Pollikey in the last moments of his tragic life. Murray's wordsmithed it just so, Hal delivering it just right. Gordie's not a madman; he's a *victim*, a simple man loved by his mom, wrestling his own demons and sometimes winning, a walking Parzilac tragedy about to lose his struggle—and take at least a dozen more with him.

Gunshots. Fire. Now the whole building's in flames. Hal Neusome is heroically confronting Gordie, helping rescue victims, pausing long enough to tell this story to the world. There's a tearful Jody Pollikey, her eyes glancing toward the innocent, pubescent face in her son's faded photo. The survivors follow, holding each other as they assure the world their people were loved, and that they mattered, and that they will be missed.

"Please! How many *mo'* gots to die?"

We're clear now. We're a hit. Hal and master-shooter Byron are the centers of attention. Everybody's excited, happy, self-congratulating, big plans for the future—all except Kristen. And me.

Reception Dude's new assistant has the place covered. I want to sneak away, head home, draw circles and squares and simple triangles for a while—nothing more—then try to drift off. I follow Kristen out to the lot. We stand at her car for a moment, a warm breeze hinting the scent of flowers and budding leaves.

Our mood is subdued, maybe even melancholy. It seems like we're the only two who still feel the tragedy we just witnessed on-screen.

"I couldn't make a career doing news," she says quietly, chirp-chirping her door lock open with a keyring remote.

"We'll just let it help pay the bills for now," I assure her.

"I'm not surprised Frank missed this for Taj."

"It seemed, you know, personal for him, the kid needing help and all."

Her eyes are glowing, headlights from passing cars making them twinkle. "I think it's that part of Frank that he's been struggling to close off ever since he lost his wife and their unborn child; he's finding out he can't do that forever, that it's still inside him, that he's powerless against it. It's caring about others, even loving them, so much that it can be overwhelming no matter how hard you try to deny it."

I remember the image of all three framed by the bathroom door. "Frank was breathing hard. She made him take some medicine." Not a very poetic comment from me, but further proof.

Kristen smiles and nods, but says nothing. She's fingering her keys, maybe feeling awkward. "I thought you'd be grabbing a chance to spend some time with Cyn."

I shrug. "She's lawsuiting. I'm going by her office in the morning to reassure her boss I'll come through with an anti-Parzilac bombshell."

She nods again, then reaches for the door handle. "I guess I should get home while it's early enough to return some of my voice-mails."

"You know, if this Parzilac tragedy stuff is hard for you, if you don't want to be involved, that's okay. You've got enough Sizemore and Weisman and Aller-Tat work. I'll cover this."

"No," she says. "No. I think I'd *rather* do it. I'll wind up watching the footage anyway, so I want to help use it to maximum effect. What got me through tonight's segment was thinking, *One more nail in Parzilac's coffin.*"

"Well, if the hammer gets too heavy, let me know."

We say good night. She drives away, leaving me standing there.

It's such a warm night, the noises of westside Chicago for soundtrack. Nobody's coming out of the studio yet, everyone still in there toasting the deaths of fourteen innocent people—recorded in *living* color. I don't want to go back in; I don't want to go home.

I don't want to stand here.

I guess I could drive out to Frank's place and see how the little monster is . . . but no. What I want is to drive out to Wanamaker and steal Cyn away from her work, maybe go out together and walk the lakefront, catch the Lake Michigan breeze . . . but no. She needs to get ahead right now, to have the lawsuits packaged by Friday so we'll have time together this weekend.

I look around some more, toward the studio, my clients' cars, traffic floating by, offices across there, the warehouses thataway, the pinpoint glow of somebody smoking a cigarette in the lot across the street, the neon arc of him tossing it aside before he climbs into his van, starts the engine, and drives away. He's got the right idea.

Go home, Danté. Go home.

I start my Caddie, then try to imagine being able to look into a back seat with baby carriers strapped into both sides. I pull out, glancing across the street again. Why was that guy with the van parked over there? That place has been closed for hours. Curse you, Flynn Durbett; you're making me paranoid.

There's not much traffic this late. I'm ready to relax a little; except I keep seeing that van back there, coming my direction, maybe following me. Impulsively, I turn south and go out of my way, watching in the rear-view as the van passes by and keeps going.

I head back north, but then I see it again. I *think* it's the same van, but I can't even be sure it's the one that was in the lot. Now there are two vans, three, a dozen—vans next to me! Vans in front of me! Vans everywhere . . .

Get a grip!

My heart is actually pounding. Should I call somebody? Flynn Durbett? What would I say?

I go out of my way again, backtrack, and circle around. There's no reason anybody else would follow this same route.

And I finally lose him.

Almost to my neighborhood, checking my mirrors more than the road, demons in the shadows, vans falling from the sky, mysterious faces watching me from the very pavement, I'm imagining a secret meeting at the M-Slovak headquarters:

"It's Roenik," a faceless suit says quietly. "He's the one out to kill our billion-dollar baby."

"Something's got to be done," another suit says. The lighting is from below, smoke curling from ashtrays.

"Something *is* being done," the first says. "Right now, in fact."

"Good. I don't need details."

"We thought about Neusome, too, but he's too high-profile. Suspicion could turn toward us. He's useless without Roenik, anyway."

"Just Roenik then—for now. Don't leave any trace."

"We never do."

I'm almost to Ravenswood now, and I see that damned van. It's a block back. I stop at the intersection and wait. The van doesn't move.

What now?

We both wait.

I need a Fantasy Patch that makes vans disappear.

Then his turn signal blink-blink-blinks its intent. Right turn, gone.

I rush down Ravenswood, pull into my drive, shut off the engine, hurry into my house, and lock the door.

Catch my breath.

Heart still pounding.

Imagine, Become, Relax.

*   *   *

Kill or be killed.

It's me versus him, or me versus them—I can't be sure how many yet.

Listen.

Are they in the house? Attach the device to my ear; activate, listen. Turn my head; scan every direction. It amplifies with a limiter, the slightest sounds clear as a bell, protecting my ears from louder noises.

I can hear my heartbeat, my own breathing. Be still, my heart.

Now I can hear *him* breathing, maybe even his pulse. He's in the house, in *my* house.

Here to kill me.

Slowly, carefully, quietly, I put on the goggles. Touch the right side, infrared. Touch again, light amplifier. Touch again, thermal scanner. Set it for three overlapping images, the best of all three ways to watch what man was never meant to see.

The faintest creak of the floor. He's downstairs, and he's moving. He's looking for me.

My hand absently touches the lump in my pocket, my keys—key-ring, really. Twist a quarter-way and I could activate the scanner/transmitter. The sensor would scan me, detect the chip glued to the inside of my molar, and identify my code. The amplifier would send the coded signal three miles every direction. They could find me then, knowing where to look. That's if they're looking for me.

Do I need help? Once I activate the tracker, all I have to do is squeeze once—twice to deactivate—and it'll send the panic call. Help! S.O.S! *M'aidez!* Urgent need of assistance . . . Get me the hell out of here!

But not yet. I'm still listening; it sounds like only one man. I've got a chance. The stairwell's a bottleneck. If he wants me, he's got to come up to get me . . . unless he flushes me out somehow, starts a fire maybe, hits me with tear gas. My mask is over there, close enough. But not yet.

I need more information, need to know what he's doing. I remove the glove from its pouch and pull it carefully onto my right hand. It's black and sheer, with little pockets on the backs of the fingers holding the sensors. I remove one, ease to my knees, reach out carefully, slowly, quietly, and set it into place looking down the stairs and toward the right. One more sensor, other side, toward the left. Now I'm backing slowly into the bedroom while another sensor watches the top of the stairs. I stretch my middle finger to the base of my palm, touch the pad, and I can see it all, split screens across the bottom of my goggles, all three angles transmitted from the sensors.

I touch several more times, select infrared, the images glowing faintly green, the lights on those tiny devices not very strong. They won't last long, either—limited power sources.

He's moving again; I can hear him, but he's still not in my three lines of sight, still not close to the stairs. He must be searching the ground floor first, confident he's quiet enough not to alert me. Maybe *he's* listening, too, making sure *I'm* not aware, not making a phone call, not escaping through a window.

Closer.

I want to twist a quarter-turn on that tracker, squeeze the panic button, then shout, "I know you're here!" Be a man, Danté. I wish my heart wouldn't pound so hard.

Movement on the left screen, the sound of feet gently pressing carpet, getting louder. He's looking at the stairs. It's one man, not very tall, dressed in something dark, barely distinguishable. I think he's a black man, but can't be sure. He's looking up the stairs, directly at my sensor-cam. Can he see it? Surely not; it's too dark.

He's holding a gun, just above waist-high, pointing it up the stairs.

He takes a step, pauses and waits. Another step, then another. It's too late now for trackers or panic buttons; it's just him and me.

And he's coming after me.

Kill or be killed.

I ease backward, crouch behind the dresser, gently remove my ultimate weapon, and aim, waiting for him, waiting, my finger on the trigger. I've never handled one before, never fired one, not sure how it'll feel, but now's the time, tonight's the night.

He's up to the top of the stairs, now only his legs visible in my last sensor. He pauses and listens, but must not yet know if I'm here or not. He looks into my bedroom and decides to try this direction first.

He takes a step, then another, then pauses.

One more step, almost within range.

I could jump out and fire now, or wait—wait until he's right in front of me, point-blank range, maximum impact.

Another step.

Another.

One more step, I tell myself. *Be ready.*

And he steps.

It's now or never.

It's him or me.

I fire.

*   *   *

"Gotcha!"

"Ha!" Jankety jumps back, pretending to cower in fear. "You sure did!" He turns on the room light.

I step from behind the dresser, hold up the 3-D spy-cam he'd given me, proof I was armed and ready, that I'd passed our little intruder-drill. "Would you like the package of eight-by-tens with that?"

"Let's check your zoom and aim first," he says, slapping me on the back and leading me downstairs to the computer he'd set up on the dining-room table. He attaches the tiny digital holo-camera to a port, then downloads its internal data. The face of one very surprised mock-intruder emerges from the front of the screen. "Perfect!" he pronounces. "You know how to zoom it fast to grab a head shot for facial recognition, or to catch a license plate on a moving van, right?" He taps the keyboard, turning the camera into a hot-cam, the moving image of this room showing up in three dimensions from the monitor. I swing it around, zip and zoom, and we're looking at the head of a miniature, jeweled dragon on one of my shelves. I click, that image appearing in a little box in the corner of the screen. Jankety grins, pulling off the black mask and running his hand across his head.

"This stuff is kinda fun," I gush. It is, too.

Jankety takes a deep breath. "Listen, Danté, you want to have fun, go to one of those paint-ball places with your friends. I'm trying to protect your life here. Like I said, you need to include a weapon."

I'm shaking my head. "I need to detect, yes, to track even. I'll admit I feel better knowing I can call for help if it gets real hairy, but I mostly want a way to get some proof and find out who it is—if there really is somebody following me. Then I can let the police handle it."

Jankety shakes his head resignedly. "It's a proven fact," he says quietly, "police aren't much help if they're elsewhere eating donuts when your adversary pulls the trigger."

"Point taken," I allow, still resolute.

"Well, let me show you how to hook the camera to your goggles. Then you can record data from infrared and thermal images, too, plus show your own perspective. That's good for evidence, like when there's an issue of what you could see and how much in danger you were."

"I left it upstairs." I turn to head up and retrieve it, adding, "It's amazing how easily I could detect that you were in the house—and knew where you were and what you were doing. I coulda blown you away and you'd never know what hit you."

"Yeah, well," he shouts after me, "that's because I'm the *only* other person in the house!"

I hurry into the bedroom and reach for the goggles.

Click.

I half-turn and find a gun aimed right at my face, just inches away.

Shaking his head with disapproval, Flynn Durbett lowers the pistol and offers a bit of advice: "Don't get cocky."

CHAPTER 14

Lawsuiters and suited looters.

Such is the swarm at Wanamaker, Salterfin & Brock, P.C., Cyn's law firm. A twenty-story, tan-brick with classic sidewalk canopies at two entrances, it's the old YMCA headquarters complete with luxurious gym and saunas, a minute's saunter from Clark Street, City Hall, and the county offices. *Mayor's Row*, a cluster of restaurants around the corner, is where the political hacks meet and greet and pause to eat. The rare warm-weather times I get to have lunch with Cyn, we take carry-out across to Daley Plaza with its fountain and massive Picasso sculpture, then relax and watch the melting pot swirl around us—walkers and talkers, hawkers and gawkers, sellers and yellers, and those hip-hop fellers.

Cyn greets me formally, allowing the briefest hug and peck on the cheek, then takes me up a floor to wait for the attentions of one Mr. Rob Salterfin, big kahuna and senior of the still-living partners, the good ole boy of the boys' club where my good young girl wants full membership.

Salterfin eventually deigns to greet us. "Miss SiCauge, Mr. Roenik, I appreciate your accommodation." He's short, balding, overweight, and slightly stooped, with little brown beady eyes and overlong arms that look somehow simian. He gestures us to seats across from his desk. I can't help but notice the wet dribble down the crotch of his thousand-dollar wool suit.

"First off," he starts, dropping into his overstuffed chair and moving papers on his desk, "nobody is eavesdropping or taking notes. The substance, content—actual and implied—of this meeting is entirely confidential, limited to the parties present in my office. Say you the same, Mr. Roenik?"

"The same, I say." Oyez oyez.

"Good then." He presses a button. A woman appears, our servant whose happiness and sense of fulfillment depends entirely on satisfying my coffee needs. I pass. "Tell me about this satellite meeting regarding Parzilac," Salterfin says, right to the point.

"My work for my clients is confidential," I spar. I guess I don't like his demanding tone. Cyn shifts uncomfortably.

Salterfin eyes me warily, tense, considering, then . . . grins. "Good."

"As I understand it," I continue, "the purpose of our meeting is to speculate about what information might become public through the news media, say Hal Neusome, for example, whose sources are confidential."

"I agree," Salterfin says, "but another purpose is to brainstorm, hypothetically, what information *we* should pursue—from the defendants—in the early stages of a possible lawsuit."

"By *we*, do you mean Miss SiCauge here?—because I don't know you, sir, and my interest is in helping *her* achieve her career goals."

"Um, oh yes, yes. I see. Yes, let me be clear that Miss SiCauge will be the lead attorney on this lawsuit."

"Miss SiCauge will play the role of exclusive firm spokesperson with the media?"

"Well now," he blusters, "I can't limit comments about the firm."

"No, but you can refer all questions and interviews about this suit to her."

"Yes, she will participate in all media commentary, but I or another partner may also be present."

I snort and glance disdainfully toward Cyn. It's not my *tooth* he's pulling. "I've seen flunky-propping before," I tell him. "It's too easy for you to step in front of the microphones, then later argue that you fulfilled this obligation in spite of leaving her standing there like a doofus. No, Mr. Salterfin, with all due respect, we are talking about risking my career for the advancement of Miss SiCauge's. My interest in yours is merely tangential."

"It must be understood that I will maintain normal control over communications as senior partner in the firm. Miss SiCauge will stand before the cameras, but time and place and outlet, and the nature and tenor of the comments, that is something over which I maintain veto."

"This is fair," Cyn says.

"About your other demand—" he tells Cyn.

"I've made no demands, Mr. Salterfin."

He waves her off. "About your *suggestion*, I talked it over with the partners and we agree. Your elevation will be announced Friday morning—" Cyn's about to wet her pants, trying not to show it. "Then you will file your lawsuit in the drugstore-driver wrongful-death matter Friday afternoon. We will hold our partnership dinner for you Friday evening. Monday, you will file all fourteen suits against M-Slovak, amid much fanfare I expect."

"You don't want me to continue negotiation over the girl's death with the insurance company and the driver's estate?"

He shakes his head, pulling a file from his in-basket and passing it over to her. "The results of our investigation," he explains. Cyn's looking at a printout of some kind. "The drugstore family is heavily in debt; even the widow's house is double-mortgaged. There's nothing there to go after. As long as the insurance company thinks there's the possibility of sharing the burden, they'll drag their feet. We need to use court-ordered discovery to bring out the family's indigence and show the insurance company they have the only pockets."

"But doesn't that bring it out?" I ask, gesturing toward the report.

"That is very unofficial," Salterfin explains. "It can't be used legally."

"How do you pressure the insurance company to settle?"

Cyn answers, "Stir up community outrage; raise the stakes."

Salterfin nods his head. "I was thinking press conference at the site of the accident."

I don't like this. "No way. I want all publicity to clarify that the driver is *not* being blamed, that it was an *accident*, an unfortunate accident and this lawsuit is just a necessary step toward collecting the insurance to which the little girl's mother is entitled."

Cyn looks toward Salterfin, who shakes his head. "High-profile cases," he counters, "demand to expose a villain."

I suggest, "Then let's paint the insurance company as uncaring, unfeeling, denying this little girl's family the protection they deserve."

Salterfin purses his lips, makes a chimp-like face, then nods, absently scratching his ribs. I expect to see him press another button and summon somebody to examine his balding pate for nits. "Done. Now let us consider the M-Slovak assault. How can you help us craft effective interrogatories?"

Say what? This boy just likes to draw.

"I'll file each summons and complaint," Cyn quickly explains, "then submit initial interrogatories—questionnaires, actually—demanding such and such information they're required to turn over. I have to be very specific or they'll weasel out of answering. In the meantime, they'll start filing a flurry of motions seeking to have it dismissed. If the interrogatories scare them enough, if they hint that I might be on to something, M-Slovak might even start making go-away offers."

Salterfin picks it up from there. "Likewise, we need to begin scheduling depositions—" He notices the blank look on my face, clarifying, "—taking pre-trial sworn testimony which becomes a part of the record. We need to know whom to subpoena and what kinds of questions to ask."

"You willing to pony up and bring in a pharmaceutical expert?" I ask.

Salterfin grimaces. "Mr. Roenik, a firm cannot issue such a challenge without the resources and resolve to commit at least several hundred-thousand dollars and countless staff hours. Our reputation will be on the line, too. I'd like to see your cards."

So I show him a ten, a list of presenters *and* the entire audience for the Parzilac roll-out. My jack is access to Murray, the knave who can tell exactly what questions to ask. I play the queen with Rex's secret compendium of all Parzilac violence. He's practically drooling by the king, a list of eighteen success stories and one witnessed suicide failure—whose mom is now Cyn's client. "I'll show you some of my ace footage, and you tell me if it looks like a royal flush."

I pull a disk from my little satchel while Salterfin practically leaps to his equipment cabinet and flings open the doors. "Do you know how—?" he starts to ask.

"I can figure it out," I assure him, much to his relief.

So we watch some footage, the two lawyers rapt. I don't need Jankety's listener to hear their hearts pounding.

There's Gordie and his mom, talking about how afraid he used to be, how Parzilac gives him confidence to speak up, to make decisions and carry them through, to take control of his life. Then we cut to him accusing off-camera demons of *doing this* to him. We watch him go berserk, firing his gun, sloshing gas, setting fire, now on the fire escape, still shooting, then climbing into a window to die in his own flames. Everybody has seen most of the post-fire interview with Jody Pollikey, so I included just a short clip of her crying, looking at his picture, shaking her head, and pronouncing, "It was the Parzilac. He struggled against it for so long; then it finally beat him."

"Imagine the impact," Salterfin breathes, "this would have on a jury."

Then the screen comes alive again, a montage of family photos showing our suicide girl, a brief voice-over by Murray imitating Hal Neusome, talking about this wonderful child who grew into a young woman with so much potential, who then joined the Parzilac trial experiments. The last photo is of her standing in the living room of the trailer, an image which dissolves into the same angle from Byron's camera. There is no voice-over now, only ambient sound, the voice of the mother concerned because her daughter never showed up for work. We move down the hallway, into the room, and we see the shattered mirror, a bleeding woman on the floor. I'd managed to get enough of this shot in even after editing out the part where I kneel down, holding her arm. There's her face, her slashed neck, her final spasms, Byron's shot finally drifting up to reveal a pill bottle on the nightstand—tipped and spilled, pink capsules.

Cyn has tears in her eyes—we've talked about this footage, but she's never seen it before. Salterfin is breathing hard, almost panting.

Cyn strikes while the iron is hot. "I want maximum publicity," she tells her boss, "straight to the federal court, then move for immediate consolidation to class-action so it's easier to start signing more plaintiffs all across the country. How many victims on your list?" she asks me.

"More than two-hundred incidents of violence, many with multiple victims."

"This could reach *billions*," Salterfin gasps.

"With my help," I point out.

"And me in the lead," Cyn reminds him.

"Mr. Roenik," Salterfin says, my buddy, my pal, "we would like to hire your agency to handle publicity for us, and to shoot video of her filing, then have copies available for anybody who attends a press conference here."

"We can handle that," I tell him, "but we're not cheap." My salute to Frank.

Salterfin's bobbing his head, still sitting in front of the monitor. "Put together a plan; coordinate with Miss SiCauge." He turns to Cyn. "Be sure you run it all by me first," he reminds her.

"I have a lot of research to do in the next few days," she says.

He shakes his head no. "You'll be a partner by the end of the week. Research is what associates are for. You work up your complaint, handle the media, and nurture your clients." He reaches for the disk, but I intercept. He looks sheepish, but acquiesces, still talking to Cyn. "Your highest priority is face time with your plaintiffs. The more public this goes, the more they'll be approached by others. You want solid, tight relationships. You're their friend, their champion, the one who would never make the mistake of failing to keep them apprised, assured, optimistic. Visit them; sit with them; become a member of the family."

Cyn wrinkles her nose. "Some of them are low-lifes."

"When you have to convince a jury that shit stinks, you better be willing to get out and step in some—"

"But—"

"*Before* it hits the fan."

*   *   *

The guy holds a gun to my head!

He jumps into my car and, just like that, he's got a gun aimed right at my head. I never even saw him.

"Damn, Flynn, you scared the hell out of me."

"Not enough," he says. "Drive."

I reach for the ignition, though my hand's not very steady.

Then I stop.

I've seen the movies. What if the engine hesitates before turning over? Would I have time to get out and away before the explosion?

"Ain't nobody messed with your car," Durbett says, reading my mind.

"Where we going? To the hideout? Meet Black Bart and the 'slingers?"

He doesn't think that's funny. "Frank says you're due at the studio."

We pull out. "What are you doing here?"

"We were looking for a tail, see if anybody followed you."

"Nobody followed me this morning," I assure him.

"*Two* vehicles followed you from your house to this lot, and one man followed you up to a meetin' at the law firm upstairs."

Huh? "Who was—I mean, were they—?"

"They were me and Jankety." We're heading west now. Durbett cracks the window and gestures with his hand. A small foreign car passes us on the right, Jankety at the wheel scrupulously not acknowledging us. He turns off onto a side street, but will probably fall in behind me again in a minute or so. "Them fellers who blew the drugstore were professionals brought in from Houston. I got nothin' on the woman dosed him with ricin yet, but she wasn't no amateur, neither. Then *you* see a van followin' you, yet you climb in your car today without so much as a look-around, and leave the door unlocked." He shakes his head. "I'm tryin' to keep you alive—at least till you get my infomercials made."

"You really think M-Slovak would go after me?" He just looks at me. "What does this have to do with the drugstore guy getting killed?"

"Culler's done found one possible connection." He's watching every direction at once, now signaling something out the car window. "Where all did you shoot them videos about Parzilac success?"

"Most were in Chicago. The rest were Grand Rapids and Milwaukee."

He nods. "Your drugstore guy used to have a contract with M-Slovak's testing company. He was recruitin' people to be in the Parzilac program. When M-Slovak canceled the deal, he filed a lawsuit to make 'em pay him off. Culler found this by checkin' civil court records. It was settled, according to the file, but it was like pulling teeth to get the son to admit this. Culler figures he's worried about bein' connected to the Parzilac testing, bad public relations after what's happened and all, but I don't know. He says it wasn't much money, helped make a few payments is all."

"Cyn's boss found out the family's deep in debt. No wonder they keep their cash in a safe instead of a bank."

Durbett looks at me, thinking. "Eleven more stores, eleven more safes, maybe one in the house, maybe one in the son's house, who knows how many safe-deposit boxes . . . Maybe they got nothin' else; maybe they got a lot more stashed. Makes me curious."

"So maybe they were greedy. Still, revenge seems like a weak motive for a dispute that didn't amount to much."

"Drastic reactions usually come from fear. Maybe they were afraid of him. Maybe he was tryin' to shake 'em down some more. Maybe he knew something about the testing, or had a bone to grind over that girl who killed herself—I don't know. But the son sure don't like Culler askin' about it."

"Can't *you* get him to talk?"

"Well, yeah, probably, but Culler's watchin' to see what he does today. We're thinkin' of maybe payin' him a visit later tonight, at his house, him not expecting it."

"Let me know what you learn."

"You just be careful in the meantime."

"Look, there's almost no chance M-Slovak or anybody else is out to get me. If so, they could've done it by now."

"Maybe they've tried—at the drugstore, at Wicker Park, maybe last night—except you spotted 'em and spooked 'em."

"You're trying to rattle me," I accuse.

"Scared mighta saved your life last night."

"You really think that van was after me?"

"No."

"Then why the big deal?"

"*You* thought it was—and then again it *mighta* been. Coulda-woulda-shoulda is a game you only get to play if you live to throw the dice again."

"You can't train me to be a soldier of fortune overnight."

"No, I wouldn't try. But you need to accept that you *could* be in danger and do three basic things about it: avoid what you can, prepare for what you can't, and *be aware* so you'll know the difference."

"Pay attention," I echo, "assume the worst, and don't panic if I think I'm in a jam."

Durbett nods, allowing the slightest smile. "There's advantages to ridin' with the man with a plan, but my druthers is one keeps his wits when the shit hits the fan."

"I won't panic," I protest.

"But you need to pay better attention. Hell, you could have a killer ridin' right beside you with a gun pointed at your head and you wouldn't even know it."

I start to speak, but he makes a gesture. I look to the left and see Jankety riding beside me now, hand cocked into a mock gun pointed right at me.

He's shaking his head.

Durbett's shaking his head.

I'm just shaken.

"Bang!" says Durbett.

*   *   *

There's a skunk in the woodpile.

Murray's chopping word-wood while Kristen prepares to shoot piles of video using the big soundstage—today is anti-merger day. I barely have time to greet Melissa, find out the clinic prescribed a milder cream for Taj's fungus infection, learn our medical insurance starts in thirty days, then pick up my pile of phone messages and mail before Frank pulls me into his office to meet Ollum DeForest of Parmenter Publishing along with a writer-beast from her stable of non-fictionizers. Is it Friday already?

"Ollum has something hot to discuss," Frank explains, "so I said she could come down this morning—just no tour today since we're shooting confidentially for an important client." He glances toward the writer, a signal he's the confidentiality concern, the skunk in our woodpile.

Ollum and this gnomish, rather heavyset white guy both stand to greet me. Our book editor is of African descent, light-skinned, built like a Sherman tank with fallen arches and a fashion-scoffing dependence on support hose. She has a puffy lower lip, a big lower jaw that juts out pugnaciously, and little beady eyes to rival Rob Salterfin's—but hers have a sparkle to them, a casual way of sizing somebody up while acting real friendly-like. She's wearing a suit, longish hair pulled back in a bun and affixed with some kind of device. "Danté, I have been impressed by your work, and I eagerly anticipate your contributions to my imprint's catalog of print, audio, and video." Her accent rings with a bit of the old British, I must say. I'm figuring her for one smart, happenin' gal.

"We've been cutting deals," Frank explains, glancing down at paperwork spread across his desk. "Seems we're talking quite a few more projects than I'd expected. One series alone will be twelve thirty-minute videos over the next three months." One a week, about what we're already crunching for Durbett. Yow. *Ka-ching!*

"My purpose for interrupting your routine this morning," Ollum continues, "is to introduce Bentley Crabtree."

The gnome pumps my hand. As if he'd been assembled from leftover parts, nothing about him is symmetrical, one eye higher than the other, a big ear that sticks out while the smaller one doesn't, teeth that would either terrify or delight an orthodontist—he even stands crooked.

"I am in awe of your news-media work this past week," he says with a thick, precise voice. "I have become a devoted fan. Bravo!" No applause. Just throw money.

"Bentley is a three-time best-selling author," Ollum explains, "currently riding the charts with his *Fat Skeletons: Scandal And Cover-up In The Diet Industry* published by my house."

Bentley quickly adds, "With editorial assistance by the *nec plus ultra*, our pre-eminent Ms. DeForest."

Ignoring the gush, she explains, "He's been working on a book about scandal in the pharmaceutical industry, but it was floundering."

He puts his shoulders up and shows me the palms of his hands like he's been caught short of facts and is ready to confess. "But the machinations done by these purveyors of chemical medicaments—" He speaks like an expressive Frenchman, slowly measuring his words for effect. "They do not arouse concern in a way that creates a best-seller. That is, until I started looking more closely at one category, one compound in particular, as pernicious a catalyst as—"

"He's researching Parzilac violence," Ollum interrupts. Her glance says she understands I'm busy today, and that she's intruded. My glance thanks her; then I toss in some raised eyebrows to show my intrigue.

"Yes, Parzilac and Parzilac violence," Bentley Crabtree confirms. "This is the juncture at which my subject impacts many readers, rousing suspicion and alarm. My research had focused extensively on the process by which the drug was developed, the horrific methods M-Slovak used to skirt safeguards and circumvent the test-trial procedures, the political manipulations that secured FDA approval in an expeditious yet incautious rush to market."

"He doesn't have much yet on violence, which I think is the more sellable half of the book," Ollum explains. "Your recent exposés have created such a profound interest in the subject, I'd like to get something on the shelves as fast as I can, certainly before the inevitable competition. You already have a lot of information, including anecdotal victim stories I regard as highly impactful, so I rang up Frank and convinced him to admit you have already compiled considerably more research on the subject."

"Les likes the idea," Frank says to me, referring to Briggs's PR dude Les Casapell. He's letting me know there's a green light to help our gnome create one more high-profile outlet for burying Parzilac, for tossing it out with yesterday's biscuits, so to speak.

"You got a half a book's worth?" I ask Crabtree.

He smiles, bowing his head slightly. "M-Slovak pioneered the shift toward subcontracted clinical testing—a critical step in determining safety and effectiveness, particularly for achieving FDA approval—a step previously under the purview of in-house laboratories. I have several alarming case studies, several catastrophic failures, evidence of altered data and deleted files, interviews with two former employees, and a fairly thorough compendium of the litigation saga which led the corporation to offer indemnity for prescribers."

"I propose fifty/fifty," Ollum says, right to the point, another pea from Frank's kind of pod.

"How does the money work?" I ask.

That earns me a complicated explanation that, frankly, sounds like blah blah *cash advance* blah blah blah blah.

"Agreed," I say.

Everybody lets out a breath. "I'll call Bentley's agent and handle your representation contract for you," Frank offers.

Crabtree is pulling several tomes from his bookbag, copies of his *Fat Skeletons*, autographing them for Frank and me with a flourish of self-importance. I hope if I ever act that way, Frank would hold a pillow over my face until long after I've quit squirming.

"I like this new emphasis," Crabtree pronounces, "though I regret limiting my focus to M-Slovak's shenanigans for now. Later this week I expect to witness one of the most nefarious political schemes ever perpetrated to obtain FDA approval. It would have made an interesting chapter."

"Whose scheme?" I ask. "For what?"

"Briggs Pharmaceutical. Friday's the big vote on their Fantasy Patch."

CHAPTER 15

Sound the trumpets! Hail! The triumphant knight-errant returns!

I and my trusty squire sally forth to the Kingdom of Kehoe, in the Land of Lundy, domain of Dragon Dib, where dwells Sam, his evil troll. We shall consort with Fair Maiden Meg, princess of print, merchant of media, damsel of the mystic airwaves.

"It's gonna feel weird walking in there as a client," portends my sage squire, Sir Rupert of the clan Allup, newly consecrated to the Kingdom of Dellman/Roenik, where majestic battlements overlook the Wooterlands, the potion-blooms of Briggs Meadow, the rippling azure of Loch Sizemore, a realm where the learned scholars of the wizened Faritzka peoples share wisdom of the ages.

"Yeah, weird," I agree.

"Make sure you use my title," beseeches my faithful servant with barely concealed modesty. *Malus pudor*, young Rupert.

"Ah yes, from scullery boy you've risen to king's governor, minister of all matters important."

"Huh?"

"Chased away as a serf, you return with a barony," I explain.

"A what?"

"Fired from your flunkie job, you get to come back as a boss-man."

"Cool, huh?"

We're almost to Elmhurst, traversing the moors surrounding Castle Kehoe, when my cell-phone rings.

"Danté!" Ah, my inveterate intelligencer, the Earl of Jankety. "Nobody followed you. But there's a recording you should hear before you go in."

We rendezvous at a dispensary of fossil fuels, dismounting to stand beside Cadillac, my faithful steed.

"Go ahead," Jankety tells his phone, pressing a button to activate speaker-mode, dialing the volume low.

"Aller-Tats," we hear Dib Wardley saying. It's kind of scratchy.

"He was driving," Jankety explains. "Calling Sam Cox at the office."

"Good, we can set them up, sabotage the account," Cox answers.

"No, this is a double-edged sword. That meddlesome know-it-all Ferman brought it in, which means he's watching how we perform, which means Frank has some kind of alliance with him. No, we better let this play straight."

"Crap," Sam blurts. He wasn't describing his creative efforts, either—though he could have been.

"He must know Danté, too, because he wants info on some of Danté's work, wants to see everything he'd done for Wooter, plus wants a run-down on the whole Wooter-creative history."

"Why Wooter? You think he's considering bringing Danté back to handle that?"

"Naw. I doubt it, but— No, I can't see Danté coming back here."

"How about if I put Danté's name on the crap and the rejects, make it look like he was moved over to Frank's group because he couldn't cut it here?"

"Yes! Good. I need to make Ferman wary of both of them."

"Can't you find out what they're up to? What about the bug?"

"It's still in their damn conference room. Ellmata's getting only one or two conversations a day, nothing we can use so far."

"We need to get another bug into Frank's office."

"He's working on it."

They start talking about somebody requesting some vacation days or some-such, so Jankety cuts it off. "Take me in with you," he says. "I'm not dressed to be an account guy, so call me one of those TV people—"

"A PA—production assistant," Rupert supplies.

"Yeah, a PA, here to meet whoever I'll be bringing TV commercials to."

He rummages through the piles in my trunk and settles on a tote full of videos, plus my satchel, which he stuffs with some extra cable, adapters, odds and ends. We mount up and sally forth to the castle.

"Danté! Rupert!" Lorette the receptionist leans across the counter to hug us. "Darla said send you straight up to Mr. Wardley's office. He wants to welcome you as—" She smiles and wags her brows suggestively. "—As Kehoe/Lundy's newest and *valued* clients." She's enjoying this.

Darla's a bit more formal but no less enthusiastic welcoming us. She buzzes Wardley, then leads us straight in.

"Danté! Rupert!" He's glad to see us, thrilled to meet Jankety, oh what a glorious day. "I know you've got a lot to do downstairs, but I just wanted to say how proud I am that you guys are doing so great—ever since New York made us, you know, *downsize*." It's a swear-word.

"This is our family here," I gush. "That's why we're bringing new business, working together, charting our mutual success, questing for the holy billable grail. Besides, we Chicago-huggers gotta stick together."

"Ain't it so, ain't it so."

We're all still standing, Jankety awkwardly shifting his packages around. Then our ersatz PA loses control and spills the satchel, mumbling apologies, setting the video tote on Dib's desk and gathering up his miscellany.

"We need to get down and see Meg," I beg off.

Dib walks us through his reception area, out into the corridor. "You guys need *anything*, you just let me know."

Meg is waiting for us. She takes us to her office for an emotional howdy-do, a group of her people milling around, anticipating our meeting. Meg is, well, Meg. She's skinny as bamboo, slightly stooped—probably from too many teen years trying not to stand head and shoulders above the boys—with a beak nose that would stick out farther than her breasts—if she had any to speak of. Mousy brown hair, plain features—she made the perfect witch at that Halloween party Darla threw last year. But what shines about Meg is her heart, pure gold, a woman with too many cats and dogs because every stray deserves her love. She's a ruthless negotiator who'll scrape every dime off a media package, get free overnights thrown in, then send homemade brownies with the contract. She's past forty now, never married—not even close I think. "I have my babies," she once told Kristen, referring to her animals. The two of them hugged after that; I never heard the rest of the conversation.

Meg's eyes light up as she lets me shake her hand, lifting mine almost to her heart. Next, she shakes Rupert's, and actually pets his head. Introduced to Jankety, she shakes but doesn't pet—though I suspect she quickly inspected him for fleas. New dog and all.

We file into the meeting room where Frank and Rupert's Aller-Tat roll-out plans are spread around the table. We all take seats, then zip through every detail over the next thirty minutes, never stopping for air, taking no prisoners. Meg's on a quest, for the glory of this brave knight come home again to bosom and hearth, and neither hemlock nor sword will deter her crusade.

"To recap," she says, "we've already put feelers out on more than half of this, we have verbals on three magazines which we need approved by tomorrow, we all agree on the time/action plan I've assembled, and Mr. Allup—Rupert—will have signatory authority on behalf of your agency and clients. Our most pressing need is final 'stats for the magazines—by?"

"Friday," I start to promise. "Oh, we still need disclaimers warning people about anaphylactic shock to be boxed at the bottoms."

Rupert's already on it. "I've been pushing Les," he offers. "He says legal researches the hell out of those, so he's predicting next Monday or Tuesday."

Meg says, "The magazine standards-and-practices people will want to see at least a mock-up before they'll lock up the space."

"If we don't have it by Friday," I suggest, "let's just box generic language that says here's where we'll warn buyers their kids might go into shock and die from using this product, then when we have the approved language, we'll cut it in, make new 'stats, have Rupert sign off before they're sent, and we should have no trouble meeting your deadlines."

We wrap up on a cheerful, excited note, the king's regiment ready to launch concept-laden siege engines at an unwary public. In the moment Meg hurries over to fetch copies for us, Jankety whispers, "You trust her—she a friend?"

"Oh yes."

Meg hugs me, shakes Rupert's hand while petting his head, then accepts Jankety into her brood with a shake and a pet, too.

Jankety looks around like he's confused. "I think I left my satchel in your office," he apologizes, hurrying to fetch it before anybody can react, returning with his parcel and looking sheepish by the time Meg finishes hugging me again. She pets *my* head this time.

My tail is wagging.

The buyers crowd around to cheer us off again, the royal cortege following us into the corridor. And me without my suit of armor.

Through the drawbridge and over the moat, we get out to the cars, Rupert remarking how well that went.

"Good people," Jankety agrees, nodding his approval.

"You planted a bug when you went back to her office, didn't you?" I accuse. For some reason, I'm feeling uneasy about the idea.

Jankety is indignant. "I did *not*. I *retrieved* the one I'd planted the first time we were in there."

Rupert's surprised. "You managed to bug her just in that few seconds—in front of everyone?"

Jankety just smiles.

"Why retrieve it?" I ask.

He looks at me like I don't understand. "We *never* spy on friends."

*   *   *

Time to hit the ground running.

People are running all directions, projects piling up. Danté the creative director is in the building, here to answer this, explain that, feedback, suggestions, brainstorming, vetoes and approvals.

Hal Neusome is running, the day before his next big *Newsline* gig. "Word's leaked about Parzilac and Pollikey," he gripes. "Jody's neighbors have been interviewed, some mentioning she blames the drug."

"Then you have to address it tomorrow night instead of revealing it Sunday," I point out.

"Nobody knows that he was part of the pre-approval trials, though. If we can get her to shut up about it, I could get by with just repeating what everybody else has and still save my bombshell for Sunday. Too much Parzilac talk could mess up Cyn's lawsuit surprise, too."

"Jody Pollikey won't care that I'm helping Briggs orchestrate a Parzilac slam in time to launch Fantasy Patch, and she's not going to lose sleep over your reinvigorated news career. She wants her son's name cleared, the blame laid where it belongs. If her lawyer tells her she's tipping off the culprits and giving them a chance to spin before Cyn's ready to expose them, that ought to shut her up."

"You get her to do that—*now*—and I'll downplay the issue as still waiting for toxicology reports from the police."

Run run run. A stack of invoices—Frank is running through them, Melissa trudging, the accounting guy wading.

Kristen is running—running anti-merger edits, helping Hal run his *Newsline* edits.

The Hale-Bopp Graphics people run in and out with a stack of renderings for me to review and approve.

Murray's Sizemore writer runs me through his outlines and drafts, everything coming along fine, lots of fun. Turns out the simulator guy is shipping one of the machines here later today so the writers and production people have a chance to feel the experience.

I run into Tony Faritzka, who mentions that his Briggs work has expanded substantially, things going great, we might want to think about adding a fourth edit suite in the near future. Frank's ears are probably burning.

I run through the drafts of Durbett's Weisman Company scripts.

"I wouldn't mind helping your book project," Murray offers, "if you want. It might be a good experience for me; plus it's a subject that cuts close to home." He still feels guilty about writing much of the M-Slovak Parzilac roll-out.

"I was counting on it," I tell him, relieved actually. Sure, I worry about this venture failing, but how could it? Look at who we have. If we lose all our clients, we'll find more. If we get too much work, we'll get help. Ms. Moeroff talks about art, but consider the artistry in assembling a primo team—an ensemble like a dance troupe—one that's in perfect sync, each bringing what's needed to the mix, an assemblage that functions smoothly, makes adjustments, self-repairs, turns out great product and feels good about it. What a contrast with Cyn's situation, all back-stabbing and mistrust, people helping each other only to the extent of their own self-interest. I'm sure not all law firms are like that—some are probably like our little group here—but it's hard for me to understand Cyn busting her hump and putting so much of her personal life on hold for something that doesn't seem very fun, where you can't trust your own teammates, where every step forward requires watching your back.

Which reminds me to call my *habeas girlus*.

"Yes, I'm already on it," she assures me. "I told her not to mention Parzilac to *anybody* anymore, and act stupid if somebody brings it up."

"Is she holding up okay?"

"Yes. No. I don't know. She seems to be, though she started crying on the phone. I had to agree to come out and sit with her for a while tonight. What a pain in the butt."

"Cyn, you're the one pillar of strength she's got right now, not only helping clear her son's name, but the one keeping the media away, arranging funeral and burial—you're all she's got."

"Isn't it great? Talk about having a client in your pocket—"

"I don't mean client—I mean a *person* who's distraught, who lost her only child, somebody who needs a friend—"

"She's *got* friends—the kind who cook yucky casseroles, from what I can tell. I'm her lawyer."

"If I can free up in time, I'll try to go out there with you tonight."

"Good. Maybe you can keep her occupied while I get some work done."

Sigh.

They say ambulance drivers get to where they can scrape mangled people off the pavement and keep their feelings separate. The same must be true for ambulance chasers.

Reception dude buzzes me that the drugstore son is on the phone. "He sounds drunk."

We greet solemnly. He's slurring his words. "Are you at the funeral home?" I ask him. His father's funeral is tomorrow. We're planning to collect a few shots for Hal.

"Naw, screw it. I'll go in a while. He ain't going anywhere."

"But your mom—"

"Listen. You wanna know what the real—what the *real* fuggin' deal is? You wanna put it on the news?"

"You mean what happened with the robbery? The—"

"All of it. *All* of it, dammit. I gotta go to the funeral home now, but you bring your camera to my house at five—no, six o'clock. How much can I get paid—how much money for a story like this?"

"Like what? What do you—" *Click.*

I go to my office and retrieve Durbett's secret-agent phone. I press the red button. "Hello?" I ask when it clicks.

"Danté Roenik?" It's an unfamiliar man's voice.

"Um, yeah. Is Flynn Durbett around?"

"Not available. Is this an emergency?"

"No."

"Something somebody else can help you with?"

"Jankety?"

"Not available. Anybody else?"

"Uh, probably not."

"Flynn will be available between six and seven. Would you like him to call you?"

Hmm . . . I might be shooting then. "No, but will you let him know I'll call him around that time?"

"Definitely before eight?"

"Yes."

"Okay. If there's no communication by eight, he'll contact you." This guy takes appointments seriously. Give *him* my lost planner.

Do I call Lieutenant Detective Heath Culler? Durbett says you should know what you have before you decide if you want to give it to police, or how and when you turn it over. No, I better see what our drunken, grieving son has to say first. Besides, he might clam up if I show up with a cop. He called *me*.

Byron and I agree it would be smart to show up at 5:30, maybe catch him off guard, at least be ready if he doesn't arrive until six. I change into casual on-the-road clothes and shoes, which still leaves me running with twenty minutes to spare. I don't feel like working, and I can't get hold of Cyn, so I wander around, but everybody's too busy to bother.

"Grrrrrr!" It's Taj.

Ah, just enough time to hang out with the young'ns. Taj puts in a *Monster Bin* video, so I pull up a bean bag to share with the lad. The other kids gather round, and we all giggle, then laugh, then growl until we've managed to pretty well spray enough spittle to spread even the most reluctant virus.

Taj settles down and finally sits still, and it's nice for me to quit running—if only for a few minutes.

What a great kid. Melissa's so lucky.

I wonder if Jody Pollikey used to watch cartoons with her chubby little boy.

*   *   *

That's the van!

We're being followed, Hal and Byron and I in our production truck, heading out to interview the drugstore son.

I'm sure it's the van that followed me the other night. It's imprinted on me, like the big fake-eye spot on the tail of a fish, the odor of a doctor's office, the sound of a dentist's drill, the flashing lights of a traffic cop, the letters *IRS*. We're pulling into the driveway of our target house, also on a cul-de-sac like his mother's. Front and side doors are closed up, curtains drawn, no sign of life.

"Keep going," I tell Byron, watching the side-view mirror. He circles and takes us back out. "There." I point down the long crossroad. The van's stopped one intersection up. I'm fumbling in my bag for the special camera Jankety gave me. "Drive around; see if you can lose them."

"Wouldn't you rather try to get behind 'em?" he asks.

"Hell no, they could be after us, or me."

I can hear the *click-click* of Hal unpacking the video camera. "You realize we're the prime target," he says. "The reporter, the shooter, the producer/director—the ones setting up M-Slovak for a major fall."

No sign of the van. We sit for a minute at a cross street.

"How sure are you?" Byron asks. "It could've been just any van—"

"There it is!" Two blocks down, it just went through the intersection.

"Move—he saw us!" Hal says urgently.

We turn right, head down a few streets, turn right again, then circle back. No van.

"You're right," Byron says. "No logic to his route. He's driving around, maybe following us or looking for us."

I want to say let's get out of here, but I'm riding with a guy who'd shoot his own demise and a news hound who's caught the scent. "Okay, they're not going to ambush us in a neighborhood like this; let's try to rush up behind them so I can shoot their license plate."

"Or get a side shot, show the occupants," Hal adds.

"But a camera in the face would prove we've blown their cover. They might react violently."

"Or a camera might *stop* 'em from reacting," Byron counters.

We drive around, but don't see anything. We're over by the mom's house now. No van.

A blue car. A van—but not the same one. I'm getting jumpy. Still driving around.

"He's gone," I say with some relief. "We spooked him. Now we're late. Let's go do this interview and get out of here."

No van. We drive back to the cul-de-sac— There it is! Coming at us, it flees the cul-de-sac and nearly runs us off the road. Around the corner, it speeds away at five times the limit. I fumble with the camera, but can't get a shot in time.

We turn around fast and try to follow, but it's long gone.

We head back to the house and pull into the drive. The side door is slightly open, but there's no other sign of anybody home. Hal and I get out, then look at each other and at the door. Byron's setting up the hand-held camera. We all stand there until he's ready. Still no movement, no sound. The camera's running now, catching a shot of Hal at the door, peering inside.

"Hello?" he calls.

Nothing.

"Maybe we should call the police," I suggest—like these two would take me seriously.

"Could be somebody in jeopardy," Hal remarks, his head now in the door. He knows the official rationale for unauthorized entry. He's inside, two steps up into the kitchen, Byron right behind him. I'm watching the street, expecting a van laden with machine-gun-toting gangsters to cut me down.

Hal's in the kitchen now. I follow, noticing the mess, a broken gin bottle on the floor against the wall.

"Hello!" Hal calls. "Anybody here?"

A sound—I think. A scraping, dull sound. They heard it, too. There's a phone right there. "Nine-one-one," I say.

"Don't know what to tell them yet," Hal whispers. "Need to investigate."

"Anybody here?!" he shouts, loudest yet.

Another sound, down the hall, I think. We all look at each other.

"It's Hal Neusome!" he tells the noise.

Nothing.

Hal takes a tentative step, listening, another, another.

Thunk. It wasn't loud, but it was definitely a sound from the last room down the hall.

A few more steps, now we're to the door, Hal in front, Byron far enough back to frame the shot, me right behind him.

"What about the rest of the house?" I whisper. Suddenly, it feels like they're all around us, and now we're trapped in the hallway, a box canyon with no escape.

"Urr-rrg," comes the sound, definitely a person or animal.

"Hello?" Hal says quietly. "We're coming in now."

He waits. No hail of gunfire.

Waits.

Hal touches the door, pushes tentatively, a few inches.

A few more.

The hinges squeal a low moan. It's a bedroom, messy, unkempt, with nobody in sight.

"Hello?"

A scrape, behind the bed. Hal stretches to see, but has to step a little closer.

Closer—

It moves! A bloody hand grabs the edge of the bed—then it disappears.

"Oh damn!" Hal shouts. He's around the bed now. "Call an ambulance!"

It's the drugstore son, crumpled in a pool of blood, his head and face crimson. Hal's down beside him, trying to see, not sure how to help. Byron's on the shot. I grab the phone on the nightstand and dial 9-2-2, have to try it again. 9-1-1.

"Urr-rrg," he says, blood dribbling from his mouth. There's a pistol on the floor next to him. Hal gently cradles his head, revealing a bleeding hole several inches above his ear.

"Wanna tell," the man gurgles. He's shaking now, twitching, squeezing his eyes open and closed. "Tell—"

"Did you try to kill yourself?" Hal demands.

He twitches and reaches for his head, then looks blankly at Hal and shivers violently. "Couldn't—any—more—" He's panting now.

"Couldn't what?"

"Couldn't—"

"Help is on the way," Hal reassures him. "You'll be okay."

"No!" he says, shaking his head from side to side, gurgling and wincing from the pain. "No! Had to—had to—"

"Had to what?" Hal prompts.

"Stop— Stop—"

Blood is dripping from his chin. I feel queasy, dizzy. Byron's steady as a rock, kneeling closer, still on the shot.

"Stop what?" Hal prompts.

"Stop—stop M-Slovak. M-Slo—"

"Stop 'em from what?" Hal demands.

But his head lolls, and his body shakes again. He claws at his head, crying out in pain.

"Hold on," Hal breathes. "Hold on." A siren is drawing close.

"My fault," he says, calm for an instant, then twitching again.

"Did you do this?"

He gurgles and says something, stiffens, then stops breathing. A vehicle pulls into the driveway, lots of noise—

"Here!" I shout. "In here! Hurry!"

Med techs rush into the house, into the room, and shoo us out of the way.

"Change disks, Byron," I tell him. "Need to dub fast."

He loads another one and continues to shoot from the hallway, then from the living room when he's hustled out by two policemen.

I rush out to the production truck and pop in the disk, a blank in another machine, and start laying off a dub to keep. I don't want to lose our original, but the police will need the evidence.

Oh damn, it looks even more real on the screen than it did from across the room—bright color, so much blood, the raspy sounds of his breath, the convulsions a counterpoint to Byron's steady frame.

A man dying in front of our camera.

We can't broadcast that, but with editing, we can show enough to tell this story, to capture this moment of tragedy.

His last words. What did he say? I re-cue the master and turn it up.

He convulses, blood spilling from his mouth, a gurgle . . .

"Par—Parzilac."

CHAPTER 16

I'm still feeling queasy.

Durbett shows up about the same time as Detective Culler. They talk to me briefly, stick their heads into the van, and watch the dub I made. I present the original disk, good citizen I am.

"We need to leave soon," I warn them. "We can't stick around for questioning; we have video to transmit."

Byron's shooting some of the action from outside. There's another crew here, WBMF News 9, a hand-held camera, no transmission truck, probably already in the area and heard the call on a scanner. They won't get much, and there won't be any good quotes tonight, so a shot of them bringing the body out is about all that's left to see.

"A suicide, is my way of thinking," Culler pronounces.

Durbett nods. "Dying murder victims usually want to say who did it. Suicides usually want to explain, leave a message, give instructions—or apologize. The gun's there next to his hand; killers ain't likely to leave the weapon."

"Suicide," Culler agrees, "unless it was a murder made to look like one."

"Wasn't more than a few minutes," Durbett points out.

"Maybe five or six," I say, "between us pulling in the first time and coming back to fnd the van leaving."

"You didn't actually see the van at the house?" Culler asks.

"No, just rushing out from the street."

"Might not be connected to the death," Durbett says, "since he was the one following you around. Maybe he got down that street, realized it was a dead end, before you could trap him."

"That's my way of thinking," Culler agrees, stretching his misshapen back.

"The best evidence is inside," Durbett decides. "Techs'll look close. Still, I wanna see the scene while it's hot."

Culler thanks me for the disk. Durbett says he'll be in touch later. They both head inside. Hal's doing a stand-up in front of the house now, recounting the events, parroting the suicide/murder observations he'd just heard us discuss. We wrap, pack, and leave for the studio—driving like Frank.

"I didn't mention the van in my stand-up," Neusome points out. "I don't think it's related, and I don't want to draw attention to it until we can nail whoever's following you. Don't want to spook them."

"Like hell we don't. I'm tired of being bait. Spook 'em right out of Chicago, far as I'm concerned."

The phone Durbett gave me rings. "Hello?"

It's him. "You're not going to broadcast what the victim said about M-Slovak right away, are you?"

"No. The bloody hand, shots of the scene, maybe a few words, but I'd rather save M-Slovak for Sunday's show. We won't let New York have the portion where he spoke."

"Give it at least a day or two," he suggests. "If M-Slovak did the wet-work—had it done, I mean—it's a bigger story than just Parzilac. If it was a suicide, he had something to hide and was ready to tell you till he changed his mind—or had it changed for him. Get your facts straight before you run off half-cocked."

Good advice. Whole-cocked is the only way I like to run.

We hit the studio running and do the news fandango in conjunction with New York. This one's not big enough to do break-ins nationwide, but it'll be lead story on most affiliates at eleven. The NBS news director is very impressed. Hal plays it like all his extensive investigative work is what's keeping him and a camera close to the action. He stresses there's a van after *us* and hints he's in great personal danger as he toils tirelessly to bring NBS the big stories.

"I want two segments out of you tomorrow night," the director tells him. "Update us on the drugstore saga, now with a suicide or possible murder, and the other one an in-depth look at the Wicker Park tragedy."

"I'll give you plenty to work with."

He's satisfied, hurrying off to coordinate the video feed.

I call Cyn's cell phone and catch her leaving Pollikey's. "Gawd," she says, "I'm glad to be out of there."

"How's she holding up?"

"She's a wreck. She's mostly telling insufferably boring stories about Gordie growing up, a stack of photo albums punctuating her little multimedia trips down memory lane."

"You think you helped her feel better?"

"I made her feel confident I'd expose Parzilac, clear her son's name, and get her a wad of cash so she can mope in Maui. I don't want her cried out before a jury gets to see some of it."

"Doesn't it bother you—I mean, what she's been through? I can't hardly stand to watch the video of her—"

"Danté, you get too close. I don't know this woman, didn't know Gordie. I'm her lawyer, not her friend. I'll just put on a good show for the jury."

"Yeah, I guess you're right. Like a surgeon who can't let the sight of blood get to him."

"He can't if he's going to be an effective surgeon."

I still feel queasy.

*   *   *

It's a beautiful, sunny day with birds gliding high in blue sky, frogs croaking in the distance, hungry bass rippling the cool, indigo water. The Briggs Marketing VP, silver-haired Doug Moore, and I strap in for a leisurely ride in the Sizemore *Wave-Slicer*. Little does he suspect.

We've lost the suit jackets, rolled up our sleeves, tatooed our arms with flaming skulls—apparently neither of us allergic to various synthetic and natural substances—and concluded we're just two happenin' dudes. When the blowers come on and muss his silver hair, he's going to look like the VP from hell.

"You now have samples of three classes of antigens in twelve of your tattoo designs," he tells me. "I'll have the rest Monday, mass production to begin by middle of the week." He greets the pilot stepping aboard, but gets only a smile.

"What's this about testing the legal disclaimer?"

"We have four drafts from legal we're running by focus groups." They're actually market-testing the fine print! "One stresses the one-in-seven-thousand odds, lists signs of shock, and recommends immediate medical assistance like injection of epinephrine."

"That'll scare people off."

He nods agreement. "But it's the one they say covers our liability best. The second one recommends it only be used under supervision of a physician. That way, if they choose to do it themselves, at least they were warned. The third lists detailed symptoms of shock to watch for and says seek medical assistance immediately."

"That's not bad. Accurate, helpful info. Not giving the odds might sound like it's a frequent problem, though."

"That's why I like number four, and think that one will test the least aversive: a warning this shouldn't be used by anybody who's previously ex-per-ienced extreme allergic reactions—the shock. Then it says experiencing the following symptoms requires immediate medical intervention, and for use *only* under adult supervision."

"Yes! Make it sound like it doesn't apply to whoever's reading it, but still give the info just in case."

Moore grins, his silver hair now dancing in the wind. He's impressed by the realism of our little boat excursion. "That bastard Casapell doesn't like any of them. He wants fine print too small to read, written in medicalese nobody can understand. I have nothing against packaging the warning in a consumer-palatable way, but they do need to be warned—not just to avoid liability and satisfy the FDA, but because it's our responsibility to safeguard the users of our products."

"You're not a fan of Les's, huh?"

"Whoa!" Moore's hanging on as the *Wave-Slicer* picks up speed and does a few maneuvers. "I was being groomed to succeed Rex when he steps down next year, but I think Les is getting the nod now."

"Doesn't Rex own the company?"

"Well, it's privately held, but there are hundreds of shareholders, mostly senior employees, with a board of directors, Rex as both chair and CEO."

"How did Les get ahead of you?"

"I really don't know—"

That's when all hell breaks loose! An explosion on the far shore, a man running toward us, waving his arms frantically—

"He needs help!" the pilot shouts.

Pfoom! Pfoom!

Moore is loving it. We leap from the cove, zig-zagging, pressed into our seats.

By the time we pull up to the pier and that mysterious door opens, Moore is out of breath. We climb out and stand there grinning.

"That's something else. Now we need to figure out how you can simulate a drug experience." Fire up the virtual hookah.

We head toward my office, stopping to shake hands with Frank, then meet Melissa and Taj.

"I was wondering about testing my son," Melissa says earnestly. "He's got asthma, and so far *nobody* can tell me what causes it."

"All the kids want to try them," Frank interjects, "and the parents want to see how they work."

Rupert scampers off to round up everybody while we go sit in the kid room, Moore admiring our little day-care fantasyland.

"Selling the allergy tests directly to consumers fits right into your philosophy, eh?" I ask him.

"Well, actually, I had pushed for creating a consumer *demand*, but I thought it should be left with the doctors to apply. We'd sell lower numbers, but charge more and tap into insurance revenues. I was spooked about the potential for anaphylactic shock. We'd been debating OTC marketing for six months, with Les wanting to go the way you suggested."

"No wonder they jumped on board so fast."

"What made the difference," Moore says, "was the way you wowed 'em with the tattoo idea, and how fast you saw the angle. You were the right guy to do it; plus, advocating the direction Les and finally Rex wanted to go anyway landed you front and center. Politically, it knocked me down a notch and elevated Les one, putting you between us."

"Give us time; we'll fix that," Frank promises. He knows exactly what Moore's talking about. Good thing one of us does.

The crowd is assembled now, so I make my own advisory speech. "Anybody who's ever had any kind of severe allergic reaction to anything should *not* try these tattoos. There's a one-in-seven-thousand chance using one will cause shock for which we'd need to rush to the hospital and get a shot of epinephrine. We try only one each day to give it plenty of time to work."

Two parents are hesitant, but the kids whine and convince them to let them try. Upward pressure, from the consumer to the buyer, that's the kid market. You gotta love it.

"Okay, so far we have three categories," I explain, listing the groupings for them.

"Since Taj has asthma," Melissa volunteers, "he should try the inhalants one—bacteria, molds, pollens, and dust."

It seems somehow fitting that Taj gets a little monster with big fangs. Melissa puts it on his arm. We all hold our breaths . . .

Watching . . .

But there's nothing, no shock, no reaction. Taj beams with pride, showing his arm to the little golden-haired girl.

"Wear it all day and see if a little red welt forms under one of the colors," I explain.

"Me now!"

"Me next!"

The kids are lined up. By the time everybody's wearing one—with Taj's little girlfriend sporting Ms. Moeroff's ballerina—we've had only one reaction. One of the older boys gets a welt from the plant-resins tropical-fish tattoo.

"Excellent," declares his mother, our CG operator. "We already knew about this, but look how easy the Aller-Tat made it to find out."

Everybody's impressed, Moore grinning, Frank's head bobbing. Rupert's putting a wizard on his own arm.

Melissa's off to the side sitting on a beanbag with Taj in her lap, watching his tattoo for *any* signs of reaction. She's distracted, maybe disappointed. This is good news, but it doesn't solve the problem. She needs answers, and after the tattoo had looked like a good way to get them, she's back to square one.

Taj just likes the monster.

"Good work, Danté," Moore congratulates me. "This'll be a major hit."

"Just remember us," I admonish, "when Frank helps maneuver you into taking over for Rex next year."

Moore shoots us a sneaky look, pretending to peer around for eavesdroppers. "You guys pull that off, I'll make sure you get *all* the Briggs accounts."

*   *   *

Best-selling author Bentley Crabtree lives in a nice, older home set back from the road. He leads me into his work area, a large den stacked with books and papers, filing cabinets shoved into corners, a hundred framed book reviews nailed to every inch of woodgrain-paneled wall.

"First," I start, setting my own stack on the table, "before we talk Parzilac, I'm curious what you meant about tomorrow's Fantasy Patch approval being a scheme."

"Oh, nothing illegal—just sneaky. Frankly, you have to admire the finesse. I've been following Fantasy Patch for three years now, ever since my mole who used to work for Briggs started feeding me information."

"He's not there anymore?"

"She works for a big lab in France now. A lot of those jobs are going overseas. Anyway, there are two ways Briggs managed to get this far without, in my opinion, enough safeguards to protect the public. One trend in the industry this past decade has been to subcontract clinical trials to independent testing firms."

"These are the tests used to show a drug's safe?"

"And effective, too. Safe and effective for whatever the drugmaker claims. Of course, once it's approved, there's nothing illegal about drug companies pushing doctors to prescribe for off-label use."

"You mean other uses it wasn't tested for?"

"Yes, or other classes of patient. For example, Parzilac was approved for treatment of severe depression, but M-Slovak pushes it even for people who just feel a little blue sometimes, and for other problems like attention-deficit disorder, panic attacks, you name it."

"What do you mean by other classes?"

"The biggest one is children. Parzilac is prescribed for more than a hundred-thousand children a year, but it still has never been tested on minors through clinical trials, data collected and presented, nor has the new class been approved by the FDA. In fact, one ploy is to wait until a patent is ready to expire, then apply for an extension so it can be tested on children after the fact."

"Wow."

"Until recently, the drug companies did all their own clinical trials. Oh, they might contract for recruitment, use locals for administration, spiff doctors and universities and hospitals who place large orders by letting them have a piece of it, but it was still under the control and supervision of the drug company. The credibility and integrity of the results had the whole company behind them, with the vulnerability that a lawsuit uncovering fraud could put them out of business."

"But using small independents makes the paper trail more complex," I venture, "and as long as the drug company doesn't officially know about shenanigans, they're safe from liability."

"And the small independent, which isn't worth much in assets, can close up shop or liquidate. Nothing stops those people from opening again under a new name the very next day."

"And that's how the Fantasy Patch testing was done?"

The little gnome grins. "It was a work of art. I've been trying to track it for three years now, and I still get surprised every time Briggs presents data to the FDA. It's always better and better results."

"Is there something *wrong* with Fantasy Patch?"

He shrugs. "Some experts have concerns, but I'm not one to judge. I'm just highly suspicious about numbers being cooked, unfavorable data never being presented, positives skewed more than they deserve—like your Parzilac girl who committed suicide at the last minute. You didn't present nineteen cases, eighteen successes and one failure. Your sample group simply shrunk by one, eighteen total, all good results, as if that girl never existed."

He's done good research if he knows about that. "So what's so nefarious about the approval process?"

"Briggs first applied more than a year ago, and the patch was denied due to inadequate testing. The director of the FDA unit recommended formation of a special scientific advisory committee to look into some of the issues raised. But that never happened, and those issues were never included in the reference info staffers assembled for the standing advisory committee. Smells a bit crooked, but I can't prove that."

"And it might have just been sloppy work."

"You're right. We *are* talking about the feds, often both corrupt *and* sloppy. Could go either way, but I have my own bias. Anyway, they met and voted for approval again, the question being: Is the drug administered through this patch safe? It lost, nine to four. After the meeting, when most had left, the director asked the few remaining if they would have voted for approval had they considered effectiveness, too—a ratio of risk versus benefit. There was sentiment that slight risk might be outweighed by the incredible results Briggs was presenting, especially for controlling violent impulses and suicide-level depression."

"Nothing in this world is entirely safe," I point out.

"But when you know the dangers, you should make every effort to make it as safe as possible."

"Fair enough."

"So they've scheduled another vote—and here's where it gets slick—to happen on the same day that many of the committee members will be high-paid presenters at the annual Neuroscience Association symposium in Seattle, *sponsored by Briggs Pharmaceutical.* I didn't expect it to come up again until next month."

"Now it's tomorrow."

"And I'm predicting the voted question this time will be benefit versus risk, and it'll pass six-to-four or six-to-five. Then Briggs will push it for every off-label scenario they can cook up, well beyond the ones approved."

"What were the issues? What made some of these advisors think it might be unsafe?"

"It's kind of obvious when you think about it. If you have a patient trying to learn to control his violent urges, you slap a patch on him and he takes charge of himself. It gets easier, he calms down, he's a new man. *Voila!* Success! But what about the guy who *wants* to kill his boss, but maybe doesn't have the nerve? Maybe the only thing stopping him is fear."

"But if you can *imagine* your boss dead, even if you'd never had the balls to do it—"

"Just slap on a Fantasy Patch."

*   *   *

By the time I leave Crabtree's, it's pouring rain. Bring your surfboards.

I'm on my way to meet Hal and Byron at the drugstore son's house. Durbett called to say it looks like somebody might have run through the back yard and jumped the fence, escaping along a drainage ditch that runs under the next street. Byron's supposed to be getting shots of that, but this driving rain is a problem.

I find them on the next street over, shooting out the truck window, up the ditch toward the back of the guy's house. I have to park in a giant puddle, so I change into my running shoes before I trot across and climb in with my shooter and reporter.

"Flynn's in the house with Culler now," Hal says. "He almost got us inside for more shots, but Culler vetoed it."

"I heard another guy," Byron adds, "call Durbett *Inspector.*"

Interesting.

"It's probable suicide," Hal summarizes, "but still suspicion of murder—off the record. That won't change before tonight's show unless somebody stumbles in and confesses."

"What about the open door?"

"Flynn said the guy could've opened it himself," Byron explains, "right after we pulled up, so he could see who we were—except by then we were driving off. There was no sign of forced entry."

"Then why suspect murder?"

Hal answers, "Flynn's suspicious about how and where the gun fell. That and the safe in the bedroom closet was open and empty."

Byron's finished with the shot, so Hal drives around to the house.

"He could have emptied it himself," I suggest, "in advance—*if* anything was in it. He *was* planning to reveal *something* to us, and might not have wanted anything incriminating in his house."

"Flynn said that, too" Hal counters. "He also said somebody could've been in there the first time we arrived. Maybe our guy was forced to open his safe at gunpoint. After we drove away, he was shot. Then the killer fled out the back way, jumping the fence and meeting a getaway car."

"Or getaway blue *van*," Byron adds.

Durbett comes out and climbs in with us. "I need to see whatever shoes you all had on in the house," he says. "We got a partial print that had traces of blood on it."

We're all wearing them, so he quickly examines each one. "Looks like a fourth person was in the house," he pronounces, "but I need to take your shoes to be sure."

"A hundred bucks," I demand. These are my new running shoes, good gosh and golly.

Without missing a beat, Durbett counters, "My guy already gave you a new pair just like these." Touché.

"My dress shoes are in the car. I can change."

"I have boots in the back," Byron confirms.

"I have a complete change of clothes at the studio," Hal admits. "If we pull the truck into the loading bay, I can sock it in."

"Good. Lemme have 'em. May be a while before you get 'em back."

Hal asks, "Can you get Culler to make a statement for me to use on the show tonight?"

Durbett sighs, thinking for a moment. "In and out, five minutes," he says. "Just you two," he adds, casting me a glance.

They drape the gear in plastic to run through rain to the house; then Durbett comes back alone. "Let's get your shoes changed," he suggests.

"So it looks like a suicide, but murder's not ruled out," I venture.

"Culler can't tell the truth yet," he says, "and Hal can't report it."

"Report what?"

"This is definitely another murder."

Wow.

When it rains, it pours.

Chapter 17

I feel like Agatha Christie's Inspector Poirot, the portly Belgian investigator and mystery-crime solver. He usually deduces a solution quickly, but then builds the puzzle piece by piece until he has absolute proof before he exposes the perpetrator—or goads the killer into revealing himself.

Hal and I know more about the drugstore son's demise than Flynn Durbett will let us report. At this point, we're not even allowed to call it a murder, though I'm firmly convinced. If Durbett says giraffes are purple, I'll consider it gospel and spread the word. Hal's been on the phone trying to get anybody important at M-Slovak to answer Jody Pollikey's assertion it was pink capsules that made her son kill, and kill himself, but goading the perpetrators into flinging some rhetoric seems highly unlikely.

No comment from the Parzilac purveyors, not for Poirot or anybody.

I guess that's smart public relations for now. Thou shouldst protest not too much, nor even acknowledge heinous accusations. That just makes the story bigger, gets the sound bites picked up on more news outlets, and lends credibility to what truly for now is little more than innuendo.

But fret ye not, Inspector Roenik does have some very volatile footage he's holding back, a big piece in that puzzle he's building. M-Slovak's henchmen may be goaded yet.

Actually, it's good Parzilac's makers are choosing for now to ignore Hal on the record. We didn't want to drop that Parzilac bombshell until Sunday, the big lawsuit show with Cyn, maximum platform for our success-story surprise, the program with Hal's name on it. But it's these off-the-record responses that have me worried: people around me are dropping like mayflies.

The advertising biz normally doesn't involve body counts.

After two hours in the control room assembling stills and other elements, I'm ready for a bathroom break. That's where I find Frank and Taj, the youngster standing on the countertop with his shorts tugged down an inch or two to expose the blotchy rash encircling his waist. Taj is reluctantly clutching a tube of cream, eyeing it warily like it's the evil orb in some fantasy epic.

"I know it stings a little," Frank soothes, "but that stops after a few minutes, right?"

The little one nods reluctantly, his eyes glistening in anticipation of outright tears.

"It'll make it better," Frank reminds him.

Taj reluctantly uncaps his tube, awkwardly squeezing some white goo onto his fingers, then stoically rubbing it around his waist, succeeding in his determination not to cry. He caps it again and adjusts his shorts, then folds himself into Frank's arms, the white-haired dealmaker holding him tightly an extra moment or two before depositing him gently on the floor. Frank breathes a sigh of relief, a mannerism immediately mimicked by Taj. I'm washing my hands now, feeling like I've intruded on something private.

"Show coming together okay?" Frank asks. Back to business.

I assure him we're on schedule, on target, on the dime, on a roll, whatever. "Hey Taj, mega-*cooooool* Aller-tat! *Grrrrrr!*"

He smiles, holding his arm out to inspect the miniature monster, the stinging around his waist now pushed to the back of his thoughts. He points at Frank's arm, tugging at his jacket. Frank rolls his eyes, then takes it off and rolls up his sleeve to show me that he and the little guy have matching monsters. Frank's gone completely over the edge, but I think he likes the view from there.

Detective Culler arrives for his on-cam interview, Flynn Durbett right behind. "I've got myself worried," Culler says. "I'm thinking maybe it looks too much like I'm cooperating with only one news outlet."

"It's the other way around," Hal assuages. "We're the ones who have footage that's helping your investigation. We're going out of our way to make it and our facilities available to assist you."

"Why don't we shoot," I suggest, "as if you're here going through other video looking for anything that might be helpful. Hal's cooperating; we turn on a camera, and capture the discussion you two have as you look at shots. It's not an interview, but more a collaboration, a thinking-out-loud, the audience witnessing the process of deduction and discovery just as it happens. You're not holding press conferences or releasing official statements yet, but after the competition sees this on *Newsline* in a few hours, you will be available and more than happy to answer everybody's questions."

Culler glances at Durbett, who nods his approval. "Good. That's good then. What about the van?" he asks him.

Durbett shakes his head. "I wouldn't mention that yet. You got nothin', so why spook 'em. They might come around again."

"Off the record," I ask, "what *do* you know?" Hey, it's *my* butt they seem to be after.

"We have two neighbor witnesses who saw the van, a blue Ford with no rear windows except in the back door—which was curtained. Neither got the plate number, but it was Illinois, that much they could say. Two white people in the front, probably men, dark-haired, both of them."

"There's more than seven-hundred in Chicago alone," Durbett explains, "white male owners, though ain't nothin' says it had to be the owner driving it."

"A dead end for now," Culler says, "unless something new turns up."

"We found a file folder in the house," Durbett says, "marked *Hal Newsome* in the son's handwriting. Inside was a bucknote written by somebody else."

Culler finishes, "It said *Research Surplus.*"

"We're trying to get writing samples from key people at M-Slovak without them knowing it," Durbett adds. "Can't let anything about the note be known at this time."

"What *can* we say?" Hal asks, a bit frustrated with all this holding back.

"That it was murder," Culler answers pointedly, "and you can show 'em how we're sure of it."

"We need the footage of the son at the hospital," Durbett says.

We get everything set up and cued, then start recording a shot of Culler as he examines the video from the crime scene, noting the position of the bullet wound, right side of the head, just above the ear. "Examiner says angle of fire is downward, about forty degrees if he was standing straight up or kneeling. That's suspicious, because a suicide's likely to shoot straight sideways or slightly upward." He demonstrates on himself with his own weapon, the likely way to aim and fire, then showing the awkwardness of lifting the butt higher and shooting downward. Next he has Hal scan the video forward to show the position of the gun next to the dead hand, Hal pretending to lay off the segment, then making stills for our Afro-Poirot—like he doesn't already have oodles of crime-scene photos of his own.

"Something looks suspicious about the position," Hal prompts, our tenacious reporter digging out the facts.

Culler says, "That's my way of thinking." He demonstrates his hand holding the gun, then dropping down onto the table surface, the weapon coming loose and resting several inches away. He gestures toward the shot on the screen.

"It's backwards," Hal pronounces.

Culler nods. "Like it was placed there to look like a suicide, but the killer didn't account for the fact that he was facing the victim, forgetting to turn the gun around, is what I'm thinking." He demonstrates holding the gun backwards, almost impossible to fire, then having it fall the way we see it on the screen. "Don't work like that," he sums up.

"This is strong evidence," Hal says, "but is it enough to conclude murder?"

Culler has Hal play the video from the hospital, pausing here and there to point out what Flynn Durbett had been first to note before even watching it unedited. It was plain as day, when the son picked things up, reached for the door, wrote down some contacts for Kristen to interview . . .

"He was shot on the right side," Culler says, "gun lying by his right hand."

Hal concludes, "And he was left-handed."

*   *   *

And we're live!

It's an excellent pair of segments, Hal Neusome here in Chicago updating two important stories, that *Newsline* team coverage we all count on.

First we recap the Pollikey tragedy, showing more video than before—*exclusive* NBS footage—better victim bites than any competitor's, background on Gordie that's more personal than others have managed to assemble from records and interviews.

Hal can't ignore Jody Pollikey's Parzilac rumor, especially since he has it recorded. His plan to wait and reveal it in a big way Sunday would make him look like he got the lead from his competitors, like he got scooped. No, he has to report it now, tonight—just a teensy bit, anyway.

We roll the bite of Jody accusing Parzilac. Hal explains, "Though we're still waiting for toxicology reports—and we promise to bring you those results—we must be cautious at this time about assigning blame. I can say, however, that our investigation has uncovered some alarming information which warrants scrutiny. We'll know more Sunday evening when we take a closer look at the controversy surrounding a possible role of Parzilac in this awful tragedy, so watch *Neusome on the News*, which will be carried on these NBS affiliates nationwide as part of a special *Newsline* presentation."

And the Parzilac blitz begins. Not bad publicity for Neusome, either. Too bad Hal doesn't have a book to promote, too—or a garage sale or lemonade stand.

We play the same gambit with the drugstore story, showing more shots of the murder scene than before, one more card in this game of media poker. Hal wanted to end it with the bit about the son being left-handed, evidence it was a sloppy murder, the cover-up interrupted by our veteran reporter arriving at the scene to ferret out more facts, but he deferred to my suggestion, agreeing it's stronger to end with emotion rather than information.

Our final shot is outside the funeral home, an overcast drizzle-looking day, loved ones and friends, strangers drawn to offer their support, protesters fed up with the senseless violence.

A grieving widow—the distraught mother suffering two horrible losses within a week—emerges from the funeral home, supported by Reverend Falluson at her arm. The crowd parts, growing silent in respect.

Hal narrates quietly under the shot, reminding us the drugstore-chain founder's funeral has been postponed. The widow smiles weakly, acknowledgment of all these people showing their love. Somebody hands her a single rose. She wobbles, Falluson's strong arm around her, holding her up.

She nods to the crowd, then turns and lets the reverend lead her back inside, Hal concluding:

"To plan another funeral, a double funeral, so her husband and now her only child, casualties of the senseless violence in our communities, may be buried side by side."

*   *   *

"Why did Hal talk about Parzilac?" aren't the first words out of Cyn's mouth, but they're pretty close to first.

"Didn't have a choice. Actually, pointing out there's nothing to substantiate it yet did more to help it die down for a few days than ignoring it would have."

"Well, Salterfin was pissed. All day, he kept saying, 'Your boyfriend better deliver on Sunday.'"

We have a bit of a snack and settle on my couch; then she spends two tedious hours overplanning her appearance on Hal's show, running ideas by me, rehearsing, trying out her on-cam style . . . I'm so tired, and so tired of Parzilac . . . I just keep drifting . . .

"That's enough about that," she announces. "Tell me the best thing that happened to you today."

"Um . . . Okay, if you'll carry me up to bed."

We climb the stairs, help each other undress, then crawl in and stretch out. She cuddles close. I'm so tired, so very tired . . .

"So tell me something good," she prods.

"Frank and Taj."

"That's Melissa's child?"

"Yeah. They moved in with Frank after the fire—"

"They're still there?"

"Um, yeah. Where else are they gonna—? Hey, what about including Melissa and the other people who were made homeless? Shouldn't they be part of your lawsuit, too? Melissa lost everything she owned."

"No, not worth it. Not enough money to justify the trouble."

"But they—"

"Let them wait until after I get what I'm after."

"That could take years."

"That's how it works. So what about Frank and this little boy?" She seems impatient, like maybe she wants to jump my bones.

"Taj has this bad rash around his waist, in his underpants—"

"Eeew! How perfectly yucky. But how do you know this?"

"Me? Oh, I've seen it. That's what I was trying to tell you. Frank is being so protective of Melissa and Taj—"

"What's Frank have to do with this, this rash?"

"Well, Frank had him in the bathroom, up on the counter, coaxing him into putting his medicine on it." I'm yawning. This non-story is taking too long to tell.

"Isn't that rather inappropriate?"

"Inappropriate? Why would that be—?"

"Well, for one thing, it's not his child. Besides, it's gross. Why would he want to?"

"It's not gross. It's a rash. And he'd want to because he loves him." I'm feeling exasperated.

She shakes her head like she doesn't get it. "Small children are so gross, all snotty and stinky, always a mess at both ends. It's repulsive."

What can I say? She's right. Little kids can be gross.

And I can't wait to have my own.

My kids will probably be a mess at both ends, and I'll be there to help clean them up. But if the worst happens to me, I'd be glad to know somebody like Frank, as good a man as Frank, would be there to coax my fatherless little boy into putting his medicine on, and hugging him and drying his tears when it stings.

She's taken my pause as a chance to change the subject back again. "What if I created a graphic for the show? Maybe bullet points showing the elements of a summons & complaint?"

I'm too tired. I'm in a bad mood.

Tomorrow's another big day . . .

I hope Taj's rash is starting to heal . . .

Frank already has enough to worry about.

*   *   *

Today Taj Norrow wears the lizard.

So go the rest of the boys. The golden-haired girl chooses the tropical angelfish, and so go the rest of the girls.

We all watch.

We all wait.

Zip. Nada. Nothing. Whew!

Everybody's relieved except Melissa, who shakes her head in disappointment. Another set of antigens, another set failing to react on Taj. Of course, we need to wait all day, and there may still appear a tell-tale mosquito bite later, but Messy-hair had said nearly all reactions will occur within minutes. Twelve hours is the fail-safe, which is why it's good that kids will want to wear them until they rub off anyway.

As the crowd disperses, Melissa quietly asks, "When will you get the other sets?"

"Should have two more ready today. Since Rex Briggs and Les Casapell are both in Washington for the big Fantasy Patch-approval vote, I think I'll tag along when Rupert meets with Moore and Stockbridge; then I can get you some tattoos to try tomorrow and Sunday."

Grateful, she calls her son over. "Show Danté your hands," she whispers. He shyly holds them out, exposing ugly red welts from his fingers to his wrists. "His other rash isn't getting any better, either."

"Maybe that clinic was wrong. Maybe it's time to try another doctor."

"I can't get an appointment before next week anyway, so let's try the other tattoos this weekend first."

I nod agreement. We're still in the kid-room, raucous play all around us, cartoons blasting from one of the monitors. Taj is helping the golden-haired girl build a block tower. We whisper as we watch the young'ns play. "How's it working out, staying with Frank?"

She gets a far-off look in her eyes, the picture of serenity. "Frank and Taj are such buddies now, and Frank has been wonderful to me." She chuckles, then gets serious again, telling me stories of their time together, and I'm struck not just by how good Frank has been for them, but how good they've been for him. Eventually, she sighs and decides it's time to get back to work.

But I linger for a minute, watching the kids, thinking, *This is where I work?*

And the little golden-haired girl is impressed as the boy with big brown eyes, a multi-hued lizard on his arm, stands on his toes to make his wood-block tower reach for the sky.

*   *   *

This place would take a lot of soundproofing to make a production stage. Those center supports would have to be knocked out, too, smoother flooring put in, but it sure is big enough. Or it would be ideal for a passel of twelve-year-olds to sneak around shooting paint balls at each other.

One of the many Briggs warehouses, it's a distribution center shared by the company's subsidiary wholesaler. Next door is a smaller building where million-dollar machines are cranking out the initial runs of Aller-Tats, soon to be shipped across town or down to Tennessee for packaging.

Stockbridge and Moore come down a steel stairway from the foreman's office, a glass-enclosed area overlooking the entire facility. Moore's carrying two small boxes of Aller-Tats, samples of the other antigens. "Let's put these in your car before we look at the video."

I check one of the boxes and discover full-colored wizards on top, an achievement of mucho coolness.

"I'll take them," Rupert offers. "Where should Duke unload the DVDs?" he asks Stockbridge.

"They're already packaged in shippers?"

"All you need is to label and send. We could've arranged that, too, you know."

"Rex doesn't want the mailing list out of company hands," he explains. They wander off on their secret mission, so Moore and I go up and watch the videos five or ten times.

"I don't like doing this," he says, "but that's not my get. Competition is supposed to be the best products at the right time for the best prices. Shipping anonymous DVDs feels shady."

I consider for a second, then decide what the hell. "If you're in such a righteous mood, tell me what you think of this patch approval going on in Washington today."

He's surprised. "Well, getting FDA approval is a critical step—"

"No, I mean changing the committee's question, maneuvering another vote when some of the detractors will be at a Briggs-sponsored symposium out west."

"I have nothing to do with that."

"Aren't you concerned about the Fantasy Patch being potentially dangerous?" Rupert and Stocky have joined us in time to hear the answer.

"Yes," Moore says. "I'm concerned about all of our products—as I should be. But research and trials have never turned up even one example of negative reaction. That doesn't mean it might never happen, but everything—I mean *everything* in life is part of a risk/benefit ratio. Even getting out of bed. Vaccinations harm thousands of children every year, but they save tens of millions of lives. These Aller-Tats might create a medical emergency in one out of many thousands, but medical care can remedy those few while countless others reap the benefits. If the patch caused as many problems as Parzilac, I'd be the first to demand we pull it off the market." He's indignant now, maybe a bit angry, like I'd questioned his honor.

Rupert's squirming at my lack of client finesse. When the customer says the sky's purple, the proper question is: Would that be lavender or violet?

"Good," I answer. "Good. I count on your integrity. That's why I can bring this up just among us friends. I can't sell deadly products. I won't sell them. I just want to know from somebody I can trust to be straight with me."

The tension's gone now, replaced by camaraderie, we four lads up here in our clubhouse, in a world of cool boys and icky girls and strict parents and bullies named M-Slovak.

"That's why at first I was reluctant to go OTC on the allergy tests," Moore says quietly.

Stockbridge pipes in, "And I admit I was reluctant to have Blaine be the first kid in the world to try them, but my wife and I talked it over last night, and today he's wearing the monster."

I admit, "I was afraid to let the kids at work try them, but the parents were okay with it, and one kid with an allergy proved these things work."

Rupert says, "I'm wearing the monster right now." He grins like a schoolboy with his first A+, everybody chuckling.

"I didn't mean to jump on you," I apologize to Moore.

He looks me over, allowing a slight smile. "It just proves you're the right guy to do this job."

"I think we need to barbecue some steaks at my house, say next week-end?" Stocky offers, our diplomat, our master of protocol. "Bring your womenfolk or youngsters if you got any." He hastily scribbles a map to his place in Park Ridge and photocopies a second for Rupert. I'll get to party with these two after all.

We don't swear any blood oaths or shoot paint balls at each other, but we do get five-hundred DVDs out for delivery Sunday and Monday. I have the rest of the Aller-Tat samples, another round of kid-testing in the offing. I'm pleased with Moore's reaction, somewhat mollified now about my patch-safety concerns. After all, Fantasy Patch must be prescribed, and only after careful screening. Moore knows what he's talking about . . .

If they've told Moore the truth.

But I'm distracted now, driving back to the stage, the stakes in this boy's game of hide-and-seek just raised again. I've spotted it twice so far; though I think I lost it a few miles back.

But I'm sure that blue van was following us.

$$*\qquad*\qquad*$$

I need a cage!

I once dived Shark Alley out of Lucaya Beach, Grand Bahama Island. Talk about a trip, the divemaster using dead fish to stir up a feeding frenzy, our small group suddenly surrounded by man-eaters big enough to swallow you whole and still have room to munch your Uncle Earl for dessert.

This feels about the same, me here in the fifth-floor conference center of Cyn's building, surrounded by a voracious school of feeding lawyers, their docile wives playing the role of remora. I'd just as soon be Cyn's suckerfish, but Rob Salterfin won't let me blend in. Frankly, I'm still distracted, wondering about that blue van that followed Rupert and me earlier today. Whoever it is must be trying to unnerve me.

And it's working, dammit.

"Let's talk," Salterfin suggests, leading me toward the bar. "If you'll excuse us," he says politely to Cyn, who's already surrounded by her own coterie of celebrators, congratulators, litigators, prognosticators, mushy gushers and at least one gushing lush.

"I have an idea," Salterfin says, having separated me from the protection of the school. He orders us another drink, like I need more.

"I like ideas," I tell him, "when they're good ones."

He's moving me off to the side to talk in private. "We should keep a back-up copy of that video here in the safe." Now there's an idea.

"No," I answer, offering all the explanation he deserves.

"What if it gets lost—or stolen?"

"It won't."

"Listen, son, don't underestimate the kind of hardball M-Slovak will play once we go public with this." Fatherly advice from dad, delivered with a menacing glare.

"I knew what kind of game we were playing when I threw out the first pitch."

"Somehow, I'm afraid you didn't. I'm worried about you and your fiancée. I wish you'd let me help."

If you've ever scuba-dived "Stingray City" in the sound at Grand Cayman Island, you know how I feel. You go down with a tub of chopped squid to feed the giant stingrays. They're like big puppy dogs, your buddies, your pals, coming by for a snack. Then you run out of squid, or try to hold back, and they get a little more aggressive—still all friendly-like, but nudging, sneaking up from behind, trying to look in your sack or under your buoyancy compensator—and if you lose control of your squid for even a split second, they'll have them and be gone before you know it. "Just stick to your part of the bargain," I tell him.

"I already have," he says. "She's partner a lot sooner than she could've earned it."

"There's still more," I correct him.

He waves that off. "Listen, I have to protect the firm—*and* your little gal. When you say *more*, you're not thinking of coming back asking for a little something extra when it's time to deliver, are you?"

"You're suggesting I might extort you?"

He grins. "You already have, trading to get a bump and a high profile for your gal. Listen, what if somebody else comes along, maybe offers you some money for that video?"

"No new deals."

"Could be M-Slovak, trying to keep it away from me."

"Could be somebody working for *you*, trying to get it away from *me*."

"Could be. But what if M-Slovak has somebody threaten you?"

"I have friends who specialize in those kinds of problems."

"Yeah, I'll just bet you do. Have these friends of yours been able to solve your problem with the blue van?"

"What do you know about that?"

"I've heard things. Listen, there's millions at stake here, likely hundreds of millions. I just don't want somebody else getting that video, or for something to happen to you and that little gal of yours."

"She's your new partner," I correct him. "I don't think she answers to *gal*."

He waves that off, too. "Friggin' women attorneys—" He doesn't finish the thought. "You know, for all the money this lawsuit will cost me, for the reputation of my firm to be on the line, you better not even think about crossing me up."

"Then you better stop pissing me off," I point out.

He grins and puts his arm around me. "Hey, I'm just testing you, making sure you got the balls in case this gets ugly." Shark for a moment, the stingray has now come back.

"I've had enough testicle metaphors this week, thank you, and I'd rather you quit trying to show me yours."

He grins broadly. "I like you. We're gonna be great together. Now, let's get over there and help my new partner celebrate her promotion."

He leads me back into the school of sharks.

I need a cage.

CHAPTER 18

A little romance.

The stuff of rack paperbacks, passion sweeps two lovers, destined for each other, into magical idyll. It's set and setting, the right mood, the right moment, the right people, the right moves.

And I'm actually nervous.

"Cyn, we always decide important things together, right?"

"Mmm, yeah." She's cuddled up next to me on the couch. "What's to decide?" Nuzzling my neck, she'll have me taxiing to the runway in no time.

"Well, should we go away, say for a weekend sometime soon? Do it on the beach in the sunshine, or at night on the veranda surrounded by tropical flowers swaying to the ocean breeze? Or a fine restaurant at the top of Chicago or New York City or at Scoma's in San Francisco? Or maybe looking through some yacht's rail across moonlit waters? Should I be on bended knee? And what about the ring? I want yours to be perfect, but I don't know anything about rings or what kind you'd like. Should I surprise you, or should we shop together?"

She sighs. "You're talking about becoming officially engaged?"

"Of course."

"Oh, Danté, you're always in such a hurry about everything."

"It's time, sweet suitress. You made partner tonight. I'm top VP and part owner of my own agency—we've done what we set out to accomplish, so now we can write the next chapter, the happily-ever-after."

"As soon as we're engaged, you'll want to set a date," she teases.

"It helps to have one when you send out the invitations."

"You're such a silly." Then more seriously, "We really should wait a while longer, until I get this lawsuit under control, until you get the agency on more solid ground."

"But we don't have to wait just to get officially engaged, or to move in together—"

"But you don't *want* to move in with me. You don't want to leave the old lady here by herself."

"Why don't you try living here?"

She sighs again. "It doesn't feel like *my* place—*our* place, and it's too far from my office, and—"

"Cyn, if it's that important to you, we can look for another home, one that will be just ours. I can work things out to make sure Theta is looked after. She'd understand."

She shakes her head slightly and sighs again, but doesn't say anything. I'm not doing very well at this romantic thing. Finally, she says, "What's wrong with the way things are?"

I hesitate, finally deciding honest dialogue means being honest. "Cyn, we're in our mid-thirties. Our careers are to the point where soon we'll be able to cut back on the long hours. I want to have at least a year or two of just us—weekend trips, romantic dinners, games of spunky moray chasing bearded clam until all hours of the night—you know, before we make a little Roenik or three to keep us up late. If we wait too many more years, it starts to be physically risky for you, and subtracts from our time at the back end when we can retire together and live in a Winnebago and drive around look-ing for the world's largest paper-clip sculpture, eating bologna sandwiches while we moan about what college costs these days."

She's stopped nuzzling now.

"Cyn?"

She sighs yet again. "Danté—" She hesitates. "Danté, I'm not sure I could be a mother, that I'd have the time."

"Sure you could; sure you would. I'll carry my share. By then, I'll have the agency running to where I just have to phone in ideas. We'll have one kid who draws pictures and another who trademarks them and sues the neighborhood kids for infringement."

She shakes her head. "Please, Danté, I need more time. I'm under too much pressure."

"You're right. We both are. It's just—well, no matter how busy I am, I try not to lose sight of what matters most. And that's you, and us."

"You're so sweet." She cuddles again. "Let's go upstairs, celebrate our success." She's up and tugging at me.

But I'm distracted.

I follow her, still trying to talk. "Cyn, you always said when you made partner, when I made VP. I know the next few weeks are too busy, but I need to know . . . Has something changed?"

She sighs deeply, glances at me, and casts her eyes downward. "Noth-ing's changed, Danté. I don't understand why you're doing this."

"I just want to know we'll talk about this soon."

"You spend so much time imagining things, trying to look ahead, trying to change everything. Can't you just be happy right now? Happy the way things are? With just us? Do you have to have everything, everybody else's version of the American dream?"

My picture wavers; I'm not sure what I see anymore. But she's right. Our picture shouldn't be only mine. We must paint it together, no matter how it turns out. I put my arms around her.

She holds me tightly, nuzzles my neck, strokes my back, kisses my cheek, my mouth, shifting closer, holding tighter, rocking gently . . .

Here and now.

It's the right mood, the right moment, set and setting . . . I'm trying so hard—too hard. I'm trying to make it happen instead of just letting it.

I'm distracted.

I guess I'm not good at the just-right-now. Each moment in life is the point between where you've been and where you're going. Nobody knows the future, but we can't just let it happen to us. We have to want, to move toward, to adjust as we go, to smell as many roses as we can but keep our eyes on the mountains in the distance.

And accept that some day we can go no farther.

That's when the journey needs to have been worth it, when what you've seen and done is your reward, when the people who've shared it with you are the collected treasures you hold in your heart.

For the first time, I'm afraid Cyn and I are looking at different mountains. And I need to know, but we can't talk right now, and to look too far ahead robs us of this moment. I love her so much, I'll try my best to give her what she wants, but I'm nervous.

Please help me, Cyn. If all we ever have is this moment, I want it to be perfect. Let's write our own story.

What we need now, more than ever . . .

Is a little romance.

*   *   *

This old horse hits the lonesome trail toward work.

My romantic night with Cyn turned out better than it started—I guess. Good thing I didn't do something impulsive like spend my life's savings surprising her with an engagement ring.

I've been assured that soon we *will* talk about all those things that had me so unsettled, and I do have faith. Cyn understands. She wants it all to work out. No two people ever desire exactly the same thing, but when they're in love, they find ways to meld their visions, to chart a mutual course, to enjoy the journey as two parts of a greater whole.

But I'm in a lousy mood.

My Durbett phone rings. "Yeah?"

It's Jankety. "Morning, Danté. Listen, Flynn got mad at himself for letting this blue van get beyond our control. If you see it again, just press the red button there and talk fast. Remember, though, they probably know you're watching for them, so we should assume they might have changed vehicles. If you see a black Jeep that looks suspicious, ignore it. It'll be one of ours."

If I see the blue van, I'm running the damn thing off the road. "Thanks, Jankety."

I hardly know this man, but I trust him with my life. I like him, too. No nonsense, you know where you stand. He looks out for his buds, somebody you can count on.

I still haven't found my schedule planner, but I know that between Rupert and Hal, my morning will be booked. Then a good bit of my afternoon will be spent bemoaning the pharmaceutical industry with Bentley Crabtree. The rainy weather's gone, replaced by springtime sunshine.

I pull into the lot at *Shoot & Die*, doff my sunglasses, and spot Taj hurrying out to greet me. He's proudly displaying his new tattoo, the banana split. "You ever had a horsey-back ride?" I ask. I kneel down and hoist him up.

Yes, I swear it's true, I shake my head side to side and whinny, then gallop him around the parking lot to his squeals of delight, looking foolish but feeling good about it, not the least embarrassed to discover there's an audience spilling out from the lobby. This horsey has worked up a steam, ready for the watering trough by the time I gallop over and let Kristen lift Taj off my back.

"We better get your horsey a drink," she tells him, laughing and giving him a quick hug before setting him gently on the ground. They each take one of my hands and lead me back to the dining area where Kristen finds us three Mountain Dews to toast Taj's first day riding the dusty trail.

Hal comes in to join us, back to the real world. "I can't get any response from M-Slovak except that they recommended an expert from Michigan who can speak objectively about Parzilac. We're setting up with the NBS affiliate in Flint to have him satellite in for the show. I wish we had some weekdays left so we could take a crew to Grand Rapids and ambush their execs, get them flustery and looking guilty, even if they don't say anything. We need to put some evil faces on this conspiracy."

Kristen suggests, "We can use pictures from their annual report, at least do a quickie on who the important players are—the ones who refuse to comment."

I like it. "It might piss them off enough to flush them out, get 'em to speak and defend themselves."

Taj burps his approval, then covers his mouth and looks embarrassed. Kristen giggles, tousling his hair.

"Something interesting on the drugstore story," Hal says. "I went through those inventory logs I copied before the explosion and fire. It only covered the last seven months or so, but I discovered that twice they were shipped huge amounts of Parzilac, once twenty-two cases, once fifteen. I don't know if they ordered that many or if the shipments were a mistake, but both times they returned all but three cases. I called several other drugstores and asked how fast they go through Parzilac. It looks like two or three cases should have been about right for the whole chain, each store needing three or four bottles of a thousand per week."

"What are you thinking?"

Hal shrugs and looks at Kristen. She answers, "One mistake I can see; two seems unlikely."

Hal adds, "Guy thinks he needs a lot of capsules, then changes his mind, something must have messed up his plans."

I supply the rest. "And what else could he need so many for unless he was selling them on the black market—to people who make Pozies."

"Except the Pozie market was falling apart," Kristen continues the scenario. "Too many problems, the dealers afraid to handle them."

"Just like Culler said," Hal finishes. "So his deal falls apart once, then again, and he returns what he can, but he's stuck with the ones he dumped loose into boxes after destroying the coded bottles. He tries again, and gets set to make a delivery—except he's double-crossed. They try to rob him, something goes wrong, he winds up stabbed and running over the little girl. They come back and torch the place in case he left any evidence of their previous arrangement."

Kristen says, "Or maybe they didn't even intend to rob him, just wanted to cut off whatever the deal was, needed to make sure he'd keep his mouth shut. Maybe he tried to extort them, threatened to talk. It took two tries, finally using ricin to silence him. After they torched the store to destroy any potential evidence, the only possible threat who remained was the son."

"They didn't go after him right away, though," I point out.

Hal says, "Maybe they thought he didn't know. Then maybe he contacted them or tried to take revenge into his own hands."

"Or maybe they figured that out only when he contacted you," I tell Hal, "and offered to squeal if we'd bring a camera to his house."

"And they beat us there," he says, thinking that one over. "I can't report this on the show yet," he adds, frustrated, "but I have to tell Culler."

"Let's see what our detective can do with it before tomorrow night," I suggest, adding, "and keep very quiet about this for now. It looks like you might have photocopies of just the kind of evidence somebody killed two people and torched a store to get rid of. I don't want this place to be next," I say ominously, all three of us glancing toward Taj.

That's when Rupert lassoes me with a stack of files. Break's over.

It's time to giddayup.

*   *   *

"I've got a brain for sale," I want to whisper, but that would be silly.

I look for the gargoyle knocker, find the tiny doorbell button, press it, and listen for the gong, the howl, the scream.

Ding dong. Oh well, reality's rarely as much fun as imagination.

Our little Quasimodo, Bentley Crabtree, leads Murray and me to the cluttered laboratory for an intensive work session. We crunch and review and argue for two hours, much of that developing the final outline for the book—a table of contents with extra detail—then splitting up responsibilities. Bentley will create graphics for twenty-two sets of data—from geographic distribution of Parzilac-violence to a fold-out chronology of the drug, the initial research to its current populace saturation, seventeen-million users in the U.S. alone, more than sixty-million worldwide. Then he'll write the sections describing the process, politics, and business aspects. Murray will work with him to describe the advertising and public-relations, then on his own to detail all the legal maneuvering like the big indemnification move. I'll tell the personal stories of the victims, summarize media reports of their plights, paint the ruined lives of survivors, and work with Murray interviewing some of those imprisoned for life or longer after committing crimes of violence while under the influence. All together, it should make a compelling read, a mix of investigative reporting and human-interest stories, see appendix D,

Chart 7.

Murray has to rush off for a Weisman script meeting, but I linger for a while.

"Let's talk Fantasy Patch for a minute," I suggest to Crabtree.

He grins, digging in one ear with a misshapen finger, then fetches us some brews. "You won't let things go," he announces. "I like that. We're two peas in a pod." Sure, after radiation bombards the Earth in some '50s sci-fi B-movie.

"Was Fantasy Patch approved?"

"Seven to five, didn't even make the national news."

"It looks like I might be the point man for selling it."

"And I hope to be the guy who tells and shows the public whatever you don't, whether that be pimples or warts."

"Or a goiter," I kid. He tilts his head, taking me seriously. He waits for me to continue, to see what's on my mind. "I don't want to sell something that hurts people," I blurt out.

"All compounds hurt somebody. I trust you have been indoctrinated into the cult of risk/benefit ratio?"

"You suggest there's no validity to that?"

"Not I," he says casually. "I must subscribe myself, at times, to partici-pate in this, our consumer-frenzied social order. All is relative, my friend. Taking a major risk in the hope of curing one's cancer is more prudent than a lesser risk simply to achieve minty-fresh breath."

"Point taken."

"Then see how easily you embrace my other point. It's a concept called informed consent. I want to know the risks, the odds—or at least as much as anybody knows. Consumers who care not are left to their own lifestyles. We remaining few abhor deception, and we deserve better. My hard-earned ex-penditures confer obligation on the vendors, one that requires relevant and accurate information to accompany their products. If thou seeketh my con-sent, then ye must inform."

"Okay, we're two peas. Now explain to me how this testing process works. Doesn't it look automatically suspicious for a big company like Briggs to outsource Fantasy Patch?"

"Oh no. It's being done by many of the biggest pharmaceutical and bio-tech firms."

"This is big business then."

"It's a niche that exploded in the last decade, now accounting for nearly five-billion dollars a year. It's a way for drugmakers to cut payrolls and avoid maintaining expensive facilities when their need is sporadic."

"I take it this testing process is lengthy and costly?" I ask.

"It can cost a fortune just searching for and researching effective compounds. When a manufacturer believes in a product's potential, it begins a process that may require ten years or more and cost another several-hundred-million dollars."

"Why so much?"

"It's a winnowing process. First comes pre-clinical testing on animals for toxic effects. After about four years, less than one percent make it to the next phase, human trials. That involves three phases proving therapeutic value and safety. Only a small fraction make it to FDA submission. It's extremely long odds for high stakes, and there's only a seventeen-year window in which they own the patent. Ten or twelve years of testing, then waiting for approval, at odds of thousands to one, with only a few remaining years to profit before the generic industry takes it away—and with competitors grabbing market niches with their own products—you can understand why minimizing the cost and speeding that process is critical."

"And why anything that helps ensure positive results is possible."

"Which brings to mind AnalyClin, sole contractors for the Fantasy Patch trials."

"And Rex Briggs has something to do with that company?"

"Majority shareholder, but no sanctioned control, non-voting stock. It's helmed by the former Briggs VP of Biometrics, a Rex cohort who got his doctorate in biostatistics at Michigan when Rex was there. The competition among outsource companies is fierce right now, with a lot of industry consolidation squeezing out the smaller firms. The temptation to provide results that please the clients must be great. AnalyClin's biggest client is Briggs Pharmaceutical, its biggest contract to date: the Fantasy Patch."

"And you have evidence of shenanigans?"

"None," he admits, allowing a smile. "Just suspicion. The FDA committee raised some valid concerns, and the AnalyClin data is too perfect, and the process took only six years since the discovery of those fungus-butt caterpillars and subsequent synthesis of Lokistarrinane. Watching Briggs manipulate the approval process makes me wonder what kind of incestuous manipulation may have happened in the trials."

I'm suspicious, too, but have to admit there might be nothing shady at all. Still, though, I wonder. "Where is AnalyClin?"

"New Johnsonville, Tennessee, just outside Camden. It's a sprawling complex of labs tied to an old private hospital along the banks of Kentucky Lake. It's one-stop testing and trials. Briggs's distribution company has a warehouse next door, too."

"I'll tell you what, Bentley. Rex gave me *carte blanche* to collect background on the Fantasy Patch story. I'll look into it discreetly."

"I am amenable to feeding you information if it is kept confidential, not disseminated through other outlets, not utilized to alert Briggs how to obscure the trail."

"Agreed."

We sit there a few minutes and drain our brews. I have to ask: "You a fan of old horror flicks?"

"I have been called Igor, but I'm not in the market for used brains."

*   *   *

Chirrup. Chirrup. Chirrup.

I've always liked the sound of crickets, those little love bugs calling for their darlin's. Someday, computers will be able to translate cricketese: "Single black male desires black female companion, enjoys moonlit nights and playing the fiddle, in good health with great legs."

There's a female cricket I'm wary of. She's getting close and won't go away. Cricket LaRayne left a message asking to appear on Hal's show tomorrow night.

"She's coming here any minute now," Kristen reports as I enter the lobby at *Shoot & Die.*

"Couldn't you blow her off?"

"I tried, politely, but she's meeting with Melissa to pitch representing her as a victim of the fire—for losing her stuff, trauma, whatever."

"I guess that's Melissa's prerogative."

"Melissa wants *you* to sit in, too. I think she's worried about interfering with your plans."

"We can keep them separate." I tell our reception dude to put Cricket in the conference room and to keep her away from Hal's edit.

Heading back toward my office, Kristen wonders, "Why doesn't Melissa just sign with Cyn?"

"Cyn doesn't want to handle the property claims."

Kristen's surprised. "But this would be for Melissa." Friends is friends, after all.

"I guess it would detract from the violence and wrongful-death aspects," I explain, unconvinced.

"A legal strategy." It's a swear-word.

"Putting your feelings aside to get the job done." I'm sitting on the front of my desk now, Kristen standing close and studying me.

"Funny you should say that. I've been wondering—you never did say how you felt about me bowing out of the original Parzilac job." An odd topic, out of the blue.

"I respected you and wish I could have gotten away with that, too. Of course, now I'm glad we have videos that'll help blow this wide open, but you know I wouldn't ask you to do work that compromises your scruples."

She nods, then turns and parks next to me, staring ahead at the wall. "So, does it look like we'll be launching the Fantasy Patch?"

"Yes."

She looks disappointed. "Which is the next-generation replacement for Parzilac."

"But this one's not dangerous."

"How do you know—taking Briggs's word for it? We believed M-Slovak, too, until we watched a young woman bleed to death." Her voice catches, and she shakes her head as if to dispel the image.

"I've been looking into it with Bentley Crabtree. He says there's no evidence of problems, but we're going to keep our eyes open."

She takes a deep breath, maybe somewhat mollified, maybe not. I know Kristen, and as long as she has doubts, they'll distract her, sap her enthusiasm . . .

Like I've been feeling.

"Rex said I can shoot documentary footage," I point out, "to tell the Fantasy Patch story. We should go where all the testing was done, AnalyClin down by Kentucky Lake in Tennessee, and investigate what they're doing."

She arches her eyebrows, intrigued by the idea. "Rex's okey-dokey will give you a lot more access than an outsider."

"Let's climb right inside their undies and find out if they smell."

"See if they've stuffed a sock in there to inflate their claims," she adds, smiling.

"Check for skid marks to see if they're thorough in their methodologies."

"See who wears Depends, make 'em laugh, then abscond with the evidence," she counters.

"Find out if this patch is nothing more than a wet dream."

"Okay, you win," she chuckles. "I can't do underwear metaphors as fast as you can."

"Bummer. I was on a roll. I'd not even started on testicle variations yet."

She turns and looks at me seriously. "You're one of the few people I trust, Danté." She's satisfied, for now. "Funny you should say Kentucky Lake. That's near the Weisman headquarters. I'd considered shooting the Sizemore *Wave-Slicer* simulation there. Since Flynn's company jet operates out of a private airport near Camden, he offered to fly us and our crew."

"And if we combine it with a shoot at AnalyClin, we can start positioning ourselves as insiders." I wouldn't mind a turn sitting at the controls of the jet, either. "A private jet! I wonder if Flynn would let me—"

Buzz. "Danté, you've been invited to join the meeting between Miss La-Rayne and Miss Norrow."

Kristen flies off toward the edit suites while I taxi into the conference room. Cricket greets me warmly, such a big smile for so tiny a woman. Melissa's glad to see me. Taj is there, fascinated by some kind of *Monster Bin* applique Cricket brought him. This woman knows how to schmooze. Taj gives her a thank-you hug before his mother chases him out and closes the door.

"I've been talking with victims of the fire," Cricket begins the meeting as we sit around the table, "—the people who were *not* injured or didn't lose a loved one. Some had already contacted Wanamaker, Salterfin & Brock, but they were turned down, so I've accepted the role as their advocate. Thank you for agreeing to speak with me, Miss Norrow."

I suggest we use first names, and the motion carries. "Who do you anticipate will be your defendants?" I ask.

"That would be inappropriate for me to discuss at this time," Cricket answers good-naturedly. "Besides, Melissa is not yet my client."

"Are you considering signing with her?" I ask Mel.

"Well, she seems like she really wants to help, and she is representing the others—and my son likes her," she adds with a smile. "I guess I am."

Cricket matches her smile, sliding a document across for her to sign. "I'd like to appear on Mr. Neusome's program tomorrow night," she mentions matter-of-factly.

"That would be up to Hal."

"How can I convince him?"

Like my grand plan to launch Cyn as a national media star has room for a small-time wannabe who doesn't even have a defendant. I might as well give her a straight answer. "It's not going to happen."

"I thought not," she admits, unflappable. "I wanted the lead reporter to have first access is all—and maximum exposure for my firm and our clients—but I understand. It is not unreasonable, then, for me to offer my commentary to competing media outlets, to talk about my plans as the other lead attorney in this tragedy, and to remark about whatever Miss SiCauge chooses to announce."

She's right—but I wonder why she's telling me. Leverage? A threat? Covering herself? Laying groundwork for a deal to team with Cyn? Huh? "I understand."

She rises, so we all get up. She gently hugs Melissa, assuring her, "I'll do what I can, hon. I trust you're okay for now? Good then. You have good friends. You're luckier than most. Thank you for your time, Danté. Give my regards to Miss SiCauge. Revealing the truth, helping those who've been harmed—we all share the same goals."

After she's gone, Melissa points out, "She's sharp about making connections."

Is that really what this was all about?

I need a computer to translate cricketese.

Chirrup. Chirrup. Chirrup.

CHAPTER 19

It's alive!

I've created a monster! And she's mine—*mine I tell you!* All mine! FrankenCyn!

She knows I'll be tied up tomorrow helping Hal and Kristen put the show together, so tonight—damn near all night from how it's looking—we've been rehearsing her. She's got 3X5 cards, outlines, lists, different outfits to try on, different looks to affect—a special appointment to have her hair done tomorrow morning . . . This babe is going to be ready.

"Will you be playing all the footage on the show?" she asks. "Everything from your Parzilac launch video, I mean."

"No way. This is for TV-America, the attention span of nits and gnats. Hal will summarize the big picture succinctly, with shots and graphics and font, then we'll show some of the juiciest bits."

"I can't get away with that during the trial."

"That's why having control of the original disks is so important for you, why you hold all the cards. You have to provide the whole shebang in court, and be willing to show it *all* to a jury."

"Hal Neusome's summaries and opinions aren't testimony," she agrees. "Yours would be, to some extent, since you were there and helped create it, but if all I have is the highlights that appear on TV, those can be impeached because they're taken out of context, not accurately reflecting the entire body of evidence."

"And Hal, technically, is the ideal repository for this information. He's got First-Amendment shields that make it harder to force him to turn over everything to your defendants."

"They'll get access to it all eventually, but I can be much more effective if it's on my timetable, under my terms." She gets sexy when she's in her power mode.

"You know, all this rehearsing can do more harm than good. Sharp lawyers need to think fast on their feet."

She takes the hint and leads me up to the pleasure chamber. Cuddling in bed, she rubs her face against my neck. "I'm sorry," she whispers. "I was just awful when you tried to talk, you know, about us. We'll consider making it official, just not right now—I hope you understand."

What timing. Right now I'm about to that point in which, historically, men have been known to make decisions with no basis in reality, no consideration for tomorrow. She wants joolokky bitummba? Sure, whatever you want, dear. Joolokky bitummba sounds good to me.

Yow.

Doubt ye not, she is alive. Me, too . . .

Power up the monster; lightning is about to strike!

*   *   *

It's Sunday, show day, and that blasted news director at NBS has been busting our chops all day. This was supposed to be a cakewalk after all of Kristen's and Murray's and Hal's work. Now since it's a special *NBS Newsline* presentation, picked up and fed nationally, it has to meet their standards for *accuracy* and *fairness*. Right now, those are both swear-words.

"Okay, we agree the lawsuit and the attorney will be the focus," he says, a conference call between him and our foursome on this end. "She can pretty much say anything she wants, and we're not responsible for it. A lawyer is *supposed* to be biased, has more latitude to make accusations, plus she presumably knows what she can get away with in order to shield herself. From there, we're presenting facts and expert opinions—the Pollikey-murder rollins showing how her plaintiffs became victims, the M-Slovak meeting footage that forms the basis of her suit, the suicide-girl shot that supports her claim, and an overview of Parzilac-linked violence across the country. You have an opposing point of view with the expert M-Slovak presented, but you really need an opposing legal opinion."

"M-Slovak had their chance to provide one," Hal argues.

"Yeah, but you blind-sided them."

"No, the lawyer did."

"True. And we're letting her manipulate *us*, too."

I'm getting tired of this. What I see on news programs every day boggles my mind for its one-sidedness, its propensity to draw conclusions based on innuendo, opinions, scant evidence, and so much bias a reasonable dissenter could readily argue the alternative if not the opposite. We're not manipulating info to further an opinion or pander to common morés; we've uncovered the truth about a dangerous product. Our manipulations are merely to give maximum impact to a story a lot of people might otherwise ignore without realizing the importance it has for so many. We've got M-Slovak dead to rights, and letting their lawyer deflect and obfuscate and spin would be deliberate dilution of our important information, all in the interest of painting the image of fairness. The only reason I'm even letting their pharmaceutical expert pontificate is because I look forward to watching him squirm when Hal hits him with all our facts.

"She's the one with a story," Hal reminds him.

"Yes, and that's why we're letting her have all the rope. Lucky she has a lot to back her up; we'd look foolish doing a special show for the privilege of watching her falter, then hang herself with it."

"All the more reason to avoid having an opposing lawyer on."

Bull's-eye! Our news director carefully avoids that point. "So you'll have the reverend there to moan about lost souls and ruined lives during the victim portions."

"We're going to let him call for justice, too, and throw the support of the community he represents behind our lawyer's cause."

"Good enough. Now, what about the drugstore murders?"

This one had taken some finesse. Hal wanted to press the point that Parzilac is so dangerous it was even being used in the manufacture of a new designer hallucinogen, then was considered by pushers to be so risky and unsafe that it's even faded from that scene. But Rex is worried about backlash against the whole category of prescription drugs, so Hal finally agreed to embrace my alternative.

"We don't have enough evidence to link the murders to the manufacture of street Pozies," Hal explains to our NBS watchdog, "so we're going with how the drugstore owner had previously contracted with M-Slovak to do clinical trials, then had sued after the drug company withdrew. We'll provide that as background and let the audience draw their own conclusions."

"You better be careful not to draw any for them."

"We will. At least we'll have the investigating detective on to provide context for our footage."

"I'm surprised you snagged him."

"He was reluctant, but we're playing it like he's appearing so he can ask the community for help in the investigation, like he's too busy for the media, except that we're a potentially valuable tool in reaching people who might have information."

"Perfect. Now what about this writer—Crabtree? You've got him promoting his upcoming book?"

"He's our best source—credible source—for the big picture on Parzilac violence. There's a lot of data I've had no time to confirm, so he'll be the expert who presents it. If he turns out slightly off on any details later, then it was him, not me."

"Okay, you can use him then."

Who does this guy think he is? I'll damn well put Taj on there to offer a four-year-old's opinion if I feel like it. All this NBS yahoo could do is cut the satellite feed and look very foolish about it.

"We're going to promo Hal's next show," I announce, "which will have the actual filing of the suit, reaction from the opposition, plus whatever all this exposure flushes out this week—"

"And we expect a lot," Hal interjects.

"—Unless you'd rather make it a *Newsline* segment Tuesday or Thursday. Then we'll promo that instead—that's if Hal wants to, him still being independent for now."

"Okay, I'll bite. Let's just call it this week, though, and not name the day. I'm stacked here, and there's no telling what other stories may break or even how much you'll have. But we'll do something by the end of the week. That okay with you, Hal?"

Good, pucker up and kiss. I think he needed to be reminded who needs whom.

All settled, we break for final preparation.

"Last chance," Kristen ribs me. "Say the word and this baby's yours." I'd insisted she direct the show. She'll do as well or better than I, plus I like showing off her talent, the depth of our capabilities here at Dellman/Roenik.

Besides, I hate doing news.

Cyn is worrying me to pieces asking questions, wanting to rehearse, trying to learn what-all is going to happen.

Then Rob Salterfin shows up. I hope he peed before he got here. I send them to my office with a copy of the run-down so they can fret over all the details.

So what do I do now? I go over all we'd just decided with Kristen, then slip in and hang out with Taj for a few minutes, clear my head, mellow out, try to remember my mantra—which is probably written in my missing schedule planner.

Here's something you don't see very often: Taj is sitting quietly, absently twisting a rubber band, rocking just perceptibly, the little golden-haired girl showing him drawings in a picture-book, the only two children here this

Sunday afternoon. He's not feeling well, some trouble with his asthma, needing to use his inhaler. He's wearing another tattoo, but still getting no reaction, four sets of antigens down and one to go. The rash on his hands is worse now. Melissa tried the medicine once, but he cried hard, so she washed it off. I gather from listening that the little girl is turning the pages so Taj doesn't spread his rash to her. Our little guy is embarrassed, even ashamed that something is wrong with him.

I'm glad Melissa has an appointment for Tuesday.

I surprise them by pausing for some hugs. First I hug her, such a sweet, delicate little child, like holding the fabled sugar and spice. Then I hug Taj, careful to avoid his waistline, but making sure I touch his hands and prove to both children that he's no leper, that I'm not afraid to touch him, that he's okay, he's lovable and loved, no matter what.

Uncle Danté needs to work now. I've got a major corporation to bring down, a legendary newsman to revivify, families who need the comfort of my images, an American public to outrage, and my star lawyer's career to launch.

I pause and look back. The little girl is patting Taj's hand now.

I'm geeked. I've never felt more excited in all my life!

Cyn, we are *this close* to having it all.

*　　　　*　　　　*

Thirty minutes.

We've started the thirty-minute countdown and everything is go. Everybody's been through make-up, geeked and ready to run—all except Lieutenant Detective Heath Culler. He hasn't shown up yet, nor do we have the toxicology and autopsy reports he'd promised. I try calling again, this time finally reaching him.

"Listen, Danté, I should have those in about twenty minutes. Problem is, I'm getting heat about coming down there. It would go much better for me if you can transmit it from here, is my way of thinking."

Panic! "I don't have microwave capability on such short notice."

"Well, at least I'll try to get you those reports."

"I can come there and shoot you, then rush back with the video. Find a good spot and turn on all the lights. I'm on my way."

"Well, okay."

Byron sets up the camera so all I have to do is power it and shoot. I grab a wide-eyed PA to drive and lug gear.

"Tell Cyn I'm chasing shots and wish her luck," I tell Byron. "And thanks."

"Just remember to point with this end of the camera," he advises with a smirk. Smart-ass.

As we race out of the parking lot, I notice a black Jeep pulling out not too far behind. Ah, my escort. Breathe a sigh of relief.

Out to the Wood Street Station, we find Culler in his office, ready to talk, but no reports yet. We set up a tripod, play with the lights, plug in a portable monitor, and watch the beginning of the show.

Montage of shots, quick run-through of who-all will be speaking—Kristen uses a still of Culler—intro the stories, new surprises and the latest information, tragedies with far-reaching consequences, the alleged poisoning of America. It's working; I already know this stuff, but I can still feel my blood pressure rising over M-Slovak. It's working.

Cyn gets most of the spotlight early, our tireless advocate for the victims, hurt so deeply by the pain and suffering she's witnessed, the heartache that will touch us all—if not consume us—should M-Slovak be permitted to continue this carnage.

"We're out of time," I tell Culler. "Let's shoot it without referring to the reports; then if they get here before I have to leave—"

We grab the shots, his stunning revelations that the drugstore son's death has been classified as murder, that not only was his father a murder victim, too, but there are strong suspicions of a second attempt on his life at the hospital. He admits the bombers fit the profile of professionals. The destruction of the drugstore was definitely more than retaliation for a little girl's death, possibly intended to murder Walt, the pharmacist who may have had knowledge about the robbery and stabbing. The police need help—we all need help—people to come forward with information, to solve these crimes before more are killed. He can't confirm if all this violence was related to the illicit drug trade, and he certainly can't conclude that Parzilac is to blame, but numerous leads are being followed and the investigation is still very much open.

I have nearly four minutes' worth—

And the reports arrive!

We grab Culler's last comments and run like hell, loading the van, pulling away just ahead of that black Jeep. I edit while my wide-eyed PA streaks toward *Shoot & Die*.

I've missed most of the show, our newly revealed footage of the Gordie tragedy, Reverend Falluson wrapping his spiritual arms around our communities—and around Cyn for standing against the maelstrom on behalf of those who need her help. I've missed Cyn detailing the suit, how Wanamaker, Salterfin & Brock will challenge the virtually limitless resources of the most pernicious of all mega-corporations.

I've missed Crabtree painting Parzilac's trail of violence and heartbreak across the country—indeed, around the world. I've missed the revelation of secret anti-merger videos appearing at homes and offices, and Crabtree telling us what these mean, why they're important, how he'll analyze this in-depth in his book—which he anticipates hitting the shelves in some four to six weeks.

I've missed the pharmaceutical expert telling us about all the painstaking research and testing M-Slovak had done, how the drug works, how the FDA had approved it, and how it still runs the gantlet of meticulous scientific examination. I've missed Hal asking him to explain why the indemnity absolution was so necessary, why M-Slovak had to assume liability for all this senseless violence just to assure physicians and psychiatrists they could write more prescriptions for more reasons without fear of accountability, no reprisal for their actions. I've missed the expert stammering—not appropriate for him to comment on legal matters—then Hal having to go to his only attorney-in-residence, my favorite lawyeress, Cyn SiCauge, and let her explain M-Slovak's position . . .

Slam dunk, kablooey!

I've missed the fatal volley, the clips from the satellite Parzilac roll-out, executives talking about running roughshod over the marketplace in their insane quest to shove pink capsules down America's collective throat, and all those success stories, the never-before-seen footage of a young woman writhing in a pool of her own blood, gasping her last breath, a bottle of pink capsules tipped and spilled.

I've missed the best-of-Gordie, the montage before and after, the chubby teen loved by his mother, the earnest young man hoping Parzilac will help him overcome his shyness, the story of how it overtook his life, the shots of him—now drug-crazed and under Parzilac's control—glaring into the camera that had once recorded his success, accusing, "You did this to me!"

We have eleven minutes remaining when I rush in during a commercial break. I run my disk, edited into four short segments, into the control room, dashing a 3X5 card out to Hal so he knows what to say. We hear background, comments from guests, our detective revealing even more, Hal Neusome with yet another scoop, and another, then another! Culler is holding up the reports, declaring: "There's no question. Hair and tissue tests show long-term use. Toxicology shows extremely high levels in his bloodstream. At the time of this firebombing, the shootings, the murders, Gordie Pollikey was unquestionably on Parzilac."

Grand slam!

A kick in the balls, if I may use another testicle metaphor.

Last comments, a personal observation by Hal—our veteran reporter who has seen so much this past week—a final montage of our horrendous footage, the wrap with NBS in New York, and we're clear.

Frank's had champagne and hors d'oeuvres set up in the conference room. Everybody is celebrating, Hal the center of attention. Cyn embraces me, Rob Salterfin pumping my hand till I think he's gonna pull it off—and bill for the pleasure—then our lawyers rush back to their office to handle incoming calls and requests from media outlets for statements, to be ready for the cameras showing up to do live remotes for the 11:00 news.

Kristen and I manage to sneak into my office so she can tell me about the segments I missed.

"It was flawless," she reports, "not as good as I'd like it to have been—" That's my director! "—But flawless."

So I'm caught up in the moment and hug her. She is, too, and hugs back. Whew! What a relief. Time to sleep for a week, another big one crossed off the list, a thousand new projects looming on the horizon.

Or hurtling down the hill toward us.

"Is it okay if I leave early?" she asks. "I'm not up for schmoozing."

"Neither am I. Let's glad-hand our way through the crowd one time and alert Frank we're out of here, then break and run for the door no matter how many are nipping at our heels."

Melissa catches us on the way out, more serious than the raucous crowd in there drinking to American tragedy. "I didn't realize—" she starts. "I mean, I knew what you were working on, but—" She takes a deep breath. "I'm glad you're doing this. I'm proud of Dellman/Roenik."

She hugs me. She hugs Kristen. We all hug each other again.

Out to the parking lot, another warm night, the noise of Chicago our soundtrack, Kristen says good-night.

"Listen, we only have the one escort. We'll both follow you home; then when you're safely inside, I'll head my way and let him follow me."

She breathes deeply. "That's a relief. I am," she admits sheepishly, "just a little bit scared."

"I'll talk to Flynn, see if we can't get you some protection, too, until we can solve this stalking problem."

She nods. "I hate to admit it—"

"Then don't," I tease, trying to keep this light.

She gets into her car, powering down the window. "I was worried about those Culler reports. I mean, we really would've had to dance if it turned out Gordie wasn't on the drug when he zonked out."

"That was just confirmation. The evidence was already overwhelming."

"Yeah, I guess you're right."

"Take it to the bank, Kristen—M-Slovak killed Gordie Pollikey."

CHAPTER 20

I've slept better than I have in a long time, and I'm actually humming the *Monster Bin* theme song to myself as I walk into *Shoot & Die*. I find Byron packing gear to shoot the big press conference at Wanamaker for Hal. Just then, Doug Moore and Rupert emerge from the simulator, their hair every which way, both grinning like overgrown goofs.

"I brought the last set of antigens," Moore tells me, straightening his jacket.

Melissa helps him with the collar, quietly suggesting, "Next time you boys should wear your play clothes."

Moore's still grinning. "I got the weekend focus-group results this morning—through the roof!"

We check them out—much coolness again—and commence with the daily Aller-Tat ritual in the kid-room. Taj wears the caterpillar this time—

And gets a reaction!

Two reactions, two of the segments forming welts almost immediately, so pronounced they damage the image of the critter. Moore retrieves his briefcase and fishes out the color-chart, checking the resins-and-chemicals list. "Rubber and latex," he pronounces.

"His hands!" Frank says. "He's been playing with that rubber band!"

Melissa is beside herself. "The elastic waistband in his underpants!" Then to the little one, "You hear that, Taj? We can stop your rash! Let's get your underpants off right now—you can just wear your shorts without them."

Taj is mortified, his eyes like saucers—his little girlfriend is right there!—*Mom, what are you doing to me?!*

Frank quickly intercedes, leading Taj away for some privacy to implement allergy-contingency plan number one. Melissa's hugging Doug Moore, thanking him profusely, tears in her eyes, problem identified, solution clear.

Aller-Tats, and the kids *wanted* to wear them. Pretty good product, pretty good marketing, pretty good hook, Danté.

Hal pokes his head in, so I follow him into the hallway. "The drugstore widow wants to be interviewed later today, sounds like she has something serious to say."

"Okay, set it up with Byron."

"Flynn Durbett's with her. They have something to take care of; then they'll be at her house by four. He said he'll protect her." Protect her?

Frank joins us, curious and concerned. We agree I'll go along for the interview; then Hal heads off to continue editing his highlights reel. I still have a few minutes before I need to leave for the Cyn-filing shoot, so I follow Frank into his office. He closes the door and drops into his chair, breathing a long sigh.

"What a relief," he says, shaking his head. "Danté, I've never felt so good about being in charge of launching a product. Imagine how these tattoos will help people—especially kids—all across the country, eventually around the world."

"Yeah, good for Taj."

"Yeah, good for Taj," he repeats, a faraway look in his eyes.

"Frank, you old softy."

Time to leave for the federal courthouse, our dog-and-pony show awaits. Passing by the ladies' room, I notice the golden-haired girl coming out with her mom, our Chyron operator who's carrying a small piece of cloth in her hand. She rolls her eyes at me, shaking her head and smiling.

"It's a solidarity thing," she chuckles, "to show their support for Taj. The kids have declared it no-underwear day."

*   *   *

Black hats and white hats.

That's what we need more of. You can't tell the good guys from the bad guys at a glance anymore. They're all dressed like lawyers. Of course, *my* lawyer looks great.

Cyn SiCauge, lead attorney, and Rob Salterfin, partner, parade into the federal courthouse. Byron's joined by five other news crews shooting the momentous event. This is more cameras than David got when he challenged Goliath, but then ours is the bigger story.

So the act of filing with a clerk isn't that much to look at, but our heroes do it with a magnanimous flourish, sharing grandiose platitudes, and reminding the reverent throng that a press conference back at Don Quixote Central begins in thirty minutes.

And Danté manages to get a hug and a kiss out of the whole deal. From Cyn, I mean.

The ante's been upped by the time we get over to the firm. There are twenty-some cameras waiting, including three with the logos of foreign press, and the room is packed. I should've thought to set up a concession stand and make a little money.

Cyn opens with her carefully prepared remarks, lots of buzz words like *accountability* and *liability* and *fallibility* and *responsibility* . . . We got us a billet o' billities.

Then Cyn takes questions, smoothly covering the basics, adroitly using catch phrases we'd rehearsed. She looks calm, relaxed, confident and sure, yet concerned at the right times, sympathetic at others, saddened by the heartache M-Slovak's greed has visited upon the trusting masses, those who now have their own voice, Cyn standing not behind them, not beside them, but leading the way.

"Miss SiCauge," a woman asks, "will you be working closely with the other attorney?" She checks her notes. "With Miss Cricket LaRayne?"

"She's not affiliated with Wanamaker, Salterfin & Brock, the law firm handling the bulk of this class-action." Low and away.

From another: "Care to comment on what Cricket LaRayne said on *The Morning Show*? She talked about you being too quick to jump to conclusions, that she intends a more thorough investigation before making claims."

Cyn smiles condescendingly—oh, isn't that cute; some youngster is playing attorney. "I think the evidence speaks for itself. I anticipate there will be many more revelations as we pursue justice."

"LaRayne is saying that, based on Detective Culler's comments, it sounds like Gordie Pollikey might have overdosed. If he were misusing the medication, wouldn't that hurt your claim?"

"I studied the autopsy reports," Cyn shoots back. "The evidence shows that Mr. Pollikey had taken only the prescribed dosage within his last twelve hours." Good, she's done her homework.

From another man: "Miss LaRayne claims that many of her clients are people you refused to help, those who lost their homes, who don't stand to collect as much damages as the ones you're willing to represent."

I can tell Cyn's getting angry. Right now wouldn't be a good time for a cricket to trundle across the floor in front of her. "We have turned nobody away," Cyn lies. "Our first priority has been to address those who lost loved ones, but we are open to helping anyone who has suffered from M-Slovak's negligence in distributing their potentially dangerous product."

Cricket, Cricket, Cricket . . . She's the cricket in the ointment. Another good guy, but this one's wearing a black hat.

Hal interrupts with a generic question and gets the session back on track.

There's a clarifier or two, Cyn summing up, time to shut this thing down.

Afterward, Cyn and Rob Salterfin are somewhat pleased, but the Cricket situation has them miffed. "Listen," Cyn instructs me, "you tell Melissa to dump LaRayne and sign with me, and for her to help me approach the others in her building, too—the ones who went over to that little bitch."

I can sympathize with Cyn, but to me it sounds like Cricket's just doing her job, no differently than I would expect from Cyn. Actually, the first time I laid eyes on her, I was impressed by her compassion.

Of course, anybody who can haul your butt into court is dangerous. Black hats and white hats . . .

They all look like lawyers to me.

*   *   *

It oughta be a smoke-filled room.

That's how I always picture this kind of gathering, four big-money players rolling up their sleeves to argue over how to divvy up the world.

Frank and I are meeting with Rex Briggs and Les Casapell. No Rupert right now; he's out Kehoeling with Meg to lock up oodles of media buys, his Aller-Tat ad mock-ups in hand. Rex and Les are here signing stacks of proofs, media logs, lots of paper and numbers which I think—I hope—Frank understands. I'm a bit distracted, it being such a nice, sunny day, that big window, beautiful grounds below, some kind of crane or heron or something standing in the pond out there by the waterfall . . .

The high-class version of a smoke-filled room.

"I need the approved legal disclaimer," Frank admonishes, "for Aller-Tat. I need it *yesterday.*"

Rex glares at Les, who manages to squirm without sacrificing too much of his panache. "Get me that sum-bitch on the phone!" He presses a button and barks orders at his minions. Within seconds, there's a man's voice speakerphoning into the room. "What's the hold up?" Rex demands.

"We were ready Friday, Rex, but a big decision just came down in the U.S. District Court out west, one we think might affect us. We're researching it. We have to do this right."

"What time today?" Rex demands.

"Wednesday, Rex."

"End of day tomorrow," Rex declares, "or I'll find something else you can research." Calm down, boy.

Rex wonders what I can show him on patch marketing—like I've even had time to sneeze in the last three days. I pull out my list of possible product applications so we can at least brainstorm, narrow it down, and find out just how much Briggs is willing to claim the Fantasy Patch can help without it getting too outrageous. I have things like: great sex; handling more responsibility with less stress; increasing confidence; focusing attention; overcoming phobias and performance anxiety and obsessive compulsions and anxiety attacks; controlling temper; curing addictions; affecting motivation, learning, self-esteem, and post-traumatic stress disorder; handling grief; managing pain, depression . . . *Diabetes? Acne? Cooties?*

Rex is liking the list. What the heck, think of more. Name 'em all. Fantasy Patch . . . *Imagine, Become, Anything!*

"Seriously—" Rex grins. Ah, he was joshing me. "Let's prioritize. Start with the approved applications: depression, obsessive compulsions, and anxiety. Then for the others, we'll have to rely more on testimonial. We'll be pushing docs hard to write off-label, but we can't make unsupported claims directly to consumers. Like your great-sex idea—we can't back that up with research yet, but after six months we won't have any trouble finding photogenic people willing to claim Fantasy Patch jazzed up their sex life."

We kick around a few more ideas and agree this needs to pick up some steam to meet our timetables.

"There's something else we need to stay on," I point out. "I'm hearing grumbles about the FDA approval last Friday. M-Slovak is going to come under intense scrutiny for its Parzilac testing, which could draw attention to the new patch on the block."

"Public relations will be part of your account," Rex says.

"Exactly, which is why I want to anticipate, and be ready for damage control."

"Good. What do you see as a problem?"

"For starters, it looks like you manipulated the FDA-approval process, side-stepping the suggestion for a scientific advisory committee, then got the voting question changed and sponsored a conference to lure away members while the others slammed a quick vote with barely a quorum."

"You've been doing your homework," Rex says, concerned but pleased. "Public doesn't give a damn about that."

"They might, especially with a zillion news hounds sniffing around for pharmaceutical scandals right now. So what's the deal? Did you get a dangerous drug approved just to put it on the market?"

Rex doesn't like that. "They're all dangerous," he snaps. "Even the damn tattoos are dangerous. It's risk versus benefit—"

"But it looks like the FDA didn't take a thorough look at that—"

"Look, Danté," he interrupts, a bit condescending now, "that's how it gets done. You want to put up a building, need a zoning variance, need some slack on the inspection; then you play the game, grease the wheel *before* it gets squeaky, tweak the politics when you have to. Try opening a restaurant with the health department on your ass, or a trucking company with the unions making demands, or putting a good drug out there on a seventeen-year patent. I spend hundreds of millions of dollars on research and testing and marketing, only to have some damn bureaucrat who pulls down eighty-thou a year—paid with *my* tax dollars—telling me to sit still for years, costing me millions, letting my competitors get out there in front of me, just so he can pretend he's providing a public service." I'm guessing this is a sore point.

"So you bribed and connived to get this through," I summarize.

Frank's about to wet himself. "Well, I wouldn't call it—"

"You're damn right I did. Just like M-Slovak bribed and connived to hold up my approval for more than a year. The FDA is nothing but extortion, and I gotta pay it one way or the other. Might as well be the quick way."

Les steps in, a bit nervous. "Danté, if you have a problem—"

"I never said that."

"Oh, not at all," Frank adds.

I explain, "I need to know what I'm dealing with. You never lie to your shrink; you never lie to your lawyer; and you don't lie to the PR guy who has to paint your keister pretty colors if you get it caught hanging out the window."

Rex grins, then reaches over and claps me on the shoulder. See, I can talk like these mover-shakers. "Fantasy Patch is a big keister. It needs to be *real* pretty."

"I want to do some serious shooting at AnalyClin," I tell him. "I'll be right there on the lake later this week anyway, filming for Sizemore. Let me put together the patch-testing story, be ready to counter anything negative that flies at us."

Rex nods to Les. "Set him up, free run." Then to me, "Needless to say, you get something that smells bad, you run it by us first, or make it go away."

"I'll bring perfume," I say by way of not answering his remark.

"Are we done then?" Rex asks, getting up. Get ye out, ye boreth me now. The smoke-filled room is closing.

"Our secretary's kid just used the Aller-Tats," I mention, "to solve a serious rash problem—turns out it was a rubber/latex allergy."

"Great!" Rex says, grinning.

"No problems?" Les asks.

"They're terrific," Frank confirms.

Rex adds, "I sure hope we're fully distributed before the first anaphylactic shock."

*   *   *

Road trip.

Cruising out on these remote shoots with Hal and Byron is starting to feel like those college-days road trips; load up and trek; party down. This time I'm the one driving. Where's the beer?

"She's nervous," Hal says. "I think she knows something about the murders of her husband and son, and she's scared. Why else would Flynn be protecting her today?"

But I'm distracted. I've just spotted the blue van!

"Blue van," I say with forced calm. "Call."

Byron's on the red button like he knows the answer to *Mortal Danger for a thousand, Alex.* "Danté sees the blue van," he says into the phone. Then he tells me, "They know. Flynn says they're tracking it." Byron listens for a second, then gives me the phone.

"You wanna get it on camera?" Flynn asks.

"Get what?"

"We're gonna catch 'em."

"Um, sure."

"Make sure Byron doesn't show me." He directs me which route to take, where to pull over quickly and let Byron get out to run behind a building, the blind driveway I'm to go through, and where the ambush will be. I don't like the sound of this, but Byron's already powering up the cam. "Don't get us gunned down, Flynn."

"Be ready to duck fast," he advises. Sounds like he's kidding, but I don't think he kids about this stuff.

This ain't no college road trip.

I lose sight of the van for a while, thinking—hoping—I've lost them. No, I take that back. Let's get these guys once and for all. We'll catch them in the act, then squeeze until they lead us right back to M-Slovak. What a scandal! Then I could have Cyn sue them on *my* behalf, all this stress I've been through, physical endangerment, blah blah.

There it is. No doubt now, no way somebody would be following the same circuitous route I'm taking.

Byron's ready to jump out. Hal's combing his hair. *Combing his hair!* I think he'd take a bullet to be in the shot, no pun intended.

Pulling in, straight back, farther. Yes, they're down the street, hesitating, seeing where I go. Around the corner, stop!

Byron's out, trotting around the other side. I can see him reach the big bricked-in sign where he'll be crouching, but I have to keep moving. I quickly turn around and come back out, heading the other way now, pulling into the next lot. Durbett's picked two shuttered manufacturing places so there are no cars or people around. I hope.

And there's the van.

I see a black Jeep not far behind it.

"Go ahead," Durbett says from the phone.

Circle back; turn right, between the buildings. As I pass the back corner, I see another black Jeep waiting off to the side, yet another coming toward me, pulling off to the other side.

"Keep going," Durbett says. "Take your time. Make sure they can see you."

I'm pulling into the back street now. The only way through is between these buildings. I look like I'm driving away.

Too far now, I can't see the van, can't tell what's happening. "How many are in the van?" I ask Durbett. "Four? Five?"

"Two."

"Are they coming?"

"Not now, Danté—I'm working." Yeah, I guess he's busy.

Screech! A squeal of tires, banging sounds, shouting.

No gunfire . . .

"Clear, Danté. Get over here with Hal if he wants to get in the picture."

And there they are, the blue van pinned between buildings by black Jeeps, several armed men crouched and aiming with deadly rigidity, the passenger spread-eagled on the ground, Durbett—wearing a headset for talking to me—standing in the open driver's door, a pistol to the head of one terrified-looking tubby. Byron's several feet back getting the shot, past Durbett's body so only his arm will show.

Hal's up there now, me not far behind. "Why are you following us?" he demands.

"We—we—we just wanted—" Tubby is hyperventilating, slowly stepping out of the van at Durbett's insistence. "We just wanted—just wanted to get some—get some, too."

"Some what?" Hal demands, but then we all see it. He's wearing it across his back. He figured we knew where to get the shots.

His jacket says he's a news shooter.

WBMF News 9.

*   *   *

It looks like a regular dining-room laboratory.

Flynn Durbett has set up equipment here in the home of our subject, the grieving drugstore widow/mother who'll be returning any minute. Dr. Arnie Stewart, expert at both gas and liquid spectrochromatography, is typing into a computer. Byron's set and lit to shoot, Hal ready to interview. A black Jeep arrives, Jankety escorting today's newsmaker.

Exhausted and nervous, she sets a file folder on the table and takes her seat, steeling herself to face the camera. Hal sits across from her, and Byron starts rolling.

"We're here," Hal begins, "because you have information about the murders of your husband, one of his pharmacists, and now your son."

"I'm afraid," she says, taking a deep breath. "I'm afraid I may be next. My son decided to tell the truth, and look what happened—" She closes her eyes for a moment, fighting to keep her composure. "They—they killed him."

"Who killed him?"

"The drug company—M-Slovak, I think." She hesitates, then continues. "I don't know. That's what he was afraid of, but he didn't say anything more about who might be after him."

"You believe he had information they wanted kept secret?"

"It started sometime ago when my husband—" She looks away from Hal. "Well, it seems he owed some people, and they started demanding certain . . . favors."

"Extortion? What did they want him to do?"

"Substitute samples of new drugs in place of Parzilac, something about solving the problem with violence, a way to test breakthroughs that aren't patented yet. He would take capsules that look like Parzilac and mix them with the real ones."

"Illegally testing a new pharmaceutical compound," Hal intones, "without FDA approval, on unsuspecting subjects, local citizens being used as unwitting guinea pigs."

Durbett looks at me, and suddenly it makes sense. M-Slovak would want to sire a new billion-dollar baby before the old one's patent expires, so why not find the best compound before starting the clock ticking on a new patent. Then years from now, they could time it to sail through the approval process on a sure thing, introduce it just before Parzilac goes generic, and continue dominating the market for another decade or more. If current Parzilac users can't tell they've been switched, M-Slovak will know it has a winner ripe for smooth transition.

"And this arrangement soured at some point?" Hal asks her.

"The pharmacist there on Madison—Walt, the one who was killed?—he was involved, too, but when he came back after caring for his terminally ill wife, he refused to participate anymore."

"When was this?"

She thinks. "Two, two-and-a-half months ago."

"But nothing happened right away?"

"My son said they stopped receiving them after that, but there were still some in the store. My husband filled in behind the counter one day while Walt went to an appointment. When Walt returned, he discovered my husband had opened a box of the counterfeits and used them to fill a prescription. Walt became furious and threatened to go to the police, so my husband called my son and had him come take the box, instructing him to destroy it. Walt never knew there were more in the cabinet in back, boxes my husband kept as possible evidence in case they tried to pressure him again."

"What happened the night of your husband's accident?"

"My son said he worried the store might be robbed, so he was bringing a box home to put in the safe. He, um, never made it . . ."

"And the store bombing?"

She drifts for a moment, then focuses her attention back on Hal, wiping the tears from her eyes. "My son believed that allowing you and those TV cameras inside the store that night made them think Walt was blabbing to the media, so they killed him and destroyed the store to get rid of any remaining evidence."

"Is that why your house was ransacked, too, the evening of your son's murder?"

"All I know is, my son decided to come forward. He told me don't worry, he would tell the truth, and we wouldn't have to—and I wouldn't have to . . . live in fear anymore."

Hal remains quiet for a moment, then quietly asks, "You have some evidence for us today?"

She slides the file folder across the table. Inside is a simple Post-It note with handwriting scrawled across the front: *Pi-ethym-lorenazol* and *Research Surplus*. "This was stuck on the underside of one of the boxes." She glances toward Jankety, who opens a hard-shell case and sets out a wrapped present, sliding it in front of her.

"And what is this?" Hal asks.

"I disguised it as a gift," she says, "and asked a friend to hide it for a while." Hands shaking, she carefully unwraps the paper to reveal a brown box just like those we found in the locked cabinet.

"Is that—?" Hal starts to ask, but she's already nodding her head.

"It's the box my husband gave my son in front of Walt, the one he told him to destroy." She opens it to reveal thousands of loose pink capsules.

Durbett is shaking his head and looking at me, leaning over to whisper, "Every sample I grabbed from those boxes tested as pure Parzilac."

"Maybe it registers the same on tests," I suggest, but he gives me that look. What, a pillow-case won't break my fall?

Byron adjusts his shot, Hal introducing our expert by rattling off a list of credentials. "Dr. Stewart will help us analyze samples of the alternate drug disguised as everyday Parzilac."

Stewart breaks the seal on a rack, exposing a hundred miniature test tubes, then goes to work. Hal has him explaining liquid spectrochromatography to the audience while he slices capsules, adds water, then takes readings. To me, it sounds like a catechism in Latin interspersed with Amazon Yanomami and Waodoni poetry.

And we hold our breaths as he feeds the data into a computer, each new screen resulting in several pages emerging from the laser-printer . . .

Finally, he announces the results: "Pi-ethym-lorenazol—that and an inert buffer. Pure Parzilac."

And we all take a breath.

He finishes inputting the results of a hundred samples, all pure Parzilac.

Video still recording, Hal asks, "Can you explain what kind of data you're reading?" A typical newsman who's lost his story, he talks authoritatively about what we *don't* know. Let's find some outraged neighbors and ask them if they'd ever suspected anything . . .

"These detail molecular composition," Stewart explains, showing us a graph with a long, flowing line, many tiny bumps, and one big spike near the center. "And this lists the chemical breakdown," he says, showing us some printing below. It still looks like Yanomami to me.

"What is this?" Hal asks, gesturing to another of the pages.

"Composition of the sample, total mass, ratio of compounds, solubility of the buffer—see here, this one was a hundred forty-nine and eight-tenths milligrams. A little over seven milligrams—or four percent of it—was pi-ethym, the remaining ninety-six percent being buffer."

Durbett smacks the wall. Hal glances at him for permission to bring it up, then says, "Samples we tested earlier showed *eighty*-percent pi-ethym, only twenty-percent buffer."

Stewart looks surprised, then starts rifling through a binder, finally declaring, "Four percent is about right. What you're describing would be the equivalent of twenty doses in one capsule, three weeks' worth taken all at once." He starts sorting the printouts, checking the pages he'd ignored earlier, explaining, "I understood we were only looking for a different drug." He pulls out one, then another, then a third page. "Samples twenty-six, thirty-five, and eighty-one," he breathes like a treasure hunter discovering lost booty. "My God, three out of a hundred samples, eighty-percent pure! This amount approaches serious toxicity. I can't imagine what they would do to someone, especially a brain already biochemically imbalanced."

"Like maybe suffering a psychotic break?" Hal asks. "Even becoming violent?"

"That's not my field," Stewart cautions, "but just imagine that happening to somebody who doesn't understand, and who has no control over it!"

"Why might M-Slovak be testing the effect of such large doses?"

He shakes his head. "It makes no sense. They already know the toxicity levels. This looks more like product tampering than testing."

The widow is crying now. "I'm sorry," she says, shaking her head. "I know my husband hated M-Slovak."

Hal says, "He once filed an unsuccessful lawsuit against M-Slovak, did he not?"

"I don't— It must—" She suddenly looks very resolute. "I don't think I should answer any more questions." She hurries down the hallway and disappears into a bedroom.

Byron stops recording and starts playing with the monitor, attaching a small receiver/tuner, presumably to check for breaking news. Hal looks pleased with the outcome, but Durbett is shaking his head.

"This could be a ploy," Durbett says. "M-Slovak could have been looking to lay blame on tampering as a way to explain all them cases of violence."

"You think there's more of the extra-pures out there?" I ask.

Durbett looks skeptical. "No, I do believe the family quit playin' ball a few months ago, which is why all this trouble, but just to be sure I'll put a team out to pull all the Parzilac from the family's stores, then follow up with their customers. We need to do some investigating, but you all need to remember: whether or not you want to bring in Culler or the feds right away will affect how fast you give up your exclusive story. That's your choice, not mine."

"I want the facts first," Hal declares. Yeah, those would be nice. Where do we place an order for pure, unadulterated facts?

"We've been trashing M-Slovak all week," I point out, "and now it looks like they might be the victim, too, the victim of a man we've been whitewashing and varnishing, a man who even lied to his own family to cover up his crimes."

Byron turns up the sound on a shot of Cyn at her press conference . . .

"M-Slovak is poisoning America! They *will* be held accountable!"

CHAPTER 21

All this technology plugging us into every aspect of each other's lives, and I can't reach Cyn because she's busy with interviews, her cell-phone turned off. I land at *Shoot & Die*, program her number to auto-dial through the switchboard, then ask reception dude to punch the button every few minutes and buzz me if Cyn answers.

Frank sees me and pulls me into his office. Rupert's there taking notes while Jankety plays a surveilled conversation between Dib Wardley and that least creative of creative directors, Sam Cox. It seems like I'm plugged into everybody in the world right now—except Cyn.

"This is from an hour ago," Jankety explains.

Wardley's voice is saying, "Ferman busted my chops, all right. Bottom line: we're to present nothing new to Wooter's people for now."

"That's *our* account," Sam grumbles. "Either he's planning to pull us off it, or worse, Wooter's looking to take a walk."

"I think it's worse. After that he chatted about several minor things, then casually asked about Roenik's work, how he is with clients and coming up with ideas on the fly. He must think Frank's group are going to be serious players after all, as in maybe they'll have more business like the tattoo job to bring Kehoe."

"I hate to see Ferman kissing their butts. If we don't put them out of business soon, he'll be expecting *us* to kiss next. I think I have a way to knock 'em out."

"It can't be something that'll come back on us."

"Hey, I'm slicker than that." Yeah, if you consider the definition for *unctuous*. "Meg had Charles do the 'stats for five tattoo magazine ads, but there's some language missing, so he red-stamped them *Sample* and typed in a slot saying a disclaimer warning about the danger of serious shock would be inserted in the final proofs—you know, so each publisher's standards and practices people can sign off in advance of last-second drops going directly to lay-out."

"You're thinking of making sure the finals arrive late so the campaign falls apart?"

"Better," Sam gloats. I can almost hear the malevolent grin. "Here's the good part: Meg and Charles were goofing around with Rupert Allup, trying to get him to relax and talk about his new job. For laughs, they made some versions of the ads that say look out, this stuff can kill your kids." Sam pauses for effect. "You think Briggs would fire them if *that* hit the nationals?"

"Heh heh heh," Dib says, and it's not the chuckle of an innocent joke. "It would kill their reputation, too, and put them out of business." He pauses. "I don't know, though. They could probably lay the blame on us."

"Not if Rupert signs off on the wrong finals."

"Oh yeah?"

"When he calls in the disclaimer sometime late tomorrow, Charles is supposed to drop it in and have the 'stats ready for approval before they're Fed-Ex'ed Wednesday morning. Instead of reshooting them, he can just strip in the changes, and Rupert's just an inexperienced kid who won't know the difference."

Rupert stiffens at the slight. Frank nudges him, saying, "You've hit the big time, kid—insulted by jealous hacks." Jankety grins, but Rupert's not amused.

Sam continues. "With the right kind of fixative, that new disclaimer could peel off, you know, accidentally—from *all* the copies going out."

"What if Rupert wonders why the file isn't just updated and reprinted?"

"Once you open a file, everybody from proofreading to the clients have to sign off again in case a stray keystroke or data error alters some other part of the ad. There's no time."

"I don't know . . . Rupert still might figure out what happened and blame us."

"Hey, Charles's story will be that he did reshoot them. When Rupert comes over here Wednesday to sign off, he's supposed to pick up a stack of old Sizemore print-ad proofs and silverprints Billy says he wants archived at his new, uh, *agency*." It's a swear-word.

"The reshoots will be mixed in," Dib says, finally racing ahead. "Heh heh heh." Man, I hate that laugh.

"And when it blows up in Dellman/Roenik's face, Charles will suggest they check the Sizemore pile and make sure *Rupert* didn't mix them up."

"Do it," Dib says.

Jankety cuts off the recording. "The rest is about their other clients—none of your business." There's that spy code of ethics.

"So let's do a switchback," I suggest.

Jankety grins. "Just make sure it looks like Rupert's the one who caught on, not that you had surveillance."

"I would have anyway," Rupert says, still indignant.

"One reason you're here," Frank says, poking him in the shoulder. "Well, we know we can trust Meg. She's no fan of Cox or Wardley."

Rupert says, "I'll arrange for her to ship the good ones, and maybe have a little fun with Charles."

Jankety says, "Sounds like a plan, but every secret operation needs a name."

Rupert has a suggestion, nothing fancy, but certainly to the point: "Let's call it *Screw Sam And Dib Day*."

*   *   *

Kristen is waiting in my office, not working, not taking notes, not doing anything—a rare sight, indeed.

"I talked to Hal," she says. "You have to go public about the fake Parzilacs—right away."

I shake my head and drop onto the divan beside her. "That could be playing right into M-Slovak's hands."

"But you don't know."

"I do know somebody can't make the contents of a capsule *more* pure, so there has to be *some* reason they sent this guy eighty-percenters."

"And there could be more out there."

"Just in case, Durbett accessed the stores' computer records, then sent people to round up all the 'scripts, replace them, and even issue generous Weisman Catalog gift certificates under the guise of a promotion. He's holding on to the last doctored case for evidence."

"But you're letting Cyn destroy Parzilac's reputation. We put a media steam-roller into motion, and now it's out of control with Cyn aboard. You need to go public, even if it's to admit you don't have answers yet."

"Look, we're dealing with a handful of stores in Chicago, and Cyn's addressing a long-term problem all over the country. Handled wrong, this could kill her case."

"And the steam-roller just keeps on rolling."

"I have a call in to Cyn," I reassure her. "As soon as I hear from her, I'm going to tell her to back off a bit, at least while Hal and Durbett investigate."

"What if she won't?"

"She will. You don't know her like I do."

"No, I don't," she admits. "But I do know you, Danté, and I expect you to do the right thing."

"I will," I promise.

"Even if it means stepping in front of the steam-roller."

*　　　*　　　*

I need to get out of here, so I hit the road toward Cyn's office downtown. Reception dude is ready to transfer the call to my cell-phone the minute she checks in.

Ring. Yes!

"Danté? Hal Neusome here." Rats. I need to talk to Cyn, not Hal-the-Nuisance. "What did you decide?" I ask him.

"We're keeping it under wraps for now. The researcher was working for Durbett, so that's confidential. The widow's in no hurry to talk to anybody about anything, but if she does I'll explain my delay as *still investigating.*"

"You can't sit on this too long," I caution him.

"No, but when I told NBS I had a potential bombshell, they gave me a slot on *Newsline* Thursday night. That gives me three days to figure this out."

"In the meantime, Cyn is spending money and risking her reputation out there trashing Parzilac."

"But she's going after M-Slovak now, not the local drugstore guy. She can focus on those cases all over the country."

"But the suit is based heavily on Gordie and the suicide girl having been in the trial groups, the impact of that footage on a jury, the potential for public-relations damage scaring them into ponying up. If that connection falls apart—if it looks like M-Slovak can claim those even *might* have resulted from local tampering—then the limb Cyn's out on will break out from under her."

"Then it's already starting to crack. I checked with the moms, and it turns out both Gordie and the suicide girl got their test-trial Parzilac through our guy's drugstores—and Gordie was still getting his there on Madison Street."

*　　　*　　　*

After a long, lonely drive downtown, my thoughts going a thousand miles an hour, I'm waiting for Cyn, hoping to catch her as soon as she gets back.

"Mr. Salterfin and Miss SiCauge will see you now." I feel privileged.

They're pleased to see me, but I proceed to displease them with my tale of product tampering.

"You have no proof of this," Salterfin says, glaring at me. "An isolated incident at best, not linked to the circumstances impacting our lawsuits, probably planted by M-Slovak to divert blame." He remains standing behind his desk, so we're all standing, me across from him, Cyn off to the side. "We cannot allow them to get away with this. This information must be contained." Cyn's nodding agreement.

"Well, it's in the hands of a news reporter—"

"One who is in your pocket," he reminds me.

"He's going to sit tight a few days until more can be learned, but in the meantime, you need to back off."

"Look," Salterfin says, "somebody duped the widow. She realized she'd been taken in once you tested the capsules. A few of the right words to her about the liability against her husband's estate and she'll shut up and go away. There's no police involved yet. Hal Neusome can't prove anything either way. You're the one in control." Salterfin comes around his desk and stands three feet from me, those beady eyes narrowed to a laser stare. "Make it go away."

I glance toward Cyn, but she's looking back and forth between us, near panic in her face. "We can trust the investigator who's—"

"You're not listening," Salterfin repeats. "What part of *contain this now* do you not understand?"

Now he's pissing me off. "The part where it's my decision and not yours," I tell him. Cyn's shoulders slump dejectedly.

Salterfin goes back behind his desk and sits down. "Let me explain something to you," he says condescendingly. "If you insist on going forward with this, I can have an emergency motion to compel discovery filed within an hour—and I'll name *you*. You're not a news reporter; you're a source whose identity has become known. I can get a judge to order you to turn over *all* your videos, your information, the names of everybody involved. I can subpoena and depose you. I'll get enough to pursue M-Slovak without you, plus go after you and Dellman/Roenik and *Shoot & Die* and every one of your little cohorts."

"On what grounds?!"

"Have your expensive, asset-depleting team of attorneys call me and we'll discuss that. I'll remind you that I have a recording of our initial meeting here in my office."

"But you said it was confidential."

"And it was—until after I said that. I got most of the rest, though, except the parts that might be embarrassing to me. Everything else is my word against yours—and your fiancée's here—who by the way could find herself out on the street so fast she won't have time to think about her chances of ever again getting a job with a reputable firm—especially after I sue her for collusion."

"She's got the clients."

"Not when her license is suspended for investigation of ethics charges," he spars.

"You're overreacting. In a few days, this will probably—"

"When I have to play probabilities, I move to increase my odds—no hesitation."

"Then I guess it *will* be my word and Miss SiCauge's word against yours."

"Unless she decides to salvage her career and back *me* up," he says, never once glancing her way.

"Danté," she says, "let's go somewhere and talk about this."

"I won't be convinced to play cover-up for Mr. Dribble-Trou here—and I *won't be bullied*, either."

"He doesn't care about you," Salterfin says to her, still focusing his gaze on me, a game of chicken who-blinks-first. "He'd permanently destroy your career before making the smallest concession that won't even hurt his own. There's a way here that everybody wins, but he doesn't care enough about you to take it."

"Danté—"

"But there's the ethical solution," I tell him, "and Cyn won't sacrifice her ethics for somebody—or for a firm—that obviously doesn't have any." I'm moving toward the door now.

"That's her choice. If she walks out of here with you now, she's through."

I'm at the door, looking at Cyn. She's biting her knuckle, but hasn't moved.

"You got too much of a promising future," Salterfin says, finally looking at her, "to leave now."

"I have space for you to open your own office," I tell her. "You don't need this."

She looks at him.

She looks at me.

She looks at him again.

"Danté, just go home and cool off for now. We'll work this out tonight."

It's a long, lonely drive home, and I don't know what to think.

*   *   *

I pull into my driveway, followed by a black Jeep. I'd rather be on some tropical beach somewhere, thousands of miles away from it all.

I invite Durbett inside. He says he's only going to stay a minute, and wants to know if everything's all right. I tell him about my problem with Rob Salterfin, downplaying Cyn's ambivalence and wavering loyalty.

"Give me your videos," he suggests. "Don't worry about him serving me with a subpoena. That'll happen only if and when I want it to. It's up to you, but you might try playing with him. Make copies of only what's been shown on the news; then dump them at his office; tell him you're out of the news biz; tell him to go to hell. Maybe he'll run his mouth and say something stupid, something you can use against him."

We talk about it for a bit, and I wind up agreeing with him before he leaves. I don't know how my talk with Cyn will go tonight, but I know I can't trust Salterfin—and neither can she. I call Byron and ask him to arrange to have somebody pull a late-night dubbing session.

Hoping Cyn will arrive soon, instead I receive two surprise visitors. Kristen looks sad, tired even, but Cricket appears to be absolutely exhausted. "She hasn't slept in two days," Kristen explains.

"Please," Cricket interrupts her, "let's not take up too much of his time."

"He needs to know what you've been doing," Kristen tells her.

"I'd like to know, Cricket."

"I have eighteen families—nineteen including Melissa Norrow and her son, Taj. She's the only one who's landed safely, a good place to stay, financial support, no concerns about feeding or caring for her son. I've been trying to get people into shelters or temporary placements, cajoling landlords, fighting bureaucracies, trying to get aid for them—I even have one mother and her little boy—about Taj's age, he is—staying at my tiny place for now. Mr. Ritenour has let me spend some of the firm's money, and I've exhausted my savings, which wasn't much given my law-school loans I'm still paying off . . ." She takes a deep breath.

Kristen continues for her, "Now some of her people are asking her to help arrange—or pay for—transportation downtown to see Cyn. They've heard she said on TV that she's now willing to take them. They all think she's going to make zillionaires out of them."

"I understand Miss SiCauge is planning to meet with two of my families later this evening," Cricket adds.

"I don't think that'll happen tonight," I assure her. Cyn and I have our own agenda, a much higher priority.

Cricket looks somewhat relieved. "Mr. Ritenour thinks there'll be a big settlement with M-Slovak down the line, but these people need help right away. On top of it, if some go over to Miss SiCauge, then that will be my fault and I'll probably lose my job and not be able to do anything for the others. I've looked into the building's insurance, but that won't help, and I've niggled a few other ideas, but can't come up with anything substantial. I assume Miss SiCauge has enough damning evidence to bully M-Slovak into settlements, and I hope to ride her coattails if that's true, but I can't be sure, and I can't make promises, and I . . . need help."

"She has two questions for you, Danté," Kristen says.

"Yes," Cricket says. They've decided in advance to keep this simple and to the point. "First, off the record if you must, I need to know if there's anything in your videos or information, any suggestion of other sources for collecting against liability—like other people involved, sprinkler system that didn't come on in time to save the building—I'm clutching at straws, I know, but I'm out of time." I don't know what to tell her. Sensing this, she continues, "And the second question is, should I tell my people honestly that they are better off signing with Wanamaker Salterfin? I'll drive them down there myself if it's a way to get them taken care of right away."

I get up, glance out the front window, think . . . "I'll let you watch the videos, Cricket—but I don't think you'll find anything you don't already know." I turn in time to see her shoulders drop. "I have an idea." I call Reverend Falluson on the speaker phone and quickly explain Cricket's problem. He's indignant.

"I thought these people were being taken care of by your fiancée's law firm. Miss Cricket, you should have come to me sooner."

"If you and your people," I offer, "and the community can rally around and help these people, I'll document your efforts and make sure you get some exposure for your good work." I know which buttons to push on Falluson, I sure do.

"That won't be necessary," he counters. "Most of the people I'll involve would be embarrassed by the attention. If you want me to say something or arrange something good to see, I can do that, but let's not go overboard on this."

"Um, sure. I'm a little surprised, though—"

"Danté, you see me manipulating the publicity machine sometimes because that's what I gotta do. If I don't, somebody else will, and I happen to believe strongly in what I do. My people expect me to be out front and be their voice when they need one. Sometimes I speak for the cause; sometimes it's to enhance my own prominence—but that's only so more people will listen next time. I've tried to be a part of what you're doing because what you're doing is right, finding justice amid these awful tragedies, your belief in the truth paramount. Cricket dear, you get me a list of what you need, come on out here tonight if you can, and we'll work on this together." He pauses. "You're not alone, child."

Cricket shows the hint of tears welling in her eyes. So does Kristen. We thank him and say good-bye.

And I still have another question to answer.

"Cricket, go with your instincts. If you believe Wanamaker Salterfin wants to sign your people because they can do more for them than you can, and can do it faster, then you wish them the best and send them on their way." I lean forward and fix her with my eyes. "But if you believe, in your heart, that they'll get the attention they deserve from you, that their best choice is to trust you, then you fight for 'em. I promise you that any information I have will also be available to you. You're not alone, Cricket."

She takes my hands and squeezes them, her eyes glistening. Kristen is smiling through her own tears, reminding our crusader, "Let's get going, Cricket. We have a lot to do tonight."

Cyn arrives just as they drive away. She melts into my arms.

"Danté, I am so sorry. Rob's a son of a bitch who had no right talking to you like that."

"Or to you," I point out, pulling back enough to look in her eyes. "God, I missed you, Cyn," I whisper.

She's surprised. "Silly!—I just saw you a few hours ago."

"But you were a long way away these past few hours." She doesn't understand.

"Listen," she says, shifting into her business mode. "I can't stay long. I have to meet a couple of those damn low-lifes who signed with Cricket. They called our office looking to jump, so I have to make good on what I said in the TV interviews. I really don't have time for this. I'm on *The Morning Show* tomorrow, and I need to be ready—"

"Cyn, aren't you going to back off a few days? You know, until we know if Parzilac really is to blame?"

She's crestfallen. "Danté, please don't start that again. I hope you realize Rob is right, that you can't reveal anything about this, that you should destroy that video showing tampered capsules. I called Hal Neusome and he said as far as he knows, it's a hoax or a ploy, and that he can't broadcast anything about it unless something new comes to light."

"But when something does—"

"But something *won't* if you'll just back off," she blurts, frustrated now. "Danté, I don't understand. You're messing up everything we worked for. We've come so far."

"How far? How far have we come, Cyn? Are you ready to commit even to being engaged to me, right here, right now, tonight?"

"Oh, Danté, Danté—we've already discussed this."

"No, we've avoided this! Come on, Cyn. I love you, and I'm tired of careers and everybody else's problems getting in our way. Why do we have to wait? *How long* do we have to keep waiting?"

"Look," she says evenly, "if you'll let this thing about tampering die so I can get on with the Parzilac lawsuit, we'll get engaged as soon as I finish discovery."

"That could take years."

"Okay, after the interrogatories. Probably six months, tops."

"Come on, Cyn, how much am I bid for each of our children?"

"You've just gotta have a rugrat, huh? Okay, after the suit is settled, if the doctor says I can handle it, we'll have one child."

Now I'm angry. "You're gonna negotiate our happiness, too? Shouldn't I have my own lawyer here to represent *my* interests?"

"Everything's a joke with you, isn't it?" she growls. "You're never happy to leave things the way they are, always gotta push me into something I don't want—" She stops short, catching her breath, maybe realizing she was going too far.

"No, Cyn," I say quietly. "Unless we both want something with all our hearts, we'll never have it." I'm shaking now, breathing hard, my heart pounding.

"I'm late for my meeting," she says.

"Cyn, don't sign those people. You're not going to help them."

"Screw those people. It's public relations. That bitch Cricket has been blasting me; I'm gonna blast her back by showing off on the news that her clients are jumping over to me."

"Please don't sign them, Cyn. Cricket's going to help them. You don't need the PR."

"I have to go," she says. "I'll call you tomorrow."

And go she does.

Out to her vehicle, she gets in, slams the door, starts the engine, races out of the drive, and never looks back.

I sit on the couch, my eyes blurry now, and it's getting harder to see. I can hear the back door quietly open, somebody coming into the front room. Ms. Moeroff sits beside me and puts her arms around me.

Neither of us speaks, but she hands me a tissue. My nose is runny for some reason.

She whispers in my ear, "Draw me some pictures, Danté."

I have to chuckle, sniffling so I don't snot the front of my shirt.

"Please?" she asks, more serious than I thought. I let her lead me upstairs to the artboard, where we sit side by side.

"What do you want?" I ask, getting my composure back.

"A picture of you, someplace nice."

I have to chuckle again. Okay, sure. I draw a simple sketch of me sitting on the beach, the gentle whitecaps washing up onto the sand, a flock of gulls circling overhead, a sand-castle nearby, the sun hanging low in the sky, reflecting across the water. I'm calming down now, feeling a bit more relaxed. Theta-therapy.

"You look lonesome," she says, eyeing my sketch. "Are you all by yourself?"

That earns a mild snort. She's something else. "My friends are running around, playing on the beach."

"Ah," she says, nodding. "They're just beyond the frame, leaving you with your thoughts. But they're close by, right?" She's looking at me earnestly.

"Oh yeah. They're always close by."

"Is Cyn out of the picture?" Just like that. She speaks her mind.

I let my head hang a second, eyes blurry again. "Yeah."

She leans over to look at me closer. "Is there nobody to sit beside my young friend?"

I shake my head no.

She stands, gives me a final hug, and asks, "Are you okay now?"

"Yeah."

"Good, I'll leave you alone. You have a lot to do."

I look up at her as she pauses in the doorway. She looks back at me with the face of a mom, bless her heart, this old lady who loves me at least a much as I love her. "A lot of *what* to do?"

She smiles, turning to leave, and answers, "You haven't finished your picture."

CHAPTER 22

Strip me naked and spray me with de-louser.

Take my belt and shoelaces, too—might as well, the way this feels. Metal detector, pat down, running my box and papers through an X-ray . . . "You can't put the videos or data-disk through that thing," I warn. I'm not used to such treatment just to meet with a lawyer. Who'd have thought Wanamaker, Salterfin & Brock would have a room set up like this? Besides Flynn Durbett, I mean.

Now the smartly dressed goons are using one of those devices that checks for radio and electrical signals. They're scanning the videos, the disk, the box of bottled Parzilac, then me again for good measure. They have to make sure I'm not sporting false gotchies.

One goon removes the videos from their cases one at a time, peering into the windows of all seven 8mm videocassettes to make sure they contain rolled tape. He's stymied by number eight, the odd-sized tape—"Betacam SP," I explain—until I show him the tiny button on the side to hinge open the protector and see the tape where it runs along the front. He has no idea these formats are practically antique to professional shooters.

"He's clean," a goon assures Salterfin as I'm ushered into the office. "No wires, no listeners, no weapons, no devices of any kind." Just a pair of thoroughly scanned gotchies.

Actually, now that I think about it, I am still using Durbett's key ring with that little twisty thing, but it's not activated for signal, and I don't plan to attack Salterfin with it.

The door buzzes, then opens as Cyn enters the room.

"Nobody else," I tell him. "This is *our* meeting." I avoid looking at Cyn.

He nods toward her, tilting his head sideways. Get ye out. She's not happy, but studies me curiously for a moment, then retreats.

Now Salterfin's eyeing my goodies as I spread them around his conference table. I pull tapes from their cases, empty the files to display a stack of laser prints, and open the Parzilac box, then set one of the bottles beside it for dramatic effect, the disk neatly displayed below. It looks like a product shot.

"So you decided to save your little gal's job," he says.

"I'm not here to negotiate for Miss SiCauge. I'm here for myself. Yesterday you threatened to sue me and my company and all my people. I want your agreement to go away and leave us alone. What do you want in exchange?"

He looks me over, both of us still standing by the table; then he grins. I'll be glad to have this S.O.B. out of my life. I don't need him. I don't need all this crap. I just like to draw.

"I want the tapes that support my claim against M-Slovak."

"I can't give you most of the originals. All but that one are controlled by Hal Neusome. But I had dubs made last night. Pick one." I power up his video cabinet, then play a minute or two of 8mm.

"What kind is that one?"

"Betacam SP, the format we sometimes shoot when gathering news. What else do you want?"

"Everything on the tampering," he says.

"If I just hand it over, you could take it to Hal's competitors."

He snorts. "I hardly think so. That would scuttle my claims against M-Slovak for the harm done by Parzilac."

"So if I give you *all* the tampering evidence, you'll destroy it?"

"Well, let's talk about this evidence. What all is there? You've got the tampered capsules—these I assume." He rummages through the box, pulling a bottle to peer inside before replacing it. "What about the data from the analysis?" I show him the stack of laser prints, the disk. Nodding, he continues, "The video you guys shot—" I gesture toward the Betacam tape. "—And *the witnesses.*" I don't like how he said that.

"The widow hadn't realized what she was bringing us. Now she's had a change of heart and wants it to go away. She doesn't want M-Slovak suing her."

"Or worse," Salterfin says cryptically.

"The only other people were the scientist, Hal Neusome, and me." He doesn't need to know about Durbett. "I don't know the scientist, but he was paid for a *confidential* consultation, end of story. Hal has no actual evidence of this hypothetical tampering scenario, and all it would do is hurt his big story, the one that was helping him make a comeback. He doesn't even remember being out at the widow's house." Nudge-nudge wink-wink. "And that leaves me."

"And if you give me the tape and the disk and the printouts and the Parzilac, telling your story wouldn't amount to anything," Salterfin says.

"Even if you kept copies of the disk and the printouts—even the video—without the Parzilac, all you have is an alleged scientist telling you hearsay. It could have been staged. It could have been capsules that you tampered with yourself . . ." He's thinking out loud.

"But if I give you this stuff, you could hold it over me, threatening to turn me in for obstruction of justice."

"Trust me; it won't be around for long."

"So you intend to destroy the evidence?"

"Of course, you idiot."

"Then destroy it now."

"How do I know what's on the disk and that Betacam tape?"

"You don't, but the bottom line is, you want the drug samples destroyed. That's the corroborating evidence. I don't care what you do with the rest."

"It'll be destroyed by the end of the day."

"No, by the time I leave your office, or it goes with me."

He looks me over. "How?"

"You can flush it. You have a private bathroom in there."

I never thought I'd let myself stand that close to Dribble-Trou, in his bathroom, *at his toilet*. But I hand him bottles while he dumps and flushes. Dumps and flushes.

"You think you might come up with any more evidence?" he asks when we're finished. My buddy, my pal.

"She said there was only one tampered case."

"Let me know if there are any new developments." He tries to shake my hand as I leave, but I pass. I don't need warts.

Down the elevator, through the lobby, across the street to the small pull-off, I step into the back of a panel truck—illegally parked, but miraculously unmolested by the police. Durbett and Jankety are at a wall of electronic equipment, the latter wearing headphones.

"You were right, they scanned for bugs," I announce. "Smooth plan, tying the activator to the release button on the tape case. I waited till after he scanned, then tricked *him* into pushing it for me."

Durbett nods. "You're just lucky they didn't have the right kinda machine to try playing that size tape."

"I knew they wouldn't, but I was worried they'd try turning the wheel to see if the tape moves. They never suspected it was packed with surveillance gear. Did you get it?"

"Oh yeah." Jankety grins, doffing his headphones and pointing to a rather poignant freeze-frame on the video monitor.

"We need to make sure he's not near the tape case when we destroy the bug," Durbett says. "What say you call him, make sure he's at his desk so we can do the melt?"

"I got a good part cued up," Jankety says, handing me the phone.

It takes a minute to get Salterfin on the line. "Hey, where's that Betacam tape I left there?" I ask the lawyer.

"Still on the table—why?"

"Don't go near it. Listen, you wanted to know if there were any new developments. How about some new video with full audio?" I nod to Jankety; then the voices are playing over the phone:

"So you intend to destroy the evidence?" I hear myself asking.

"Of course, you idiot."

Jankety cuts the recording. Now it sounds like Salterfin is going apoplectic—heck, maybe even anaphylactic, far as I know. "But how—?"

"Don't get near that tape," I warn him. Then I hear a woosh and crackling sound over the phone line.

"What the hell?" Now's he's coughing; then the line goes dead.

"Burned a hole right through his table," Durbett predicts.

"Ba-woosh!" Jankety apes. He's loving it.

"I hope it sets off his sprinkler system," I add, all three of us nodding approval.

"Okay, you're done with him," Durbett pronounces, gesturing Jankety to climb up front so we can drive away.

Done with Wanamaker, Salterfin & Brock . . .

Put my clothes back on; I've been de-loused.

*   *   *

Sitting in my office, trying not to think about Cyn, I need a road map pointing the way out of this depression—and I don't mean the fantasy found in some patch.

Every time I look up, Rupert's rushing in with something else for me to do, the stacks piling here and there, this way and that. This time it's a fax from Bentley Crabtree including—of all things—a map, a colorized geographic distribution of the U.S., the ratio of Parzilac violence—incidence and prevalence—compared to population. There are several big blank gaps on it, mostly the Plains states and the Southeast. Attached is a note: *Data incomplete.*

Please get stats for Atlanta, New Orleans, Memphis, Birmingham, Jackson Miss, Nashville.

Rupert comes in again, this time with a fat file—and of course a map—detailing the regional print-ad roll-out of Aller-Tat. It's data sent over by Ted Stockbridge showing where and when shipments will go, plus data from Meg listing all the publications, ad specifications, and deadlines. What a daunting pile. There's a Post-It from Stockbridge that says: *Rupert, this covers the six-week mfg run, any surplus to Chicago, Detroit, and Cleveland.* "Meg went a little extra on the ads in those cities," Rupert explains.

I'm distracted for a minute. "Do you have the map to Stockbridge's house he made so we can come to his barbecue this weekend—handy I mean?"

Of course he has it right there in his satchel, clipped between the appropriate pages. Something's bothering me about it, a sense of déjà vu.

Frank comes in with Hal Neusome and Jankety. "I want your opinion on this, Danté," he says. "It means calling in a big favor from Tony Faritzka."

Hal waves a stack of papers at me, apparently the shipping and inventory records he'd copied before the fire. He spreads some out. "Remember I found out too many cases of Parzilac were bought, then returned—twice?" He stabs at the photocopies to show me. I don't like the sound of this. "I want to get into the distribution company's computer system and figure out where they shipped those excess cases."

Frank explains, "Remember how Stockbridge said the system grew up over the years? Briggs owns the company that distributes Parzilac to most of the country."

"And Tony Fariztka's people are doing that big software upgrade," Hal says, "and designing training programs for using it. He has people inside Briggs right now working on those computers with full access to everything. We want Tony to put Jankety on his team—*today*—so he can do some exploring for us."

I don't like the sound of this. "Frank, where did Stockbridge say Briggs *doesn't* do any distribution?"

"He named some southern states, um, Louisiana, Mississippi, Alabama, Georgia, Tennessee—I think that was it."

I'm looking at these guys, but the room is spinning. To Hal, "Do you have a copy of that note the widow said was in the case of loose Parzilacs?"

He flips through his file, pulls it out, and now I feel sick to my stomach. I show him the map to Stockbridge's house. He's confused. I show him the Post-It on the Aller-Tat distribution file, then the buck note we got from the widow.

"It looks like the same writing," Hal says, everybody's jaw agape.

"Compare the word *surplus*," I tell him, my head in my hands now.

Nobody says anything.

"Tell Tony we need Jankety in there fast," I say quietly.

Everybody stands there. Frank says, "It looks like Stockbridge wrote that tampered-Parzilac note."

"My God," Hal breathes, "this could be bigger than Chicago."

"Nationwide," I say, the room still spinning, "coast to coast, except five or six states in the south, which is why there's no violence data for Atlanta, New Orleans, Memphis . . ."

Rupert's catching up now. "You're thinking Stockbridge has been tampering with Parzilac?"

"But Stockbridge has a good job," Frank says. "Why would he do something like this? So his company stock would be worth more?"

"Who wants Parzilac to go down?" I practically shout. "Who wanted us to do PR and help protect the guy who was doing the tampering before something went wrong?"

"Rex?"

"Rex Briggs?"

They're all looking at me. Ask the last question, Danté. Say it: "Who would want the competition knocked out right when he's ready to launch his Fantasy Patch?"

*   *   *

Ashes ashes; we all fall down.

The kids are playing all around me. I can't get any work done. I can't get that stupid *Ring Around the Rosie* song out of my head. I don't like waiting like this, waiting for Jankety to report back, waiting for Durbett to show up so we can pay a little visit I seriously dread.

Taj is back from the doctor, his rash already improving after a night of wearing draw-string drawers, a bottle of antihistamines promising complete relief. Aller-Tat is a good product that will help a lot of people—especially kids—if it ever gets into the marketplace.

Fantasy Patch might be a good product, but I don't know. Maybe I'll learn more about it Thursday when I shoot at AnalyClin—*if* I shoot down there.

If Briggs is still my client.

All we have at this point is suspicion, weak and circumstantial evidence, a picture that changes with every shake of the kaleidoscope.

Maybe even Parzilac is okay in that great risk-versus-benefit scheme of things. Maybe not. How can I take a stand when I don't know?

Rupert comes in and shows me the approved disclaimer language, then says he's heading out to see Meg. He's enjoying the skullduggery—oh, to be young and enthusiastic again . . . "You moving your office in here with the kids?" he jokes. I just might.

Kristen is watching me from the doorway. I look at her, a slight nod, tacit permission to come sit with me. Taj is on her like icing on cake. She holds him in her lap and cuddles him, both giggling a little, both relaxing and content. The way she holds him seems so right . . .

"You okay, Danté?" she whispers.

"I don't know." She's not up on the latest developments.

"I like to cook every now and then," she says, an odd observation. "I think I try a little too hard not to make a mess." She's looking at me, maybe a little sad, maybe searching for my reaction, maybe just thinking out loud. "It's not as fun, but it's a lot easier than cleaning up."

"Yeah, I imagine so."

She leans toward me. "Of course, if I *do* make a mess, I can't let it sit. I *have* to clean it up. You're like that, too." With that, she hugs Taj again, then stands him up and tousles his punkish haircut. She stands to leave. "You okay, Danté?"

"I don't know." Ashes ashes; where's the Phoenix?

"You will be."

"Yeah."

She tousles *my* hair.

*   *   *

"Danté?" Melissa stirs me from my reverie. I think I was watching cartoons. "You need Frank for anything?"

"Huh? Oh, no."

"I'm sending him home. He's not been feeling well all day."

"You may have to threaten him."

"I already did. I locked the files, forwarded his phone, then locked his desk and hid the key. He's getting the hint."

"Tell him I'll check in with him later."

She studies me a second, watches Taj, then watches me. "Is there anything I can do?"

"You good at cleaning up messes?"

"I have a four-year-old." She rolls her eyes.

"Make Frank go home and get into bed, and make sure Taj is taking his medicine. I can't think of anything more important."

"That's easy; they both know better than to cross me." She leans over and uses her fingers to straighten my hair. "Let me know if I can help on the hard stuff."

*   *   *

You see those mob movies where the kingpin is holed up in the penthouse, layers of security protecting him, goons and guns, maybe a few booby traps, certainly electronic surveillance. The good guys need to penetrate, neutralize each layer, and move inexorably closer until they reach that last line of defense . . .

"Hello?" It's a chubby eleven-year-old, and he doesn't appear to be armed.

"Hi, Blaine," I greet him. "I'm Danté. This is Flynn. We're friends of your dad's. Is he home?"

He bobs his head, lets us in, and shows us to the living room before scampering off to find our target. We've penetrated the final layer, and we're in.

The Stockbridge homestead is spacious, comfortable and homey. Durbett's studying the room like he's checking for booby traps, mapping routes of escape, gathering evidence. I wish Jankety had succeeded in computer-tracking the information we want. He couldn't decipher some of the critical access codes and still manage to remain discreet. Now that we know there might be more bad Parzilac out there, we're in a hurry, no time to play games—though Durbett's way of saying this is a bit more eloquent, if not indelicate. He wanted to take Stockbridge from his office, isolate him, then squeeze him till he popped and the access codes oozed out. But our target had left early to take his son for an appointment, something about an allergist and, according to his smiling secretary, "Those Aller-Tats worked!"

"Hey!" It's Ted Stockbridge entering the room, Blaine watching us from the hallway. "What a pleasant surprise!" He's pumping my arm like the well's dry and the crops need water. I introduce Durbett as a consultant. "Hey, great! You've met my son." Stocky urges him over, standing behind him and holding his shoulders while the lad dutifully shakes our hands.

"I drew your Aller-Tat," I tell him.

"Wow, cool!"

Durbett says to Ted, "We got questions we need answered right away."

"I was just on the phone with Doug Moore. He's stopping by for a beer, but I think we've already got a quorum, so will it be glasses or bottles?"

We agree cold bottles are better than warm glasses, so he hurries off to tend bar, leaving his son to entertain us.

"You enjoying your day off school?" I ask.

He smiles knowingly. "Mom doesn't like me playing my Wooga-Woppers Wargame, so Dad keeps it hidden and we play when she's out of town—that's if he ever lets me have a turn." He rolls his eyes again with a mischievous twinkle.

"And she's in Cleveland tonight," Stockbridge says, returning with a tray, "so we'll be wopping woogas till the wee hours." He turns and high-fives his son. I picture them bumping bellies, this chubby kid and his big-kid dad. "So what kind of questions?" he asks.

"Well, they're confidential," I start.

"Oooo," he says, peering sneakily at his son, "secret plans. Blaine, we need to talk privately, so you go up and download some more woogas."

Blaine politely shakes my hand, then Durbett's, then suffers a merciless noogie from his dad until he squirms and giggles himself free and scurries off. We all watch him go, but I glance around in time to see a sadness in Durbett's face.

"Boy needs his dad," the mercenary says. "It's a shame, fathers that don't care enough to be around for 'em."

"I can't imagine," Stockbridge says softly, and he means it. "My wife is a wonderful woman, and the greatest mother in the world, but me and my son . . . well, we're the guys in the family. That's our jobs, the big guy and the little guy. We look out for each other."

I'm trying to smile, but I'm not sure I have the stomach for this. I want to leave, to forget the whole thing, but Durbett pushes ahead.

"I think you need to start rethinking your future." Durbett sounds sympathetic, but there's a quiet force behind his words. "Your wife and son gonna be okay without you?"

Stockbridge is taken aback now, confused, even a bit angry. "Flynn, what are you—?"

My turn. "Ted, we don't want to see your son suffer any more than necessary. It's going to be hard on him, and on your wife, but you need to accept the fact that they'll probably have to get by without you."

"But why?"

"Because you're goin' to prison," Durbett says, more edge to his voice. Stockbridge is getting red in the face, now jumping to his feet. "Sit down," Durbett tells him, and it's not a request.

Stocky is flabbergasted. "What the hell are you talking about?"

"Research surplus," I say. "Pi-ethym-lorenazol. Product tampering leading to murder. We have the proof."

He's blustering now, beet red, starting to sweat. Then he lowers his head, shakes it, and finally looks up at me. "It might have been illegal," he says sadly, a far-off look in his eye, like he can see it now, and it's not a pretty picture, his new future . . . "But nobody got hurt. I don't know what you're talking about—murder."

"What did you think distributing eighty-percent pure Parzilac would cause?" Durbett asks evenly. "Some nice little overdoses where nobody would get hurt? What about people like Gordie Pollikey?"

Stockbridge is stammering. "Eighty-percent? I thought you were talking about the research surplus."

"Which was what?" I ask.

He spreads his hands. "Parzilac. That's all they were. We had boatloads left over, so they were slipped back into the system. I won't say it's never been done with other drugs. I don't like it, but that's not my choice."

"Who decides?" Durbett asks.

Stockbridge starts to say something, then narrows his eyes, suspicious again. "I don't understand. What am I being accused of?"

Durbett says, "You've already admitted putting the tampered Parzilac, called *Research Surplus* in your own handwriting, out there in the marketplace. Now you're saying you were told to do this. By who?"

"You're saying the ones I distributed were tampered with?"

We backtrack for a minute so I can explain the scenario. Stockbridge is sitting there stunned, now white as a ghost, his hand trembling as he reaches for the beer bottle. He changes his mind without drinking, setting it back down. The situation is very tense—

And the doorbell rings. It's Moore.

"Get rid of him," Durbett suggests.

Stockbridge shakes his head. "No, we go way back. He can hear this. If

I'm in something over my head, I may need to count on his help."

It's a grim situation that our normally good-natured, silver-haired gladiator walks in on. It's Stockbridge's turn to tell the whole story, as much as we've covered so far, and he leaves nothing out.

Moore is astonished.

"Most were shipped more than a year ago," Stockbridge says, his voice quavering. He's ready to spill his guts. "Two smaller shipments since then were the last of it."

"Those went to the murdered Chicago drugstore guy?" I ask.

He nods. "I've been a nervous wreck since then, especially after I heard the accident might have to do with stealing Parzilac."

Durbett asks, "Where else have you shipped it?"

"There was a list of nine stores spread across the U.S. I had nothing to do with setting up their end, just getting them out. All I knew was, we had hundreds of cases of surplus from doing research on the M-Slovak drug, and I was to send them only to certain people who understood they wouldn't be in bottles."

Durbett says, "Our priority has been to eliminate any more tampered capsules that might be out there."

All eyes are on Stockbridge. "More than a year?" I repeat. "Except only those two shipments, right here in Chicago?"

He nods, swallowing hard.

"We've contained those," Durbett says. "We managed to exchange every prescription that came from his stores in the last sixty days."

"What about the returned cases?" I ask. Then, to the Briggs duo, "Twice in the past year, the Chicago guy ordered way too many cases of Parzilac, then returned them."

"My God," Moore says.

"They coulda been altered before they was returned," Durbett points out.

"What happened to those cases?" I demand of Stockbridge.

"They would go back into inventory for redistribution."

"One was about seven months ago—"

"Those would have all been delivered, prescribed, consumed by now," Stockbridge says.

"And two weeks ago."

His face lights up. "Those we'll still have. It's a monthly cycle, so they would have to be reinventoried before placed back in the shipment pool."

"We can intercept them," Durbett pronounces. Then to Stockbridge, "On whose orders were you acting?"

He stammers. "The first time, it was Rex, in his office, with Les Casapell. After that, it always came directly from Les."

"This is going to bring down the company," Moore says, shaking his head, "but it's got to be done."

Stockbridge looks like he's going to cry. "I'm going to prison," he breathes, looking up toward the stairs, toward where his young son is wopping woogas and waiting for his dad to come up so they can wooga-wop together.

"Not necessarily," Durbett says. He leans forward, the mien of ice-cold hell. "Is this the truth?"

Tears break, crawling down the portly distributor's cheeks. He's trembling, but he looks back at Durbett, resolute. "Honest to God. If I'd known— I would never—" He wipes his face with both hands, then looks toward the stairs again.

"Then you need to cooperate," Durbett says.

"Whatever it takes," he says, almost a whisper.

"Count me in," Moore declares. "I can always get another job somewhere, or maybe it's time to retire. I can't—I won't work for Rex anymore, and I need to help Ted here look out for his family." There's an intensity in the man's face, and I believe him.

I believe them both.

"Let's bring down Rex and this Les Casapell," Durbett says, "but try to save the company." Moore's nodding vigorously. Durbett adds quietly, "And hopefully save Ted." Stockbridge is wiping his face with a tissue, gratitude in his eyes. Right now Durbett could tell him to jump in front of a bus and I think he'd do it. They both would. "We need to know how this happened. Why would M-Slovak sell Briggs eighty-percent Parzilac?"

"They wouldn't," Stocky says. "We made our own batches—which is why, when we had too much, it should've been destroyed, not sneaked into the system. We couldn't just return it and admit its source."

"Somebody in manufacturing would be in on this?"

"No, they just follow the order-runs. If this was cooked for the research department, that's where the stock would be delivered. Later, they would send any leftovers to me. I arrange to destroy, stock, store, or ship."

"Could somebody in research be in on it?"

"Well, they wouldn't *have* to be," Stocky decides.

Moore muses, "The order-run could have specified sending them directly to you."

"So we need to know if research was involved," Durbett says.

"The head guy over there and I are tight," Stocky says. "You remember him, the messy-haired labby who was worried about anaphylactic shock. He's always been a safety freak, worried about side effects and unforseen problems. Given his druthers, he'd almost never release a drug for trials, so I can't imagine him being in on something that hurts people."

"Call him," Durbett decides.

Stocky talks on the phone for a few minutes, some pleasant chatter, just needs to clear up some confusion in his records. He hangs up, anger in his face. "They've never done any pi-ethym research at Briggs," he grinds out. "Not on humans or animals, not for toxicology, not at any dose. I mentioned eighty-percent pure, and he laughed, said I must be mistaken. Nobody would test something that strong."

We all look at each other for a moment, then Durbett breaks the spell. "We need to document who's been placing the order-runs, plus everything about where and when you shipped 'em to those nine stores."

"That's all computer files," Stockbridge says, "but I'm off work tomorrow—it's a school holiday for Blaine, and my wife's away, so I took the day. Even if I was in there, I'd normally ask somebody to pull those kinds of records—not do it myself. It's going to attract attention if I start duplicating files."

"We just need your access codes," Durbett tells him, "and a road map of where to look so we can get in and out fast."

"It's not tied to any external network," he cautions. "You have to be on a company terminal, one ported to the distribution system."

"I'll take care of that. You give me the info; then be ready at this phone tomorrow morning." He hands him one with a red button. "A man named Jankety will call you if he has any questions. Don't even hesitate; tell him whatever he needs."

"What can I do?" Moore asks.

"Nothing for now."

"Wait, I have an idea," I chime in. "Can you get me in to see Rex in the morning, say to get his reaction to a new merchandising display?"

"I'm already on his schedule for ten-thirty," he says.

I look at Durbett, his eyebrows up. He nods recognition, asking, "You can do something that fast?"

"I work with the best," I pronounce. "My simulator guy—exhibits and displays."

"Dad?" It's Blaine at the top of the stairs. "Can I come down now?"

Stockbridge motions to him, the lad tentatively coming in as we all stand to leave. Our portly distributor surprises his son by standing behind him, not with hands on his shoulders, but wrapping him this time with his arms, holding him tightly. I feel queasy about how we squeezed him, but it had to be done, and fast. We needed the truth; this is how Durbett could be sure.

It's time to plan our escape.

Blaine asks, "Um, is everything okay?"

I smile reassuringly. "It is now, thanks to your dad."

*   *   *

I built my share of model planes and cars when I was a lad, but that was nothing like this.

We're here in the workshop of my simulator dude, and there's a whole team trying to build this little thing, to fulfill my vision. I'm drawing while he blueprints, five artisans cutting and edging and coating and covering and detailing, Jankety wiring and modifying, Moore giving feedback and clucking approval, and Kristen providing moral support. We don't really need her—actually, maybe we do—but she wanted to come by and watch, and she's enjoying herself.

The challenge is not just in getting it built, equipped, and functional, but in making sure it looks good—damn good, the Danté standard. If it doesn't impress, then it'll defeat its purpose.

So the hours drag on, and we make steady progress. I keep slipping away to try calling Cyn. I've left more than a few messages at her various numbers, all to no avail. I try one more time, only to hang up the phone and just sit there in the simulator dude's office.

After a moment, Kristen slips in and sits with me, trying to cheer me up. "I've been on this side of the phone more times than I can count," she muses. Self-deprecating. I'll bet she learned that by the time she was in middle school, two heads taller than all the boys.

"It's a new feeling for me," I return, wishing I hadn't said that. It's like asking: You fall down a lot? Get hurt a lot? Yeah, well I never have.

Suddenly, I feel very protective of Kristen. I wonder how many times she's been hurt—and why anybody would allow himself to hurt her. She's beautiful, admittedly taller than most women, but she's as smart as anybody else I know, and she's got the best personality, so much empathy, so giving, so caring, strong and independent with a lot of savvy. When I watch her with Taj . . .

"She'll come around," she reassures me. "You know that quote: Something something set it free, blah blah it was meant to be—something like that. She cares about you too much to let career matters make her forget."

She's right. I know she's right. I'm looking at her and thinking about Cyn and suddenly recalling a thousand good times and our plans for the future, and I know Kristen's right. Isn't she?

I shake my head no.

Then I hear Jankety calling for me.

And Kristen hugs me, saying, "Trust me; it will work out for the best."

The display is done, pretty good for a rush job, and it's time for everybody to head home.

The drive seems longer than usual. I'm not thinking about blue vans or Rex Briggs, but wondering if Cyn will call me tonight. And with every minute, with every mile, the more I think about it, the odds keep going down. Kristen had smiled at me reassuringly as she said good-bye in the parking lot, so confident all would be okay.

For such a smart lady, this time I think she's wrong.

But I just don't know for sure.

My house feels empty, lonely somehow, as I check my voice-mail, disappointed none are from Cyn. I walk back and check on Ms. Moeroff. She's tired, so I don't linger very long. I don't mention what's on my mind, but I think she knows.

She puts her arms around me and whispers, "The more I see who you are, the more I love you. That won't be true with everyone you meet."

"Same for you, Lady Theta," I tease her.

She smiles, reaches up to tousle my hair—why's everybody playing with my hair lately?—and says, "What matters most is that now you're seeing more of yourself. That's who you have to love first."

"Where have I heard that before?"

She shrugs, "Probably some rock-song lyrics."

"You know everything, don't you?"

"Took you long enough to figure that out." She stands on her toes to kiss me good-night on the cheek.

"What did my horoscope say?"

"Big changes in the offing. Career, travel, and romance are in your future."

So I sit in my house and watch the late news, and there's a clip of Cyn. She's trashing Parzilac, now voicing over some of my footage. Salterfin must be gambling I'll just go away and not cause them more problems. An impasse. A draw.

I'm not going to leave her any more messages tonight.

I go to bed and manage to drift off at some point.

It's really late now, or early, and the phone is ringing. *4:18am* the clock glows.

Ring. Cyn has finally called, but I hesitate.

Ring. No, I need to answer it.

"Hello?" It's Melissa. "Danté?" She sounds like she's crying.

"Melissa! What's wrong?" Oh God, Taj . . . ?

"Danté?" she repeats.

"What is it?"

"I thought he was just sick!"

"Who? What are you talking about?"

"Frank—Oh, Danté, it was his heart."

CHAPTER 23

Bright fluorescent glare.

I'm used to lighting sets and scenes, making sure everything is clear, so I notice how areas are lit, and here in the hospital waiting area it's as harsh and unforgiving as lighting can be. Bright fluorescent glare.

Melissa and Taj are sitting forlornly in the far corner. Their eyes are swollen, their faces red. They both brighten some as Ms. Moeroff and I approach.

"Oh, Danté," Melissa breathes, now in my arms. Theta's wrapping Taj in a similar embrace. "He's alive is all I know," Mel whispers.

"Let's go find some juice and snacks," Ms. Moeroff's telling Taj, leading him away so we can talk.

"What happened?"

"He's been skipping his medicine," she says, "then today it caught up to him." We sit in adjacent chairs, holding hands. "He kept getting worse all evening, admitted his arm was numb, but he wouldn't go to the hospital, wouldn't let me call a doctor—" She screws her face into the consternation of a mom angry over spilled milk. "Oh, he can be so stubborn!"

A doctor suddenly appears. "You're the daughter?" he asks Mel.

"Yes," she says. He leads us off to a small room just around the corner, Taj and my old lady watching us go. "He's okay for now," the doc says. Melissa practically faints. He explains what kind of heart attack it was, how thinners managed to break up the clot, the problem with an artery, more tests over the next few days, probably that catheter balloon Friday or Saturday, hospitalized four or five days, then wait and see how he does for a few months, gonna have to make a few lifestyle changes, take better care . . . "You got him here just in time," he assures her.

"When can we see him?"

"Right now, but five minutes tops. He'll be groggy."

Theta abstains and says she'll wait, so the three of us go in together.

Frank looks so old and frail. I've never seen him like this. He's tethered to IV's and various machines, beeping blippers and blipping beepers, and I have a stomach-wrenching sense of déjà vu, recalling the last moments of the drugstore guy's life.

Melissa's trying to compose herself, Taj moving cautiously up to hold

Frank's hand, afraid he might hurt him.

"You'll do anything for attention," I tell him. "Pitching the local HMO account, are you?"

Frank grins weakly, then looks toward Melissa. "Told 'em you were my daughter," he said, "in case decisions had to be made."

"Well, decisions *have* been made," she admonishes him, "and there's gonna be some changes in how you take care of yourself." She's holding his other hand now.

"Yes, ma'am. I'm okay, Taj," Frank assures the little one. "You can't climb in with me now, but I'll be home any day—"

"Don't be in any hurry," she cautions him.

"I wouldn't think about crossing her, Frank," I tell him.

He chuckles again. "No, Taj and I know better, don't we?" He takes a deep breath. "She's not gonna let me work any more this week," he tells me.

"We'll cover. I'm gonna cancel my trip—"

"*No*," he asserts, almost straining from the effort. "No, *do not* let this slow us down. *Operation Screw Sam and Dib* is today, and you've got too much to do before you fly to Tennessee tonight. I'll be willing to let Mel mother me for a while if you promise this won't slow down the company."

There's nothing more to say . . . except, "You've put together a crack team, Frank. We'll use this as a chance to dazzle you."

He chuckles yet again.

"One minute," comes a voice, urging us to wrap and git.

I squeeze the hand Mel's been holding. She leans over and kisses his forehead, assuring, "We'll be close by."

"Leave Taj a minute, okay?" he asks.

We go out to the hallway, trying not to be obtrusive, but we're both sort of watching through the glass alongside the door. Taj leans over the bed while Frank scootches a little closer. They whisper back and forth for moment; then the little one wraps his arms around Frank's neck. Frank encircles him with his own arm, virtually wrapping him in wires and tubes. Frank has tears in his eyes.

Taj comes out, pausing in the doorway to look back, he and Frank waving bye-bye to each other. Taj takes his mother's hand, then mine with his other.

We walk slowly down the too-white antiseptic hallway, people scurrying this way and that. Tears streak Melissa's face, but Taj is stoic, the determined little trouper. I'm having trouble seeing, but I think it's because there's too much light. Nothing is clear anymore . . .

In this bright fluorescent glare.

*   *   *

It's a warm sunny day, yet I'm driving in a fog.

Then I sit in my car at *Shoot & Die* for a minute, steeling myself to bear bad news, but I finally have to go in. I inform our reception dude about Frank just as Kristen and Murray and Rupert are blowing in from the parking lot. They're stunned, and Kristen even cries. I think Rupert does a little, too, and I'm having trouble seeing again. We all stand there for a minute, trying to find the right way to vow we'll bust our humps while he recuperates, but then the phone rings, breaking the spell.

"It's Miss SiCauge," the reception dude informs me.

I head back to take it in my office. "Frank's had a heart attack," I tell her.

"I'm not surprised. Did he die?"

"No, he's in the hospital."

"I assume you know the videos you gave Rob only show the edited clips that have already been on TV."

"Yeah, that was intentional."

Her voice drips with malice. "Yeah, well, that means you lied to him."

"Actually, no. Listen to his recording and you'll notice I talked like a lawyer."

Now sarcastically, "I really appreciate your support. Did you know Cricket LaRayne is making claims on your behalf?"

"What claims?"

"She's assuring people she'll have access to the same information as Wanamaker, Salterfin & Brock."

"I made her that promise, yes."

Extended silence. "Why would you do that?"

"She was in danger of losing clients to your firm. I believed in her commitment to help them."

"Oh, and not in ours, is that it?"

"Something like that." I feel so sad. This is like talking to somebody I don't know.

"I hope you realize I've been working hard on this end to keep Rob from going after you. He wants to file a flurry of discovery-related motions, subpoena you for deposition, then sue you and your company. I think I might have cooled him down for now."

"It's a bluff, Cyn. I collected proof that he planned to destroy evidence that would exonerate your defendant, and that he actually did destroy what he thought was evidence, with that intent. He may be running his mouth, but he's scared of me. And you know, Cyn, I'm in no mood for this today, so don't do anything on my behalf. Tell him I dare him to file anything on me—*anything* that might make me get even madder. I'm ready to slam-dunk somebody right now, and he'd be a very easy target."

"But what about me?"

"Quit the firm. Quit right now, and walk away. It won't hurt your career, taking the high road, refusing to be part of a conspiracy."

"But if you come forward with this proof you claim to have against Salterfin, then it'll ruin me, too."

She's not going to quit. She's not going to walk away. She'll let her ship sink with that rat aboard.

"Then keep him off me," I advise.

Pause. "I don't understand, Danté. I thought you loved me."

"I do."

"Then prove it."

"I just did."

Pause.

Click.

Long Pause.

Dial tone.

Fog.

*   *   *

Meg shakes my hand, then winds up hugging me and, just briefly, stroking my hair. I feel like purring.

"Rupert should be down any minute," she reports, a hint of smile betraying her complicity. "The courier is waiting downstairs, ready to head straight to the FedEx terminal at the airport."

Rupert comes in loaded down with a huge stack of mounted Sizemore photostats, grinning like a kid clutching too much ice cream. "You should have seen Charles's face when I started thumbing through these ads. I made it a point not to notice the Aller-Tat 'stats buried in the middle, but I sure took a long time doing it. Then when I said I'd bring them with me, he fell all over himself offering to have them trucked over instead."

We sort through the pile and, sure enough, there they are, magazine and newspaper ads for Aller-Tat including the Briggs-legal, Moore-tested, new-and-improved disclaimer warning about anaphylactic shock. Meg sets about packaging them with contracts and sundry paperwork, affixing pre-printed mailing labels, tape tape tape . . . We offer to help, but we're in her way, so we let Rupert regale us with the detailed version of his dalliance with Charles down in graphics. He's painting us a fun picture, a real hoot.

Meg's phone buzzes twice. She hits the speaker button, a young woman's voice coming on. "This is Jenny—down in the mail room? I checked on that for you, and we can get it out as late as seven o'clock."

"Thanks, Jen," Meg tells her. Then to us, "That's our signal. It means Pam has the packages ready to send out."

She leads Rupert and me—like I've forgotten the way during these past thirteen days as *The Artist Formerly Known As A Kehoe Employee*. We walk into the mail room and find Charles over in the packaging section grinning and flirting with Pam, a small stack of mailers at the end of the counter.

"There's been a change," Rupert announces. I'd like to have been the one to say it, but this one's his—insult the savvy of my account supervisor, dare they. "We'll handle it from here." He scoops up the pile of goodies just as Meg hands a memo to Pam stating that her clients from The Dellman/Roenik Group will assume responsibility for the shippers.

"But they're ready—" Pam starts.

"Everything's been changed," Meg interrupts, feigning exasperation with a roll of the eyes.

"Thanks anyway, Pam," Rupert says. Then he positions himself in front of Charles, shaking the surprised man's hand with mock sincerity, fixing him with an enigmatic expression. "Thank you so much for your assistance, Charles. I can't say enough about how much you've helped."

*   *   *

Look for the man in a panama hat, carrying a newspaper under his arm, with a carnation in his lapel.

Or just wait at the gas station closest to the Briggs headquarters and Durbett will come find me . . . And there he is, in that familiar panel truck. I climb into the passenger side, asking in my mysterious secret-agent voice, "You got the goods?"

He gives me a funny look. "I brought the Aller-Tat display." Same difference.

We pull in at Briggs and park near the main entrance. He helps me unload the rack. It's nearly three-feet high, a slick display with tattoo cartoons ringing the top and bottom and down between rows, little slots to hold the packages and brochures. Not bad for a rush job.

I lug it inside and hurry up to Rex's office. Doug Moore is waiting in the anteroom with a box of product packages, so we go in together. Les Casapell is already in there.

"Hey, that's pretty slick!" Rex greets us, eyeing the display. Les looks pleased, too.

"Is it okay if I leave it set up over here for a few days, let you get used to it, see what you think? We won't be making any decisions until I get back from Tennessee."

"Yeah, yeah. That's fine."

I set it up quickly, helping Moore fill some of the slots. He passes a few over to Rex and Les for them to examine.

"You got my approval already," Rex says, Les clucking a similar sentiment.

"Good," I answer. "Then we have only a few topics to cover before I fly down tonight. I need the contact info for our AnalyClin shoot tomorrow morning."

"I'm flying down this afternoon," Les says, checking his watch. He passes me a small file. "That's a map and basic info. Just meet me there, and I'll coordinate whatever you need."

"One last thing," I bring up. "I need to noodle how the marketing for Fantasy Patch can incorporate assurances that it's tamper-proof."

"Why the interest in tampering?" Rex asks, taking the bait.

"Hal Neusome won't tell me much about it, but he says somebody might have been doctoring Parzilac, which would cause all the violence." I wave it off dismissively. "It's probably a dead end, but he's pretty worked up about it. I just want to make sure that if tampering becomes a controversy, Fantasy Patch presents the image that it offers an extra margin of safety."

"Good," Rex says. He's flustered, though. I need to play poker against this guy.

"Yeah, good," Les agrees.

"Very good," Doug Moore echoes, and we're up shaking hands, looking forward to a good shoot down south.

I straighten up some packages in the rack, touch the panel at the base, and hold my breath, half expecting some buzzer to go off, men in flak suits to come rushing in . . . Nothing.

I follow Moore down a floor to his office. We look at each other, afraid to talk for the possibility of listeners. Right on cue, Ted Stockbridge wanders in nonchalantly. He's not wearing a panama hat, no newspaper, no carnation in his lapel.

"Hey guys," he greets, closing the door behind him. "Everything going okay?"

"Fine," Moore says.

"Uh huh," I agree. Gosh, we're slick.

"That friend of ours," Stocky says, "—he got what he was after."

*   *   *

I'm feeling ultra-paranoid as I walk out to the panel truck. At least I'm not scared of blue vans anymore.

"Is it working?" I ask.

Durbett just grins, starting the engine and pulling out. "I made arrangements to park down behind the gas station. We have to stay close," he says. "Climb in the back and monitor; let me know if the signal starts to break up while I'm driving."

I comply, and I must say I'm blown away. There on a monitor, in full color, wide-angle shot, is Rex's office. He's still at his desk, Les across from him, and I can hear them talking—in stereo! And that image! The shot of Salterfin in 540 was impressive, but this is high-def! I never imagined a concealed pinpoint camera lens a sixteenth of an inch across—attached to a fiber optic wand, attached to a processor board, attached to a short-range transmitter—could possibly shoot with this level of resolution.

"We'll get Roenik to spin a tale," Rex is saying, "about Pozies. There's gotta be an angle there—"

"Dammit," Les says. "We don't know what he knows."

"I'm gonna call Neusome, feel him out."

"Hold off, Rex. Wait for Ellmata."

Durbett parks behind the gas station, then peers into the back. Satisfied with the integrity of his signal, he shuts off the engine and sits beside me on a hard cushion.

"How much longer?" Rex is demanding.

"Mr. Ellmata will be here in ten minutes, sir," comes the disembodied voice.

Durbett is manipulating the controls of a videodisc recorder in the rack.

"Dual back-up," he explains. He's going to play me what we already have without interfering with the other two masters still recording.

"Danté can spin it," Rex is saying on the live monitor. "He's so worried about the agency right now, he'll do whatever it takes to keep our business."

Now I'm watching two conversations at once. The playback monitor starts from when I pressed the activation button on the Aller-Tat display. As soon as Moore and I leave, Rex goes berserk. "How the hell did Neusome come up with this?" he demands.

Les is freaking. "I don't know! I don't know what he has!"

"Get me Ellmata here—*now!*" he tells the air.

"Yes, sir."

Live-monitor Rex is saying, "Had to be the wife. Dammit, he swore his mother didn't know anything about it."

"Had to be her," Les is agreeing. "Who else knew?"

"What kind of proof could he have?"

Playback-monitor Rex says, "Should've just paid off the son of a bitch when he tried to extort us."

"Should've let Ellmata whack him," Les counters.

"Yeah, wound up having to anyway. Of course it got screwed up. We're just damn lucky they had a way to get to him in the hospital."

"Ricin," Les agrees, "nature's little problem-solver."

"Should've whacked all three from the beginning."

Live Rex says, "It was that botched job on the son, is what it was. Our little suicide solution sure as hell turned into a murder investigation."

"You can't blame Ellmata's people," Les argues. "That damned Neusome busted it up before they were done. That could've been—almost was—a lot worse."

Playback Rex says, "I thought paying off that pharmacist—Walt or what's his name—why didn't he get the boxes out of there like he was supposed to?"

"Because the little girl got run over. Ellmata said Walt panicked, thought he could wait a few days till things died down. *You're* the one who sent Danté and a damned TV crew out there to sniff around. If running over the little girl hadn't given Ellmata a way to make it look like vigilante backlash when he had Walt killed and the store torched, we'd be in deep with no way out. At least he got rid of the eighty-percents still in the store."

"And that should've been the end of it until that back-stabbing son tried to blackmail us."

"He said when his mom got suspicious, he told her it was M-Slovak testing a new drug, and to keep her mouth shut or she'd lose everything she has."

"Yeah, well, now it looks like he lied. He must've told her everything, or how else could she know?"

Live Rex pronounces, "Kill the bitch. Whatever it takes, Ellmata's got to get somebody close enough to shut her up. And for once, try to make it look like an accident."

"What about Neusome?"

Live Rex orders the air to get Neusome on the phone. Playback Rex is caught up to where we started watching, so Durbett stops the first disc.

The live voice announces, "Mr. Neusome's on vacation and not available until Saturday."

Les says, "Doesn't sound like somebody who's chasing a big story."

"I don't think he has anything, but we should still remove the wife, just in case."

"What about the rest of the eighty-percents?"

"They're still in the New Johnsonville warehouse, right? Just fly down there for Dante's shoot at AnalyClin like nothing's wrong; then when you have him out of the way, get next door and personally see that they're destroyed."

Buzz. "Mr. Ellmata is here."

A short, heavy, Latin-looking guy bursts into the room carrying a briefcase. He closes the door behind him.

"That's him," Durbett tells me.

"We need the wife dead fast," Rex says.

"Shut up!" Ellmata orders him. He pushes aside papers on Rex's desk and plops the case down, flipping it open and removing a small device.

"He's gonna scan!" Durbett blurts, jumping up to punch in a code on a computer keyboard. All the monitors go dead, colored lights on equipment blinking out.

"What did you do?"

"Shut it down. It can't be reactivated remotely either, only by pressing that button on the display again. Good thing I set it up that way. They won't know we got 'em until you're ready to let on." Good thinking. "Besides, you got what you need."

Need for what? What am I going to do now?

Durbett's on his secret-agent phone. "Has she been moved?" he asks the phone. "Good. They're planning to kill her. Keep her secure." He hangs up, then asks me, "What's the plan?"

Think, Danté. Did they teach this in college? Conspiracy 101? Sting Operations 410? The *Don't Get Yourself Killed* Discussion Group? "I want to get it on camera," I pronounce.

Durbett grins. "I wouldn't expect anything less."

"You got room on the jet for Neusome?" He nods. "Do you, um, do you have the *contacts* to arrange a raid down there tomorrow morning, to seize the adulterated Parzilac supply?" He nods again. I use his secret phone and call Hal.

"You were right. They called looking for me," he reports.

"Get out of there," I warn him. "Pack to travel, bring your foreskin and your make-up, then disappear for a while. Meet us at Durbett's jet at—" What time was Kristen going to be there with the crew? Oh yeah— "Meet us at Midway by six-thirty." Durbett gives him directions to a private lounge in the terminal, a secure place to wait for us. "Durbett will arrange to have the police—"

"The feds," Durbett corrects me, "—using a carefully orchestrated—shall we say *anonymous*—tip, none of which can become part of the news."

Hal heard him, and agrees.

"Then," I continue, "when the feds swoop in for the big raid and arrest Les right on the spot, I'll already be standing there with a camera crew, and you'll appear out of nowhere to be the only reporter on the scene. You combine all that with the footage Durbett and I just shot—!" I'm about to wet my pants.

I think Hal does wet his.

Durbett asks, "What about Billy's simulator shoot?"

"Kristen will handle that. I was only going down to shoot AnalyClin and glad-hand Sizemore in place of Frank."

"I got some things to do tonight and first thing in the morning," he says, "but I'll send Jankety to be part of your crew. He'll be extra eyes, and be armed, in case something goes wrong. I'll try to be out there by the time the raid goes down, but *do not* get me in the shots."

"We'll do our best, Flynn, not to turn you into a moving blue dot."

We climb into the front, pull out, and head toward *Shoot & Die*. I call the reception dude. "Track down Cricket LaRayne and Bentley Crabtree. Get 'em to come there, ASAP, whatever it takes. And make sure Murray and Kristen are around. I'm on my way. Any word on Frank?"

"Melissa just got in with her son, said he's doing fine."

"Don't let her leave. I need her in this meeting. Oh, and send a courier out to my house in a few hours to pick up my luggage. I don't think I'll have time to go home and pack."

I call Ms. Moeroff. "I need a favor," I tell her.

"Calm down, Danté—you're panting." I thought I *was* calm. "What can I do?"

"I need a travel bag packed, two casual outfits, and two look-nice but dress-down outfits, plus all the usual toiletries and such. I'll have a courier out there to pick it up in a few hours."

"I'm glad to help, Danté," she says sweetly. Then quietly, "Is everything okay?"

"No, but I'm working on it. What's the horoscope say?"

She hesitates. "It says there's an old lady who lives in a carriage house who loves you very much, and that now you have a good chance to make her extra proud."

CHAPTER 24

If you want to grab people's attention, just promise the *possibility* of something grotesque.

From the most pious Bible-thumper to the lowest back-alley rump-humper, anybody'll pause to look toward the ledge and gawk at some suicide jumper—not to see him be talked down, not to watch as he's walked down, but just in case there's a plummet, and then a splat to be chalked around.

Why do people watch those real-life police shows on TV? To see camera-conscious constitutionally couth coppers calmly collaring culprits? *Au contraire.* It's for the possibility of gunshots and car chases . . . explosions and fires and blood—oh my!

This is why I'm trying to figure out how to make sure the big raid tomorrow will be a camera-worthy event, exciting to watch, full of action and suspense, pageantry and drama.

Mental note: talk to Durbett. Maybe he can set off some smoke bombs or something during the raid.

But first: the mundane details, taking care of business before I leave town. We need to prevent panic at Kehoe, so Rupert and I are standing in the closet at *Shoot & Die*, talking for the benefit of a bugged chair. It doesn't get much sillier than this.

"So what's the story behind the hold-up on the ads for Aller-Tats?" I ask.

"It's a budget thing. Somebody didn't dot an eye or cross a tee or something. Should be resolved by tomorrow."

I can just hear Dib Wardley and Sam Cox doing their *heh heh heh*, thinking their little scam is going to work after all.

We join Kristen, Byron, and Melissa in the big conference room, the one with a Durbett scanner that monitors for listening devices. There are no bugs snug in our rug. I still don't know how we'll be alerted if somebody does smuggle a bug, but Durbett assured me we'll know, no doubt about it.

I explain that we're planning a video ambush on our clients. "We now have video-confession proof that Rex Briggs and Les Casapell engineered the Parzilac-tampering scam—"

Buzz. "It's Jankety, Danté."

I assure our spy-hacker that he's clear to talk over the speaker phone.

"We got it all!" he exclaims. Sounds like he's enjoying himself. "I not only downloaded disks of all the evidence and printed hard copies, but by using Stockbridge's access codes, Faritzka's guy showed me how to set up three security layers and initialize new pass codes. Ain't nobody gonna be able to erase those files before the federal marshals get to 'em."

"What did you learn?"

"Nine drugstore chains around the U.S., each shipped the so-called *Research Surplus* on three different occasions. They used to order way too much Parzilac every now and then, then return it a week later for redistribution to other stores throughout the region. Our guy in Chicago was the first one doing this, going all the way back to the Parzilac trials when he had the contract with M-Slovak. The others were added later, one at a time."

"You think there's any additional danger to the public?"

"Extremely unlikely. There were a lot of file moves and some amateur attempts to cover up the trail right after that girl got run over a few weeks ago. The last returned cases were sent to Tennessee for storage. It's a good bet Rex shut down the whole system after things got weird up here, at least until he saw if there would be any fallout."

"Since then," I point out, "it's been one problem after another for him. He probably had the other drugstores destroy any remaining eighty-percents; then he had the store up here fire-bombed after Walt got cold feet. Rex called what's stored in Tennessee *the rest of them*."

"And even if there were more," Jankety finishes, "I'm sure he's warned each store in the past hour. I'll bet eighty-percents are now harder to come by than Pozies. Still, there'll be records showing the pattern, probably even a paper trail."

"Can Flynn predict what time the raid will be?"

"Since they have other locations around the U.S. to coordinate now, it's looking like mid-afternoon. It's cumbersome because Flynn has to act like an anonymous tipster who's simply supplying info."

"Speaking of info, can I get the list of drugstore targets?"

"Be careful nobody gets tipped off," he cautions me. He tells Melissa how to run the data line through my red-button phone so it'll decode his encrypted signal. "We got 'em!" he gushes before hanging up.

Byron's squirming, so I explain, "You're going to shoot the AnalyClin stuff with me. When Durbett gives the signal, Hal will appear; then we'll rush next door to Briggs's distribution warehouse in time to catch the raid and the arrest of Les Casapell."

The news director is on the speaker phone now. I tell him, "Hal's going to need at least twenty minutes on *Newsline* tomorrow night for a *major* late-breaking story, live from the studio here, footage you'd die for."

Sounds like he's smacking his lips. "What is it?"

"Extremely confidential," I warn him unnecessarily. "Product-tampering scandal of the century, and Hal will be in Tennessee with a camera to shoot the arrest and warehouse raid. Warn the news operations at nine of your affiliates to have microwave trucks ready and waiting. They'll be the only news on the scene when the local raids and arrests happen. I want stand-ups from each site reporting to Hal Neusome in Chicago. You cut 'em together; Hal will intro them during *Newsline*; then afterwards your affiliates can use them during live field reports at eleven."

"Excellent! When do I get the info?"

Melissa's back with print-outs now, so I read the list of cities to him. "Melissa Norrow will give you precise locations approximately two hours in advance, so you *must* make absolutely sure the crews wait down the street somewhere until the last second so nobody gets tipped off."

"You got it." He hesitates. "Who's taking the fall—M-Slovak?"

"I can't say any more right now. I've risked too much for the good of *Newsline* and Hal Neusome as it is."

Buzz. "Mr. Doug Moore and Ms. Cricket LaRayne."

I shoo out everybody but Melissa, my team scattering like so many *Wave-Slicers* at full throttle, then invite the visitors to come in together.

"I got the estimate you wanted," Cricket says, glancing nervously toward Moore. I urge her to go ahead. "Rex Briggs is worth in excess of a hundred-million."

I turn to Moore, who looks like he's not slept since, well, since the ice age. "How tight are you with your board of directors?"

"Very," he says. "I had eight of twelve committed to voting me CEO when Rex retires, but he's been working to fill four vacancies that open next year, using his own cronies, people who'll back Casapell."

"He won't be in the running," I point out, "and Rex is going down along with him."

Moore takes a deep breath. "If the job opens before Buchanan retires next year, then I'm in. He virtually controls seven votes and influences most of the rest. Problem is, it doesn't sound like there'll be a company to helm, unless I'm to be a captain who goes down with the ship."

"Is the company cash-rich?"

Moore nods. "Have to be, in this biz, what with research costs."

"How much?"

He winces. "Two, maybe three-hundred mill."

"This Buchanan—does he think fast on his feet, ready to deal?"

Moore's sitting on the edge of his chair. "That's what I like about him."

I turn to Cricket. "You can't approach clients of Wanamaker, Salterfin & Brock, can you?"

"It wouldn't be ethical—"

"But Melissa can, right?—one victim to another?"

Cricket smiles. "I suspect our Miss Norrow can be very persuasive."

"How much are dead people worth?—in a settlement, I mean."

Cricket winces now. I don't have time to be delicate. "These people don't factor very highly. I mean, there are formulas for anticipated life span, earning capacity, support of dependents, and so on." Seeing I want more, she continues, "If I had Miss SiCauge's clients, I'd try for the stars and moon, but I'd be shocked to get a million per, and wouldn't be surprised if mediation came in at two- or three-hundred thousand—tops."

I tell Moore, "If she sued Rex, Les, and the corporation jointly, it would be smart for the company to settle out right away for, say, a half-million apiece, fifty-grand for the property losers like Melissa, then let Cricket go after everything Rex and Les have of their own stashed away in order to sweeten the pot."

There's a lot of wincing going on today. "It would have to be non-disclosure," he says, "to discourage nuisance suits."

"That's why if they settle in the next day or two, based on a demand letter before the company is publicly named as a defendant, then the spotlight would stay on Rex." Moore takes a deep breath. I lean toward him in all sincerity, adding, "I'm trying to save the company."

"We can't possibly do any better in the long run," he admits.

"No, and you'll need to slide Dellman/Roenik a huge wad of cash to help clean up your public relations after this breaks open."

"It'll take a lot of whitewash, but I'll bet you could find a way to pull it off." He takes another deep breath. "I'm going to have to sell all this to Buchanan, you know."

"Can you, without me having to show him all my cards? I'm a bit busy today."

"All I can do is try." He stands up. "I need to use your office."

"Just make it clear there's only one shot to keep the whole corporation from going down, and that you're risking everything—including federal obstruction-of-justice charges—to do what's best for the stockholders and employees."

"That's a language he understands," Moore concedes.

After he leaves, Cricket asks me, "Miss SiCauge doesn't know about this yet?"

"No. She and Rob Salterfin will learn at the same time as everybody else—on Hal's show tomorrow night."

"But why—?"

"You're looking to help people, aren't you?"

"Yes."

"Then let's figure out how. You already have the family of the little girl who got run over, and now you have a defendant to collect from. If Melissa starts calling Cyn's clients, one victim to another, and says she just settled, cash on the barrel head, and that she heard anybody who dumps Wanamaker Salterfin and signs with Cricket can have their money by Monday, you think they'll jump?"

Cricket smiles. "I think they'll call Miss SiCauge first to see what she has to say about it."

"Wanamaker Salterfin's got no defendant. Is there any way they'll get a settlement out of M-Slovak before the news breaks tomorrow night? You think they'll *ever* get one from M-Slovak?"

"I'll have to keep the source of this money confidential at least until after the news breaks." She's thinking out loud.

"No question. We can't risk tipping off Wanamaker Salterfin that they've got the wrong defendant, and we can't tip off Rex and Les."

Moore comes back in. "It took some serious dancing, not being able to tell him the details, but he can see the gravity of the situation and he trusts me to act in the best interests of the board. Only problem is, it's got to be a verbal commitment until Friday. For him to document it sooner means calling an emergency board meeting, which Rex would be in the middle of. So if Miss LaRayne—" He's looking right at her. "If you'll take my word for it, we have a deal. Rex gets arrested tomorrow; the board convenes Friday to fire him; then they vote to approve the settlement we've negotiated here today. Buchanan guaranteed me the votes."

"What about Rex's job?" I ask him. "Who'll get the nod?"

Moore looks very serious, but there's the slightest hint of smile. He shrugs. "I was already the front-runner; plus I'll be a hero for heading off the company's collapse . . ."

"We can make this work, Danté," Cricket tells me, her eyes deep with gratitude.

"I'll deliver the clients," Melissa vows. I'm betting on her.

"And I'll get the CEO job," Moore declares.

"Which agency will wind up taking over *all* of your ad accounts?" I ask him.

Moore has to smile. "Why, The Dellman/Roenik Group, of course."

*   *   *

Okay, listen up, class. Are you prepared for today's quiz?

That's how it feels, zipping toward Midway Airport to fly south and condemn two tycoons to long-term detention. Have I studied every angle, thought of everything, brought what I need? I feel like it's the day of the big test and I've crammed the wrong subject.

Durbett greets me when I arrive, pulling me into a private lounge to make the transfer. "You left one copy here?" he asks, referring to the dubs I made from the video of Briggs and Casapell admitting their heinous roles.

"This contains the original disk for the feds, plus a dub for you to hold for safe-keeping. The only other dub is in my desk at *Shoot & Die*. Melissa knows to retrieve it and turn it over to Sally for editing as soon as I signal that the raid has started."

"Good, we don't want your employees knowing any sooner—too much chance of leaks. Too many people know as it is." He castigates me with a disapproving frown, reminder he was against involving Hal and NBS. "Remember, Hal *cannot* know I'm setting up the raid, or that I have anything to do with turning over the video to the feds."

"Yes, I know. Hal got an anonymous tip, and knows nothing of the chain of information."

Durbett's private jet is way cool, plenty of room for him and our pilot, me and Hal, Kristen and Byron, and—arriving at the last second with a grin but no luggage—Jankety. It's set up like an elongated sunken living room, with office area at the front, comfortable bathroom at the rear. I could get used to this kind of travel, especially a flight time from Chicago to Camden, Tennessee of less than an hour.

We strap in and lift off, Jankety reporting, "Les Casapell flew commercial-carrier to Nashville where he was picked up by the Briggs company chopper—a nice Jet Ranger, I might add—then dropped off at AnalyClin. Two flunkies took his bags to the company condo at New Johnsonville and brought back a car for him. Should I arrange further surveillance?"

Durbett shakes his head. "He's not going anywhere. Luckily, he's too busy painting a pretty picture at the clinic for the interviews, so he doesn't have time to destroy the stock of bad capsules until after Danté's gone."

Ring ring. Jankety answers the phone and hands it to me.

"Danté?" It's Melissa. "Les Casapell called to see where you're staying, so I gave him the name of the motel. He said he's going to leave his condo phone number with the desk clerk in case you want to get together tonight. If not, he'll see you in the morning."

"Thanks, Mel—"

"I have a message for Kristen, too. Tell her the film crew has arrived in Nashville, the *Wave-Slicer* is in Dickson for the night, and that Billy Sizemore won't be there until tomorrow evening. I didn't let on that you'll be heading back here by then."

"And Frank?"

"Complaining because they won't let him out of there."

"Sounds like he's doing fine."

"Taj takes a boxful of toys every visit so they can play. We got Gramps a *Monster Bin* overshirt."

"Make him behave himself, Mel."

"Easier said then done. Between the two of 'em, Taj is the mature one."

I report to the crowd, everybody pleased the old man's too ornery to let a heart attack get him down. Kristen gives me a special look, her eyes sparkling, nodding her head. She's been worrying about Frank—a lot. We all have.

Byron and Jankety are into the bar now, the clink of ice cubes echoing through the quiet hum in the cabin. I'm lost in thought, still not quite prepared for the big test. "So when do I get to fly this thing?" I ask Durbett.

"You look like you got something on your mind," he answers, "so let's go give the pilot a break."

Durbett takes one set of controls—I should've expected as much. The pilot steps back into the cabin, so I close the door to the cockpit and slide in behind the other controls. Within minutes, I'm actually flying it, not unlike a kid sitting on his parent's lap holding the steering wheel, ready for the pole position at Indy.

"How can we make sure the raid will be visually exciting?" I ask Durbett.

"You can't. If it goes well, there won't be much to see."

"That doesn't make good news footage," I point out.

"You'll get the agents going in, then bringing out cases of capsules, and Casapell being arrested. That's doin' pretty good."

"Will they be breaking down doors, weapons drawn, and so on?"

Durbett takes over the controls, giving me a sidelong glance, but not answering.

"Helicopters, armored vehicles, men in flak suits?" I press.

Durbett snorts his disgust. "Ain't you learned nothin' yet? This ain't about puttin' on a show for you; it's about shuttin' down a deadly operation that's poisoning innocent people."

"Well, yeah, but—"

"But hell." He's annoyed now—and that's when I get the *quiz* I've been dreading. "What is it you want, Danté? Are you looking for justice or to make news? Are you trying to save lives or Hal's career? Are you repairing the damage *you* did to Parzilac or just trying to sell your Fantasy Patch?"

Yow.

I take a deep breath, think it over, embarrassed at being called out. Then it hits me—

Oh oh oh! I know the answer to this one!

"All of the above."

*   *   *

It's really starting to hit me now. I'm sitting by myself in the motel room, the warm night-time air wafting through the window, the fragrance of lake and woods, the sound of crickets—I have to chuckle at the image *that* conjures—a mosquito buzzing near my ear, moths flinging themselves against the screen . . .

I want to call Cyn.

But I can't. I'm still trying to see our future together, somehow working past this problem, maybe after all this commotion has blown over, when she realizes she was wrong, that we were both wrong . . . If she ever realizes.

But I just can't see it.

Ring.

"Danté?" It's Kristen. "Are you all right? You looked so down."

"Yeah. Pre-sting jitters, I guess. I get this way the night before I topple corporate giants and get people sent off to prison."

"I was thinking of walking over to the diner, having a piece of pie or something. Want to come along?"

She's being a friend, and it does sound like a good idea. Maybe a slice would fill the piece missing from my life, if just for a moment. So we perch ourselves in the duct-taped vinyl booth of some gawdy, lime-green, fluorescent-lit level of Danté's Inferno, snarfing chocolate cream, all the while talking about nothing.

"It's Cyn, isn't it?" she finally says, looking at me sympathetically.

I start to brush her off, but she's earnest, trying to show she cares . . . Oh the dangers of having a director who can read the producer's mind. I nod, staring at my choco-smeared pie plate.

And wouldn't you know, my eyes are getting blurry on me yet again. I need to have them checked.

"It'll work out," she whispers, and she means it.

I shake my head. "Not this time."

"But you love her, don't you?"

"Yes, I love her . . . but you can love someone and still not be able to have a relationship."

She nods slowly, conceding the truth of my words. "And sometimes you can have so much relationship with somebody, you forget to notice you love them."

We look at each other, and I can see we're both embarrassed by the uncustomary intimacy. "We should get some rest," I say, the tension broken.

"Yeah," she says.

We walk back, not saying anything, nothing more to say.

I bid her good night, then start toward my own room, but I decide I can't stand to sit in there by myself right now, that I need some air, to clear my head, stretch my legs, whatever. I walk down the road, then head down a side street that goes toward the lake. There's not a soul around, my solitude an uncomfortable fit, ready to be broken in.

The black gauze of night shrouds me with an orchestra-tuning cacophony of buzzes and chirrups, the harp-strokes of fat bass and hungry bream breaking the surface, the basso rumble of bullfrogs harrumphing from the reeds, the choir hum of a boat trolling its way around the coves, the gravel-crunching percussion of a vehicle coming down the road behind me . . .

Of all things, it appears to be a blue van. I have to chuckle.

Then it pulls over just past me, the back doors opening. Three men in dark clothes jump out and grab me, one putting a rag over my nose and mouth!

I struggle, but the rag stinks, and my legs turn to rubber—

CHAPTER 25

Strapped down. Wrists, ankles, belly.

Smooth leather restraints. IV needle in the crook of my arm, bag hanging on a hook. Somebody's drugging me.

Painted cinderblock walls, dirty green, like hospital scrubs. Door with tiny, barred window, food-tray slot. Tile floor, scuffed and cracked, a San Andreas buckle down the middle. Small, elongated window near the ceiling, grated over, dark outside or painted black.

I'm trying not to puke, dry heaving, demon pie burning in my gut. Feel like an elevator falling too fast, dizzy, now floating . . .

Fluorescent light fixture above me, two long tubes, one flickering on and off, buzzing, waves spreading every direction, the whole room dancing, rocking back and forth, now falling again.

Calm down, Danté. Focus. Relax. Try to remember . . .

I never finished that drawing for Ms. Moeroff. I feel really bad about it, ashamed even, tears blinding my eyes. How could I do that to her? She wanted me to finish it; but then she left, and I never did.

A drawing of me, sitting alone on the beach, my friends nearby, the sun and the sand and the surf.

Me, strapped down now, slowly poisoned, about to die, alone.

Would Ms. Moeroff forgive me for not finishing the picture? Yes, but she would be sad. I really messed up on Parzilac, but I was trying to fix it—you know that, don't you, Kristen?

Can Frank save The Dellman/Roenik Group without me? Of course he can. Nobody needs me. I did leave some loose ends to wrap up, though. Had 'em written down somewhere. Ha! Probably in my schedule planner, wherever that is. Never did go electronic—afraid I'd lose it, or spend all my time organizing it.

What did I forget to tell Kristen?

Sally the TV psychic has me on the line. "Hello, Danté!"

"Psych me, sweetheart."

"There's somebody powerful in your life, someone important . . . A woman? A man?"

"Rex Briggs."

"Right, a man. He's—what? Your boss? Your—?"

"My client. Mr. Fantasy Patch. Have you heard? *Imagine, Become, Escape!*"

"It's about the Parzilac?" she says, but she's a man now.

"No, it's about the Patch. Market share. Sowing fear and selling salvation. Praise be. Did you know?—I'm the preacher-man, the minister, the missionary. Just ask Danté, he'll tell you. He'll show you how to cover your nakedness, pray to the pills, stop being human in the quest for something more. Evolve ye. Go forth and prescribe. Scripture's in the fine print at the bottom of the ad. Become the image—"

"What about Rex Briggs? You made a video, didn't you?"

"Yes, Mr. Les Casapell. I know who you are now. Yes, I made a video. *Gotcha!* You *and* Rex Briggs—"

"Where's the disk?"

"Hidden—Hey! How'd you know I made a video?"

"Ellmata got suspicious about your Aller-Tat display, asked how long it'd been there, took a closer look. Where's the disk?"

"Hidden."

Frank's lucky. He found a daughter, a grandson, wasn't even looking, didn't know how much he needed 'em. Good for Melissa. Good for Taj. "Grrrrrrr!"

"Oh, that's how it is then?"

"Grrrrrrr!"

"Where's the disk hidden?"

"Secret."

"Does Hal know where?"

"Nope. Hal don't know squat."

"I guess he was telling the truth."

"You're not the psychic; you're Les Casapell. You look like a big dick, you know that? Wear a turtle neck; pull it up high for that—"

"I've already killed Hal Neusome 'cause he wouldn't tell me where the disk is."

"Hal's dead?" I can feel tears in my eyes again. What if he kills me, too? I had plans. I was gonna make sure Ms. Moeroff is okay when she gets real old, the gerbil who'll probably outlive me. Guess now she will—

"Where's the disk?"

The elevator's falling faster and faster. I forgot to tell Kristen—

"The disk?"

Dammit, I'm crying now. How did I lose Cyn?

"Disk?"

I'm sorry, Ms. Moeroff. I shoulda finished the picture. I'm sorry—

"Danté!"

"Kristen?"

Falling faster and faster—

"Disk?"

"Kristen?"

Faster.

"What?"

"*Grrrrrr!*"

*   *   *

Smells like barf in here.

I pry my eyelids open and discover I'm slumped against the wall next to an old, rusty-cracked porcelain toilet bowl, a basin of like condition above it, corroded pipes. I'm behind the table where I'd been strapped earlier, the area I couldn't see. It's the toilet that stinks, and me a little, until I rinse my mouth and face, then flush. Apparently the heaves are what got them to unstrap me—that and I must not have been much of a threat when my purple haze was busy kissing the sky. Chocolate pie. 'Nuff said.

There's daylight filtering through the barred window now. It has that *dawn* look about it.

I'm a bit wobbly, but not too bad considering the chemical wallop I've been through, fuzzy drug buzz from a doozy bug drug.

Locked in.

Keep quiet while I think. They killed Hal because he didn't know—

I remember telling Les the disk was in my desk at *Shoot & Die*.

They have no reason to let me out of here. They have lots of reasons to make me disappear for good. Why am I still alive? In case I lied about the disk in the desk, in case they have to squeeze me harder. I'm imagining the phone call:

"Yeah, we got the disk, but it's marked *Dub*. What the hell's that mean?"

"Means it ain't the original."

"What do we do?"

"Hold tight. I'm gonna talk to Roenik again, sandpaper his eyeballs, clamp electrodes to his gotchies, then get rough."

Still queasy, I have to sit. I wonder how much time I have. Where am I? Maybe one of the old ward buildings of the sanitarium that's now AnalyClin.

Seems deserted; nobody's walked by, no activity in the hallway.

My group is supposed to meet for breakfast at eight, so they probably don't even know yet that Hal and I are missing. That's if we're the only two who were snatched.

Kristen?

I have to lie back now, the room too wobbly for me, the San Andreas floor threatening to open and swallow me whole. Wish it would; might be a way out.

Durbett would come looking for us . . . but how would he know we're here? No access, no way to be sure— The RFID chip on my tooth! The key-ring! Yes, just twist a quarter-turn and activate, press twice to signal distress!

I jump up—steady, steady—claw at my pocket, yank out my key— It's the motel room key. My own key-ring is sitting on the TV back in my room.

Damn.

There was no reason to take my personal keys for a pie-snarfing with Kristen.

What if they grabbed Kristen, too? As the director, she would be next most likely to know where hides the disk, but she doesn't. Would they hurt her—or worse—for having no useful information?

I feel like I'm falling again, actually trembling now. My eyes are blurry. I test the bolted door, then sit on the edge of the restraining table, stare at the floor, and try to calm myself. I need a plan.

But what?

Staring at my lap, my hands clenching and unclenching.

I'll never again laugh about Durbett's silly safety and protection devices. Still, I shouldn't need them. I'm not a private detective or somebody who's in jeopardy day-to-day. I just like to draw.

Durbett and those devices of his. Staring at the floor. His high-tech tracking chip, even glued to my tooth, turns out to be worthless if I don't have my super-duper spy key-ring.

Staring at my shoes.

How's that molar microchip gonna help a kidnapped child if he loses his key-ring?

Staring at my shoes, and it's so obvious I must be stupid. Which shoes did you pack for me, Ms. Moeroff?

Which shoes?! I'm yanking them off, pulling frantically at the soles.

Nothing.

The other— And there it is, a small rod, twist to activate the battery. Now it should be reading the data on my molar-chip, transmitting a locator signal up to three miles.

Whew!

Now, is anybody looking for me?

Will Durbett know to check for a transmission?

Will somebody help me before Casapell comes back with the electrodes?

Smells like barf in here.

Is Kristen okay?

*   *   *

Okay, I'm ready.

I've been waiting quite a while. Come get me. Any time now would be fine by me.

Preferably sometime today.

Tired. Whipped and tired. —But alert! Whipped and tired, tipped and wired. Whew . . . Still woozy, could use a snoozy.

I stretch out on the table, thinking. Les hadn't mentioned Kristen, and I figure if he kidnapped her, he would have said something, if only to shake me up like he did by admitting he killed Hal. But then, maybe he grabbed her after I'd told him where the disk . . . No, no reason to unless he knows I didn't give him the whole truth and nothing but the truth. If he figures that out, he'll come back to confront me first.

I sure need the troops to come rescue me—any time now. I'm ready. Let's go.

Gosh and golly, I hope somebody picked up my tracker signal. Surely they've realized I'm missing—but do Durbett or Jankety even know I'm glued to a molar-chip, or that I'm carrying an ID transmitter? Durbett's busy this morning. Where did Jankety go?

Pink Floyd: *Is anybody out there?*

Drowsy, still tingling from the drugging, lying on my side now, eyes closed . . . Have to stay alert.

I can hear somebody at the door. It's opening. Don't move—figure out what's going on first.

"Wake up, Roenik!" It's Les Casapell, that felonious phallic feller.

I open my eyes slowly, pretend to be dazed and confused, my tribute to Led Zeppelin. There's a guy in a lab coat looking me over. Beside him, farther back, is a large goon hovering protectively next to Les Casapell, Monty Python's Bigghus Dickus.

"Huh?" I respond. Good line—I wrote it myself. Now to start composing my epitaph . . . My heart is pounding, but I need to act like I'm still bug-drugged. Stall. Kill time . . .

Before they kill *me*.

"The disk in your office is a copy!" Les accuses. He's up to speed now.

"Huh?"

"How many copies did you make?" he demands.

I ignore him.

Goon steps forward and slaps the daylights out of me. Man, he moves fast. I prefer to *keep* my daylights, thank you very much.

"What?!" Another of my better lines.

"How many copies did you run?"

"Of what?"

"Of the video you made of Rex and me in his office."

"I made a copy," I tell him.

"What copy?" he snarls.

"The one in my desk."

"Where's the original?"

"I don't know." This much is true. I have no idea where Flynn Durbett is. What I do know is that he's not here to rescue my sorry butt right now. He said he would be busy this morning—might not even still be in Tennessee—

Goon reaches to hit me again, his fist clenched this time—

"I don't have it," I mumble.

"Is it in your house? Somewhere in the studio? Where?"

"Let me bust him up," the goon says, fixing me with the glare of his eyes. He's like some trained dog fixated on a bowl of treats, waiting for the command to pounce.

"Dose him again," Les says. "I can trust the answers better that way. Then if he doesn't cooperate, you can smash him a piece at a time until he decides to share secrets."

The lab-coater steps forward and reaches like he's going to strap me down again, just for an instant standing between me and the other two.

Kick!

I kick him hard in the gut, knocking him into the others, all three off balance— And I'm out the door, slamming it, sliding the bolt-bar into its slot just as goon bounces off the steel.

Thump! He hits it again, then takes out a handgun and shoots at it. I jump to the side, but there's no penetration, no movement, nothing. This ancient Mesopotamian relic of a door overmatches anything short of a grenade.

"Oh! Now I remember where it is!" I shout at them, my daylights fully recovered. Enough taunting for now, it's time to beat a hasty retreat.

I run down the dingy corridor of this obviously deserted building. Down to the corner landing I huff and puff, four steps up to ground level and the door out—

And it's locked.

And chained and padlocked. I trot past it another thirty feet, under the stairwell, dead end. Rats. Time to backtrack—

But there's a second goon, and he's letting my prisoners out. Great, I'm the one with a molar-tracker and they're the ones who get rescued.

They're running my way, and I'm trapped.

Up the stairs, Danté—yes, two or three at a time would be prudent.

Another corridor, opening into a wider area that looks like a hospital ward, evenly spaced pillars floor to ceiling, grated windows, debris piled against a wall.

Keep moving!

Through some kind of examination area, old cabinets along the wall, into another ward, a hallway with storage closets, the doors missing, a landing and stairwell. Too risky to descend so close, they might have split up to cover both ways down.

Keep moving toward the other end of the building. My side is cramping up. I'm panting.

Another ward, pause and listen.

Oh no, the sound of somebody running toward me from ahead.

Turn around, retreat, run like the wind—like quiet wind, trying not to let them hear me, or track me.

The middle stairwell again— Chance it?

A door opens below, poignant response to my question.

I run again, back to where I came up. They're dead-ending me.

I notice a steel pipe in the debris, grab it on the fly. It's no gun; it's no can of chunky tuna in water, but it's all I've got.

To the stairwell, pause, listen, no sound. Ease down quietly.

Nobody, no sign. Move forward a few feet . . .

And there they are, Les and both goons stepping from the alcove across from the doorway, all three training pistols on me. They're right in front of the door, blocking my way, not like I could get out through that chain, anyway.

"It's over, Danté," Les gloats. "Tell me where the disk is and I'll let you live."

I don't believe him. His credibility is shot, far as I'm concerned. "What guarantees do I have?"

Boom! One goon shoots above my head, cinderblock dust poofing into the air, dandruff settling on my hair.

"You're guaranteed to die if you don't."

"You're gonna kill me anyway!" This I believe, and he doesn't have to draw me a picture.

"Wound him," Les says, stepping back a pace.

Second goon takes aim—

Ka-boom! The door blows in, goons splatted against the opposite wall, Les running the other direction with a bit of a limp in his stride.

Durbett peeks his head in just as Les disappears from sight. He steps inside, Jankety right behind him.

"It's about time!" I'm trembling, but hoping it doesn't show. Mr. Cool in the face of death, that's me.

"Where's Neusome?" Durbett asks.

"They killed him!"

"You know this for sure?"

"No, that's what they said—"

"Where were you?" He's talking urgently.

"Down there on the left, the open door."

He inspects the first few doors, all damaged and unboltable. "Most ain't secure," he pronounces. "Neusome could be in any of 'em."

"What took you so long?" I ask.

"Waiting for back-up," Jankety answers, but then your signal started moving fast, so we figured you were loose and in trouble—"

"Get him out," Durbett commands, "and move the boat out of position. I'll cover you; then I'll look for Neusome. Come back to just beyond the pickup point when I signal."

"Let's go," Jankety commands, tugging me toward the door.

"Watch that damned camera," Durbett warns him.

Bright daylight, and Jankety points down toward the water's edge where Kristen is waiting in the Sizemore *Wave-Slicer*, Byron in the back shooting

Steadi-Cam our way. Loud rumbles echo in the sky. "Run!" Jankety commands. "I'm right behind you, out of the shot."

Durbett steps behind him just as we bolt for the shore.

The rumble is a helicopter, lifting over the buildings from the other end of the complex!

I'm running like a wild man, jumping into the boat, the chopper almost to us now. I glance up to see an arm and a gun—

Boom! Jankety's hit just as he stumbles into the boat!

Boom! Boom! Durbett's firing, Kristen powering up and backing the boat away from the shore. The chopper's been hit, a man falling out the side. The body's snared by the branches of a tree, right above where the boat had been.

The chopper veers away just as Kristen jams the throttle, and we take off at a thousand miles an hour. That guy's still in the tree, not moving.

The chopper circles around behind the building to get away from Durbett, then comes after us with a vengeance.

Jankety's down in the boat, bleeding. Byron's shooting video of the chopper gaining on us—the man's a maniac.

"I'm all right," Jankety assures me, but I'm not convinced. He hands me a pistol, then gestures in the direction of the chopper. He's breathing hard, panting.

So here we are in the world's fastest consumer-model speedboat, fully equipped with the next generation of tri-dimensional projected data imaging—from below-surface sonar and thermal-sensor scanning to satellite mapping with course/route logic and a host of other programmed applications.

And I'm on my knees pressing Jankety's shoulder, trying to stem the bleeding—

"Shoot him down or we're dead!" he shouts at me.

The chopper's gaining, bullets rain-splatting the water now. Kristen's intent at the helm, punching icons on the Sizemore 4000, manually overriding the throttle.

Pfoom! Pfoom! They're gonna hit us—

Boom! I fire, losing my balance in the process. It's enough to make the chopper veer a little and lose some distance.

Now it's off to the side, trying to come up beside us. I can see Les in the open door aiming his pistol right at me—

Boom! I hit the bubble! At least it made them veer again.

"Jankety!" It's Durbett's disembodied radio voice. "You okay to decoy?"

"Better off in the woods than bouncing in this boat!" he shouts over the roar.

Boom! I miss the chopper completely, but I'm keeping it wary, not too close.

"Into a cove!" Jankety shouts at Kristen. "I'm going into the woods! Danté, be obvious about throwing me one of those blank disks soon as I'm out—"

"But you're—!"

"Do it!"

Kristen roars up into a cove and back-throttles, riding a wave into a clump of trees at water's edge. Where did she learn—?

Jankety's climbing out, me helping hand him up. The chopper's circling close— *Pfoom! Pfoom!* One shot hit the bow of the boat. I grab an empty disk case and, making sure the chopper can see, toss it into the woods where Jankety's clutching his shoulder. I lose my balance and fall to the deck as Kristen roars back, spins us, and zooms out of the cove.

It worked. The chopper's hovering over the woods, trying to spot Jankety, looking for which way he's gone with the coveted evidence—or facsimile thereof.

I scrabble up next to Kristen. "You heading back?"

"Durbett said stop just beyond where he rescued you!"

Rats! The chopper's heading our way again. Les done figured us out.

"Be ready to shoot at them!" Kristen reminds me.

Point with the narrow end; pull the trigger. How many shots left in the clip? And to think I've been drawing pictures when I could've been at the firing range. I'd rather draw prison bars around Les—

The chopper's gaining. It's going to be a race. I can see what's ahead of us in that tri-dim projection from the Sizemore 4000. I touch the icon that raises our perspective to encompass more sky than water. I can see the trees and a bird flying high—

Pfoom! Les isn't close enough to hit us yet; he's just trying to shake us up—

Almost there. Kristen's slowing now, the chopper almost on us. Hal Neusome runs out from the building where I'd been held, dropping into the tall grass like an old lady on a patch of ice. Kristen back-throttles to cut our speed, then roars into an arc toward the shore, now facing the chopper. I can see our 3-D adversary in that Sizemore projection. Byron's *still* shooting Steadi-Cam.

The chopper slows to hover. Les Casapell leans out, weapon in hand—

Psst! Psst! Boom!

The chopper's hit! Durbett and several other guys have appeared in the brush along the shore— *Bam! Bam! Bam!* They're *wailing* on Les.

The chopper starts to smoke, turning slowly, losing control. It tries to escape, flying toward the building, then starting to spin faster and faster, losing altitude . . .

Toward the corner of the roof—

Kristen is nosing into the shore, Byron up on his feet now, still shooting—

Crash! Right into the edge of the building. *Ka-Boom! Whoof!*—a fireball, debris raining every direction, images echoed in the tri-dim projection, tiny three-dimensional remnants showering the holo-grounds.

Byron is running toward the crash site, and there's a just-rescued, rather disheveled Hal Neusome just ahead of him—*in the shot!*

I could smile. I mean, well, maybe someday, looking back.

Then Kristen and I run toward the conflagration, wondering about survivors, but there's no chance, no way. The dead man in the tree is the lucky one. They won't need his dental records . . .

There's no sign of Durbett or his minions. I head back toward the shore and find him crouched in the brush.

"We're gonna move out," he says. "Make sure Byron keeps the camera off us." He touches his vest. "Jankety!"

"I'm okay."

"Go get him," Durbett tells me. "Then you two meet me at the jet. I'll have a doctor there for him. You and me's going back to Chicago."

"But the raid—"

"Leave everybody else here to shoot it. Just you is going." He signals; then three guys jump up and follow him around the other side of the building. I run up behind Byron to make sure he doesn't catch a shot of them.

"Let's get Jankety!" I shout to Kristen. "He needs help!"

We race to the boat and take off at a thousand miles an hour. Several minutes later, we pull into the cove and find our dark-skinned mercenary waiting patiently on a log jutting over the water. He's tied his shirt around his shoulder. It looks like the bleeding's stopped. I help him climb in.

"Flynn shot 'em down," I gush.

Jankety's grinning as Kristen backs out and throttles. "I know! I could see it from here! What a show! Did Byron get it?"

"Every frame! Flynn said rush you to the airport. He'll have a doctor there."

"Ah, yes—our own Doc Hayward."

"Then he and I are flying to Chicago."

"We'll cover the raid and get set up to shoot Sizemore!" Kristen assures me over the roar. "Take the disks with you. There's two DVRs still on the plane—you can edit during the trip!"

We zoom past the scene of the downed chopper, then head to the boat launch, a mile south, where Kristen left a rental car. She unlocks it while I walk Jankety up and help him ease into the front seat. She hands me the keys, then suddenly surprises me with a brief hug. "Be careful," she cautions, looking into my eyes.

Before I can say anything, she turns and bolts for the *Wave-Slicer*, jumps in, waves and smiles, then backs out and guns it.

I'm standing there watching her zoom away when Jankety reminds me, "I'm bleeding, you know!"

And we're off to the airport where a small group greets us. They make room for a short fat guy with a doctoring air about him. He quickly examines Jankety right in the front seat, then pronounces, "We can move him in my car."

"Hell," Durbett jibes Jankety, "I thought you was hurt!"

"Just enough to miss the fun," he allows.

The pilot is powering up the jet while Durbett and I thank everybody and clasp hands with his troops. Then he and I climb aboard and seal the hatch.

"Why Chicago?" I ask, strapping in. "Why the hurry?"

"Hal said he heard Les tell somebody the disk was only a copy, that they might have to hit the studio to find the original."

We're accelerating down the runway.

"So send your people—"

"I got Detective Culler headin' there," he says, looking at me very seriously. "I sent my own people to *your* house."

"But why?"

"Hal also heard 'em say they found an old lady at your place when they got there."

CHAPTER 26

Time to get busy.

We're at about thirty-thousand feet, zooming toward Chicago, and I can't reach Ms. Moeroff by air-phone. Durbett's still not heard from the people he sent to my house to check on her, to look around, get the lay, watch for lurking bugs and burly lugs. So far all is clear at *Shoot & Die*, but everybody there is on alert—and Durbett's sending somebody else that way, too. The man's got hordes of cohorts.

Time to get busy, see what Byron shot, lay off some footage—

Hank! I try calling Hank Barnahay's house to have him check on Ms. Moeroff, but again no answer. Hank has a cell-phone, too—he brings it when he works in my garden—but I don't remember the number; it's written in my missing schedule planner. Durbett can access it through a database, but that might take a while, so he starts the process, just in case.

Time to get busy and edit some shots.

We're ten minutes from Chicago's Midway Airport when Durbett gets the call from the operative he sent to my neighborhood. He listens, then directs the caller to sit tight because we're on our way. He hangs up and tells me, "Your house and the carriage house out back have both been ransacked. There's no sign of the old lady."

"Oh God, what do we do?"

"It's time to get busy."

*   *   *

Tick.
Tock.
Tick.
Tock.

Few things are more relative than time. Time flies. Time drags. Time marches on.

Time stands still.

The fastest jet isn't fast enough. The best espionage and guerilla gear isn't good enough. The most sophisticated communications equipment echoes silence when there's nothing to report.

Tick. Tock. Tick— Ring! It's an operative, finally checking in again.

"No sign of Hank," Durbett tells me after clicking off. "Said his car's gone, but his house is wide open like he left in a big hurry. They still ain't found your phone book—"

Ring. They found Hank's cell-phone number! Durbett tells his man to have one guy stay there while the other one skedaddles to meet us at the airport. Then Durbett tries to call Hank, putting it on the cabin speaker phone so we can both talk.

"Yeah!" Hank answers.

"It's Danté!—here with a friend! What happened?"

"They took her! There was two cars at your house, people inside. I started to walk over, but they was leaving, and Theta went with 'em. She looked toward me, but didn't act like she seen me. She was hunched over like an old lady who needs a walker, but I could tell she was faking, that something was wrong, so I followed 'em, staying way back so they wouldn't see me." He uncorks the Barnahay curse bottle and lets the expletives flow for a moment, finally explaining, "Then I lost 'em." I learned some new words, plus new ways to use the old ones.

"Where?" Durbett asks, calmer than I feel. "Which way?"

"I'm in Stickney, on Cicero Avenue. They went somewhere in the warehouse district, but I been driving around looking for their cars and haven't seen 'em yet."

"Briggs has a warehouse in that area," I tell Durbett. "I've been there."

"Tell him where."

I give Hank directions—it's only a few blocks from where he is.

"Yes! I can see their cars now, parked at the side."

"How many people with her?" Durbett asks.

"Three guys, but they didn't look too tough. I was thinking I could—"

"No," Durbett tells him. "We'll be there soon. Don't risk her safety moving too fast. Just stay close, don't get yourself seen, and be ready to follow if they take her outta there. Hit *reply* to tell us if anything changes." Durbett clicks off and asks me, "You know your way around there?" He's retrieving a vid-disk from a padded case.

"No, but Stockbridge does."

"Here, make another copy in case we need to trade for Moeroff." He's punching in another phone number. "Get Stockbridge on the line."

I go through a secretary, then finally hear Stockbridge's voice. "Hey, Danté—" he says.

"Ted—" I start.

Durbett cuts in, "Need your help *fast*. Meet us a block north of the Stick-ney warehouse."

"Um, okay—"

"Fast, Ted! Leave right now!" *Click.*

Durbett's digging some phones from another case, all with red buttons. He calls somebody, asks for the time, then hangs up. "Raid won't be for another thirty minutes," he tells me, referring to the Tennessee bust soon to go down. "Get Rex on the phone, find out his game. Remember, he's prob-ably recording you. I'll listen but won't talk."

I speak with Rex's secretary, who puts me on hold, then says Rex will call me right back. I have to give her the number Durbett mouths for me.

"Switching to secure equipment, maybe getting people out of his office," Durbett explains. "He can't tell where you are by the area code, but you can admit you're on the jet, that you can meet him for an exchange if that's his plan."

Ring. "Where are you?" Rex asks.

"Flying back to Chicago."

"You know what I want."

I'm thinking fast. "Yeah, and you woulda had it, too—except Les messed up big-time."

"Why'd you do it?"

"It wasn't me. It was the guy looking for info for a book he's writing, but I found out and got the video before he even got to see it. I made a back-up copy for safety and took it to Tennessee, hoping I could schmooze Les with it, firm up our commitment for all your Fantasy Patch business."

Rex hesitates. "You haven't done anything with it?"

"If I'd turned it over to the cops, would you be talking to me right now?" Now a Frankism: Divert his attention from the possibility before he has time to mull it. "I have too many plans for getting rich off the Briggs accounts, but that idiot Casapell had me kidnapped and drugged—pretty bad treatment for somebody who pulled your butt out of the fire and was going to give you back your evidence."

Rex hesitates again. "Well, it sounds good, but I want the disk in my hands before I believe it. Where you gonna land?"

"Midway."

"What time? I'll have somebody there to get the disk as you get off the plane."

We've already started our descent; I can feel it. We'll be landing any minute now. "Thirty minutes," I tell him. Durbett grins, liking what I said.

"You know I have something you want," Rex hints.

"Yeah, a whole lotta business."

"No, your old lady stopped by to visit. She's a bit disoriented, though, needs directions home. Soon as I verify the disk, I'll make sure she's sent on her way."

"Ms. Moeroff! You have Ms.—?!"

"Don't screw this up, Danté," he warns, cutting me off, then hanging up.

"Good thinkin'," Durbett says. "I'll send the jet back up, then have it land again when Rex's guy gets there, but let it sit on the tarmac while he cools his heels."

"But why? We'll be to the warehouse by then."

"Something could go wrong, or delay us moving in. This way, plan B is already workin' for us." He unpacks a tracker like I'd seen at the studio last week, explaining, "Your job is to get the old lady somewhere and hide. I'll use this to find you when it's over. Now, let's strap in."

"What's the plan?"

"Don't know yet. Got any ideas?"

Tick-Tick-Tick-Tick . . .

*   *   *

Ted Stockbridge and Hank Barnahay are eyeing each other warily from opposite ends of the parking lot. Flynn Durbett and I arrive in one of his black Jeeps, neatly stacked cases from the jet filling the cargo area. We pull in and park, signaling them to come join us. They climb into the back seat; everybody's introduced, no need to stress the urgency of our situation.

No need to draw them a picture.

"Rex just arrived," Stocky reports. "There was another guy with him." The man he describes sounds like Ellmata.

"Ellmata," our mercenary pronounces.

"One of the guys with Theta," Hank reports, "just left before Ted got here."

"Which way?"

"South on Cicero."

"To the airport," Durbett surmises.

"That leaves two guys holding Ms. Moeroff along with Rex and

Ellmata," I sum up, ever the detective.

"How do we get in?" Durbett asks Stocky.

"My pass-card gets us through the gate. That small brick area attached to the front is the office. My key gets us in there. The warehouse will have lots of open doors this time of year."

"She's probably bein' held in the offices," Durbett guesses. "How's it laid out? How's it connect to the warehouse?"

"That part's unused unless I or one of my people comes here to work. The reception area's inside the door, with maintenance locked off behind it. The stairs to the right lead up to two offices, a couple of storage closets, and a small meeting room, all on either side of a hallway that leads to the door into the foreman's nook, a glass-enclosed cubbyhole overlooking the floor of the warehouse."

"From there?"

"Iron stairwell straight down onto the floor. Against the wall is a smaller stairway leading up to the gantry-crane catwalk."

"That door's the only way out the back, and the front door's the only way out this side?"

Stocky nods.

Durbett has Hank hand him one of the cases from the back. He extracts some tiny devices, then has the two back-seaters pull up their shirts so he can tape pinpoint cameras with microphones to their chests, positioning them to peek out their shirt fronts. He links them to tiny transmitters in their pockets, then straps on one of those video-screen visors I tried the night Jankety trained me. He grabs another for me to wear.

I point out, "If we go in the front, they can escape out the back." I'm quite the strategist. This visor is cool. I can see in front of me, but there are small windows in the lower corners showing miniature views from Stocky's and Hank's chests. I can hear our conversation reverberate in my right ear.

"How many people in the warehouse?" Durbett asks.

"Not more than a dozen at this end; it's all storage. There'll be thirty or more back in manufacturing."

"Fire alarm?"

"Big red buttons scattered around."

"How close to the foreman's overlook?"

Stocky thinks for a second. "Right outside the door, up on the wall."

"We need to separate the ones holding Moeroff, if we can."

I say, "Ted's the only one who can walk in without raising suspicion."

"That's why he's wearin' a wire. He'll go in and find out the lay of the situation while we visor-watch. Hank stays out of sight at the front entrance so we'll know if they come out that way—"

"I got my Colt," Hank reports, showing us his pistol.

"Yeah, I noticed," Durbett says evenly. "Only if you absolutely *must* use it," he stresses. "It's more important you be eyes and ears for us. If they get out the front, it's better you follow than to get yourself shot and leave us no way to know which way they went."

"Where you gonna be?"

"Danté and I's goin' through the warehouse." To me he instructs, "You stay by the door and watch. Once we know what's happening inside, I'll hit the fire alarm, clear out the bystanders, try to draw out one or two from the office and take 'em down. With any luck, that'll leave only Rex and Ellmata with Moeroff. I may go in right then, or I may signal you to go around and enter from the front, carrying that disk like you've landed early and Rex's office said you could find him there."

"Depending on what?" I wonder.

"Instinct. I'll see how it feels. Maybe it's best I move fast; maybe I'd rather have another distraction. If I *don't* signal you to go around, then you're covering the warehouse to make sure they don't get out your way—you know, in case I get cut down." He has Hank grab another case, from which he hands me a small pistol. "Keep it in your waistband out of sight." It's not a request. "Don't shoot wild," he adds.

I start to protest. I'm not a shooter, don't know how to handle a gun . . . but that's Ms. Moeroff in there. I'll do what I must.

Durbett looks at each of us, assessing, calculating, sizing up. "Remember, the job is to get the old lady out and get away. Nothing else, for now."

I'm thinking, *And don't get killed.*

"Any questions?" Durbett asks.

I have a thousand questions . . . but there's nothing left to say.

Durbett puts the Jeep in gear. "Let's do it."

*   *   *

Through the gate.

Back near a loading dock, park.

Stockbridge walks toward the front, his picture in my visor bouncing sea-sickly, the view in front of him. Hank follows behind him, his camera showing a lovely view of Stocky's butt.

Durbett leads me into the warehouse. It still looks like a cool clubhouse for a gaggle of twelve-year-olds.

I move behind a stack of crates, peering around the right side, watching Durbett. He disappears from sight for a minute, then suddenly materializes at the foot of the stairs, gliding up and into position.

Visor view: Stockbridge turns at the front and waves his arm, probably motioning where Hank should wait. He opens the door, hesitates—the lobby's empty—then steps inside.

Durbett's looking at me, nodding. One or two warehouse workers notice us but don't pay much attention.

Visor: Up the stairs, nobody . . . nobody . . .

Durbett's holding something in his hand, a weapon maybe, real smooth, not obvious to curious workers.

Visor: "Who are you?" It's Ellmata.

"Ted Stockbridge. Who are *you*?"

"You got a reason to be here?"

Stockbridge, sounding annoyed, answers, "I run this place. Who *are* you?"

"Wait here."

The man turns and starts down the hallway. Stocky follows.

"I said wait—"

Glimpse into the meeting room, two goons, the leg of another at the edge of the frame, probably Rex.

"I don't work for you. What's going on here?"

The door's slammed shut. Ellmata's in Stocky's face now, crowding him back. Stocky turns toward the only closed door, kicking it. "Theta?!" he shouts.

"In here!" It's muffled, but that's my gal.

Durbett hits the alarm. *Woo Woo Woo Woo Woo* . . .

The door behind Ellmata opens. "What's that?"

A voice in the room, Rex: "It's the warehouse."

"Check it out!" Ellmata shouts, lunging at Stockbridge. Our portly dude's fairly spry. Now the camera's bouncing—

Warehouse door opens, goon glances out.

Workers are scattering, exiting the premises.

"Open the door!" Ellmata shouts, wrestling Stocky toward the room where Ms. Moeroff—

Second goon reaching for the door, camera veers away.

First goon steps into the foreman's overlook, out onto the stair landing.

Whomp! I didn't even see Durbett move, but I heard the blow. He pushes the unconscious—dead?—goon over onto a beam, glances my way, holds his finger up.

Wait.

Visor: Door opens, Stocky wrestled inside—and Moeroff's out! My little old ballet dancer practically climbs over Stockbridge *and* Ellmata!

Durbett crouches.

Visor: Stocky's locked behind a door now, pounding on it. Where did Moeroff—?

She bursts out the foreman's door, running up to the catwalk. The second goon is right on her; Durbett can't shoot. He leaps onto the catwalk, but the goon turns and fires. Durbett jumps behind a support pillar, one foot on the walk, one hanging in the air.

Hank in the visor: "What's going on? Where's Theta?" He's at the entrance now.

Moeroff's sprinting. I want to fire at the goon, but I'd shoot too wild. It's too risky.

End of the catwalk, Moeroff climbs into the girder lattice-work and dead ends.

Durbett leans out to fire, and the goon ducks behind the next support pillar, same position. It's a stand-off, Moeroff trapped beyond the end, goon between her and Durbett, neither man able to move without being vulnerable to fire.

"I'm going in!" Hank bellows as he charges in and up the stairs.

I run around the crates and find a position closer to the overlook.

Hank's visor: *Boom! Boom!* Hank's firing wild. Rex is right in front of him now, then Ellmata. Hank swings at Rex, his blow deflected. Rex and Ellmata run down the hall and through the doorway, Hank right on them. All three burst through the foreman's office, onto the stairs. Ellmata's got a gun out now. He whirls at the bottom of the stairs—

I rip my visor off and drop it behind me.

I can't shoot toward Hank!

Hank swings his pistol up—*Boom!* Hank's hit!

"Hank!" Moeroff screams.

Hank falls.

Boom! Boom! I hit Ellmata! He whirls, staggers, and collapses.

Where did Rex go? He got to the skids, somewhere in front of me.

I look to Durbett. He returns a look that says he doesn't know, but he's scanning, watching, dividing his attention between the action on the floor and the man behind the other pillar, waiting for his chance.

Oh God, Hank's trying to crawl, smearing a pool of crimson. It looks like the bullet pierced his chest—

"Oh Hank!" Moeroff screams, sobbing now.

He's trying to crawl toward her.

Boom! A shot ricochets from the beams around Moeroff. She crouches behind a girder, a folded spider disappearing from sight.

It was Rex who fired at her, giving me a hint where he is.

Around to the left . . .

To the next stack of skids . . .

Around the left—

Durbett tilts his head urgently to the right. I pull back and ease around to the right side. I can hear something moving maybe thirty, forty feet away, several more sets of skids.

Look to Durbett, nothing there. He can't see Rex anymore. He raises his hand and aims, reminding me to keep my weapon up and ready.

I freeze and listen. The only sound now is Ms. Moeroff crying, her quiet sobs echoing through the cavernous warehouse. I can't see Hank anymore, and I don't hear any movement.

I listen.

I wait.

Something makes me suspicious. My instincts say go back to the left. I don't know why.

No sign of Rex. He can't get back toward the stairs and the foreman's door without me seeing him. He can't get to the open bay door without Durbett having a shot. I figure there are about ten sets of skids he could be lurking around.

I move to the next one. Now there are maybe eight, tops.

Right or left?

I listen.

I wait.

Nothing from Durbett.

I've never heard Ms. Moeroff cry before, and it's tearing a hole through me. Oh, Hank . . . How did I drag you into this? I'm sorry, Ms. Moeroff. All I ever wanted to do was look out for you, to make sure you were loved and comforted from now until the day you danced beyond the final curtain call.

I've let you down—

A slight sound, to the right.

Move around the left, another set of skids. No more than six stacks now.

I'll kill the monster who hurt my old lady, who took away the man she loves, a couple of gerbils they used to be. I'll blow his head off.

I'm trembling with rage, but I have to calm down, to relax my breathing. My heart's pounding. Listen, Danté. Just listen . . .

Don't let Ms. Moeroff lose two of us in one day.

I have to wipe my eyes on my sleeve, have to see clearly, have to stay calm.

Have to listen . . .

Wait.

Ease around the left, the next set, the last two. Rex has to be this way or that way. There's no place to hide.

It's him and me.

My trembling has stopped.

Ms. Moeroff's quiet now.

My heart pauses; there's nothing but a calm stillness, a quiet serenity.

It's time.

I ease around the first corner to the left—

Rex charges around from the right and jumps me from behind! My pistol slides across the concrete. We roll and struggle, moving closer to the gun. I can see Durbett now, aimed and ready, but there's no clear shot.

Rex is on top of me now. He outweighs me by a hundred pounds, on my chest— Can't breathe— Crushing . . .

I'm trying to squirm, beating and clawing at his back with my right hand.

He's reaching for the gun.

I can't get my arm up high enough to pound at his head— Can't breathe—

He's got the gun. My left hand is holding his wrist, pushing his hand away. But he's stronger, and I can't breathe—

The gun's closer to my head.

Closer.

I see a flash up on the catwalk, Durbett leaping to a girder, dropping and firing, grabbing the underside of the grated walkway. The catwalk goon's head explodes crimson, his lifeless body turning slowly, then falling to the concrete below.

Boom! Rex is firing! Concrete shatters next to my head. Still pushing against Rex's wrist, losing my strength— Can't breathe—

Durbett's in the seat of the gantry crane, jamming the control levers. The cabled hook is swinging my way, lower, closer—

My whole body's tingling—

Boom! Concrete sprays into my eyes.

The big iron hook hits my hand. I grab it, twist.

Boom! Grazed the tip of my ear.

I hit Rex in the back with the hook, twist it around, snare his belt.

And Durbett's pulling him into the air, lifting him off me. I'm gasping, but I hold Rex's wrist for dear life, dragged up with him, twisting it—

Boom! He missed!—and I twist the gun free!

"Danté!" Rex shouts, sailing away from me. "Dammit all! I—"

And his belt pulls loose, the CEO dropping face-first to the concrete like a sack of cow-plop, his head crushed, a splat of blood.

"Call for an ambulance!" I scream to the crew outside, running to Hank. Durbett's heading up toward Ms. Moeroff. Stockbridge can sit in the closet a few more minutes. None of this action was grabbed on camera, but I don't care. Not right now.

Hank's face-down in a pool of blood, but he's breathing. "Don't move," I warn him.

"I'll get help!" Durbett shouts, leading Ms. Moeroff to the stairs, then disappearing into the offices.

"Theta?" Hank asks weakly.

She's running down the steps.

"She's okay, Hank," I tell him softly. "You saved her."

*   *   *

It's one helluva show. *NBS Newsline*, the full hour, Hal Neusome front and center.

The footage from the big raid in Tennessee is excellent; the helicopter chase plays like an episode from some big-budget movie. We cut together the whole story with a library of shots that seems inexhaustible.

The local NBS news affiliate has two crews standing by "live on the scene," one location that strikes me as silly—the Briggs warehouse where nothing is going on anymore—but the other is one that's very important: live at the hospital where Hank underwent surgery earlier today.

"We expect full recovery," the doctor reports for our viewing audience. He goes on to say there's serious damage to the something-something artery, pointing at a plastic model, but I'm not listening anymore. I can see a tearful old lady in the shot, and now she's hugging the doctor. It's hard to describe how much I love Ms. Moeroff, but I don't have to tell her. I show it, and she knows.

The guests on our program are great, especially Cricket LaRayne, sitting beside the Reverend Falluson, people dedicated to making right what once went wrong. I think they will, too.

Doug Moore's another guest for a brief statement. It seems an emergency board meeting was held, and Briggs Pharmaceutical has a new silver-haired gladiator of a CEO. He pledges to cooperate with the authorities and work with Ms. LaRayne, not only to assure the public's safety, but to make amends for the pain and suffering Rex and Les wreaked on unsuspecting Americans.

The other guest is a blond-haired dude who claims he just likes to draw. *Danté Roenik*, they call him, but he's been called other things many times before—and will again, I'm sure. I have to admit I do more than just draw:

"As a creative director and dabbler in public relations, it's my job to make sure my clients and their products are put forth in the best light. In this business, we're all guilty of trying to manipulate the news media, but luckily Hal Neusome is above that, presenting the truth as he sees it, always digging tirelessly, always willing to consider that he might be wrong. It was quite an adventure we went through today, our lives being saved by that incredible Sizemore *Wave-Slicer* and Sizemore 4000, and all that Weisman-catalog gear we used in the warehouse, all of which you can read about in the coming months when Parmenter Publishing features the exclusive story in Bentley Crabtree's new . . ."

After the show, I give our director one major hug, telling her how proud I am of her.

"You better be," Kristen joshes, "after leaving me to do the work while you talked on the phone all afternoon. What was that about?"

"You'll know soon enough," I tease. "Hey, I'm going to sit with Ms. Moeroff tonight, a hospital vigil till they kick us out, then back at the ransacked ranch. If you're not too busy—"

"You saved me from having to offer."

It winds up being a long, emotional night, and I'm exhausted, and I don't even remember falling asleep. I do recall watching those two sitting together on the couch while my favorite old lady tells my friend and director, the one who can read my mind, all about Hank, comparing him favorably, one at a time, to each of Ms. Moeroff's husbands through the years . . .

I already know this script . . .

CHAPTER 27

"There you are," Frank greets me. "It's about time you remembered the old codger who pulled your arse off the unemployment line."

I pull a chair over by his hospital bed. "Watch what you say, Frank. Dementia's not pretty."

"Impressive show last night."

"Yeah, but Kristen gets all the credit."

"I know," he says, a twinkle in his eye. "She came by this morning to soak up the accolades."

"Are you doing okay?"

"Out of here tomorrow, take it easy a week or so, back in the saddle again. Actually, yes—I'm doing much better after a talk I had with Melissa this morning."

"Oh?"

"You know she'll have that fifty-grand from Briggs in a few days. She won't need me anymore."

"Oh, like a place to live is all she needs you for?"

"Well, no—and she made that very clear this morning. We've worked out an arrangement where they stay on at the house. She'll spend some of that money on something frivolous, then bank half of what's left for herself and put the rest in a fund for Taj."

"She deserves—they both deserve—to have some fun with it."

"Yeah." He's looking off into the future. "I'm going to have a lawyer write me up a will, and set up a trust, too, so they'll both be taken care of. I don't have anybody else, you know."

"They're more than enough, Frank."

He grins. "Yeah, they are, aren't they? Anyway, they'll stay on with the agreement that if one or both are still there when I get too old, they'll prop me in a corner and dust me occasionally."

"I don't think you or Ms. Moeroff will be gathering dust any time soon."

"I hope not, but I feel better knowing I'll do right by Mel and the little monster."

We sit quietly for a minute, then both start to speak at the same time. I insist he go ahead.

"Kristen says you spent all afternoon on the phone, and that you disappeared this morning. What's up?"

"I've been taking care of business, you being laid up and all. In fact, the visit's over; now it's time for a meeting."

"Oyez oyez."

"This is just a formality, because I've been on the honker with Hendon and he votes with me on all the proposals. That's fifty-two percent. I'm just giving you the courtesy of being listed in the board minutes as unanimous."

"Take advantage while I'm laid up, huh?"

"You'd be proud of me."

"I am."

"First order of business: Your stock and my stock don't fully vest for a year. I proposed we vest as of today, and Hendon agreed."

"How could I turn that down? It's unanimous."

"Second: We're holding twenty-two percent of the stock for employee incentives. I propose we divide that five ways and pay it out immediately to Kristen, Byron, Rupert, Murray, and Melissa."

"But what about—?"

"They earned it, Frank, and I'm too busy today to debate it. Just say yea."

He chuckles. "My arm hurts, you twisting it like this. Okay, yea. So what's all this have to do with where you've been today?"

"I went to see Karl Ferman. I played him the audio of Dib Wardley and Sam Cox conspiring against us, sabotaging our client's ads out of personal vendetta. Needless to say, he was quite upset."

"I'll bet."

"I told him the audio-disks will remain confidential if Sam and Dib and their two cohorts in graphics and shipping are sent walking. He pointed out that the recordings were obtained illegally. I told him I could take the legal heat if he thinks he can stand the public-relations and suspicious-clients nightmares."

"Sam and Dib are history, aren't they?"

"End of the day today, so we're supposed to keep it confidential until then. Seems they have an appointment with Ms. Kirloot at five."

Frank chuckles again.

"Next proposal: We sell The Dellman/Roenik Group to Ferman's parent company, to be merged immediately with Kehoe/Lundy."

Frank sits upright, surprised. "But Dante—"

"There are some contingencies to the deal. First, you stay retired, but come in as a consultant emeritus—write your own job description. You don't get to take it easy yet—a man looks stupid juggling only one ball."

"I'm listening."

"I take over as grand exalted pooh-bah agency senior-VP creative director and pool boy. The rest of our crew gets offered very nice jobs. The staff at *Shoot & Die* stays on."

"I thought you liked having your name on the letterhead," Frank joshes me.

"I do. We can't give up the Kehoe name due to reputation and continuity and all, so the new agency will be called Kehoe, Lundy, Dellman & Roenik."

Frank beams. He likes that, I can tell. "Is it an attractive offer?"

"Well, I asked for the stars and the moon. Ferman balked, but I pulled a Frank on him."

"Oh?"

"I had a series of calls set up—that's why I was on the phone all afternoon, making arrangements."

There's a twinkle in his eye again.

"It was fun," I continue. "Seems Ollum DeForest's publisher pledged volumes of business to our new alliance. Then Billy Sizemore made a splash, promising waves of ad jobs floating our way. Then some feller name of Durbett spied the chance and lobbed in a money grenade, blowing five million and stressing his clout with other bigshots around the globe."

"Good old Flynn."

"Yeah, and good old Tony Faritzka, too. He trained Ferman's attention on the feasibility of keeping *Shoot & Die* in the black just on his account alone."

"Tony's a good man."

"That he is. The next news-flash was a commitment from NBS to produce and broadcast locally from the other half of *Shoot & Die*. We already need to start planning an expansion."

"I'll bet Ferman was impressed."

"He was—somewhat—until Briggs CEO Doug Moore wrote out a five-year prescription to dose us with at least *ninety-million dollars*, possibly twice that. Old Ferman had a woody, I'll tell you."

"Wow. You think Moore can deliver?"

"He's cut from your cloth, Frank. That's why I'm in a hurry; I have to get out to Briggs. Seems they have some pressing PR needs."

"I'll say. So Ferman jumped at what you put on the table, huh?"

"That ain't the half of it. The clincher was what I threatened to pull out."

"Oh?"

"I plugged in a Texan, name of Woot Wooter. Seems he climbed down off his llama long enough to promise that if we put his account under my tutelage, then he'll call off the agency review. If not, he's gonna play somewhere else."

"I bow at the feet of the master," Frank kids me.

"I was just pretending to be you, Frank."

He smiles, and he really does look like a proud father. "How much?"

"Well, there are still a few contingencies."

"How much?"

"Hendon's real pleased."

"How much?"

"Twelve."

He's stymied. "Twelve what?"

"Million."

His jaw literally drops. "But— How—"

"I pulled a Frank."

"You mean I pocket more than three million right off the top?"

"And Melissa and the others can walk away with a half-million each—though they've all said they intend to keep working. Something about having too much fun to quit now."

Frank's clutching my hands, trying not to laugh too hard, his eyes glistening. He takes a deep breath, then finally remembers to ask, "The other contingencies?"

"There's two. First, Tommy the security guy gets a big bump in pay."

"Why?"

"He helped me carry my stuff to the car when I got the Kirloot boot. I promised him a big raise when I came back and took over the place."

Frank laughs. "Well, I'm sure—"

"Have to keep my word, Frank. You taught me that."

He rolls his eyes. "What's the other contingency?"

"I design the new icon-logo for *Shoot & Die*."

"What's that?"

"It's a critter wearing a holster, a camera in one side, aiming another camera with his flipper."

"His flipper?"

"It's a catfish, Frank."
"Wearing lipstick?!"
"And Nehru jacket."

EPILOGUE

To capture imaginations . . . I start with an image. To capture my own . . .

But first, business: I return Doug Moore's call. He lets me know to start concocting creative ways to inform the public that Briggs Pharmaceutical is delaying the introduction of its Fantasy Patch until key trial-test results can be replicated, customer assurance from a concerned manufacturer.

Next, legal: I check back with Cricket to find out the good news. It seems the judge granted her lawsuit class-action status, effectively freezing out Rob Salterfin's pathetic attempt to get a piece of the settlement she just negotiated with Rex's widow. Rumors of an ethics investigation have sparked a mass exodus from Wanamaker, Salterfin & Brock, résumés piling up on Cricket's desk.

Finally, personal: I call Ms. Moeroff, who's packing to move into Hank's house for a while to help him recuperate when he's released from the hospital. She's thrilled with the progress of our hero, so she wants me to quit worrying and have a good time, to see the sights, capture an image or two. My horo-scope said good time to travel . . . You gotta love her.

Okay, it's time to hit the beach.

Picture Frank's sixty-fifth birthday celebration. It's a week after merging our new company with Kehoe, and we're here at his condo on Florida's Sanibel Island. Flynn Durbett lent us the jet so our gang could relax and enjoy a long weekend, unwind, regroup, maybe think up a few ideas for the Weisman promotions . . .

I walk out onto the white sand, pause to lob *attaboys* at Murray Rivner and Bentley Crabtree, two paste-legged wordsmiths sprawled in chaise-longues, their laps topped with laptops, arguing over how to write the chapter on the ricin murder.

I look off to the south and see Melissa and Rupert walking together along the shore, Frank's protégé finally taking an interest in something other than clients, Taj's mother still learning how to relax, to focus on herself, and to let friends look after her son.

Several little kids run by. I imagine a dazzling array of allergy tattoos adorning their chubby little arms, replaced by Fantasy Patches when they're old enough to nurture anxiety and angst. I walk past some tourists staking out a parcel of sand, several sun bathers, one or two bun shavers. That fanny-floss G-string leaves nothing to the imagination. What a picture . . .

I pause and watch Taj playing with Frank on the beach, the youngster burying Gramps in the sand. Frank waits patiently, then jumps free and grabs the little one, both wrestling and giggling, my funeral shot replaced by the image of a white-haired Phoenix rising, grandfather time cradling the child he adores. There are no bad hearts, no painful rashes, just a birthday to celebrate, and friendship to share.

Taj stops laughing long enough to announce, in his very best *Monster Bin* Q-Tawzh voice, "Goo-lah! Foo-lah! Woo-lah! Grrrrrrr! Q-Tawzh gonna eat up Grandpa Frank!" The old man gives him a growl retort, and they're wrestling and giggling again. I sure hope he doesn't grow up *too* fast; I like seeing him like this—Frank, I mean.

I walk on, find a patch of beach close to the water, and have a seat. The gentle whitecaps are washing up onto the sand, a flock of gulls circling overhead, a regal sand-castle posing nearby, the sun hanging low in the sky and reflecting across the water. I'm calm, relaxed. Theta-therapy . . .

Just like that picture I drew for her—the one I never finished.

"You look lonesome," Ms. Moeroff had told me that night, the image of me sitting by myself in paradise.

Nothing ever seems to turn out like I pictured it, but I have to keep trying. Start with a sketch, add some color, shading, texture and background, then a subject that always changes. When I dare to put myself on the canvas, I must repaint it every day, to reveal how I grow older, to search for the smoldering embers of my lost youth, to capture grief and pain as contrast to happiness and joy, lines to half-tones, shadow to light.

I've spent many years drawing Cyn into my picture, imagining our life together, our careers, our family, our old age . . . I think I wanted it too much, so much that all I could see was the picture I painted, smoke and mirrors, special effects, a deceptive ad. Cyn's not in the picture anymore, so here I sit without her, the portrait of a man alone on the beach, just as I'd drawn it for Ms. Moeroff.

"There you are!"

It's Kristen!—one bodacious bikini-clad gal, bathed in the warm glow of sunshine, the most beautiful vision I've ever beheld. She's bringing a small package and some cold drinks for us. I smooth the sand for her to sit beside me, accepting a glass and sipping from the nectar of unrealized potential.

"What'd you bring me?"

"It's Frank's birthday," she says, "but you get a present, too."

"*Moi?*" I open it, and of course it's a monogrammed, leather-bound schedule planner.

"I heard some of the pages were missing when they found your old one locked in Dib Wardley's desk."

"I love it," I whisper, already planning to misplace this one, too—at the first opportunity.

"Check today's date," she prods.

I flip to the page, and there lists my plans for tonight:

> 1) Dinner with Kristen.
> 2) Moonlit walk on the beach.
> 3) Waterbed snorkeling (optional).

I put my arm around her. She rests her head on my shoulder. We watch the sun hang low in the sky and think about framing a new image, staging a new shot, bringing some animation to this still-life, co-executive producers with no script.

Life is always good, and with the right people it can be great.

So this didn't turn out the way I pictured it, but could it possibly get any better?

I can only imagine.

Read Flynn Durbett's Early Story!

Invigilator
By Stephen Geez

A Tennessee teen in the mid-1990s, Eugene Weisman enjoys pretending to defend a so-called "alien"—until the game turns deadly and his life depends on what others believe.

Hand-picked to helm *Program Invigil,* Colonel Chester McGovern takes responsibility for detection, isolation, and eradication—then unleashes enormous inter-military power cloaked in black-helicopter secrecy.

Tiring of the clandestine wet-work biz, soldier of fortune Flynn Durbett settles down to run a weapons-smuggling ring for governments and underground patriots—but then old obligations renew, and his own opinions matter less than standing up for others'.

As Eugene attracts followers who declare him the true savior, McGovern lays siege to American citizens while searching for the missing black box in his obsessive mission to preserve life as we know it.

Do we really need to be protected? And who will deliver us?—the military, or a loosely organized rag-tag militia? Is it all fantasy, or a threat greater than we ever imagined?

Everybody has the right to believe, but only one can be the *Invigilator.*

Fresh Ink Group
ISBN: 978-1-9 36442-08-9

BEEN THERE, NOTED THAT:
Essays in Celebration of Life

Observations, Inspiration, Remembrance,
& Noteworthies To Share

By Stephen Geez

The simple lives of everyday people in a mundane world prove extraordinary in this collection of 54 personal-experience essays by novelist Stephen Geez. The eclectic mix of memoir, commentary, humor, and appreciation covers a wide range of topics, each beautifully illustrated by artists and photographers from the Fresh Ink Group. Geez catches what many of us miss, then considers how we might all share the most poignant of lessons. *Been There, Noted That* aims to reveal who we are, examine where we've been, and discover what we dare strive to become.

www.FreshInkGroup.com
ISBN: 978-978-1-936442-05-8

More Books by Stephen Geez

General Fiction
Dance of the Lights
What Sara Saw
Papala Skies
How It Turns Out

Mystical Adventure Series
Rich Mr. Fixx: *Crystal Clear* #1
Rich Mr. Fixx: *Spider-Boxed* #2
Rich Mr. Fixx: *Hot Doggies* #3
Rich Mr. Fixx Graphic Flashback #1: *Shell Game*

Science Fiction
Invigilator
Zhasou Pure

Essay Collection
Been There, Noted That

GeezWriter
How-to Series for Authors

The Fresh Ink Group

Publishing
Memberships
Share & Read Free Stories, Essays, Articles
Free-Story Newsletter
Writing Contests

Books
E-books
Amazon Bookstore

Authors
Editors
Artists
Professionals
Publishing Services
Publisher Resources

Members' Websites
Members' Blogs
Social Media

www.FreshInkGroup.com

Email: info@FreshInkGroup.com

Twitter: @FreshInkGroup

Google+: Fresh Ink Group

Facebook.com/FreshInkGroup

LinkedIn: Fresh Ink Group

About.me/FreshInkGroup